Cubana

Cubana

JaQuavis Coleman

www.urbanbooks.net

Urban Books, LLC
300 Farmingdale Road, NY-Route 109
Farmingdale, NY 11735

ISBN 13: 978-1-64556-282-5
ISBN 10: 1-64556-282-4

First Mass Market Printing February 2022
First Trade Paperback Printing November 2020
Printed in the United States of America

10 9 8 7 6 5 4 3 2 1

Distributed by Kensington Publishing Corp.
Submit Orders to:
Customer Service
400 Hahn Road
Westminster, MD 21157-4627
Phone: 1-800-733-3000
Fax: 1-800-659-2436

Cubana

by

JaQuavis Coleman

Prologue

Duality

Five little monkeys jumping on the bed
One fell off and bumped his head
Mama called the doctor, and the doctor said
No more . . . monkeys . . . jumping on the bed

The young child gleefully sang the lullaby as she smiled, playing patty-cake with her imaginary friend. A little brown girl sat Indian style on the floor, wearing a long, white pajama gown. Her skin was ebony, but her eyes . . . Her eyes were ice-cold blue—a rare combination; however, a beautiful one. Her angelic voice echoed through the sparsely furnished house. Four pigtails hung from her head. She looked to be no older than 6 or 7 years old. She continued to sing the children's song, merrily clapping the air as if there were someone else directly in front of her. The happiness in her eyes was innocent and pure.

The open windows allowed her voice to travel onto the streets of Havana, Cuba. The dilapidated homes lined the block, which sat on a long, dirt road. Stray monkeys hopped around the streets playfully along with kids without a care in the world. The simple, familiar, lullaby was majestic and loud. It was peaceful and highlighted the Sunday morning. Loud enough for the man just outside to hear it as he walked toward the home. He had a small, leather duffle bag in his hand as he made his way toward the house. As the man approached the door, he glanced around and peeked down the block, watching while the kids played stickball in the middle of the street. He also saw young girls jump roping and others playing tag; some of them barefooted. It was a harsh but lovely sight to behold. The blissful adolescents were having so much fun, although they were impoverished, not even being able to afford the bare necessities of a simple pair of shoes. Their innocence wouldn't allow them to understand the extent of their own dire situations.

Some of the houses had openings where windows should have been. Roofs were damaged, and each house looked like it was one strong wind away from collapsing. What the city lacked in wealth, they made up for with pride and tradition. The graffiti-littered surfaces on the side of houses and buildings were ugly but also stunning—duality at its finest.

The man scanned further down the street and saw various domino matches being played at small tables. People congregated outside of some of the homes, laughing and speaking Spanish. Groups of men huddled around the small tables and hooted as the beaming hot sun seemed not to bother their golden skin complexions.

Saint Von was the man's name who scoped the neighborhood. He simply went by Saint. He was visiting from the United States . . . New Orleans, Louisiana, to be exact. Saint felt the burning sun shining down on his neck as he pulled the bucket hat down snugly onto his shiny, bald head. He tried to block the sun from his eyes and then straightened the gold-rimmed sunglasses on his face. A toothpick hung from the left side of his mouth as he twisted it using his thumb and pointer finger. He carried a small duffle bag in the other hand. Sweat beads dripped from his brow as he made his way into the house where the angel-like voice was coming from.

Saint wore an open, white linen shirt, and his tattooed body was on full display as a bulging belly somewhat stuck out over his belt buckle. Saint wasn't flabby by any means, but his belly slightly poked out and served as a trophy for his years of good living. His neatly trimmed, full beard hung down to his Adam's apple, and his bear-like face was highlighted by beautiful white teeth on the top row, with a gold row across the bottom.

Just before he stepped into the doorless home, he heard the sounds of monkeys panting and making noises just above him. It made him look up and notice the wild animals hopping around on the roof of the five-story building next door. They were moving frantically, play-fully beating on their chest. He shook his head and entered the home. He couldn't get used to the wild animals blending in with society as if normal. It was a far cry from his upbringing in Nola.

As he stepped inside the house, he saw a dimly lit hall. A creaky flight of stairs was right in front of him that led to the second story of the flat. The long, dim, and damp hall was one that Saint had been in quite a few times. He had made it a habit to come to see the woman they called Pandora every time that he visited Cuba. It was always his last stop before heading back home. As he climbed the stairs, the sound of the child's voice grew louder and louder. The smell of burning incense filled Saint's nostrils as he approached the door at the top of the staircase.

As Saint entered the room, he saw the young girl on the floor, playing. He paused and then smiled as he walked past her. They locked eyes, and Saint's bright smile triggered her to return one as well. He headed toward the back where long, flowing beads separated the rooms as they hung from the door's overpass.

Saint slowly walked into the room. The sound of the beads tapping one another always soothed him. He entered. The deeper he got in the room, the less and less he heard the young girl's voice. He squinted his eyes and tried to focus on the dark figure that was in the corner. As he got closer, he heard the sound of a match being lit, and a large flash of light followed it. The flame was connected to a long, wooden matchstick, which was held by unusually long, manicured nails. Each nail was at least four inches long.

A woman's face appeared as the match's flame slightly illuminated the room. Saint's eyes locked in with hers. Her beautiful, big, penny-shaped pupils and full lips let him know exactly who it was. The familiar face soothed him as he walked closer to the light, exposing her face more clearly. The gorgeous woman before him was none other than Pandora. She wore a multicolored silk wrap around her gray locs, which hung out from the top of it.

"I've been expecting you, Saint," Pandora whispered as a small grin formed on her face. She spoke clear English but with a heavy Spanish accent. Her skin was the deepest ebony Saint had ever seen. Her eyes were a rare blue color. They were oddly gorgeous. In this beautiful country, it was a usual combination; however, the States had stripped Saint's interpretation of what Black looked and sounded like. A Black woman's physical characteristics had limitless shades and mixtures, and Pandora was the evidence of that. He was standing there in pure amazement.

Pandora was simply majestic to the naked eye. She was nearly twenty years his senior. However, one couldn't tell by her looks and smooth skin. It was when she opened her mouth that her age showed. Pure wisdom flowed from her mouth, and the strain in her voice showed her years on this earth. She proceeded to light the candles that were spread around the table where she was sitting as Saint stood before her.

"Have a seat," she instructed as she blew out the match and focused her undivided attention on him.

Saint's eyes followed the smoke from the match, and it led directly into her blue eyes. Her gaze was piercing and unwavering as she stared at him, almost as if she were looking *through* him rather than *at* him. An intense chill crept up his spine, and he felt his shoulders becoming more relaxed at the end of it. A small flutter happened in Saint's heart, and like always, he was mesmerized by her presence. He slowly took a seat and gently set the duffle bag on the hardwood floor next to his chair. Saint placed his hands on his lap and took a deep breath as the smell of burning sage and incense calmed him.

"Hey, Pandora," Saint said, as he got comfortable in his chair and looked around the room.

"Hello, handsome," she said as she strategically spread the small crystals around the table. Saint looked at the little gems as she aligned them and incoherently mumbled things under her breath. Pandora closed her eyes and slowly swayed back and forth, and then she stopped abruptly and froze. A small smile formed on her face, and she opened her eyelids, focusing directly on Saint.

"Our ancestors are ready to speak. But before we do what you came here for, let's talk. I feel something is on your heart. Something other than what's in that bag down there," she said as she nodded her head in the direction of the duffle bag full of plastic-wrapped kilos.

Saint was taken aback because it seemed as if she were reading his mind. He usually would come to get his "bricks baptized" by Pandora. He would ask her to separate any Karma or harm that would come to him by way of the bricks of heroin he was about to distribute back in the United States. However, on this particular trip, he had a few extra things going on in his life that he needed help with.

"Damn, you always seem to know what's on my mind," Saint said, shaking his head in amazement.

"No, I always know what's on your heart. I can see it through your eyes. So . . . Come on, talk to mama," Pandora said as she winked and attempted to lighten the mood. Although Pandora was highly spiritual, she had a way of making people feel comfortable with her. Her motherly spirit was one of comfort. She had a special skill for making people open to her.

"There are a few things. I ran into some legal trouble a few years back, and the case came back up. My trial starts in a few," Saint admitted.

"Oh, I see. You're on trial for what cause?"

"Murder," he answered in a low tone as his eyes dropped, breaking their gaze.

"Did you do it?" Pandora asked blatantly and without hesitation. Saint nodded his head in admittance.

"Yeah, but in self-defense," he whispered, genuinely having regret for what he had done. He had sorrow but not for defending himself. Rather, for taking the life of someone that he knew personally.

"I can see that your words are pure, and you have re-morse," Pandora said, as she clasped her hands together. She paused and just stared at Saint before speaking again. You could tell that she was analyzing him and choosing her words wisely before she spoke.

"I will ask for guidance from our ancestors, and if I can help you . . . I will. You will have to come back after the sun sets," Pandora explained carefully. Saint nodded in agreement and reached down to go into his bag and placed his hand on a brick. He was about to put them on the table so Pandora could bless them, but Pandora waved her hand, signaling for him to pause.

"There is something else on your heart. What else is troubling you?" she asked as she rested her hands on top of his. Saint closed his eyes and paused, realizing that he couldn't get anything past her. He took a deep breath and sat upright. He chuckled to himself and shook his head, realizing that Pandora was very good at what she did. He couldn't get anything past her. He slightly showed the golds in his mouth with his partial smile.

"I'm getting married. Well, if I'm not in prison . . . I'll be getting married."

"Ooh, here is the *good* stuff," Pandora said playfully as she sat upright as well. "Do tell . . ." she said.

"There's really nothing to tell. Shorty is the truth. I just don't know if I'll be the man she wants me to be. I never did anything like this before," he honestly admitted.

"Okay, I see. You have cold feet, eh?" Pandora said as she nodded slowly, understanding exactly what was going on. "Well, you need some advice, not divine intervention." Pandora slowly waved her arm across the table, clearing all the stones and gems so it would be a clear pallet. She placed her hands on the table with her palms facing up.

"Come on," she instructed as she glanced down at her hands, wiggled her fingers, and then looked up at Saint. Saint placed his hands inside of hers and listened carefully, knowing that she was about to lay some game on him as she always did.

"What's your worries, Saint? Do you not love her?" Pandora asked.

"Of course, I love her. She's a real one," he admitted.

"So, if she's the one . . . Why the hesitation?"

"That's the million-dollar question. I don't know exactly. I dream about her in colors that don't exist." He paused as he let his words marinate. "She's been there with me from the beginning. I just want to reward her with everything. She deserves to be happy. She has been through it all. She held me down every single time and never once made me think she wasn't in my corner. Even when it was hard," Saint said, feeling the urge to tell Pandora every single emotion he was feeling toward his fiancée.

"Okay, so why don't you want to marry her?" she asked.

"I do. I just don't want to hurt her. My life is real, ya hear me?" Saint said as his New Orleans drawl emerged in his dialect. He was good about hiding his strong New Orleans accent, but when he spoke from the heart, it always seemed to peek its head. He continued, "This life is not fit for marriage. I'm knee-deep in this shit. I want to wait until things slow down for me so that I can focus on her. But on the flip side, I can't make her wait forever. Does this make sense?" Saint said, seeking guidance. Pandora gently squeezed his hands and took a deep breath.

"You ever lie to her, you ever lied to this woman you speak of?" Pandora asked.

"Yeah, I have. Only to protect her feelings, though," he replied.

"She's found out about these lies that we speak of?" Pandora quizzed. Saint simply nodded his head, confirming her suspicions.

"Let me tell you something about a woman, and I need you to listen closely," Pandora spoke. She paused and turned her head to the side, staring at nothing in particular, searching for the correct words.

"Be careful about lying to your woman. Every time she forgives you, you will love her a little more. However, with your lies, she will begin to love you a little less. So, the day you love her the most will be the day that she will love you the least." Those words sent shivers throughout Saint's body, and the heaviness of his heart resonated deeply within his chest.

"Now, that advice is on the house. Something to grow on," Pandora stated as she released her grasp and focused back on the crystals that were on the table. She realigned her crystals, placing them correctly. Saint thought about her words, and just that quick, he made a decision. He decided if he beat his current case, he wouldn't waste any time in marrying his woman.

Saint smiled and placed the bricks on the table as Pandora began the baptism. As always, Saint just sat back and watched. The process never took too long, and some would say it was a waste of time, but ever since his connect suggested this, he had never been pinched by the law. Therefore, he never took his chances and skipped the process. He had a routine, and it had been that way for years. He would see his connect, and, on his way out, he would always stop by and see Pandora. Some would call it superstitious, but Saint called it playing the game the way it was supposed to be played. He listened as she chanted . . .

Afterward, Saint carefully placed the bricks back into his leather bag but not before sliding an envelope filled with cash over the table to Pandora. She smiled and received the money. Saint gathered himself and his bags, then stood up. He bent down and kissed Pandora on the cheek as he always did and then headed out.

As Saint reached the door, he turned back and found Pandora looking at him while smiling. He returned the smile and proceeded out. As he glanced at the wall just by the exit, he saw writing on the wall. The word "*Duality*" was written in what seemed to be a kid's handwriting. It stood out because it wasn't a common word that a child or someone of an adolescent age would write, and the word stuck with him. Saint never used the word before, so he was somewhat unfamiliar with the term.

"The more you live . . . the more you'll understand. I'll see you after dark for that other matter," Pandora said as if she were reading his mind as he tried to ponder about the meaning.

Saint said nothing and walked out. As he entered the hallway, the sound of the young girl's voice picked back up, getting louder with each step. She was singing the same lullaby as if she had never stopped singing. Saint noticed that the sound was slightly different than what he remembered. It now sounded like multiple voices were singing the song in unison. As he entered the main room, he saw the little girl sitting on the floor. However, this time, she seemed to be sitting across from another young child. They both had the same look, same gown, and same skin tones. The other child was a boy with a short haircut.

Twins? he thought as he walked past and eyed the two. With the girl, he could see her face fully, but the other child's back was turned to him as they playfully slapped hands while singing. Saint thought it was odd. He started to second-guess his memory, knowing that there was only one girl before. He shook his head and chalked it up as a mental lapse. As he walked toward the exit, he turned back to look at the children. All of a sudden, they stopped singing, and it grew eerily silent. The little girl that faced him smiled, showing her big blue eyes. Saint smiled back, and as the young boy slowly turned around, Saint held his smile, ready to greet him as well—but when he saw him, a wave of fear and confusion swept through his body.

What the fuck? Saint thought as the smile quickly faded from his face. The young boy had no facial features—nothing. No eyes, no mouth, nose, or eyebrows. Saint's mind spun rapidly, trying to make sense of what he was seeing. He looked at the girl, and she was smiling, like there was nothing unusual about her counterpart's deformity. The faceless little boy vaguely turned his head sideways, tilting his head to the side. This freaked Saint out as he shook his head in disbelief. He hurried out and wondered what the fuck he had just seen. Just as he reached the outside and felt the rays of the sun, he leaned against the house to catch his breath. Then, once more, he heard the kids sing. Saint looked down the block and noticed that it was now empty, a far cry from the happy, energetic scene from earlier. He took a deep breath, inhaling through his nose, and briefly closing his eyes to recenter himself.

Five little monkeys jumping on the bed
One fell off and bumped his head

Mama called the doctor, and the doctor said
No more . . . monkeys . . . jumping on the bed

Saint gripped his bag tightly and headed away from the house, but the sound of something crashing against the ground startled him, making him jump back. A monkey lay there as a maroon-colored puddle of blood seeped out of its body. Horrific-looking brain matter from the monkey's skull was splattered against the ground and instantly made Saint's stomach churn. He quickly looked away, not wanting to see the gruesome sight. It seemed as if the monkey had fallen from the building to its death. Saint looked up to see a lone monkey on the top of the roof dancing around while looking down at its dead companion.

Saint hurried away as he heard his phone ringing from his bag. He retrieved the phone and looked at the caller ID. It was his right-hand man, Zoo. His phone wasn't a usual one or even an up-to-date one, for that matter. His oversized Nokia phone had a long, rubber antenna sticking from it. It was at least fifteen years old and was totally outdated. Saint used this type of phone for many reasons, but the obvious one was its lack of technology. Older phones lacked the capabilities of being traced and were much more difficult to tap remotely. The long antenna allowed him to reach anywhere completely under the radar in North or South America. No phone towers were needed to correspond with the opposite party. It was basically a ramped-up walkie-talkie, and that's the device of choice he talked business on.

"Peace," Saint said, answering.

"Peace. We good?" Zoo asked.

"Absolutely. On my way back home now."

"God is good," Zoo said, smiling through the phone.

"Amen," Saint said, as he made his way down the block, where an antique car was waiting for him.

Saint pressed the *end* button and made his way to the end of the block. He saw the male driver just down the road. He was Cuban and stood no taller than five feet. The driver was waiting for Saint patiently as he leaned against the rear of the car with his arms folded. The man had olive-colored skin and wore a straw fedora hat. He seemed to be in his early 60s. Saint used him for transportation every time he visited the country, and he escorted him around in his 1960 Ford. The driver's name was Pedro.

The car was a faded red color, and you could tell that it had been sunburned over the years. The car didn't look like much on the outside. It had various rust spots, holes, and bald tires. It had been through many harsh days, and its war wounds proved it. Nevertheless, it ran like a horse, and that's all Saint could really ask for.

As Saint got closer, the man said something in Spanish and opened the rear door, giving Saint a clear path to slide in. Saint slid in and threw his head back in the car seat, thinking about the peculiar day that he had. Something was different about today, and it gave him an eerie feeling deep within his soul.

As they cruised the Cuban roads doing fifteen miles per hour, it gave Saint time to reflect. He watched as kids chased the car and knocked on the windows. He would pass out money usually, but today was different. He kept seeing the boy's blank, deformed face. He wanted to blame it on stress, but he knew better. Something was happening. He just couldn't put his finger on it. He prided himself on having a sharp mind, but this was an occurrence that he could not wrap his thoughts around. His brain was playing tricks on him in the worst way.

Or was it?

He thought about the words of Pandora and the day's events. He looked to his left and saw the bag that would be distributed throughout the bayou, making him a quick seven figures when it was done. He wanted out, and the main reason for that was so that he could become the man that the love of his life deserved. With what he saw this day, he knew someone or "something" was trying to tell him something. He just didn't know what exactly.

A beautiful cathedral church was the setting for the day's special event. Luxury cars lined the parking lot of the historic church. It was a gathering of bosses, family, and well-respected figures throughout the bayou. Stunning, hand-crafted statues of angels peppered the marbled floors, and tall podiums were the pillars of the immaculate haven. Three months had passed, and Saint was at a major crossroads in his life. He stared at himself in the full-length mirror and straightened up his bow tie, examining it very carefully. His shiny, bald head and huge, shaped beard were flawless. His well-tailored Tom Ford suit was all white, and the Italian cut fit him impeccably. His belly had even shrunk a size or two. He hung the expensive suit very well. He looked like he stepped straight out of a *GQ* magazine.

Today was the big day. He was marrying the woman who held the key to his heart, Ramina. The room had five other men inside, all of them talking amongst each other, sipping Cognac, and prepping for their leader's new union. They all were suited as well and accented with traditional black accessories. Saint was in the presence of his groomsmen, his team. Although none of them shared the same bloodline, they were family by way of the drug game.

Saint was a boss. He was the natural leader and the sole connect to the Cuban heroin plug. Although Saint was younger than some of his men, he held the most wisdom. He moved as if he were twenty years older than his actual age. He never did anything fast. His speech, his movements, his business moves were always slow and well calculated. Saint never spoke loudly. No one ever heard him raise his voice. He did everything on his own terms and in his own tone. He controlled "the board" at all times. Saint was the man that made the operation go. He was at the top of the totem pole, and it was the best-kept secret in the bayou.

Zoo approached Saint and straightened up his tie. He then threw his arm around Saint's shoulder and leaned in to talk to him. Zoo hugged him tightly.

"Today is the day, bruh. You finally about to do it," Zoo said proudly.

Saint nodded in agreement without saying a word. He looked at Zoo through the mirror and faintly smirked at his best friend. Zoo stood about six feet and had a slim build. His skin complexion was as dark as night—so dark that he almost looked purple. He wore a neatly cut Caesar hairstyle and 360 waves wrapped around his head flaw-lessly. He wore Cartier frames with wood grain around the rim of the glasses. He was from Flint, Michigan, and it was very prevalent in his style. He migrated to Nola ten years before, when he went to school at Louisiana Tech on an athletic scholarship. He ended up staying after his college stint and began his new career in the drug trade. In his newfound game is where he met Saint, and they had been tight ever since. He served as the underboss to Saint and was the buffer between Saint and the rest of the wolves that the job came with. Saint was more behind-the-scenes, and he moved ghostlike.

An old saying was "if you know, you know," and this term explained Saint's entire being to the fullest. He was a quiet storm in the drug game, and not everyone knew who he was, but all the *right* people knew who he was. Saint was what you called a "street king," and, on that day, the king would finally be getting his queen.

"Mina is getting a good nigga," Zoo said, having a heart-to-heart with his partner in crime. Saint slyly slid his hands in his slacks and walked over to the window that was facing the beautiful acreage behind the church. Without even looking around the room, Saint spoke.

"Give Zoo and me a minute alone," he said in his low, deep baritone. He didn't speak loudly, but when he spoke . . . people listened. Therefore, the room cleared out immediately, and Saint waited patiently as the men exited the room. Saint casually glanced back and made sure everyone was gone and only he and Zoo occupied the room before he spoke.

After the last groomsman left and the door was closed, Saint spoke. "Zoo, I'm done," he said with conviction and without a doubt. Zoo grew a look of concern on his face and walked over to Saint, joining him by the window.

"What?" Zoo asked, not believing what he was hearing.

"I'm out. I'm flying straight. I'm done with the game," Saint said.

"Wait . . . We are just getting started. How can you pull the plug? Listen, I know you on your married man shit, but we still out here in the trenches. We ain't ready to hang it up just yet. We got the entire bayou sewn up. We can't just shut down shop like that," Zoo pleaded as he was now standing in front of Saint.

"Don't worry. I'm giving you the plug. I'm done with it. It's yours now," Saint answered.

"Don't play, bro . . ." Zoo said as a wave of excitement overcame him. He shot a look of optimism in the direction of Saint and tried to read him. Throughout the years, Saint had never introduced Zoo to his Cuban plug. He always kept them separate and went alone. However, he was at a place in his life where he had enough money to retire comfortably, and he did not need the game. He was 34 years old and was ready to build a legit life with his new wife.

"Nah, I'm serious. After I get back from the honeymoon, I'm going to introduce you to the Cuban connect. It's yours now. The whole operation is yours now. I'm out," Saint said, reconfirming his exit.

Zoo couldn't hold in his emotions. He hugged Saint so tightly and firmly, understanding that Saint had just changed his life forever. With a plug like that, the sky was the limit, and it was something that any dope boy dreamed of. Zoo nearly had tears in his eyes as he released his embrace and looked at his best friend. Unlike Saint, Zoo had no escape plan for the game. He loved everything about it. All he wanted to be was a kingpin, and he was willing to take anything that came with it. In his mind, the reward of being the number one guy outweighed the pitfalls that accompanied the position. He was eating good under Saint, but he didn't have the power or the respect of Saint. And *that's* what he yearned for.

"I won't let you down, bruh. That's my word," Zoo said with belief.

As always, Saint acted as if someone were listening, so he spoke low as he leaned forward and put his lips near Zoo's right earlobe.

"We'll fly out to Cuba, and I'll personally introduce you to Alejandro," he whispered, referring to the connect. He gently tapped Zoo's cheek and continued. "Take this mu'fucka over," He then reached over and grabbed the champagne bottle that was sitting in the bucket of ice. Zoo grabbed a champagne flute, and the sound of the cork being popped echoed throughout the room. They both shared a toast as the sound of the bell rang throughout the church, which was his signal. It was time for the ceremony to start.

"Yo, quick thing. I was going to wait, but I want to get on top of this while you're away on your honeymoon. We ran into a little problem," Zoo said as he reached into the inside pocket of his blazer. He pulled out a small Baggie. Saint's eyes went directly to it, and he noticed the stamp on the front. It had a US seal on it with words underneath it. It simply read "*Cubana*." It caught Saint's attention because that was his signature stamp that he put on his heroin. However, he could tell that it wasn't his because the logo was slightly off. He knew from the jump that it was a copycat.

"You know how the game go, beloved. Niggas gon' imitate. Don't trip on that," Saint said calmly as he grabbed the pack and studied it.

"True, but this shit killing niggas. Four people overdosed this month off this pack. The mix ain't right, man. Somebody putting some shit in the game."

"You take it to Jeremy?" Saint asked, referring to their lab technician that they had on payroll.

"Yeah, he said it's bogus. It's laced with acetyl fentanyl," Zoo responded while shaking his head.

"What's that?" Saint asked as he slightly frowned.

"Fake dope. Synthetic," said Zoo.

"Who putting this out with our stamp on it?" Saint questioned as his brows frowned.

"That's the million-dollar question, my guy. We don't know. But this shit is flooded all through the bayou."

"And you say how many people overdosed off this bullshit?" Saint said as he shook the bag in front of Zoo's face.

"Four as of last night. Plus, you know the heat that bodies bring. We don't need that type of attention," Zoo answered.

Saint instantly became concerned, and his mind put a plan together. He held the Baggie up to the light with one hand and flicked it with his index finger.

"You have to get to the bottom of this. I told you what time I'm on. I'm dead serious, beloved. This isn't my concern anymore."

"I know, I know. But you know how I get down. I'm about to start shaking shit up until I get some answers," Zoo stated. Saint knew exactly what Zoo was referring to when he said, "shaking shit up," and Saint didn't want to take the leash off Zoo. Zoo was a hothead, and Saint didn't want to exchange the hands of power while in the middle of bloodshed. He knew he would have to get to the bottom of it before he completely walked away. He wanted his exit to be smooth and quiet—not like this.

Just as Saint was about to respond, the door swung open, and a petite woman that looked to be in her late fifties came in. She had a small gray Afro, and her face was made up. She wore an evening gown that matched the accent color of the wedding. Saint swiftly placed the pack of dope inside his pocket to hide it. It was his mother.

"Hey, Ma," Saint said, hoping she didn't see what he was just holding up. He especially didn't want her to see it because of her past addiction. She had been clean for only about ten years.

"Hey, baby," she said while smiling from ear to ear. Her bright smile was on full display as she waved her son over. "Come on, now. The pastor is ready for you. It's almost time to start."

"Yes, ma'am," Saint said respectfully as he nodded his head. He watched as his mom waited for him and waved him over hastily.

"We'll talk about this later, beloved," Saint whispered to Zoo. Zoo nodded in agreement, and they both headed toward the exit and prepared to go to the main chapel.

A small-framed woman stood before the cathedral's steps as she looked up at the historic place of worship. Her green eyes and caramel skin tone made her unique, and her tattooed body only added to that. She had a small tattooed heart under her left eye that was the lone marking on her flawless face. Various tattoos covered her neck, body, and even her fingers. Over thirty-five tattoos covered her entire body, which only added flair to her distinctiveness. She had a ruggedness about herself, yet was still feminine. Her Cuban descent shined through her features, so there was no hiding her heritage. Her smoky-brown skin resembled that of the people of her native land.

Tay tried her best to tame her frazzled hair as she repeatedly rubbed it down. What once was a silky-smooth mane was now brittle, wild, and all over her head. Her tattooed hands were ashy and in need of moisturizing. A wave of embarrassment overcame her as she looked up at the beautiful church before her and then down at her attire. She wore a soiled, tight-fitting jogging suit with a small jean jacket over it. She hadn't changed clothes for a week straight. She knew that she hadn't bathed in a while and probably smelled just like she felt. Nevertheless, something seemed to pull her to that place, on that day. She had to see Saint one last time before he started his new life.

Tay had heard through the grapevine that this wedding was more than just a nuptial, but it served as his retirement party to the game. The streets were speaking, and it was a day that the bayou shut down to honor its Most Valuable Player. She heard the sound of the bells ringing and instantly felt sick to her stomach. She abruptly bent over and threw up on the church steps, dry heaving as she gripped her abdomen. She was nervous and heartbroken at the same time. She was there to see the man she was in love with marry someone else. She wanted to be happy for him, but her somewhat selfish heart wouldn't allow that to happen.

Thoughts invaded her mind, asking God why he wasn't marrying her. After all that she had been through in life, it seemed like she deserved him more. The pain of meeting her soul mate, knowing that he could never be hers, was a pain that she could never have fathomed. Most people think physical pain is the worst thing in life, but try living with regret. That is true pain because there was no real end to that feeling. Regret is everlasting. It will eat you alive quicker than any cancer known to man. She knew that she had kept things away from Saint that would make him look at her differently. Therefore, she realized that she did not deserve him. The agony of knowing that was a pain that she knew would never fade away. *Too many secrets,* she thought to herself.

She gathered herself, stood straight up as she wiped her mouth, and then took a deep breath. Slowly, she walked up the stairs and then through the humongous French-style opening. She pulled the heavy doors, parting them, and walked in. The scene was breathtaking. It was something that she would only read about in fairy tales, and she was blown away. She could hear the distinct sound of the cello playing and the chatter from the guests that occupied the chapel. As she made her way toward it, she heard the sound of footsteps echoing throughout the lobby. She turned back and saw a man walking her way. He was barely paying attention to her as he made his way toward the chapel as well. As the man got closer, she saw and instantly noticed that it was one of Saint's henchmen, Gunner. She tried to bow her head to avoid eye contact, but the man had already made out who she was.

"Tay?" Gunner said as he squinted his eyes, trying to see if it was her. The young man used to have a crush on Tay, so seeing her like that instantly saddened him.

"Hey," she said shamefully as she tried to fix her hair. She slid the hair that was over her face behind her ear and folded her arms in front of her chest.

"Damn, I haven't seen you around in a while," he said nervously as he couldn't bring himself to make eye contact with the girl that he had lusted over once before.

"I know, right?" Tay said with a forced, nervous smile. Her eyes were wavering and unsteady. She, as well, couldn't bring herself to look at the young man in the eyes. She was in the middle of a drug binge and knew that it was showing through her appearance.

He couldn't believe how bad she looked. He felt a sense of pity for her. He was embarrassed for her. He could smell the absence of cleanliness bouncing off of her and dropped his head in disbelief.

The young man looked over his shoulders to see if anyone was looking at them. Then he shook his head and focused back on Tay. "Look, you shouldn't have come here. You know that," he admitted, not wanting her to mess up his boss's big day. Everyone in the hood knew what had happened the time she was around, and she was the last person that he thought would be at the wedding.

"I know, I know. I just wanted to say congratulations. I shouldn't have come," Tay admitted, and as she brushed past him and stormed toward the exit, Gunner grabbed her by the arm, stopping her.

"Hey . . . hey. Look, take this," he said under his breath as he took his free hand and reached down into his pants pocket. He pulled out a wad of money and quickly slid a hundred-dollar bill off his rubber-banded roll. He held it up in front of Tay, between his pointer and index fingers.

Tay's eyes shot to the money, and her mind instantly started to race. She thought about the drugs she could buy with that and shoot directly into her veins for the high that she had been chasing after that entire morning. Her heart pounded, and an insatiable urge overtook her. Her hand involuntarily went to the back of her neck to tame the sudden itch that overcame her. She immediately became fidgety. She looked like a full-blown fiend, and the young hustler instantly felt terrible for her. She was his age, and to see her tweak like that was heartbreaking. It was like he could see her thought processes.

It was evident that she was trying to fight the urge to take the money as she stared at it intensely. She was twitching and scratching at the same time, which was making it uncomfortable for him to watch. She was at her rock bottom, and it was apparent.

"Just take it," he whispered in a pleading voice, knowing that she needed a fix so she wouldn't get any sicker than she already was. He was a dealer of heroin, so he knew the internal battle she was going through. That same feeling that was killing her was the same one that kept him in business and paid. His only worry was that word would get back to Saint that he gave Tay money so that she could get high. However, he felt sorry for her. He just wanted to help.

Just as he was about to say something else, the doors opened, and the sunlight shined into the lobby. It was the bride coming with a group of other women through the front doors, and she was headed in their direction. It was time for the wedding.

Tay focused on the woman in the big, flowing dress. The dress was glamorous and elegant. The sheer, tubelike dress was tight fitting but opened beautifully the closer it got to the ground. She looked like an ebony mermaid. Her train dragged at least eight feet behind her, and a stylist followed her and held up the rear of the gown. Tay's heart dropped when she saw how beautiful she was. She wished deep down in her heart that she was in that beautiful dress rather than Ramina. Tears welled up in her eyes, and her bottom lip quivered. Pain filled her chest, and she felt anxious. Her breath became short, and a flutter in her heart made her feel like she was about to die right there on the marble floor. She had never felt that feeling before. She placed her hand on her chest, and it seemed like the only thing she could hear was the sound of her own breathing. It was as if the world had slowed down, and Ramina was walking in slow motion toward them. She stared at Ramina's beautiful made-up face and deep maroon lipstick and was in awe. She was absolutely beautiful.

"Come on," the young man said as he wrapped his arm around Tay. He then guided her toward the sanctuary, not wanting her to ruin the wedding. Ramina was so busy gathering herself and talking amongst her squad that she didn't even notice Tay by the chapel door. Tay and Gunner took a seat in the last row, slipping in unnoticed.

Tay glanced at the head of the church. Her eyes frantically searched for Saint, trying to locate the only man she truly ever loved. She was eager to see him. It had been almost a year since she had been in his presence, and her anxiety skyrocketed. The way that man made her feel was second to none, and no drug could compare to the high that Saint was capable of giving her. She was captivated by him and his aura. Saint was a vibe. A vibe that she couldn't get anywhere else on planet Earth. He was always calm . . . always slow motion. His voice was like violins in her mind because it never got loud or off-key. His voice soothed her. Her heart raced, just thinking about his baritone. Saint was that nigga, second to none. The most impressive trait he had was the fact that he didn't even know it. And if he did, he didn't show it. His humble demeanor made him even more appealing. She smiled, seeing him in the crisp suit. She caught a glimpse of his pearly white teeth as he and Zoo talked with each other.

"He's so handsome," she whispered as a tear involuntarily slipped down her face. She quickly wiped it away and sniffled. Although she was sad, she was happy for him because he seemed to be joyful. The look on his face told his story. He seemed as if he were content, and that was true. He had finally found peace in his life. Saint was about to exit at the top of the game, and that day served as a retirement party as well as a wedding. Tay saw the line of groomsmen and bridesmaids at the helm of the place and watched closely as Zoo and Saint smiled and whispered to each other while standing there waiting for the bride to enter. The loud sounds of the organ played, and everyone immediately stood. Everyone except Tay, that is. She sat there with her hands on her lap as the sea of guests stood up around her.

Everyone's eyes shot to the entrance and waited patiently for the woman of the hour. The sounds of the wedding song were like a dagger to her heart as she closed her eyes. Every note tugged at Tay's heart, and she thought that she would have a heart attack right then and there during the ceremony in front of everyone.

Suddenly, the large church doors swung open, revealing the bride to be. By now, the tears flowed nonstop as she started to hear the gasps and chatter. Tay chanted something incoherently under her breath as the woman made her way down the aisle. She mumbled nothings in a low tone as the tears continued to flow. She watched Ramina walk past her with her beautiful white dress. A glamorous, sheer veil was over her face, but it didn't hide it well. Her watering eyes and pretty smile were on full display as she slowly made her way to her soon-to-be husband.

Tay watched as the man that she loved waited for the woman at the end of the aisle . . . that was not her.

She couldn't take the pressure and quickly slipped out the back door once the bride made it to the front of the church.

Chapter One

A Toast to the Assholes

The sound of yet another plate being dropped by the waiters erupted. The shattering sound had become a part of the party, it seemed like. That was the third plate broken during the reception. People paused for a second to look over at the mishap but continued to finish up their meals as they ate the 5-star New Orleans cuisine, compliments of the chef hired by Saint and Ramina.

"You peep what's going on, bruh?" Zoo whispered as he leaned over toward Saint as they sat at the head table. Saint listened closely and then scanned the almost full reception hall. He vaguely grinned and calmly nodded his head in agreement. Saint always chose gestures over words if he could, picking and choosing when he spoke.

"That's exactly what I thought too. I knew I wasn't tripping," Zoo said as he sat back upright and fixed his blazer and adjusted his Cartier frames. He took a sip of champagne directly from the bottle and scanned the room. Champagne was flowing, and the reception was in full swing. It had been a few hours since the wedding, and now it was time for the celebration.

The vibe was a positive one, and the sounds of smooth R&B played in the background, acting as a soundtrack for the night. The reception was only for a selected few, and it was the ending of a great night. Only Saint's closest friends, business associates, and the waitstaff were in attendance. No extras. Although the crowd was small, there was a lot of power present in the building. Saint had earned a lot of respect throughout the years. Therefore, his guest list was one of importance. A few of the soldiers from Saint's blocks were there, but the guest list was mostly criminals. It was a den of hustlers and urban legends. At least a dozen street millionaires attended, all of whom Saint supplied, making that possible.

His wedding was a meeting of the elites. Everyone who was somebody came out to pay respect to Saint. Saint got just as many farewells as he did congratulations. He was moving away from the bayou and heading away for good, and everyone that ate with him knew this. Saint was the plug and the source of many men's life aspirations. He and Ramina would ride off into the sunset, leaving the life that had afforded him his luxurious lifestyle. Saint had sucked the streets dry and saved up enough money to retire comfortably from the life. He set out a plan, and he was at its pinnacle. His exit plan was well calculated. After his honeymoon, he and Ramina would retire in Miami.

A long table stood at the head of the room, and the groomsmen and bridesmaids all accompanied the newlyweds. Food had been served, and it was time for the best man to give a speech, honoring his right-hand man. Zoo stood up and grabbed a butter knife and tapped it against the wineglass, causing a chime to sound throughout the place. Everyone stopped moving and talking. Heads turned, and all their focus was now on Zoo. The DJ lowered the music that was playing throughout the speakers, and just like that, the entire place was quiet. The only people that were moving were the waiters who were picking up the dirty dishes from the different tables throughout the room. Zoo spoke loudly so everyone could hear him.

"My name is Zoey. My friends call me Zoo, if y'all didn't already know."

"Zoooo!" someone yelled from the crowd causing Zoo to pause briefly and then look in their direction. He smiled.

"See this nigga to my left? That's my guy right there. The best friend I've ever had. Not a man of a lot of words, but when he speaks . . . he speaks of substance. When he speaks, it means power. See, Saint and I met years ago when I was a senior in college. I had just blown out my knee and didn't know what I was going to do in life. He showed me a new way of thinking. He showed me that I didn't need a lot of friends, just one good one. And I found that in him. My mu'fuckin' partner in crime. We got a lot of money together too. We started a real estate company and haven't looked back since," Zoo said and hesitated as he shot a look over to Saint and winked. Saint smiled, knowing that they hadn't sold one damn house together a day of their lives. Honestly, that was the first time he ever heard something about a real estate company. Saint shook his head in amusement as he tapped Ramina's leg under the table. She chuckled as well, catching on to the inside joke.

"Zoo crazy as hell," Ramina playfully murmured under her breath. She whispered so low that only Saint could hear her. Saint picked up his glass and saluted Zoo, followed by a simple nod. Zoo continued.

"Saint always did right by me and showed me what real friendship is. I tell you all the time, there's not a lot of people that's cut from our cloth. Not too many niggas like us. He told me once that when it comes to friends . . . less is more, so there's plenty of us." Random encouraging shouts from the crowd came from the guests as Zoo's words resonated with them. He was preaching a ghetto sermon.

"I know that's right!" a lady yelled as she clapped her hands.

"Talk to 'em!" another man yelled as if Zoo were in a pulpit.

Zoo paused a moment and picked up his champagne flute. He raised the glass in the air and looked as the waiters continued to do their jobs, not paying him any attention. Then he picked up his speech right where he left off. "I want to wish him and his beautiful wife, Ramina, the best, as they start this new chapter in their lives. I love you both from the bottom of my heart," Zoo said as he dropped his head, signaling that he was done. But he quickly scanned the room and said something in addition.

"And another thing . . . I want to thank the waitstaff for the phenomenal job they're doing tonight. Let's give 'em a round of applause," he said as he motioned for people to clap. The crowd clapped, and a few of the waiters smiled but didn't pay too much attention. They were staying on the task at hand.

"Now, I want everyone to do one more thing for me. Raise your fist like this," Zoo said as he put his fist in the air. People were confused about what exactly he was doing. However, slowly but surely, the guests raised their fists. Zoo looked back at Saint to see if his hand was raised.

Saint just smiled and shook his head. Saint knew that his friend was a charismatic character and sat back and watched the show, not wanting any part of what was about to happen. Once Zoo saw all the hands in the air, he finished off his speech.

"Now stick up your finger like so," he said, as he waved his middle finger in the air. "All these waiters are federal agents, trying to find something out . . . but they won't. We are all law-abiding citizens in this mu'fucka. So, this is a toast to y'all bitch-ass mu'fuckas. Nice try. Spend these good folks' tax money on something that makes a difference," Zoo said with a big smile on his face. The entire room had their middle fingers in the air, and all the attention went on the mostly male waitstaff.

The waiters paused, and their pale white faces all blushed red. There was no denying what Zoo had said. It was the truth. One of the male waiters seemed to be so irate that he couldn't hide it any longer. The 40-something-year-old Caucasian man stood there in shock. He clenched his jaws tightly, and his pale white skin instantaneously turned plum red. It looked like smoke was about to pour out of his ears, he was so hot. Out of pure frustration, he dropped the handful of plates he carried and stormed off. Their cover had been blown, and it seemed almost instantly the other waiters followed suit. The sounds of glasses shattering erupted because multiple "waiters" dropped their plates and walked out. The guests, still with their middle fingers in the air, laughed uncontrollably. They literally laughed the Feds out of the building. It was a beautiful moment.

They say that the Feds have a 98 percent success rate, but on that night, they lost to the streets. It was a historic moment for the bad guys. Saint couldn't do anything but laugh as he shook his head at Zoo. Saint had known about the setup for a little over a month, and rather than complain, he let it play out. The Feds were always trying to find something on him but never could. The recent murder case that he had thrown out made them put him under a microscope. The careful and strategic measures that Saint took to protect himself over the years had all paid off. No paper trail connected him to his empire, and the only blemish he had on his jacket was the murder, and that wasn't even drug related. That incident was personal. He watched as Zoo walked back over to him and took a seat next to him. The DJ played the music again, and everyone talked among themselves at the crazy turn of events. It only added to the legend of Saint. That night was one for the record books.

It was just a few ticks after midnight, and most of the guests were beginning to exit. However, Saint and his wife were still there, enjoying the moment and dancing the night away. They must have had the DJ spin back Lauryn Hill's "Nothing Even Matters" about ten times. The two swayed back and forth as Ramina sang their favorite parts of the song in his ear while snapping her fingers to the snares. Saint's hand was on the small of her back, and her arms hung from his neck as they slowly rocked in perfect unison together. Saint's bow tie was untied, and the first two buttons on his shirt were unbuttoned. He was feeling good as he looked into the eyes of his new wife. Ramina was tipsy, and both of their hearts were full of joy as the thought of their new life had both of them in a blissful, trance-like state. He held a large bottle of champagne in his free hand and smiled at Ramina while gazing deeply into her soul's windows.

"Mi, you're beautiful. You're perfect," he complimented in admiration. He called her "Mi" for short, and she loved it every time she heard it. Her thick frame and wide hips made Saint's mind think about what they were going to do after they left. He looked at her face and admired her skin tone. Her full lips and made-up face were that of perfection like a ghetto Barbie. Baby hairs rested on her edges as her hair lay perfectly. He slid his hand down to her plump backside and cupped her ass, giving it a slight squeeze.

"You always know what to say to make me smile, Saint," Ramina said as she gazed into her husband's slightly red eyes. It made her smile, knowing that he was happy and finally letting loose for a night. He seldom drank, so he was in rare form.

"It's my truth, love. I'm just speaking about what I see. You're the prettiest girl in the world to me. You been here since the beginning, and I appreciate everything. I appreciate your loyalty. For that, I owe you the world," Saint said with sincerity, never breaking eye contact with his lady.

"You're my soul mate, Saint Von Cole," she said as she smiled and looked at her man in admiration.

"You're my soul mate, Ramina Shay Cole," he said, playfully returning the sentiment. They both shared a small laugh and continued to rock.

"Can I ask you a question, mister?" she said.

"Of course, love. Ask me anything," he answered.

"Are you going to leave it alone? Are you done? Like, done-done?"

"Of course," Saint said, as he looked around. "I'm out. There's nothing left for me to do in that world. I'm out," Saint confirmed. He spoke with conviction and was confident in his decision. He was out of the game for good. He saw the skepticism in her face, although she remained silent and nodded her head in contentment. Saint knew that, like everyone else, it was hard to believe.

"I can stay and die, or I can bow out gracefully and live the rest of my life with my best friend. Seems like an easy choice, you hear me?" Saint explained charmingly. He ran his tongue across his top row of teeth and smiled. It was contagious because it instantly made Ramina beam.

She shook her head, blushing.

"What?" Saint asked, wanting to know why she was smiling.

"You always make things so easy. Everything is so easy with you. You never cease to amaze me. You always have an answer to a situation."

Saint pulled her close to his chest and gently kissed her on her forehead. He whispered that he loved her and inhaled deeply as she lay her head on his chest, vibing to the rhythm of the beat and his soul at the same time.

Saint knew that a wise man knows how to make something complicated seem simple. Yet, a fool takes something simple and makes it complicated. Saint understood this, so he moved accordingly. Little did she know, he had been planning his exit for years. Everything that was happening now was a direct result of his strategic thinking. He would always think about a situation in ten different ways before he even told a soul about it, and this instance was no different.

As the song wrapped up, three girls dressed in bridesmaids' gowns approached the newlyweds. The song switched to what the locals called "Bounce" music. Bounce music was legendary in the bayou. The upbeat, fast tempo style was a staple in the culture of New Orleans, and it wasn't a party officially until you had the bounce. The sounds of Big Freedia pumped out of the speakers, and Ramina and her girls all come together while forming a small circle. Saint stepped to the side and smiled, watching his wife have a good time with her girls. That's when he felt the arm of Zoo wrap around him.

"You did it, my nigga," he said just before taking a big gulp from the champagne bottle.

"It feels right," Saint replied as the two stepped off the dance floor, walking side by side.

"Can you believe the fuzz came in this mu'fucka on your wedding day? They will stoop to the lowest of lows to lock a nigga up, won't they?" Zoo said, shaking his head, still in disbelief.

"They can snoop all they want. They ain't got shit on me. Let 'em come. I'm not worried at all," Saint said confidently.

"No doubt . . . No doubt," Zoo replied. He watched as the girls enjoyed themselves and yelled loudly while gyrating their backsides. He loved Ramina's crew because they were all beautiful, young, and rich. They were a power circle, and each one of them had a nice hustle going on. They were infamous throughout the city for being bad girls that loved the bad boys. Ramina was the ringleader of their crew, for sure. She complemented Saint very well by owning one of the most prominent salons in the city, and her online hair store did seven figures each year. Ramina wasn't your typical dope man's wife. She had her own, which made her even more desirable.

Zoo watched closely as the girls moved their big asses in circles in unison and eyed the one he would proposition later. But first, he wanted to talk business with Saint. Saint could turn someone from a small-time hustler into a king with the snap of a finger. Saint was the source of every drug dealer's happiness. He could change their lives with one simple phone call.

"About what you said earlier, I really appreciate that. I been waiting to take my shit to the next level. This is my way to do that," Zoo explained.

"Indeed. Indeed," Saint simply replied.

"I'm expanding," Zoo said, as he stared at nothing in particular. Saint could tell that he was planning his next move. The ambition was pouring out of him. Saint knew that was his best trait, but it also could be his worst.

"Expanding, huh?" Saint said.

"Yeah, I'm going to shoot back home and set up shop in Flint. I have a few cats out there that's moving around. They just need a steady pipeline to feed their people, feel me?" Zoo explained.

"After I get back from the honeymoon, we are on the first thing smoking to Cuba," Saint assured him.

"Cubana," Zoo said as he did a bad interpretation of a Spanish accent. He continued, "Oh yeah, I need you to plug me with homegirl too. You know . . . your witch doctor out there. I need that shit on my side, just in case shit goes left. I still can't believe that case got dropped. No trial—not nothing. Whatever you paid that woman . . . It was worth it."

"Was it worth it?" Saint asked. He was asking himself that question, more so than Zoo. "And she's not a witch doctor," Saint said as he shook his head at his friend's misconception. "It's not that simple. There's more to it than just voodoo dolls and that bullshit you see in movies," Saint said, as he had mental flashes of the things he saw on his last trip. He had been there plenty of times before, but that last time, things were definitely different.

Chapter Two

Monkey on the Back

Bums and dope fiends were scattered in various huddles under the overpass. It was in the wee hours of the night when only the street zombies and hustlers were up with their own personal agendas. A congregation spot for the city's have-nots, homeless, and druggies was under the city bridge. Two different bonfires inside old aluminum trash cans were ablaze, also known as a poor man's heating system. As the small fires illuminated the dark area, bums circled them, waving their hands over the flames in an attempt to keep warm. The scene resembled Hades with how fires danced in the air, and soulless addicts wandered aimlessly. Some of them looked like statues that leaned to the side from the effects of the heroin's potency.

Tay had become a familiar face on the scene over the past few months. She was by far the youngest fiend on the scene. Earlier, she had left the church, which was only a block away. She slumped on the soiled sofa as she could barely keep her eyes open. She dazedly moaned as she tried to sit upright but flopped back because her upper torso felt as if it weighed a ton. She immediately melted back into the couch after her failed attempt.

She felt wetness in between her thighs and looked down to see a huge wet spot in her crotch area. She groggily woke up completely from her heroin-induced nod and realized that she had pissed herself. This was a common thing among junkies. The rush that an addict felt when the drugs traveled through their veins was described as orgasmic. The sensation was like no other and sometimes caused the urge to relieve yourself. Tay had taken the money that Gunner had given her at the wedding and went straight to the dope man for her fix. Before that day, she had been clean for an entire week. However, seeing Ramina walk down the aisle to Saint pushed her to try to numb the pain. She just wanted the pain in her heart to go away, and the only way she knew to do that was to get high.

She gathered herself and stood up. She straightened her jacket and rubbed her frazzled hair. She looked around and noticed the familiar faces under the bridge and felt a sharp pain shoot through her stomach. She doubled over in pain and vomited onto the pavement. She knew her body was about to become dope sick. She was on a countdown to being in unbearable pain if she didn't get another shot of dope in her veins. The small fix that she had gotten earlier wasn't enough to keep her from going through the motions of being ill.

Her eyes scanned her surroundings, then focused on the gas station across the street. She headed that way to see if she could catch a young hustler to try to make a trade. "A trade" was a term in the streets when fiends would trade sexual favors for drugs, and Tay was open to it all. She would do anything to get the monkey off her back and prevent herself from getting sick.

She made her way across the street, where two guys stood outside of the station with hoodies on. She crossed her arms and hugged herself tightly as she made her way over to them.

Saint opened the door to his black Range Rover and watched as his newly wedded wife stepped in. They were just outside of the reception hall that was near the church where they were just married. As he took a swallow of the champagne that was in his hand, he studied his wife closely, admiring her. He gulped the bottle and wiped his mouth as he swallowed. He then walked around the car and hopped into the driver's seat, but not before pulling off his blazer and placing it across the middle armrest. A packet of bad dope fell from his pocket and onto Ramina's lap. Ramina wasn't green to the game, so she immediately knew what it was. She picked it up and examined it.

"This looks different. This isn't Cubana," she said confidently as she examined the altered stamp.

"I know, I know. It's some fake shit going around, and I have to get to the bottom of it," Saint said as he placed his hand on the steering wheel.

"I thought you were out, Saint," Ramina said as a brief wave of disappointment was written all over her face.

"I know, love. I just want to get to the bottom of it before Zoo starts shooting up shit. You know how he is," Saint expounded.

"Yea, I know, but that's not your concern anymore. You promised that this was over, babe. You promised," Ramina pleaded.

"You know what? You're right," Saint admitted, knowing that if he didn't just walk away from the game, something would always pull him back in. Instantly, Ramina smiled like a young schoolgirl.

"Well, I'll get rid of this for you. I'm going to make sure you leave this shit alone. We are about to start our new life together. We're leaving the bayou for good. So it can just be us two," she said joyfully. She tucked the pack in her purse to ensure that Saint wouldn't follow up on the street issue.

He watched as Ramina immediately took off her Louboutin stiletto heels and rested her feet on the white carpet of his car. They caught each other's eyes and smiled, both thinking the same thing. They couldn't wait to reach their home so they could make love for the first time as husband and wife. The sexual tension had been building up all night, and they were lusting after each other. He watched as Ramina giggled and worked her dress up, exposing her bald vagina. She pressed her back against her door so that she was completely facing him. She put one of her legs on the dash so that he could get a perfect view of her love box. Her big, brown legs always turned Saint on as he smirked at her voluptuous physique. She spread her legs apart as far as she could and rested her head on the window. Saint slowly pulled off.

He looked over in awe and smiled as he watched as she gave him a show. She sexily put her fingers in her mouth and made sure that she put enough saliva on them to do the job. She then circled her tongue around her own fingers, dropping them down to her box.

"Oooh," she purred. The moment her wet fingers reached her clitoris, it pulsated. Ramina smiled in pleasure as she felt the heartbeat in her love box. She tenderly tapped her vagina, causing a loud, wet sound to erupt. With every tap, it seemed as if her button grew and grew, slightly peeking from her lips. She continued to moan, all while keeping eye contact with Saint. She then applied pressure to herself and slowly stroke herself in slow, circular motions. Saint tried his best to focus on the road, but it was hard to stay on track. His eyes went back and forth from the road to his girl. He felt his manhood begin to grow. He thought about how he would bend her over as soon as they walked through their door. Ramina took her foot and placed it on Saint's crotch, searching for his growing tool. Her foot stopped when she found it, and that's when her mouth watered.

"Yeah, I'm livin' like that," Saint said playfully in a deep New Orleans accent, showing off his girth and strength. His bottom row of golds was on full display as he ran his tongue across his white top row. She wanted to taste him and took it as a personal challenge to make him erupt before they reached home. She got on her knees, in the seat, and unbuckled his belt buckle. She frantically searched for his rod, and when she found it, she let out a satisfying moan. Saint leaned back his seat slightly while keeping one hand on the steering wheel. He lifted his shirt so he could get a clear view of what was about to happen. He watched as Ramina wrapped her full lips around him, slowly swirling her tongue around his tip before swallowing him whole. She slowly made him disappear and reappear, working her magic. The slurping sounds made the experience even more enticing for Saint as he let out an unintentional moan. She wiggled her ass in the air as she pleased him, and the sight made Saint even stronger.

As Ramina pleased him, a bell sounded. Saint's eyes drifted to the speedometer, and he saw that he had low fuel.

"Damn, love, I gotta get some gas," he whispered, and he stared at the needle, pointing to "E." He watched as she slowly bobbed her head up and down, licking the sides of his shaft just before devouring the whole thing. He peeked at the huge BP sign and decided to make a quick stop before they were left stranded on the side of the road because of an empty gas tank. As he whipped into the gas station, he tapped Ramina so she could pause their session.

"Um," she hummed as she popped his tool out of her mouth. She sat up and wiped her mouth as she looked around to make sure no one was watching. They both looked at each other and burst into laughter. "Nigga, hurry up," she said playfully.

"Yes, ma'am," he answered as he made himself decent before exiting the car. He had on his dress slacks and an open shirt, displaying his tattooed belly and designer belt. His Valentino loafers clicked the pavement with each step. As he approached the store to pay for his gas, he saw a few youngsters standing by the door. He didn't know them, but obviously, they knew who he was because before he could reach the door, one of them opened it for him.

"Respect . . ." Saint greeted as he nodded to the youngsters, making sure he made eye contact with both of them before stepping through the threshold.

When Saint made it into the store, the young man that held the door open looked over at his partner with concerned eyes. He knew who Saint was and his prominent position in the streets. Saint was the plug, and every young hustler wanted to get put into position by him. Not a lot of people knew who Saint was, but if you knew . . . you knew. Saint could change a life with the snap of his fingers, so when the young dealers saw him, he was like a real-life walking lottery ticket. They just hoped that they were lucky enough to get on his radar . . . lucky enough to be a part of Saint's team. In the streets, he was a god.

However, the thought of what was going on in the alley just a few feet away was causing concern for them. They prayed to the heavens that Saint didn't notice what they knew. One of their partners was having his way with Tay in the dirty alley. It was well known that Tay was Saint's loved one, and no one wanted to be on the opposite of Saint's wrath over her—nobody.

"Move your hands," the young man said harshly as he looked down at Tay. Tay was on her knees in the wet alley.

Tears were in her eyes as she took the young boy into her mouth. She felt ashamed and embarrassed, knowing she was pleasing a 16-year-old boy just to get her next fix. The young hustler had his eyes on Tay for years and never thought that he would have her in the position that she was in now. The pimply-faced teen was as black as tar, and his demented, gap-toothed smile was on display. His skinny jeans were wrapped around his ankles, and he trapped the bottom of his shirt between his chin and chest to get a clear view. His big belly hung freely as he watched his manhood disappear and reappear from the blow job. His lustful eyes were fixated on the Cuban beauty that sucked him off. Her wavy hair was something he yearned after, and it made the experience even that more exhilarating to him. He couldn't believe he had Tay blowing him. She, at one time, was the catch of the neighborhood. Her association with Saint and Zoo made her a hood trophy, a notch under his belt.

He was having the time of his life, but Tay felt disgusting. As she slurped on the fat, young thug, a wave of shame overcame her. But then the pain in her stomach reminded her of why she was doing what she was doing. She felt the cold concrete and wetness on her knees and wanted it just to be over and done with. Another sharp pain hit her once again, but this time it was much more painful. It was so painful that she grimaced, causing her to scrape her teeth across the young thug's shaft. She jerked back and shrieked in discomfort.

"Bitch, watch your teeth," he said through his clenched teeth. He frowned and stepped back, snatching his tool from Tay's mouth. She dropped her head down in humiliation as she wiped the excessive saliva from around her mouth.

"Sorry," she whispered as she tried to grab his penis once again. He aggressively slapped her hand away. He then grabbed her forcefully by her face and made her look at him.

"Don't be sorry . . . be careful," he said with a demented look in his eyes.

Tay nodded her head in understanding and then gingerly took him into her mouth again. She worked her mouth on him, hoping that he would climax soon so she could get her fix from him. He threw his head back in pleasure as he gripped the back of her head and rammed himself into her mouth. She gagged and almost threw up because he was hitting her tonsils. He held her head and went as deep as he could, blocking her airwaves as he felt himself about to explode inside of her mouth. She placed her hands on his thighs and tried to push away so she could get air, but that's when he just held her tighter while releasing himself.

"Aaaagh," he moaned as a walnut-sized glob shot into the back of her throat. He finally released his grip on her head and stepped back, shaking his tool off as the semen flung from his penis.

Tay gagged and heaved as she tried her best to catch her breath. She fell to the ground, feeling dizzy from the lack of oxygen. Tay held her chest and panted heavily as she was now on all fours like a dog, searching for air. The young hustler put his tool inside of his jeans and laughed as he saw Tay suffer just beneath him. The sight of her gagging only fed into his ego. He wasn't a good-looking guy by any means. In his mind, it was payback for all the pretty girls that dissed him throughout his life. Somehow, treating her like shit made him feel better about the rejection.

He reached into his pocket and pulled out a small pack of heroin. He tossed it on the ground. It landed just to the right of Tay. She hurried and scooped it up, yearning to feel its power rush through her veins.

The hustler walked away so that he could boast to his friends about dogging the beauty. But before he could clear the alley, he heard her voice.

"Hey! Hey! What the fuck is this, man?" Tay yelled as she stood to her feet, examining the bag.

"It's what the fuck I gave you," the young man said as he paused and looked back at her.

"Yo, what's up with you? We had a deal. This isn't a forty pack," Tay yelled in disappointment as she rushed over to him and grabbed him by his jacket. He quickly snatched away and spat in her face. He had given her a small pack that he used to provide samples to the fiends. It wasn't enough to satisfy the intense hunger of a seasoned junkie. He had planned to short her from the jump, assuming she would just be happy with what he had given her.

"What the fuck?" she yelled again, as she wiped the spit from her forehead. The hustler walked away, leaving her there dumbfounded. He returned to post up right in front of the store, where his friends were waiting.

As the young man posted up, he saw the look on his friends' faces and immediately knew something was wrong.

"Fuck wrong wit' y'all?" he asked, looking back and forth between the two guys.

But before they could answer, Saint came out of the store. As he walked out, Tay was coming from around the corner in a rage. She was about to curse the hustler out but seeing Saint made her freeze up and become speechless. She stopped dead in her tracks and looked at the only man she ever truly loved. Saint was speechless as well. He froze when he saw his "baby." Although he didn't have the same type of attraction to her that she had for him, he did truly love her. He had more of a big brother feeling for her, and seeing her in her current state broke his heart into tiny little pieces. He looked at her eyes and knew that she had been using. The way they were sunk in and the dark circles were a dead giveaway that she was on the hunt for a fix.

Saint opened his mouth to speak, but nothing came out. He was watching his little baby tweaking, and it killed him. Tay could feel the awkwardness and just wanted to run away in pure disgrace. However, the pains in her stomach made her brush past him and approach the guy that had shorted her. Saint watched as she flew past him, and his eyes followed her as she stood in front of the group of guys. Saint took a deep breath and headed to his car and pumped the gas.

Damn, she looks so bad. Li'l baby don't even look like herself, he thought to himself, referring to her as a name he used to call her. He gave her that name because she was so tiny. Although she was 20, she had the body of a little boy. She had very small breasts and wasn't curvy at all. However, her pure beauty overcompensated for her lack of voluptuousness. Tay was his little baby, and that title had so many layers that only they understood.

He shook his head as if he were trying to shake off the concern that he had for her. But it didn't work. That love was embedded deep in his heart, and no matter how he tried to dismiss it, he couldn't. He glanced back and tried to see what was going on. He saw that they were arguing, but he knew that he couldn't get into another person's street business. He could tell in her eyes that she was fighting inner demons, and this crushed him to the core.

As he pumped the gas, he kept wanting to go and just save her, but he knew it was too late. His name was too good in the streets to break the code of it. He couldn't see himself trying to save a mere dope fiend from some petty business that wasn't his own. No matter how he cut it, it would seem as if he were being a square if he intervened.

He hopped back into the car. Ramina was sipping on the bottle of champagne and jamming to the music that she had turned up. The sounds of his speakers knocked as smooth R&B music sounded. The chill ambiance of Summer Walker's song had her in her element. She swayed back and forth with her eyes closed while snapping her fingers to the beat. She was oblivious to what was going on outside of the car and was in her own world. Saint hopped in with a heavy heart. He wanted to tell Ramina about what he saw, but he knew that it was a tender topic, so he decided to keep it to himself. He gave her a half smile and put the car in drive just before pulling off. Ramina finished off the bottle and looked over to Saint with bedroom eyes. She now wanted to finish what she had started as she looked down at his pelvic area.

"Let me get you together, babe," she said as she tossed the empty bottle in the back and then leaned forward. She licked her lips as she unbuckled his pants once again. She pulled his slightly erect tool out and circled his tip with her tongue. She knew from experience that had always got him to stand straight up in no time.

Saint drove and tried to focus on what Ramina was doing to him, but his mind was on Tay. He glanced in the rearview mirror, trying to see her, but they had gotten too far down the road. He thought that she was out of his system, but the connection was obviously still there. The look in her eyes . . . He couldn't shake those eyes. Those pretty eyes and the hurt behind them tugged at his heart. *Where did I go wrong with li'l baby? It wasn't supposed to be like this,* he thought as the guilt mixed in with heartbreak and played with his emotions. His mind drifted, and he replayed all the scenarios where he could have done something differently. As Ramina continued to work on him below, the heaviness of his heart pushed water out of his eyes. He couldn't understand why the girl's soul was tied to his like it was. No matter how hard he wanted to let her go, he just couldn't. He felt responsible for Tay's happiness, and anything beneath that felt like a failure on his part.

Ramina abruptly stopped and sat up. She looked over at Saint to see what was wrong with him. He had gone soft, and that was never a problem for him. He stood tall every single time, and his dick would get hard if she so much as touched it. But she knew what was wrong. It was written all over her man's face, and the water in his eyes was a clear indication of what she already knew. She crossed her arms as she looked straightforward, her mind churning as conflict manifested in her soul.

"Go get her," Ramina said reluctantly. She had seen Tay when they pulled up and saw their interaction as well. She decided to pretend that she didn't see it, not wanting to ruin her wedding day. But it was evident that something was bothering Saint. Ramina loved him so much that she was willing to hurt so he could be happy. Saving Tay would make him happy, and Ramina had accepted that. She knew the love that he had for Tay and seeing his pain really did something to her.

"What?" Saint said as he put his tool back in his pants. He looked at her, confused. It was as if she were reading his mind.

"You heard me. Go get your li'l baby," she said as she looked over at him, leaned forward, and gently cupped his face. "I understand. Go back," she whispered.

"I'm so sorry, love," Saint said, as he looked into his wife's eyes. A single tear slid down his face, and it simply broke Ramina's heart. She felt water build up in her eyes as the sorrow in her chest created a feeling of anxiety.

"It's fine. Turn around," she whispered, as she sat back in her seat and looked away just as the tear fell . . . just in time so that Saint didn't notice. He quickly hit a U-turn and headed back to the gas station to rescue Tay.

***

"You betta get outta my mu'fuckin' face. Take that pack and handle your business. You lucky I gave you what I gave you for that whack-ass head you gave me," the fat thug said as he looked at Tay with disgust. She had been begging him for the past five minutes, and he was growing agitated by her audacity.

"That's not fair. Now, give me what you owe," Tay said with pure rage as she balled up her fists and tears fell from her eyes. She knew that she would be in for a night of pain if she didn't get enough to keep the monkey off her back. What he had given her wasn't going to cut it. She needed more dope. She needed it bad and would do anything to get it.

"I'll do whatever you want me to do. Just please give me enough to shake this pain," Tay begged as an intense pain shot through her stomach once again.

The fat thug seemed as if Tay's agony amused him. He was about to push her away, but he got an idea when he saw the desperation in her eyes.

"Let my boys hit it. If you let all of us hit that pussy, you can have this," he said as he dug into his pocket and pulled out a pack. Instantly, Tay cried harder, knowing that she couldn't oblige to his request.

"I'm sorry, I can't do that," she said as she dropped to her knees in shame and teared up.

"This nasty bitch on her period," the fat thug said as he looked at his boys and laughed.

"That mouth still work, though," one of the other boys suggested.

"You damn right. That mouth works just fine," the fat thug said as he smirked and grabbed his junk and rubbed it through his jeans, thinking about the round two of action he was about to get.

"Okay, I will suck off all three of y'all. Just give me the dope first, so I know you're serious," Tay pleaded as she looked up with her hands clasped in a praying position. The fat thug reached into his pocket and pulled out a forty pack. He then tossed it on the ground where Tay was kneeling. She hurriedly scooped up the pack and it put it in her pocket.

"Come on," she said as she wiped away her tears and headed toward the alley.

The boys childishly chuckled and followed her into the darkness.

"I'm first, my nigga," one of the boys yelled as he pulled out his semi-erect penis and walked over to Tay, who was already on her knees. They didn't even notice the Range Rover pull up a few yards away. Saint smoothly stepped out and approached the alley. The sound of his calm, deep voice sounded.

"Show is over," Saint calmly said as he brushed past the two waiting thugs and headed over to Tay and the guy that she was about blow. He grabbed Tay by the arm and forcefully lifted her to her feet.

"Saint, let me go!" Tay yelled as she thought about getting her fix over anything else. Saint gave Tay a stern look as he gripped her tighter and pulled her close. She quickly backed down, knowing that Saint wasn't someone to play with. He had the savage look of a lion in his eyes, and it instantly sent chills down Tay's spine. After a few seconds of silence, Saint guided her past the crew and toward his car.

"Nigga trying to save the bitch. She belongs to the streets, my nigga," the fat thug said playfully while Saint's back was turned. The two other boys were shocked that he said something sideways to Saint. Their eyes grew as big as golf balls by their comrade's remark. One of the boys even tapped the fat thug and whispered, "What the fuck, man?" They understood who Saint was, but obviously, their friend didn't.

Saint heard what was said as he put Tay in the backseat. He remained quiet until he got her inside secure and shut the door. Then he calmly turned around and slid his hands in his pockets. He slowly walked over to the group of boys with a slight smile.

"What's your name?" Saint asked as he approached the fat one.

"I'm Fatboy," the guy proudly said as he poked his chest out a tad bit more than it already was.

"You know who I am?" Saint asked as he stepped closer to Fatboy, chest to chest.

"Nah, not really. *Should* I know?" Fatboy asked sarcastically.

"I know," one of the other boys said as he nervously raised his hand. They knew Fatboy wasn't aware of who Saint was. He had been locked up for the past few summers. Saint quickly put his finger to his lips, signaling that the boy should be quiet.

"My name is Saint. I didn't mean any disrespect, li'l nigga. This business is personal and—"

"Li'l nigga?" Fatboy said, cutting Saint off. He looked around at his boys like he couldn't believe what was said to him. He slid his hand into his back pocket and grabbed the small .25-caliber pistol out and transferred it into his front pocket. He intentionally wanted Saint to see what he had. He then continued. "I'm big weight out here. I advise you to take yo' ass where you came from. What you, a deacon or something?" he asked as he looked Saint up and down and saw his attire, not knowing that it was his wedding day.

"Nah, beloved. I'm no deacon. But check this out . . . You got it. You won. I apologize for the misunderstanding," Saint said politely, as he slowly put his hand on Fatboy's shoulder and patted it one time. "Have a good night, gentlemen," Saint said without one bit of malice or aggressiveness in his tone. He simply just patted the boy's shoulder and turned to walk away. He looked over to his left and saw Zoo creeping from their blind side. He didn't even bother to look over directly at Zoo. It was business as usual for them. Minutes before, Saint had called him and told him what was going down with Tay. Zoo had been parked on the side, watching the whole thing play out.

As Saint got to his car door, Zoo was preparing to blow Fatboy's brains out. Zoo knew exactly who to hit because of the discreet signal that Saint had given him by merely tapping the shoulder of Fatboy. He was nonverbally giving Zoo the greenlight. As Saint drove off, a loud thud rang off in the distance. It was the sound of a single gunshot that resonated, echoing through the air. Saint and Ramina didn't flinch at the noise, already knowing the cause of it. Tay jumped, frightened, and tried to see what was going on, but Saint had already pulled out of the lot and out of eyeshot of the homicide. In the streets, Saint was feared, and his reputation was something that he would guard with his life. Too bad Fatboy didn't know any better. He would now have to find out about who Saint was on the *other* side . . . because he was clueless in this realm.

Chapter Three

Toad You

Ramina cried a cascade of tears as she sped down the highway, pushing nearly eighty miles per hour. The top was dropped as she glided in and out of lanes on the interstate. She needed to feel the force of the wind. She wanted to *feel* it. She had to feel something . . . something other than what she was feeling on that early morning. Everything was just so heavy on her soul, heavier than anything had ever been. Her entire being was shaken, and everything that she knew was for certain somehow was now unreliable. The picture-perfect life that she finally thought she had seemed to be snatched from under her. The only man that she truly loved was in love with someone else. She could tell. She just knew. There was something about seeing those tears in Saint's eyes that told her the truth. Not his words or his actions, but those tears told her everything that she *didn't* want to know. She had been with him for years and never once saw tears from that man.

Ramina had no makeup on her face, and her natural brown skin glowed in the sunlight. Being in public like this was a rarity for her. She hadn't walked out of the house in years without being dolled up. But on this day, she just had to get away from the anguish that was back home.

She slightly raised her oversized sunglasses with her index finger and wiped tears away as she wept. She cried uncontrollably as she thought about how her husband was at home tending to that dope-sick woman, rather than celebrating their new marriage with her. The loud purr from her silver Porsche Panamera ripped through the airwaves. She neared one hundred miles per hour. The sounds of Lauryn Hill knocked through her sound system as her long, jet-black hair blew wildly in the air.

She was supposed to be on an airplane on her way to Italy for her honeymoon. Instead, she was in still in the bayou . . . heartbroken. She was there wondering if she had made a mistake by marrying Saint. *How can he be trying to put her together, while I'm fucking falling apart?* she thought as the tears continued to flow. She had loved Saint with every morsel in her body, and she knew he was a good man. The problem was that he was being a good man to someone else. Anxiety crept in. Although she tried to breathe slowly, the heartache was overweighing it all.

"Why does he love her? I fucking hate her. I *hate* that bitch. I wish she would just die," Ramina cried as she smashed the accelerator to the floor, pushing the luxury vehicle to the limit. She was now nearing one hundred twenty miles per hour. Somehow, the speed seemed to help her release the unwanted tension that had built up inside of her.

Ramina's disappointment and frustration had reached its boiling point. She felt like she was being robbed— robbed of the life that she had deserved. She stood by Saint's side and played her position the right way throughout the years. The pain slowly started to become rage. She possessed a massive flame that burned deep within her soul, all behind the man that the streets feared, and the ladies lusted after. She was drawn to his quiet power. She was addicted to him, and she wasn't going to let him go.

"Fuck that!" she yelled as she squeezed the steering wheel as tightly as her grips would allow. She let out a roar of passion that she never knew she had.

"Aaaagh!" she screamed, which turned into a gut-wrenching sob. She angrily hit her steering wheel. She wasn't a hateful person, but over that man, she would become the worst. He was her trigger. *He was her trigger*.

She felt something in the pit of her stomach rumble as nausea set in. Suddenly, the urge to throw up overwhelmed her. She was sweating profusely and dry heaving while becoming dizzy. Vomit came up in her mouth. She leaned over to spit the vomit out in her passenger seat. Her eyes grew as big as golf balls when she saw all the clear secretions that she had thrown up. But it wasn't the spit and secretions that alerted her. It was the small green frog hopping around in it, struggling to escape the thick liquid . . .

What the fuck? she thought as she tried to refocus her fuzzy vision. Her heart raced rapidly. She was confused and frightened at the same time. She shook her head and focused on the road . . . but it was too late.

The sound of a thunderous crash resonated in the air, followed by screeching tires and crushing metal. Ramina crashed her car into the back of an eighteen-wheeler semitruck, instantly propelling her body into the air like a rag doll. She was launched about fifty yards and crashed violently onto the pavement. Her body rolled over a dozen times against the concrete, ripping her flesh with each flip. It all happened so fast . . . She never saw it coming. She didn't have a chance. As Ramina lay there slipping in and out of consciousness, she was completely bloodied, and the left side of her face was skinned from skidding on the road. She tried to move, but she couldn't. The broken bones and trauma wouldn't allow her to.

She felt her life slip away, and all she could think about was Saint. She just wanted him to come and save her. She wanted him to make sure that she would make it through. Her thoughts went to Tay. Her eyes were getting heavy as her vision got blurry, and she saw an animal standing over her. She was horrified, yet she could not gasp, scream, or move. She was just there. It looked like a monkey, but she wasn't sure. She couldn't really make it out clearly. She thought that it was odd. She had never seen that type of animal up close other than in zoos, and that was behind glass. Ramina took a deep breath as her eyes slowly closed. She couldn't fight the urge to sleep . . . So she let go.

Saint sat in the chair next to the bedside of Tay. He watched closely as Tay scratched her body vigorously and fidgeted in her sleep. Her body was drenched in sweat as if a bucket of water had been dumped on her. She faintly whimpered, and she continually clawed at herself. She scratched so hard that she drew blood, making thick welts on her arms and neck, and trickles of blood were in different spots on the white sheets. Saint understood what was happening to Tay and knew there was nothing he could do about it, but just wait it out. Her body was going through withdrawals, and it yearned for the drug that made Saint wealthy. Saint was sitting in a chair right next to the bed and watched, knowing that he was helpless, and that's what broke his heart. He wasn't that much older than Tay, but in a way, he felt like she was his little baby. He felt the responsibility of taking care of her, no matter how difficult it was.

Something deep inside was telling him that he was doing the right thing. He rubbed her hair, gently laying it down and brushing it in one direction. He could feel the wetness from the sweat, but he didn't care. He just wanted her to get better. He slowly caressed her and whispered to her. "Shhh . . . shhh," he said, trying to comfort her, and instantly he noticed the murmurs slowed, and her body got more relaxed. "That's my girl," he whispered as he leaned over and tenderly kissed her forehead. He continued to rub her until she stopped tweaking altogether. He half-grinned while watching her closely. He knew that she was a diamond in the rough and had the potential to be something great. However, her past demons had a hold on her, a strong one. She had been through so much in her life, and he knew that if he didn't help her, no one else would. At 21, she had suffered three lifetime's worth of pain and despair. Her pure beauty hid her pain well, and she looked nothing like what she had been through.

His thoughts drifted to his new wife, and guilt set in. The thought of him asking her to go through this at the time of their wedding really bothered him. He felt selfish, knowing that he temporarily ignored her feelings to tend to Tay, who had a hold on him, and he could not understand why. He thought that he was the cause of her current struggle, so, therefore, he felt responsible for her. He hadn't seen her in over a year, but there wasn't a day that passed that he didn't think of her. When he saw her in that alley, he felt God was giving him a second chance to right his wrongs with her.

Although he had her blessings to help Tay, he knew deep inside that Mi had put his feelings before her own. He was so worried about Tay that he never thought about how Mi must've felt. He understood that she hadn't deserved to be anyone's second option or on a back burner. He felt a flutter in his heart as if he just saw Ramina's face. He shook his head, ashamed of himself, and headed out of the room to tell her he was sorry. He hadn't even realized he had been in the guest room with Tay all night. Not until he saw the rays of the sunlight peeking from the living room blinds did he notice that he had broken day while tending to her.

He walked across his spacious home, and it felt unusually cold. The ten thousand-square foot estate was one that Mi had made their home. Her woman's touch shined through the exquisite interior design. Her stellar creativity was one of the many things he loved about her. It was simply beautiful. Saint walked across the marble floors and looked up at the high ceiling. Beautiful baby saints were hand drawn on his ceilings. He was amazed every time he looked at it. It was Ramina's idea, and it added character to the home. It was like their mini Vatican with beautiful brown faces rather than pale ones. He reached the porcelain wraparound stairs that led to the second floor and headed toward their bedroom.

When he walked in, he expected to see Ramina in the mirror, doing her hair and makeup as she did every morning. He entered, ready to apologize for his actions, but he found himself standing there alone. The bed was perfectly made up, and the room was empty. A small note was on the bed with her handwriting on it. Just next to the note were two first-class tickets to Italy. As he read through the paper, tears formed in his eyes, but none fell. Her words seemed to talk directly to his heart. He dropped his head and thought back to how it all began. He thought about how times had changed over the past few years. He sat on the bed and just stared at the paper in disbelief. At the time, he thought that it was the beginning of a new chapter in his life. Now, looking back, he realized it was a part of the ending. He wished he had never been opened to the things that Cuba offered.

He sat on the bed and thought deeply. He remembered when things were so simple, and life seemed easy. He looked to his left and saw a Bible there. It had a sticky note with Ramina's handwriting on it. It simply read,

Give this to her . . . Matthew 11:28–30

He grabbed the Bible, stood up, and walked back to the room where Tay was. She was still in there fighting her demons and sweating profusely as she slept in obvious agony. There was an onslaught of moaning and scratching as she clawed and dug into her own skin. It was hard for Saint to watch, but he knew that she had to go through the withdrawal process to get better eventually.

He wanted to run out and find Ramina, though he knew that Tay really needed him. He was torn. Deep down in his soul, he recognized that the right thing to do was to go after his newly wedded wife. But what about Tay? What was she supposed to do without any help? She had no one in the entire world except him.

Saint looked at his li'l baby in pain, and it shook him to his core. At that moment, he realized that he truly loved her. It was because of the way she made him feel and the emotion that she pulled out of him. It wasn't a romantic relationship at all . . . Well, not in Saint's eyes. It was a complicated love between those two. Deep in his heart, he felt that he was responsible for her happiness. That was a heavy burden for anyone to have, but he knew that he owned it. He could not wrap his mind around his bond with her. It felt as if he were rooted to this girl. From the surface, it appeared as if it were a brother/sister relationship, but from Saint's point of view, he wanted to protect her as if she were his daughter. But the truth was, Tay looked at him as more than that. She was deeply in love with him, and he realized that. That's why the relationship was so toxic. His mind drifted back to the first time he met her in Cuba. It was the night that his life changed forever.

Chapter Four

Lion and Water

Two Years Before . . .

The sun was just rising, and the orange and purple hues blended perfectly on the sky's horizon. Blue water from the waves washed up on the shore and wet the entire backside of Ramina. She lay on the edge of the beach shore, just close enough to feel the water wash up. She wore a sheer cover-up robe that left nothing for the imagination. Her wide hips were on full display as she parted her thick brown thighs. Saint lay naked, right in between her legs, kissing her gently. Her red, pedicured toes were dangling in the air as she gripped the sand while gasping for air.

Ramina arched her back and moaned as Saint slowly rocked in and out of her cleanly shaven love box. He took his time, as usual, rocking back and forth, making sure he stayed deep inside of her while doing so. Ramina couldn't help to be in love. The man that was making love to her was her soul mate. Everything about Saint was perfect for her liking. His size, his girth, and his rhythm were tailor-made. It seemed as if he had been specially made for her. She loved the way he made love to her. He was never loud, he never went fast, and he was never weak. She could feel his power in each and every stroke . . . every time. She loved the weight that he put on her when they were intimate. For some odd reason, it comforted her and made her feel safe. As Saint rocked back and forth, he placed his lips by her left earlobe and whispered everything he wanted her to know. Saint was skilled and seasoned enough to know that anything you wanted to stick in a woman's thoughts had to be said during sex . . . good sex, that is. It was seduction at its highest level.

"You are my soul mate," he said in his deep baritone as the sound of the ocean echoed through the air. It was a perfect combination, his voice and nature's ambiance. Earlier that morning, he had wakened her up with kisses and, shortly after, walked her to the beach. They were just outside a private villa in Aruba. It sat directly on the beach, and Saint took full advantage of the majestic layout. He wanted to celebrate her birthday correctly, so he took her international to hail her special day. Saint and Ramina had traveled the world together and made love on different beaches around the globe. It was "their thing." They traveled several times a year and lived life to the fullest. They had been together since they were teens, and they deserved it . . . They deserved each other. Their passports were stamped up and barely had room for any more.

He gently lifted off her so that he was looking her directly into her eyes. He stretched out his arms, flexing his muscles as he repositioned himself while remaining deep inside, touching her bottom. He continued stroking her with a slow, constant pace . . . making sure he stayed at the back of her love box. He was applying that pressure, that heaviness that kept her clitoris engaged. Ramina stared at him intensely and thought about all the reasons why she was so in love with her man . . . her lion. She loved the way his full beard hung like a mane. His belly slightly poked out, but as she glanced down, she could still see him sliding in and out of her. Saint gradually changed pace, giving her longer strokes. She grabbed the back of his neck and raised her knees, pulling them back closer to her chest, thus, giving him more access to her.

She mouthed, "I love you," as a tear rolled down her face, feeling overwhelmed by his pure love and energy. Saint was just different. She had never cried while making love before she met Saint, but with him, it happened almost every time. They were not tears of pain, discomfort, or even of the slightest sorrow. She cried because she was elated. She cried because she knew that he loved her without any bias. His love was unwavering, intentional, and most of all, it was unconditional. The way he looked at her while he sexed her was almost hypnotizing. He never looked away or was embarrassed. The constant eye contact made it more dreamlike. He stared at her while slowly tapping her. This was a nonverbal language that gave her a sense of security. His confidence gave her strength, and this exchanging of energy always was food for her soul.

"Saint, I love you so much. You . . . You feel so good, baby," she moaned as the tears steadily flowed. She smiled while biting her bottom lip in pleasure. Saint's constant stroking and patience were about to pay off. He had been building up her climax for the past twenty-five minutes, and she could feel her release nearing. She adored the way he handled her. He was never rough with her; always patient.

Saint stared into his woman's eyes, and the way her breathing became rapid, he knew she was about to reach her orgasm. He ran his tongue across his lips as he felt his tool get even more erect. The sight of her curvy body and big breasts turned him on. Her dark areoles were huge, and he saw them beginning to get erect as well. He loved the way they jiggled with every thrust. He listened carefully as she whispered in between gasps.

"I'm about to come . . . I'm about to come. Don't stop. Please, don't stop," she said as she gripped his forearms and dug her nails into them.

Saint wasn't a rookie by any means, so he stayed the course and didn't change up his rhythm. Through experience, he knew that when a woman tells you she is about to have an orgasm, the last thing you do is speed up. That was a novice mistake that most men made. They had no patience. Saint had plenty. He didn't do anything fast. He understood that you should keep the same speed and stay at the same spot when a woman is reaching her boiling point. So that's exactly what he did. He steadily glided in and out of her until he felt her vagina walls contract and get tight around his pole. Ramina's body jerked violently, and that's when he knew she was there. He slid his pole out of her and tapped her clitoris swiftly with his tip. After a few hard taps, a geyser of liquid shot from her box and crashed against Saint's stomach.

"Aaaagh," she yelled loudly as she let herself go, squirting everywhere. The wet sensation made Saint explode as well. He shot his load on her belly as her final squirts seeped out. They had climaxed together and found themselves on their backs, looking at the sun come out. It was a beautiful thing. It was perfect timing.

"Happy birthday, pretty girl," Saint said as he held out his hand. Ramina breathed hard and tried to catch her breath before speaking. She couldn't help but smile.

"Thanks, baby," she answered as she slapped hands with her man. They had an unbreakable bond. Although they were lovers, they were best friends.

"I'm hungry," Ramina said as she looked over at him.

"Bitch, me too," Saint playfully said as he displayed his beautiful smile. Then both of them burst out into laughter, and Ramina rolled over and straddled him, playfully hitting him. She leaned down and kissed him after they play fought.

"This really was beautiful. It means the world to me," she said, thinking about their vacation and the thought he put into it. She was on cloud nine.

"And you mean the world to me, pretty girl," Saint answered.

Saint watched as Ramina did her makeup in the mirror across the room. She sat in front of a vanity mirror as she swayed to the music playing in the background. She wore a huge terry cloth robe with a towel wrapped around her head. The smell of sage filled the room, and the smoke danced in the air freely, setting the vibe. Saint sat at the dining table in the middle of the villa. His focus was on the scattered dead men's faces that were on the table. He put the stack of hundred-dollar bills through the money machine and watched as the Benjamin Franklin faces flickered one after another. A loud beep sounded, letting him know that the count was complete. He quickly grabbed the money out of the top of the machine and then wrapped a rubber band around it. He neatly placed the

stack in the duffle bag that was near his feet. He always re-
counted the money to make sure it was right. He wanted
to make sure that his purchase money was accurate for
his upcoming Cuba trip. Although they were in Aruba that
morning, he planned on being in Cuba by the end of the
night. Saint had been in the drug game since his teens, but
everything changed when he found a heroin connect in Havana, Cuba, while on vacation with Ramina. He had the
plug going on seven years, and his empire had skyrocketed since the pipeline was formed. He always scheduled
his Cuba trips at the end of a vacation that he and Ramina
took. That way, he could avoid the hassle of the US and being under the watchful eyes of the American government.
Saint was very strategic, and this was just one of his cau-
tious tactics to remain meticulous.

"So, listen. I'm going to meet you back here in two
days. I'm going to shoot this move and be right back," he
said as he zipped up the duffle bag.

"OK, babe, I'll be here waiting," Ramina answered as
she applied the blush on her cheekbones. She paused and
turned around so she could be facing him rather than the
mirror. She watched as he walked over to her with his
duffle bag in hand. He had a stack of money in his hand
and gave it to her.

"This is for some shopping. Zoo is downstairs when
you're ready to go. Just call him, and he'll have the car
ready for you out front," Saint said, letting her know that
he had everything taken care of. Zoo always tagged along
with them when they traveled the world.

The car service was waiting outside of the villa to
transport him to the private airport. As usual, he chartered a private plane to Cuba so he could meet his
connect Alejandro. Ramina took the money and smiled

as she examined the stack. She loved the way he spoiled her, and she couldn't wait to hit the shopping district in downtown Aruba. She stood up and jumped into his arms, instantly making him drop his bag. She wrapped her legs around his waist and wrapped her arms around the back of his neck. Saint was just under six feet, so he hovered over her five foot four frame. It was easy for him to scoop her up as he cuffed her plump butt cheeks, feeling her wobbly, soft cheeks.

"My pretty girl," he whispered as he hugged her tightly. She closed her eyes and inhaled the clean, fresh smell of his cologne.

"You're so good to me. Thank you, baby," she said just before she leaned in and kissed him. After their kiss, he let her down to her feet and just stared at her, smiling. She always loved it when he showed his teeth. It was her favorite part of his physical features. The sight alone made her want to have a replay of what they had done earlier that morning.

"You deserve to be treated well. You're perfect. Perfect for me, anyway. You just get a nigga, ya heard me?" Saint said with sincerity.

"You heard me?" Ramina mocked while smiling from ear to ear and playfully making a silly face. She loved mocking his New Orleans accent. His charm melted her, and he didn't even try. It was so effortless with Saint. He always knew how to time things perfectly to make her smile. That Creole-influenced twang got her every time. They both laughed.

"Be safe. I'll be here waiting when you get back," she said as she stood on her tiptoes to give him a peck on the lips. Saint gently smacked her buttocks and squeezed it just before he picked up the duffle bag, heading out the door.

"Forty-eight hours," Saint said as he opened the door to exit.

"Forty-eight hours," Ramina repeated as she stared into the mirror, beginning to apply her mascara. That was something they always said before he went on his Cuba trips. He always made it a brief trip when going to visit his plug.

"Hey," Saint said as he looked back at his woman.

"Yes," she said as she stayed focused on the mirror while tending to her eyelashes.

"Look at me," Saint instructed. He waited until her full focus was on him before he spoke again. Ramina slowly turned toward him and caught him staring at her, smiling widely. His whites and his golds instantly made her smile.

"Yes?" she said beaming.

"I just wanted to look at you again," he said as he stared at her in admiration. After a few seconds of gazing, he quickly left. She sat there, blushing with butterflies in her stomach, staring at the door.

"That's a man right there," she whispered to herself as she shook her head in disbelief at how he could still make her feel like a little girl. His charisma always made Ramina feel a type of way and only solidified that he was the love of her life.

Saint took the elevator to the lobby and checked his watch to see what time it was. Just like he planned, he was in the lobby at nine a.m. sharp. The private resort had some of the best villas in the country, and it was one of Saint's frequent vacationing spots. He walked onto the marble floors that led to the spacious, open lobby where staff moved about the place. The five-star establishment was gorgeous, and the sound of the live Mariachi band serenaded the morning guests. Saint wore an open linen shirt with Armani slacks, Italian cut. As he walked out on the marble floor, he looked over toward the car and saw Zoo sitting there conversing with a beautiful Latina woman. Zoo glanced over and noticed Saint and cut his conversation short to join him.

"Top of the top," Saint smoothly said as he slid a toothpick in his mouth.

"Top of the morning," Zoo responded as he slapped hands with his best friend. They both headed outside of the establishment so they could talk away from the earshot of the other guests and staff.

"How was your night?" Saint said as he gave Zoo a smirk and looked back at the lady who was sitting at the bar.

"Nigga, you see that over there?" Zoo said as he smiled and rubbed his hands together while glancing back as well.

"I see it, for sure," Saint complimented and approved. He shook his head and chuckled at his right-hand man. They had spent the previous day on a yacht together, including the Latina woman, so he was familiar with her. She looked back and saw Saint and Zoo looking at her. She smiled and waved at Saint. Saint slightly smiled and gave her a head nod acknowledging her.

"What?" Zoo asked, knowing Saint wanted to say something. "What? Spill the beans, brody," Zoo said.

"I'm just saying . . . every trip we take, you come with a different girl. Every single time," Saint said.

"Everybody can't be like you and Ramina. See, y'all got something real. All this shit is fake, bro," Zoo explained.

"What you mean exactly?" Saint asked, trying to follow Zoo's thoughts.

"I mean that none of this is real if you really think about it. She wants me because I got the bag and can take her on trips for her to post on social media. And to be honest, I only want her because of that phat ass. Simple math. It's an unspoken transaction that no one likes to talk about," Zoo expertly explained.

"I get it, bruh. I just can't lie down with a bitch I don't have a mental connection with, ya hear me? I mean, I could when I was younger, but now, I'm on some other shit. Catching a nut is only half the pleasure," Saint said.

"I feel that. But until I find someone like that, I'm keeping my options open," said Zoo. He tapped Saint on the chest playfully and looked around like he was about to tell him a secret. "Bro, I let that bitch spit in my mouth." They both burst out into laughter, and Saint shook his head in disbelief.

"Y'all into some freaky shit. What the fuck, man?" Saint asked while laughing.

"You damn right. She loves for me to choke her while I'm hitting it," Zoo explained.

"What?" Saint asked while squinting his eyes.

"This girl is wild as hell, brody. I thought I was about to kill her last night, but she didn't want me to stop. She said she comes harder when she's about to pass out. It's the weirdest shit."

Saint just stayed silent and shook his head as he couldn't wrap his thoughts around the choking thing. He couldn't see how a woman could let a man do that to her. He tried to envision himself choking Ramina but couldn't. In his mind, during sex, a woman should be handled gently and treated like a difficult math problem. This meant slowly taking your time to figure out the intricacies that please her. He knew that sex was about break-

ing a body's code, not pain. This is why he could make
a woman fall in love with him, while others like Zoo
couldn't. Before Saint could respond, he saw a black luxury car pull up. He knew that it was for him. He arranged
for the car service to pick him up at nine oh five.

"Okay, this me," Saint said as he reached out and
slapped hands with Zoo.

"Bet. I'll make sure Ramina is good," Zoo ensured his
right-hand man, knowing that would be the next thing
Saint would say to him.

"I appreciate you. I'll be right back," Saint confirmed
as the car pulled up right in front of him. One of the bell-
hops went to open the door, and Saint stepped forward
to slide in the backseat of the vehicle. The bellhop held
his hand up, signaling for Saint to pause. He then looked
past him and focused on the group of four men emerging
from the elevator, all white men of a certain age. They all
looked to be fiftyish. They wore different variations of
tropical shirts, and all had deep tans. They were chatting
among themselves and had beers in their hand as they
approached the car. They also were rolling luggage with
their free hands.

"Excuse me, sir," the bellhop said to Saint as he
slightly brushed him to the side, clearing the path for the
white men approaching. Saint instantly grew offended
and frowned at the lack of respect shown for him. Zoo
caught wind of Saint's discomfort and immediately went
into goon mode and stepped forward.

"Don't get smacked the fuck up out here," Zoo said
with his face twisted up in anger.

As always, Saint remained calm and gently tapped
Zoo's back and whispered, "It's all good. Stand down."
He didn't want Zoo to go berserk. He knew his friend

well enough to know that he had no problem with turning the small situation into a chaotic scene. Zoo took a deep breath and stepped back as Saint requested.

"Sir, I apologize, but this service is for Mr. Regis," the valet said as he didn't even take the time to look at Zoo. As the men approached, they dropped their luggage and like ants to sugar, the bellboys hustled to pick up their bags.

Who is this guy? Saint thought to himself, offended. He stepped back and closely watched as everyone seemed to want to cater to the group of men. He watched as the men all slid into the back of the spacious car, and the man with the open shirt and bone-white hair was the last to enter the vehicle. The man had a head full of white hair and a neatly trimmed goatee. His teeth were pearly white. He reached into his pocket and pulled out a diamond-encrusted money clip as he watched the last of the bags being loaded into the trunk. He then peeled off Benjamin Franklins and tipped each bellboy that was in his sight. By the way that everyone was so attentive to him, one could tell the respect level that everyone had for the man. Saint and Zoo watched as the man got inside the car and slowly cruised out of the resort's lot.

"Our money spends like his," Zoo said as he reached into his pocket and pulled out a rubber-banded knot of one-hundred-dollar bills and fifties. He waved it in their faces as he had a smug look on his face.

"Put that away," Saint said calmly and in a low tone. He then leaned over to a young valet worker and asked him the question that was on his mind.

"Who was that?" Saint questioned.

"That's Regis Epstein," he answered while leaning in and keeping his voice low. He then continued to fill in Saint. "He owns this entire resort. He actually has a few of them here and also in the United States. Big spender . . . big tipper. Everyone wants to get in his good graces to catch him on one of his generous nights. He's a fucking billionaire," the man said with excitement.

"Gotcha," Saint said while nodding, taking in the information. He then realized that it wasn't all about money. Sometimes, power.

Saint reached into his pocket and slipped the valet a hundred-dollar bill for the insight. The valet's eyes lit up, and he quickly thanked him while sliding the money into his pocket. The valet looked beyond Saint and waved over a second car to pull up. Saint followed his eyes and saw the car. He slapped hands with Zoo and watched as the valet opened the door for him.

"In a minute, beloved," Saint said to Zoo just before he smoothly slid into the backseat of the car with a duffle bag in hand. He was on his way to get on a jet to order one hundred kilos of the purest heroin in the world.

Chapter Five

Iron Eagle

Saint stood at the desk, looking in the eyes of the blond, blue-eyed receptionist. He was slightly agitated as he rested his hands on the counter, waiting for a response from the lady that stood behind the desk. He stared at her as she typed into her computer.

"I'm sorry, Mr. Cole. We don't have any charters available until tomorrow evening," she said as she shook her head as she scanned her log list, running her finger down the screen. Moments before, she had informed him that one of the pilots had called in ill, and his scheduled Cuba flight wasn't available. This presented a problem for Saint because Alejandro was very finicky about promptness. He knew it was a flight that he could not miss.

"I scheduled a flight a month ahead of time. There has to be something you could do," Saint said in a low, calm tone, thinking about the potential hiccup in business that this missed flight might cause.

"I'm sorry, sir. My hands are tied. I can check to see if there are any outgoing commercial flights. The airport is just down the street," she suggested, trying to accommodate their mishap. Saint instantly knew that was not a possibility because of the security and customs process

that commercial flights entailed. He could not chance being caught with that amount of money. It would cause a
red flag for sure. Although he didn't transport the dope
back, he did indeed directly bring the cash to the plug
Alejandro and set up the deal. This was a shopping process that had to be done by him personally, or else it just
wouldn't happen.

"That's not an option. I fly private, ma'am," Saint said
as he turned around and looked on the runway. He saw a
large Gulfstream G6 sitting on the runway with the steps
let down. It was the grandfather of the fleet and one of
the biggest jets money could buy. Saint noticed it immediately because he had been eyeing it for some time now.
His money was only long enough to charter the smaller
ones, but he promised himself he would charter a bigger
jet one day. "What about that? Is that jet available?"

"Sorry, that jet is reserved for . . ." the receptionist said
but paused when another man approached the desk. Saint
followed her eyes and noticed that it was the same man
from the resort. It was the white-haired man that Saint
had seen earlier. Saint watched as the group of men that
he was with earlier filed out of the private lounge with
a few younger women around them. Obviously, they
were having a good time. The drinks in their hands and
laughter were evidence of it. They all headed out the door
and toward the awaiting jet. Regis stopped at the desk
after overhearing the problem involving Saint.

"Hi, Jan," the guy said with a big smile on his face.

"Oh, hello, Mr. Epstein," Jan said enthusiastically.

"Hey. I didn't mean any harm earlier at the resort. We
were kind of in a rush, and the staff knew that," Regis
said with sincerity.

"No worries," Saint replied.

"I'm Regis," the man said as he extended his hand.

"I'm S—" Saint began, but Regis cut him off midsentence.

"Saint Cole," Regis said, finishing his words for him.

"Yeah, how did you know?" Saint said as he squinted and shook his hand.

"You're going to Cuba, right?" Regis asked.

"Yea . . ." Saint said, confused, not knowing how Regis knew so much about him.

"Jan, he can ride with us," Regis said as he looked over at the receptionist and winked. "Well, that's if you *want* to. We are heading over there for the weekend anyway."

"Sure . . ." Saint said skeptically. However, he wasn't about to turn it down because he needed to get there.

"Walk with me. Let's talk," Regis said as he motioned Saint to follow him outside onto the runway. Saint picked up his bag and followed him out. As they exited the building, they stood on the runway and talked.

"You're going to see Alejandro, right?" Regis said nonchalantly as he slid his hands in his shorts and casually walked.

"Maybe . . ." Saint answered, not wanting to expose his hand to the stranger. His mind started to churn, wondering how Regis knew so much.

"You don't have to worry. Alejandro is an old friend of mine. You see that logo," Regis said as he pointed at the jet with the Eagle on it. It was a logo of an eagle that read *RE Enterprises* across the bottom. "That's my logo. I own this fleet," Regis informed him.

"So, this is yours?" Saint asked as he waved at the private charter building.

"Yes, sir," Regis answered.

"Alejandro recommended that you use my company to handle your business, correct?"

"Yeah, that's right," Saint confirmed, as the picture started to look clearer to him. Saint remembered that Alejandro suggested that he fly from Aruba to Cuba and, shortly after, suggested RE Enterprise as an airline. Saint then understood that Regis's private airline was a pipeline for Alejandro's heroin business. It all made sense. That immediately made Saint more comfortable with Regis. They were both in the same business. Saint remembered that the valet mentioned that he owned the resort, and now Saint was learning that he owned the private jet company as well. *Oh, he papered up for real,* Saint thought to himself as he did the math in his head.

"You're not the only person that comes through here that Alejandro deals with," Regis explained. "You can ride with us. We will get you there. Come on," Regis said as he patted Saint on the back. They headed toward the jet, and while walking, Regis pulled out a big Cuban cigar and lit it. He puffed it slowly and held his head back, blowing smoke circles in the sky. Saint observed closely and watched the older man who seemed not to have a care in the world. The closer they got to the jet, the louder the sound of the jet propellers got.

Saint climbed the stairs and entered the cabin of the jet. He was greeted by a gorgeous redheaded woman who looked more like a supermodel than a stewardess. Her big double D breasts and long legs looked like she had stepped right off a fashion runway and then came to her job as a flight attendant. Her full lips made her look plastic. She resembled a real-life Barbie doll.

"Hello, Mr. Epstein. Welcome aboard," she said as she held a glass plate in front of her. It had three rows of a white powdery substance on it. Also, a rolled-up dollar bill next to it moved slightly around on the glass. She raised the plate so that it was chest level with Mr. Epstein.

He wasted no time as he smiled and picked up the dollar bill, putting it into his nostrils. He made a loud snorting noise, sniffing a line and swiftly tossing his head back to avoid drainage. Regis smiled and whispered, "Thanks, babe." Then he walked into the cabin, and Saint was right behind him. As Saint stepped up, the stewardess offered the plate to him, but he put up his hand, rejecting the offer. Saint didn't do drugs, and he wasn't about to start.

He was blown away by the upscale interior design. He had been on jets before, but this one was different. The pristine architecture was simply breathtaking. The smell of flowers invaded Saint's senses as a plethora of beautiful, colorful bouquets were placed throughout the joint. The plane was equipped with marble floors, neon lights, and had a full bar accompanied by a bartender. It resembled a classy lounge more so than an aircraft. Saint looked around in awe as he observed his surroundings. He thought that he was getting money, but after seeing Regis's private jet, he understood that there were levels to it. Regis introduced Saint to each of his three friends as they moved about the cabin. Saint greeted them all, and they welcomed him with open arms. Regis and Saint ended up at the bar as they both grabbed a seat on the stools.

"Do you drink scotch?" Regis asked while he grinned, displaying his white porcelain teeth.

"Sure," Saint answered as he got comfortable on the stool. Regis immediately turned toward the bartender and put up two fingers.

"Coming right up, Mr. Epstein," the Latino bartender said as he snatched two Cognac glasses off of the back display and poured the drinks. Just as Regis turned back to talk to Saint, the pilot's voice sounded through the jet's speakers.

"Hello, Mr. Epstein and guests. We are about to take off, headed to Cuba. The flight is just under three hours, so sit back and enjoy, everyone," he said just before logging off.

Saint felt the power of the jet take off, and he became slightly tense. All the others on the flight were enjoying themselves, laughing while doing blow. Regis saw Saint's uneasiness and raised his glass and waved it, signaling for a toast. Saint picked up his glass and obliged Regis. They tapped glasses, making a chiming noise that sounded throughout the jet. They then downed the drinks, and a conversation between them ensued.

"So, tell me about yourself. What are you into besides your business with my guy, Alejandro?" Regis questioned.

"This is all I know. My business with Alejandro is my only business," Saint answered honestly. He was a stone-cold hustler. That was all he was about.

"What a shame . . ." Regis said under his breath as he shook his head and downed the last swallow of his drink.

"Come again?" Saint said, feeling as if he were being belittled.

"It's . . . just . . . Can I be honest with you?" Regis asked.

"Absolutely," Saint said, looking Regis directly in the eye, trying to find out his angle, but also giving him a stern look to let him know that disrespect would not be tolerated. Regis returned the stare, but his eyes weren't ones of malice. He seemed to be sincere in his concern and tone.

"I hate to see your people get caught in the trap," he stated as he waved his hands while speaking.

"Your people? Trap?" Saint questioned, slightly offended.

"Yes. The trap of generational curses."

"Hmm," Saint said, listening carefully, wanting to hear more of what he was saying.

"Obviously, you're a bright guy. You've made it to this level of the field you're in. However, where is the maturation? Where is the growth? I mean . . . the United States was built on dirty money, so I'm not knocking what you do. Sometimes, to build a firm foundation, you have to play on the devil's playground."

"You damn right," Saint said, agreeing with what the older white man was discoursing.

"I want you to listen closely to what I'm about to say . . ." Regis requested. Saint nodded his head to affirm that he was all ears. Regis paused and looked Saint directly in the eyes and stated, "The first blocks of your foundation . . . should be the only ones that should have to touch the dirt."

"Well said," Saint replied. He understood where Regis was coming from, and he realized that he was right.

"The issue with your people . . . no disrespect . . . but the issue is the unwillingness to go legit. If you're into a shady business, there is no way your kids should be too. Does this make sense? At some point, you have to have an exit strategy and turn the dirty money clean," Regis answered straightforwardly.

Saint listened carefully and thought deep and hard about what Regis had said. He didn't know if it was the drugs or booze that had Regis so open to talk with him. Nevertheless, Saint was smart enough to comprehend that insight was better than money, and it wasn't every day that he got a chance to sit and talk with billionaires. Saint soaked up the game received from Regis, and they had an intimate conversation for the entire duration of the flight. Saint had gained an ally on that trip, and he understood the power in that. Before exiting, they traded numbers, and Regis invited Saint to his home after his business with Alejandro. Saint gladly accepted.

Chapter Six

Birds and the Keys

Havana, Cuba, was hot and dry as the sun beamed down. The tourist and airport workers moved around outside of the terminal. Cuba had no frills or fancy architectural structures. Their technology and landscapes were at least fifteen years behind the United States. It was cut and dry. They had one facility for incoming jets and planes for the entire region. There wasn't any classism in the country because almost everyone was poor and living beneath their means. Only the government or those who were connected to it were well off. That and the Cuban Cartel. It was cartel land that Saint was in, but he didn't worry because he knew the leader of it personally.

The people there were kind and humble. Having nothing usually made people appreciate life and others a tad bit more. That's one of the reasons why Saint loved the country. It always humbled him. It was in the afternoon, and local kids were scattered around, peddling Cuban-themed T-shirts and paintings to the incoming tourists. It seemed as if every product had faces of mostly Fidel Castro or "Che" Guevara printed on it. Ever since Obama had mended the United States' tumultuous relationship with the country, it became more of a tourist destination.

A little brown boy ran up to Saint and pulled at his shirt, causing him to look down.

"Dos," he said as he held up two fingers. He waved the Cuban bandanna around. Saint smiled at the kid and respected his hustle.

"Dos?" Saint repeated as he held up two fingers as well. The young boy smiled, showing his brown teeth. The boy had a black eye and fat lip, which made Saint feel sorry for him.

"Sí," the young boy said while nodding his head up and down.

"Bet. I got you, li'l man," Saint responded as he returned the smile and reached into his pocket. The young boy's eyes lit up when he saw Saint's gold teeth. He jumped up and down in joy and pointed to them as if they were majestic. In their country, seeing something like that was like seeing a unicorn.

"Oh, you're talking about my teeth?" Saint asked while smiling even bigger. "You like that gold, huh, li'l man?" Saint ran his finger across his bottom row to signal what he was saying to the boy.

Saint reached into the top of his T-shirt and pulled out a small gold chain that he had tucked away inside. It had a small charm hanging from it. It was a solid gold baby saint with Black boy features. On the back, his initials were engraved. It read *SVC.*

Saint reached around his neck to unclasp it. He smoothly unhooked it and placed it on his new little friend's neck. Saint let the charm fall to li'l man's chest, and he stepped back to check him out.

"Now, you a fly young nigga," Saint smoothly said as he crossed his hands and stood in the classic hustler's pose. The little boy was so happy and joyous as he mimicked Saint.

The child slapped hands with Saint and looked down at the gold around his neck. He teared up because he was so happy. He didn't even own a pair of shoes, so a chain was everything to him. He quickly wiped the tears away, but he never stopped smiling.

"*Gracias. Gracias,*" the young boy said, meaning thank you in Spanish.

"*De nada,*" Saint responded, meaning you're welcome. Saint didn't know a lot of Spanish, but he knew the bare minimum to get by. Saint then pulled out some pesos and slid a bill to him. The young boy, in return, handed him the Cuban bandanna.

"Yeah, this some fly shit, ya hear me?" Saint asked as he folded it up and tied it around his head. Saint put his hand on his chest and said, "*Me llamo,* Saint," introducing himself.

"*Me llamo,* Luca," the young boy said as he tapped his chest and smiled widely.

"Bet. My nigga, Luca," Saint said as he slapped hands with him. The young boy nodded his head in appreciation and walked off with his chest poking out, excited about his new chain. A group of his friends crowded around him and examined the chain in awe. Saint watched as the boys slapped fives with him and made him feel like a king.

People of different ethnicities stood on the curb, waiting for their turn to hop in a taxi. Saint stood on the curb as well and heard distant voices approaching him. He looked back and saw Regis and his party. Saint had opted to exit the jet as soon as it landed. At that time, they weren't done partying, so he excused himself, knowing he had to meet his plug. A black SUV pulled up to the curb. It stuck out because it was the only vehicle that was remotely modern on the entire street. Saint watched as they hopped in and cruised away. They were all so high that they didn't even acknowledge Saint as they brushed past him to get in the truck.

Saint recalled their conversation on the flight and realized that Regis had given him a lot to think about. During their brief encounter, they talked about everything from politics to sports, but mainly business. Saint learned that each one of his friends on that flight was a billionaire. Other than Regis, a senator, an oil tycoon, and an NFL team owner were on that jet. Saint watched them party like rock stars with the young women for the entire flight. One wouldn't know that they were such prominent figures by how wild they were. A single leaked photo from that jet ride could have ruined all of their lives. He saw someone waving from afar as he looked up the street. It was a short Cuban man with a straw fedora. He instantly recognized him. It was his usual driver, Pedro, waving him over to the car. Saint walked over to the vehicle, and the man opened the door for him.

"Mi amigo, Saint," the short man said in excitement as he displayed his snaggletoothed smile.

"Peace, beloved. Good to see you," Saint said as he placed his hand on Pedro's shoulder and gave it a slight squeeze. The humble man bowed his head and smiled, genuinely happy to see him. What he got paid to transport Saint on that one day took care of his family for three months. In his eyes, Saint was a pure blessing from God. Saint ducked his head, slid in, and got comfortable. He knew they had a long ride ahead. He was on his way deep into the jungle, where not many people went. The entire town knew whose territory that belonged to, and it wasn't to be tested. It was time to visit the plug, Alejandro.

Beautiful green leaves and vibrant flowers grew everywhere. Rich, dark soil covered the ground, and hundreds of chirping sounds blended together to make a unique, cohesive ambiance. It was nearing dusk, and the sun was falling for the day. The temperature had cooled off, and the air had tons of moisture in it. Saint took a deep breath and closed his eyes as he felt a sense of relaxation. He bopped up and down while on the back of a brown thoroughbred horse as they made their way through the jungle. His small duffle bag was by his crotch, tucked securely as they made their way through the wilderness.

His male guide led the way on a horse as well. The guide was shirtless and shoeless and looked to be in his early teens. He held a long stick in his hand as he rode, using it as a lead stick to push away the low-hanging branches and clear the path for Saint and him. As always, the guide never said one word to Saint. He just met him at the pickup location where the road ended and then took him to his boss, Alejandro. Saint's driver would always park and wait for his return, no matter how long it took.

At first, the long jungle journey used to make Saint uneasy. However, after a few trips, he started appreciating the nature trot. The smell of the damp earth combined with old, fallen leaves was unique. The earthy smell had an automatic calming effect on a human, and Saint experienced it every time. He would always look straight up through the tall trees that hovered over them to see if he could catch a glimpse of exotic birds that he probably wouldn't see anywhere else. The jungle never disappointed him. The colorful creatures would dip in and out of sight, flying from branch to branch. The small crevices through the tall treetops allowed the sky's light to illuminate the area. He knew that they only had a little while longer before it would be completely dark, and this is why arriving on time was so important when going to see Alejandro.

Saint wiped his brow as the sweat dripped off his forehead. He felt the bandanna that Luca had given him was still tied around his head. He had almost forgotten that he had it on. As Saint looked ahead, he saw the big castle sitting on a hill. The sky opened up. They had finally cleared the jungle. Two gun towers that resembled lighthouses stood on opposite sides of each other. Both stood fifty feet vertically. The towers were made of a beautiful gray stone wall, and a large light sat at the top of it for night vision. One sat on each side of the home overlooking the entire property. One gunman was in each tower, both armed with scoped high-powered rifles. The level of protection never ceased to amaze Saint every time that he visited. Unlike back in the States, the police feared the gangsters—not the other way around, and Saint could respect that, being a Black man in America. He admired the tenacity of the drug lords to rebel against the authorities. The willingness to go to war with the police was the main thing that kept the peace. The mere thought that the other side would push that button made the police think twice about friction. Sometimes, that's all you need for peace . . . the fear of knowing that the other side *would* push the button.

They made it to the entrance, which was protected by a tall steel gate that wrapped around the entire compound.

Barbed wires were at the top of the gates, and it looked more like a luxury prison rather than a home. The guide gave a hand signal to the guard, and moments later, the harsh noise of the steel moving sounded, and the gates parted open. Saint hopped off of the horse and grabbed his bag. He then walked across the land and entered the private property. As Saint made his way to the front door, he saw Alejandro's wife waiting for him. She stood there, smiling with her hands on her hips. She waved him in, and Saint smiled at her.

"Hello, Magalia," Saint said as he smiled and leaned in to kiss her cheek.

"Hello, Saint. So good to see you," she said, speaking perfect English. She was in her midforties and was a beautiful, middle-aged woman. She was about ten years younger than her husband, Alejandro. She was full-blooded Cuban, and her olive skin glowed like none other. Her dark hair was neatly pulled back, and her smile was welcoming and warming as usual. She had a big beautiful smile that warmed Saint every time he saw her. She had a single silver tooth in the far left side of her mouth, and it was like her signature. Saint always remembered that shiny cap every time she opened her mouth.

"Alejandro is in the back with the kids," she said as she stepped into the house and made her way into the back. Saint followed her as they started walking down the long foyer.

The inside was amazing to the eye. Every time Saint visited their home, he was blown away by the stunning Gothic, old-fashioned design. It almost made him feel like he was underground. The rocky ceilings and gray stonewall gave it a vintage theme. The long corridor was just ahead of him, which led to Alejandro's main living quarters. The hall resembled a high-end cave. Wooden lanterns were lined on the walls to provide lighting, and the smell of cedar was prominent.

As they made their way to the end of the hall, a large, sliding barnyard door stood there. Magalia reached for the door and slid it open, revealing their beautiful, modern home. The open floor plan gave it a grand appearance. One wouldn't even think that they were in Cuba by looking at it. It looked more like a high-end condominium in the middle of Manhattan.

The color scheme had shifted from what it was when you first entered. The white marble floors and light walls brightened up the setting. An AK-47 rifle was on the floor, propped up against the wall as if it were an umbrella. It was just casually there. Saint learned that Alejandro kept assault rifles all through the house as if they were a part of the décor. His family was so used to having guns around that they paid it no mind. It tripped Saint out every time he came over to see the ins and outs of cartel life.

Saint stepped in and saw Alejandro wrestling with his two young brown boys on the floor. They were laughing and horse playing as they reenacted a big-time wrestling match.

"Alejandro, Saint has arrived," Magalia said with enthusiasm as she stepped to the side so that he could get a clear view of their guest. She walked over to the kitchen area, put on an apron, and checked the food that she was preparing. The smell of Cuban cuisine filled the air, and Saint instantly remembered how good of a cook Magalia was.

"Aye, Saint, Amigo," Alejandro yelled with genuine excitement as he stood up from the ground and threw his hands in the air. Saint instantly smiled, feeling the love from his dope connect. Every time he came to Cuba, they made him feel like family, and it was much appreciated.

Alejandro walked toward Saint with his arms open, welcoming a hug. He wore a black silk shirt and well-tailored Italian cut slacks. Versace slippers were on his feet, and his whole style was player. He had brown skin and looked like an African American. The only thing that suggested his Cuban heritage was his soft, curly hair. He wore a five o'clock shadow for a beard and was slim built. *Look at this smooth old nigga,* Saint thought to himself as he approached and hugged him tightly. After their embrace, Alejandro cupped Saint's face and smiled, looking at him directly in the eyes.

"You look so much like my brother. It gets me every time," Alejandro said while shaking his head in disbelief and smirking at the same time. Although Saint was of no kin to him, he reminded him of his deceased brother so much. Saint was like a younger version of him, and it always blew his mind. That was one of the reasons he took a liking to Saint years back while meeting him at a local restaurant.

"You always say that," Saint responded, knowing that Alejandro always enjoyed seeing him. Saint didn't mind one bit. He found a plug of a lifetime in Alejandro, so he wasn't complaining at all. They had built a strong bond over the years, and Alejandro gave Saint whatever he wanted, as far as heroin was concerned. Alejandro owned over 500 acres of land in Cuba. He grew many things like tobacco, hemp, and his number one breadwinner . . . opium poppy plants.

Opium poppies were flowers from which heroin was made after an eight-step process. It was by far the most addictive drug in the world, and no one produced more in the world than Alejandro. His lavish home reflected his vast wealth and success as a leader of his Cuban drug cartel.

"What's good, fellas?" Saint asked, as he looked past Alejandro and saw the two young boys, both 9 years old. They were twins and Alejandro's only namesakes.

"Hey, Saint," one of the boys yelled in excitement.

"What's up, Saint?" the other boy yelled right after. Alejandro raised his children speaking English, knowing that it would be an essential skill to have. He always planned on sending his boys to college in the US, not wanting them to follow his footsteps in the drug trade. However, in the meantime, he did not hide or shelter them from what he did. He wanted them to know both sides of the game, just in case the US thing didn't pan out. Saint handed a small bag over to Alejandro. He peeked in the bag and smiled at Saint.

"You come bearing gifts," Alejandro said while smiling. He tossed it over to his son, who caught it excitedly.

"Count it up, boys," Alejandro instructed his boys. They eagerly hopped up and started dancing, loving to get a chance to play with the money machine. The boys raced to the kitchen table and dumped the money on it. One of the boys ran to grab the money counter from a closet, and shortly after, they were beginning the counting process. Alejandro looked over at his wife as she stirred the pot of shrimp in coconut sauce. She always made sure she cooked a good old-fashioned Cuban meal when Saint came around.

"How long until the meal, Mama?" Alejandro asked his lady as he looked at her with admiration. She smiled as she looked up to answer her husband of over fifteen years.

"About an hour, papi," she answered as she wiped her hands on her apron.

"Great! We have time for a cigar," Alejandro said as he winked at Saint and headed toward the door that led to his basement.

Saint followed Alejandro down the stairs. The tavern-style staircase was made of cherry oak, which led to Alejandro's man cave. It looked like an old-school cigar lounge, equipped with a pool table and an old-school jukebox. A walk-in cigar humidor was surrounded by glass. They made their way over to the humidor and stepped in to handpick themselves a Cuban cigar.

"Heard you had an eventful trip here," Alejandro said as he picked up a cigar and slid it under his nose, appreciating the homegrown optimum stick.

"Word got back to you quick," Saint responded as he picked up a cigar of his own.

"Of course. I know everything that's going on in my territory," Alejandro confirmed. They casually walked around the humidor, which had rows and rows of hand-rolled cigars and looked through the selection.

"Yo, what's the story with that guy?" Saint asked.

"Who? Regis?" Alejandro asked.

"Yeah," said Saint.

"A rich asshole," Alejandro said, sending them both into a small chuckle. He then continued. "He's a necessary evil that I use for my business. He makes it possible for me to transport my product throughout the world with ease with his private fleet. But to be honest, I don't care for him too much," he admitted.

"Oh, yeah?" Saint said, trying to understand who Regis was.

"Yeah, he has a dark side that I don't agree with," Alejandro said as he exited the room and headed over to the lounge chairs.

Saint thought that Regis was an excellent plug to have and wondered why Alejandro was down talking him.

There has to be more to the story, Saint thought as he followed him out and joined him for a smoke. Saint didn't ask any further about Regis, but he definitely was curious about his new acquaintance. The financial game that Regis had laid on him during the flight had Saint's mind open to expansion and leaving the drug game. Regis's words really stuck with Saint, and the thought of having an exit plan didn't seem like a bad idea. Saint thought that maybe Alejandro didn't like the thought of Regis taking one of his drug distributors away. Little did Saint know, however, that Alejandro was trying to protect him from the devils that hid underneath the surface . . .

Chapter Seven

Cougars

"Okay, get ready for bed, guys. Tell Saint good night," Magalia said as she cleared the table, collecting the plates off of it.

She, Alejandro, and the kids had just had dinner with Saint, compliments of Magalia's excellent cooking. While eating, they talked and laughed together about life. Not once did they speak about drugs because what was understood never needed to be explained.

Once Saint left with the bricks, he would see Pandora, and then he would leave them with Pedro. That was the routine, and by the time he returned home to New Orleans, a pallet of heroin bricks would be waiting for him by way of hidden compartments inside of a U-Haul truck. Saint never asked about the intricacies of the operation as far as the transportation of the drug. Alejandro had a well-oiled machine, and his reach was substantial. All of the people in Cuba worked together as a unit. Cuba treated drugs differently than people in the States. Drugs weren't as taboo and were almost looked at as a religion. It was their country's primary source of money, and it had its own intricate network.

Saint stuck out his hand to give the boys a pound as they excused themselves from the table.

"Holla at y'all next time," Saint said as he playfully rubbed their heads, messing up their hair.

"See ya later, Saint," one said.

"Bye, Saint," the other boy said as they both hugged their father and ran upstairs out of sight. Magalia put the dishes in the sink and then walked over to Saint.

"I'm about to get the boys ready for bed. It was good seeing you, Saint," Magalia said as she bent down to kiss him on the cheek and hugged him.

"Thank you so much for dinner, and it was good seeing you too," Saint replied as he grinned.

"You're stopping by to see my sister before you leave, right?" Magalia asked.

"Absolutely. I'm going by in the morning before I leave," Saint confirmed.

"Okay, I'll let her know to expect you," Magalia said.

"Thank you so much," Saint replied.

"You know she has a thing for you, right?" Alejandro playfully asked while smiling.

"She does not," Magalia said as she playfully hit her husband.

"She wants to be his cougar," Alejandro said before bursting out in laughter.

"Oh, hush. She just likes him. He reminds her of Bo when he was younger," Magalia said as she mentioned Alejandro's deceased brother. Alejandro and his brother had met them both at the same time, decades ago, during a double date. That was how their blended families began many moons ago.

Saint remained silent, smiled, and shook his head. Magalia gave her husband a quick peck on the lips and headed toward the stairs.

"Take care, Saint," she yelled before she disappeared up the stairs.

"You too," Saint yelled to her before focusing on his plug. Alejandro reached under the table and grabbed the duffle bag. The bag was filled with some of the most potent dope in the world. Saint could step on it multiple times and still have the best dope in the country; it was that strong and pure.

"All jokes aside, make sure you go see Pandora before you leave. It's an important step to complete the process. The one time I didn't ask for the spiritual protection . . . I lost my brother."

"Sorry to hear that," Saint said. That had been the first time Alejandro ever went into detail about his brother's death.

"It's okay, my amigo. Just make sure to remember, whatever you do, right or wrong . . . take prayers with you," Alejandro said, with genuineness in his eyes. He said it, knowing that Saint needed to hear that wisdom. He had a gut feeling that Saint was preparing to get into things that he had no idea about. Saint's chance meeting with Regis made him uneasy. If it were anyone else, Alejandro wouldn't have given two shits about it, but he saw his brother in Saint and wanted to forewarn him without coming outright and saying what was on his mind.

Saint lay in bed in his hotel, and the sounds of the simple, old-fashioned alarm clock rang. It was 9:04

exactly. It was the morning after, and he would leave Cuba in a few hours. He just needed to make one stop before he left the country. He looked over and saw his duffle bag right next to the bed, and he always got a rush when copping drugs there. He knew that he would multiply those squares, put his stamp on them, and flood the bayou in a week.

He got up and took a hot shower, letting the water cascade down his body. The hot water helped wake him up, and after a few minutes, he stepped out and wrapped himself in a towel. He stood in front of the mirror and heard his phone buzz. He looked down at the screen and saw that it was a text from Regis.

Let's have a drink this evening. Talk business . . .

Saint picked up his phone to reply.

I would love to. But flight chartered to leave in a few hours.

Saint put his phone down after pushing the *send* button. He applied shaving cream on his head to prepare for a shave. To his surprise, Regis shot a text back immediately.

Charter was changed to tomorrow night and upgraded to the G5.

Saint nodded his head, remembering the plushness of the luxury aircraft.

Bet.

Saint put down his phone and continued to shave. He instructed Pedro to meet him in the lobby at nine thirty sharp. He sped up the process of shaving, and as he ran the razor across his head, he jumped in pain.

"Fuck!" he said under his breath as he turned his head and looked in the mirror to see the damage. He noticed that he had scraped his head and caused blood to trickle from it. He quickly grabbed a piece of tissue and applied pressure to it to stop the bleeding. He took care of the scratch and got dressed, grabbed the bricks, and headed over to Pandora's district to see her.

Saint had arrived in the Santeria district where Pandora's home was located. His driver, Pedro, had parked the car at the end of the block as he always did, not wanting to drive on the block and interrupt the festivities. The sight of children playing in the streets always made Saint get a feeling of nostalgia from back when he was younger. Those were the only times, while in Cuba, when Saint was reminded of home. The look wasn't similar, but the feeling was. A child's joy was a universal language. That particular district was one known for Santeria rituals, so the sounds of music, drums, and singing were always prevalent there. It was lively. In some ways, it also mirrored summertime on Bourbon Street, just grimier and less glamorous.

Heavy doses of graffiti were drawn on the abandoned buildings and sides of houses. The symbols and drawings were ones of various crosses, abstract art, voodoo dolls, and skeleton heads. To some not familiar with the practice, it might seem scary, but most often, people fear what they don't truly understand. The uninformed would call it voodoo and think of it as spooky or satanic. However, it wasn't evil at all. Europeans gave this religion a negative jacket, but that's only because they didn't understand it. It wasn't for them. It was for the "cho-

sen ones," people of color. The religion of Santeria was
merely living descendants connecting with deceased ancestors, asking for help while also praising them.

Saint casually walked down the street, easily blending in with the locals. He carried his duffle bag full of
bricks in one hand and slightly held the other arm out.
He did so to balance himself while toting the heavy bag-
gage. Kids were running around, laughing, and having a
good time, as usual. He approached Pandora's spot, and,
like always, the entry was wide open . . . open to whoever wanted to come and get prayer or guidance from her.
Pandora was known to be a well respected *oshun*.

An oshun is a spirit, a deity, or a goddess that reflects
one of the manifestations of God in the Ifá and Yoruba
religions that are practiced heavily in Cuba. Pandora
opened her home for all of the community to come.
They held her up and protected her faithfully. She was a
treasure to the people. Oshun is the deity of the river and
fresh water, luxury, pleasure, sexuality, and fertility. She
is known to be connected to destiny and foresight. This is
why Saint needed to see her. She was his spiritual shield
and an insurance policy for the wolves of the game. He
had the upper hand on all traffickers in the States just
because of this one lone factor. Pandora was his secret
weapon.

As Saint crossed the threshold of the door, he noticed
that salt was sprinkled on the floor of the steps. Pandora
once told Saint that salt helped keep evil spirits away, and
that was the reason she did it faithfully. The crunching
noise of his shoe against the salt sounded with each step
taken.

He proceeded to walk up the narrow staircase, and when he got to the top, he noticed a broom was standing upside down while leaning against the wall. That served a very important purpose that Saint would eventually find out about.

He walked into the home, and instantly, the smell of burning sage invaded his senses. The distinct scent was strong, and clouds danced in the air, making it nearly impossible to see clearly. It resembled fog on a cold Sunday morning. Saint walked in, and the smoke made it seem as if he were in a dream. The smell of the sage relaxed him as he made his way toward the back where Pandora usually was. Although he had no number or direct line to her, she always seemed to be expecting him whenever he arrived. As Saint walked through the hanging beads that separated the rooms, as always, Pandora was in the back corner at a table waiting patiently.

The process that was about to occur was called "baptizing the bricks," and after urging from Alexandro, it was a step that he never missed. With Pandora's blessing, he had the utmost confidence that moving the batch of drugs wouldn't cause him any strife or heartache to himself or his team back home.

"Saint, I've been expecting you," Pandora said while waving him over to her as he smiled.

The room was dim because it had no windows. Only the flickering candles provided the lighting. As Saint walked deeper into the room, he noticed that it was much cooler than the rest of the house. It sent chills up his spine, but not because he was fearful. The sudden climate change caused his body to react in that way.

"Hey, Pandora. How are you?" Saint asked as he approached the table. Saint always thought Pandora was one of the most beautiful older women that he had ever seen. He always was enamored by her gorgeousness every time he was in her presence. Her head wrap was multicolored, and it kept her hair hidden . . . all accept the single gray locs that hung freely to the left of her forehead.

"I'm doing just fine. How are you doing, handsome?" she said as she stared at him with a warm smile. "Have a seat," she instructed as she waved at the chair in front of her table. Saint did as he was told and took a seat while setting the bag of dope at his feet.

"I'm good. Thanks for asking," Saint answered with his boyish charm.

"Before we start, do you want to ask your ancestors anything? Anything troubling you or you need help with?" she asked.

"Nothing more than what's in this bag. I'll save those requests for if I ever really need it," Saint answered.

"Smart man," Pandora said as she smiled and tapped her temple with her index finger. She moved the crystals around that were scattered all over the table, and Saint dug into the duffle bag. He glanced at the wall behind Pandora and noticed a Medusa head, hand-drawn on the wall. He was a big fan of Greek mythology and instantly recognized the woman's character with a head full of snakes and beautiful eyes. He had never before seen that painting while visiting Pandora. Maybe it was a new drawing that was recently added.

"Medusa . . ." he whispered as he stared at the painting. Pandora followed his eyes and looked at the drawing as well.

"No, baby. That's not Medusa. That's a painting of my great-great-great-grandmother. See, you Americans believe anything them white people tell you. Not us . . . We know the truth. That image has been made famous by white-washed tales and Greek mythology. But the truth is . . . Those are not snakes that you see on her head. Those are long locs like the ones on mines," she said as she grabbed one of the gray locs that was hanging in her face. "And her skin wasn't pale. It was dark and brown like yours and mine. Her beauty was so captivating, they switched the truth and sold it to y'all in story form. They steal everything from us and sell it."

"Are you serious?" Saint asked as his mind started to think deeper.

"Yes, I'm afraid I am. That stone that you turn into if you look at her . . . well, that's partially true," Pandora said as she looked down at Saint's crotch area and smiled. Pandora then went back to moving her crystals around. Saint smiled as his mind was blown by the new information that he had just received. He always learned something new when he visited Pandora.

As he placed the bricks on the table, he noticed that she was staring at him. It took him by surprise because she had never looked at him before the way she was looking at him on this day. She had a smirk on her face and didn't flinch or look away when he caught her staring. Pandora was too grown to hide her intentions. She was straightforward and unwavering.

He went back to placing the bricks on the table, thinking that he was tripping. As he set another brick of dope on the table, he heard her voice whisper his name.

"Saint," she said softly as she moved her hand onto his. His eyes instantly shot to her hand and then up to her lustful eyes. "You look just like him," she continued.

"Huh?" he said, pretending as if he didn't know what she was talking about, but he did.

"I'm going to give it to you today," Pandora said as she stood up, causing Saint's eyes to follow her. Now he was looking up at her as she hovered above, staring down at him.

"You are going to give me what?" Saint said, trying to understand what she was talking about. He was lost.

"My nana," she whispered.

Saint smiled involuntarily, knowing that she meant something other than what she said. He thought about something taboo when he heard the term "nana."

"I think in your country . . . They call it 'pussy,'" Pandora said, now leaving no room for misinterpretation. She said what she fucking said. Pandora turned and walked toward the rear of the room, where a red wooden door was. She had on an oversized spiritual gown, but for the first time, Saint noticed her nice lumps in the back as her wide hips swayed back and forth. Saint watched her closely and was frozen in confusion. He couldn't believe what he had just heard.

"Come on now . . . Do not keep this old woman waiting. It's been many moons since Pandora's box has been opened," she said as she put her hand on the doorknob and slowly peeled her garments off, exposing her shoulders.

Saint didn't know what to say. He was completely caught off guard. He tried to think about what to utter.

At first, he wanted to turn it down, but on the other hand, Pandora was a very enticing specimen. He also had never been with an older woman, so the curiosity was most definitely there. *Damn,* he thought to himself as he was stuck standing at a mental crossroad. He then recognized the reality of it and asked himself, *Is Pandora the type of woman you say no to? What the fuck, yo?* He pondered what would be the consequences of doing that. So, he didn't . . .

Saint slowly stood up and watched Pandora's clothes drop to the floor, leaving her completely naked body on full display. Her back was turned toward him as she stood in the doorway with her legs slightly parted. She then took off her head wrap, and long gray locs dropped down liberally. The beautiful hair reached the middle of her back. She ran her hand through them, untangling them and shook her neck, allowing them to drape freely. Her naked, thick but shapely frame was far from what Saint thought it would have been. For a 50-something-year-old woman, her body was amazingly intact. The only indication of her age was the gray hair. The shea butter that was on her body made it shine like no other, and her deep brown skin tone was flawless. Her massive butt cheeks hung down like teardrops, and her thick thighs touched. She knew Saint was watching, so she spread her legs apart a bit more, so her love box was visual from the backside. His mind was blown, seeing that hairy, meaty kitty hanging down so low. It was the plumpest he'd ever seen . . . ever.

"Come get it," she whispered as she slowly disappeared into the dark room.

Saint didn't want to do it, but his manhood had a difference of opinion. He felt the tip of his penis tingle, and shortly after, the whole shaft started to rise. He unhurriedly followed her into the room, and when he walked in, a red light lit the space. After taking two steps in, he stopped in his tracks to admire the seductive scenery. He saw the biggest bed that he ever witnessed sitting in the middle of the room. It was the size of two California King beds put together and was oval-shaped. It looked like a sex den more so than a bedroom. Red silk sheets lined the bed, and a naked Pandora was right in the middle of it. She was lying down while propping herself up on her elbow.

She held her index finger up and signaled for him to come to her. Saint felt like he didn't have control of his legs, and it seemed as if he walked to her against his will. He felt like he floated to her rather than taking steps. The only thing that he could feel was the blood circulating to his dick, which was rock hard.

As he reached the edge of the bed, he took off his shirt and then his pants. He was only left with boxer briefs, and his thick penis print was on full display through the cotton. He stood there with his member bulging and pulsating while looking down at Pandora. His eyes drifted to her big breasts, which were at least a double D in size. Her big brown areoles and nipples were enticing to Saint. She had the type of nipples that, when erect, they stuck straight out like bullets. He glanced at the gray bush between her legs, matching the color of her locs exactly.

He watched as she got on all fours and crawled toward him. Her large breasts were dangling and crashing against each other as she made her way to him. Then she reached over and grabbed him.

"Uhm," she moaned as she rubbed his thick rod through his boxer briefs. She moved her hand up to the elastic waistband of his underwear and slowly peeled them down, making his erect penis pop out like a jack-in-the-box.

"Young bull," she whispered as she held Saint's tool and studied it. His penis tip was plum red because of all of the circulation. A thick, bulging vein ran from the base of his pole, all the way to the beginning of the tip. Saint looked down and watched as it throbbed repeatedly. Pandora took her time and rubbed, jacked, and caressed it. She took her free hand and cupped his sack that was hanging beneath it. She slowly rubbed the sack while stroking his shaft with the other hand. She was using the two-hand action method. Saint threw his head back and closed his eyes, enjoying the masterful job by Pandora.

"You're ready," Pandora confidently said as she lay back and spread her legs. She put her fingers in her mouth and wet them. She then rubbed herself, exposing her chubby lips and swollen area.

Saint climbed onto the bed while never taking his eyes off the prize. He had never before seen a kitty so pudgy and pretty. The contrast of her hair and pink insides was turning him on. Her love box seemed to be raised off of her body like a mound. It was something great to see.

As he climbed onto the colossal bed, he felt like his knees sank into it. It was the softest thing he had ever been on. It was as if he were lying on a bed of clouds, but these clouds were bloodred. She pulled him up, wanting him to straddle her, and brought his penis to her mouth. He followed her lead and waved his manhood over her face as she swallowed him whole. She bobbed her head while grabbing his cheeks, controlling his pace as he stroked her face. Her mouth was so hot and wet as she did work on him. He looked down at her locs and ran his hand through them as she pleased him.

Pandora let out a loud moan of anticipation as she blew him. Saint closed his eyes and listened to her relaxing moans and slurping noises. She hummed and talked nasty in between sucks. Her voice was so clear and coherent in his mind. It seemed as if it were in his head rather than being spoken out loud. He felt like she was speaking to his soul rather than to his eardrums.

All of a sudden, she stopped and looked up at him. Saint locked eyes with her, and it seemed as if he couldn't look away from her gaze. He was stuck . . . mesmerized by her dreamy eyes. She grabbed him and threw him onto his back, swapping positions with him. At that point, she slid down and slowly straddled him. She lined her midsection up with his. Now, she was looking down at him with lustful eyes and freaky intentions. No matter how hard Saint tried, he could not break the eye contact that he was sharing with Pandora. She slightly lifted her ass and reached down to grab his hard tool. Once she found it, she let out a sigh.

"Ooh," she hummed, appreciating how rock solid he was. She then expertly guided him inside of her and sat on him, sliding him deep inside. Saint felt like his pole was diving into a heated Jacuzzi. It was the wettest and warmest that he had ever experienced in his life.

"Hmm," she moaned as she closed her eyes and flickered her tongue.

Saint instantly felt her warm wetness, and her tight womb seemed to grab him. She wildly rode him as her hands slipped down to his neck area. She leisurely tightened her grip, while crashing down onto his pelvis area, riding him like a horse. Her shapely assets waved and jiggled with each thrust. Saint couldn't believe how hard and good this older woman was making love to him. She plopped her ass up and down, her love box making wet sounds with each crash landing. She rode him with tremendous force and velocity. Her wide hips were moving rapidly. She was on a stern mission to make herself come. She repeatedly raised her big ass and dropped it down on him, making her ass wave like an ocean.

Clap

Clap

Clap

The sounds of lovemaking resonated throughout the room as her cheeks violently plopped down on him, completely soaking his balls. He had never felt a vagina as hot, tight, and wet as Pandora's. It literally felt like heaven on earth. Saint wanted to moan, but he couldn't move. He couldn't speak. He couldn't even move his hands to hold the waist of the beautiful elder on top of him. He was very familiar with that feeling he was experiencing. As a child, he would have similar episodes while in the wee hours of the night. He would wake up with the inability to move or speak. He only could see what was going on around him. He couldn't move anything except his eyeballs from left to right, up and down. Some people called it "A witch riding your back," but that wasn't the case at all . . . a goddess was riding him.

Saint could feel a powerful orgasm coming as Pandora rode him. She could feel hers approaching as well, and she didn't hesitate to tell him.

"Here it comes. Oh my . . . Here it comes," she said as small sweat beads formed on her nose and forehead. Her already firm grip had gotten tighter around Saint's neck, and she kicked it up a notch, riding him like a madwoman.

Saint stared into Pandora's eyes and seemed to get lost in them. He couldn't even blink at that point. Her hazel eyes were the most enticing thing he had ever seen, and he was mystified. He tried to breathe, and he couldn't, but he didn't care.

As the massive orgasm approached, he felt his body stiffen up and the insides of Pandora's vaginal walls contracted. Her walls gripped him tightly, and wet noises emanated from her body. The sounds got louder and louder with each stroke. She had reached her peak and screamed as she released herself. She shook so hard that she quaked his body as well. Her eyes rolled behind her head as her body jerked violently, catching her orgasm. She mumbled under her breath, words that Saint couldn't make out clearly. It was almost as if she were speaking gibberish or in tongues.

At the same exact moment, Saint released his large wad into her and closed his eyes as the sperm shot out of his pole and into her pink abyss. All of a sudden, he felt his entire body being submerged into cold water. The cold sensation sent his body into shock, making him tense up instantly. When he opened his eyes, he saw the brightest blue water around him as he kicked and flailed wildly. It was total confusion. He was literally in the middle of the ocean. He frantically looked around, and his entire scenario had changed within a split second. He was in water kicking and fighting, not being able to wrap his mind around what just happened. Oxygen bubbles came out of his nose and mouth as he looked up and saw the sun shining down through the water.

He instantly swam upward, feeling that he was running out of breath and was about to drown. His heart pounded rapidly, and anxiety ran rapid throughout his chest. So many things were going through his mind as he swam up, confused as ever. His mind was playing tricks on him. He knew that just seconds before, he was under Pandora making love, and now he was submerged in water, trying not to drown.

As he continued to swim, he felt his time was running out, and he would die. At the last second, when he believed that he would pass out from having no air, his head burst out of the water. He felt the hot sun beaming against his face. He took the biggest gasp of air and let the oxygen enter his lungs as he swung his arms wildly, trying to stay afloat.

Ring

Ring

Ring

The alarm clock sounded, waking him up from his dream—or nightmare. He wasn't really sure which one it was. He quickly sat up and looked around frenziedly and realized that he was back in his same hotel room.

He looked at the old-fashioned alarm clock, which read 9:04 . . . just like it did in his dream. He reached over to stop it from ringing and then looked down at his body, which was drenched.

"Yo, what the fuck? What the hell was that?" Saint said out loud as he swung his legs over and placed them firmly onto the floor. He looked over and saw the duffle with the bricks of dope, and the feeling of déjà vu overcame him. He had dreamed all his life, so he knew what it felt like. However, that—what he experienced—was *not* a dream.

I wasn't dreaming. I know that for sure, he thought as he stood up and peeled off his drenched clothes. He stood in the middle of the floor naked and then looked down at his morning wood. As he looked closer, he saw something odd. A long strand of hair was on his pelvis. He reached down to grab it and examined it. He held it up so that he could get a better look. He immediately knew that it wasn't his. The hair was gray.

"What the fuck?" he said again as he tried his best to make sense out of what just happened. He proceeded to the bathroom and turned on the shower while shaking his head in confusion.

He stepped in, letting the water cascade down his body. The hot water helped wake him up. The only thing he could think about was his so-called fantasy with Pandora. It was the best—and worst—dream that he had ever endured. His pipe was still rock hard as if he had a long night of sex. He couldn't stop thinking about the orgasm that he felt. He had never before come that hard, and he was sure that he wasn't fantasizing. It felt too real to him. *How could it be real, and I'm back in the hotel room?* It was all too weird for him, and he was mentally defeated. He chalked it up to his vivid imagination and lack of sleep.

After a few minutes, he stepped out and wrapped himself in a towel. As he stood in front of the mirror, he heard his phone buzz. He looked down at the screen and saw that it was a text from Regis.

Let's have a drink this evening. Talk business . . .

"Same text as in the dream?" Saint asked himself aloud as he frowned. He picked up his phone to reply.

I would love to. But flight chartered to leave in a few hours.

Saint put down his phone after pushing the *send* button. He applied shaving cream on his head to prepare for a shave. To his surprise, Regis immediately shot a text back.

Charter was changed to tomorrow night and upgraded to the G5.

Now, it was just getting outright spooky, and a chill slithered up his spine. He also got goose bumps on his arms as he felt the hairs on the back of his neck stand up. He responded to Regis once again.

Bet.

Saint put down his phone and continued to shave. He instructed Pedro to meet him in the lobby at nine thirty sharp. He sped up the process of shaving, and as he ran the razor across his head, he jumped in pain.

"Fuck," he said under his breath as he turned his head and looked in the mirror to see the damage. He noticed that he had scraped his head and caused blood to trickle from it. He quickly grabbed a piece of tissue and applied pressure to it to stop the bleeding. He couldn't believe what was happening to him as he relived the same steps as the fantasy. He was definitely ready to get out of Cuba and head home, where things weren't so unexplainable. He took care of the scratch and got dressed, grabbed the bricks, and headed over to Pandora's district to see her.

Weird, he thought as he saw the broom upside down, leaning against the wall. He looked down, and the salt was there as well, just like in his fantasy. As he entered the second floor, he made his way back to the room where Pandora was usually waiting. Sage was burning, and smoke danced in the air as he passed through the beaded doorway. Just as he entered, he looked down and saw a puddle of water on the floor, so he immediately stepped over it.

"Hello, Saint," Pandora said with a smile as she sat back at the table.

"Hey, Pandora," he responded, slightly smiling at her.

"Watch that puddle on the floor, baby. You wouldn't want to drown in all that water, now, would you?" she asked rhetorically with a smirk on her face. She winked at him, which made Saint's mind race in curiosity. *Was it real?* he thought to himself as he made his way over to her.

"Is there something different about today . . ." Saint asked as he approached the table, squinting his eyes in confusion. He was trying to figure out if Pandora was playing mind games with him. It seemed as if she knew that he was experiencing déjà vu. He wanted to know if she knew what he had fantasized about.

"Well, it will always be different in this home. Each time you come here, you'll see things differently. My home will always show you what you need to know. What you require will be laid before you. Always," Pandora confirmed with a smile as she started to move her crystals around. Saint carefully placed the bricks on the table as he took in what she said. He remained quiet and just listened carefully.

"Whatever you feel, that's just your ancestors talking to you, so don't be afraid. It's always for your own good," she said with a warm smile. Saint didn't understand what she meant by that; however, he didn't want to ask any more questions. He just wanted to handle his business and leave. That day had been too strange for him as is.

He didn't say much on that particular visit as they went through the ritual with the baptism of the bricks. He left there confused and ready to get back home to the money. However, he had to meet up with Regis later. He wanted to connect with him again. The deep conversation they shared on the flight made him curious about his future plans, outside of the drug game.

Chapter Eight

Snakes

A feast was underway, and lobsters, prawns, and stuffed swordfish were the main dishes. A long table sat on the greenest grass on the private estate owned by Regis. Tall, wicker fire torches were stuck in the ground near the table to provide light as the darkness loomed in the sky. The full moon's light bounced off the ocean, just in front of them as they chowed down. The sounds of the crashing waves created a relaxing ambiance as they gathered. The water wasn't far from them, maybe a few hundred feet from where they sat. Cuban workers moved around the place in white uniforms, serving every need of each guest. Fifty yards behind them stood a large mansion that resembled a palace. Numerous large windows were on the rear of the house, and all of the lights were on, so the elegance of the inside was on full display.

Saint had arrived shortly before and was personally escorted by a car service provided by Regis. Regis had arranged that they pick him up from his hotel once the sun went down. Although Saint had been to Cuba numerous times, he never knew about the modern, beautiful island that he was currently on.

Regis owned the small island on Cuba's soil and used it as a playground for his close friends and business colleagues. It was just off the Atlantic Ocean and sat on a picturesque beach. It only was open when he and his wealthy friends came, so it was a secret to anyone outside of the small town. Regis had flown out a few more friends for that weekend. About twenty-five men congregated, enjoying themselves. The guest list contained nothing but the elitist of the US. Everyone there was affluent with substantial political influence.

Saint was the only nonbillionaire in attendance, and it showed from his silence. However, Saint didn't feel out of place at all. His confidence made him a giant among them. He studied his surroundings, learning more and more with each sidebar conversation he eavesdropped on. He wasn't the only African American in attendance. But by the people's choice of dress and vernacular, he knew that they weren't cut from the same cloth that he was. Saint noticed immediately that their whole swagger was off. They weren't from where he was, and if they were, it had been a very long time since they had been there. He knew that he was the only street guy present, and he liked it that way.

Regis and his friends sat at the table, laughing and drinking the finest Merlot. Saint sat at the table and carefully watched as they talked about the latest stocks and real estate developments that they were a part of. As he heeded attentively, he soon realized that their conversations were different than what he was used to with his crew. They talked about millions as if it were mere dollars. A politician casually mentioned his new hotel in Miami that cost him "300" to develop. Another man at the table bragged about a new erectile dysfunction pill that his team was creating that had cost him "about 50" to produce. Saint instantly knew that the measly million that he had stashed in his floor at home was nothing in their world. Although Saint didn't add to the conversation, he listened and studied while soaking up everything.

Regis sat at the head of the table with his legs crossed, sipping his wine. The elitist of the US would come party with Regis because there were no rules there. No cameras, paparazzi, or bickering wives to be the fun police. He sat there with a shirt, blazer, and ascot on to complement his attire as he was engrossed in the group's conversation. He looked down at the end of the table and noticed that Saint wasn't talking much, so he decided to take the initiative to make him more comfortable.

"Excuse me, gentlemen," Regis said, pardoning himself as he stood up and buttoned his blazer. He looked at Saint and motioned for him to follow him. Saint took his time and wiped off his mouth. Then he stood and walked over.

"Regis," Saint said as he approached him.

"Saint, my guy. How are you enjoying the food?" Regis asked as he casually slid his hands into his white slacks.

"It's delicious. Thanks," Saint answered while walking side by side with him.

"Good. Good. I want you to take a walk with me. I want to show you something," he said as they headed toward the home. They entered, and the inside was truly amazing. It looked like a giant hotel lobby and had big podiums throughout the spacious first floor. Double wraparound stairs with velvet flooring led to the second level.

"So here it is—heaven," Regis said as he opened his arms and slowly spun around, showing off his spot.

"Yeah, this is nice, for sure," Saint said as he looked around and slowly nodded in approval.

"I invited you here because I see something in you. You're a lion. You have an aura about yourself, and I'm very good when it comes to judging character," Regis said as he stepped closer to Saint, looking directly into his eyes.

"I appreciate that. I truly do," Saint said, standing firm and returning the stare. Regis paused for a second and held the gaze, almost like he was sizing Saint up. But, of course, Saint didn't fret.

"Good. You see those men out there?" Regis said as he turned, pointed, and looked at the group fraternizing. He continued, "There is a business connection to anything you want to do in life out there. That's called a power circle. We all look out for one another and build wealth among our faction," Regis explained.

"That's a powerful thing right there," Saint agreed.

"Yes, it is."

"May I ask you something?"

"Sure thing, shoot."

"Well, it's obvious that you know what game I'm in. How can I switch the business? Go legit without having my past catch back up with me?"

"That's a good question. And by asking that, you have separated yourself from the majority of the people in your field. You have bigger aspirations than what you are doing, and that's the key," Regis confirmed. "As I was telling you on the plane, the best thing you can do is make your dirty money, clean," Regis said as he put his hand on Saint's shoulder.

"What's the best way to do that?" Saint asked.

Regis slightly turned Saint so that he could face the outside where the men were. He then pointed.

"See that guy right there in the blue suit? Red hair?" Regis asked as he pointed.

"Yeah."

"That Morris Fillman. He manages one of the biggest investment brokerages in North America."

"Okay," Saint answered as he looked at the dorky-looking, forty-something-year-old man.

"Whatever you give him, he gives half back to you. But when he gives it back, it's via check with his company's logo on it. Clean by way of investment dividends. His brokerage isn't public, so there's no way authorities can verify or double-check your numbers. Voilà . . . clean money to live and do with what you please," Regis explained as simple as he could.

"Oh, I see," Saint answered.

"Then after that, you give him that same check, and you sit back and watch him work his magic. You think moving dope is lucrative? That's peanuts compared to the stock market . . . if done right," Regis clarified.

"Well, I need to talk to him. We need to do some business together."

"Agreed. But he's real timid. You have to ease your way in with him. Take on some of his interests and then approach him with it. For instance, he's a heavy gambler. You talk gambling, and he will talk your ear off all night," Regis said, chuckling, showing his perfect, fake, porcelain teeth.

"Oh yeah?" Saint said.

"Oh, for sure. That's why he's here now. He doesn't drink. Doesn't fuck around on his wife. No drugs . . . nothing. He's here for the dogfighting. He bets a million a match," Regis explained.

"We used to fight dogs back in my hood . . ." Saint paused, correcting himself, knowing that Regis wouldn't understand his slang. He continued, "We used to fight dogs back in my old neighborhood when I was young."

"No disrespect, but this dogfighting is not like what you are used to. This is a whole different monster. High stakes like you wouldn't even imagine."

"Is that right?"

"Yeah, this is my group of friends. But there are many groups like us around the world, and one thing that all men have in common, no matter the country . . . All men are competitive. So, once a month, we meet here and fight our dogs. That's one of the unspoken main attractions in Cuba."

"Okay, I can fuck with that for sure," Saint said.

"We actually are having one tonight, if you want to come."

"One tonight?" Saint asked.

"Yeah, an old-fashioned dogfight. A few times a year, we have an event and show who's boss. Every team brings their pick of the litter and throws them in the ring."

"Yeah, I'm game. I'm down."

"Great. I have a bitch that hasn't lost in two years. She's a vicious li'l fucker too. She kills whatever I put in front of her," Regis boasted. "Then it's set. We have a few hours before that starts, so let's have fun in the meantime," he suggested.

"Cool."

"Follow me," Regis instructed as he walked further into the home. They made a quick right, and Saint saw an extremely long, narrow corridor before them. The hallway was nearly pitch dark. If not for the candles that were lit along the walls, they wouldn't be able to see. He noticed that there was a line of doors on each side of the hall. It began to make sense to Saint.

This was an old, converted hotel, he thought, as the row of doors were lined up against the wall. Regis walked to the first door and then looked back, smiling at him. As he opened the door, he stepped aside so Saint could peek in.

"Have a look-see," Regis instructed as he nodded his head in the direction of the room. Saint stepped forward and peered inside. The room was dimly lit. He was taken off guard by what he was observing. A tall, slender woman wearing an all-leather catsuit stood there with a whip in hand. She wore six-inch heels and looked like an Amazonian. She had long, blond hair and wore bright red lipstick. A naked, pale, white man was standing up with ropes tied to each limb, stretching him out. He looked like a standing starfish. A black gag ball was in his mouth, and red whip marks covered his body. His ass was as red as an apple from an obvious beating, and the sight alone made Saint cringe. Loud, heavy metal music played as the woman wearing leather cracked the whip against his backside, causing a loud slapping noise to erupt through the air. The woman shot a look at the door and noticed Saint.

"Get your ass in here, you little bitch," she said to Saint as she cracked her whip in the air, making a loud, snapping noise. She then ran her tongue across her top lip seductively.

"What the fuck?" Saint said under his breath as he was in unfamiliar territory. Regis saw that he was uncomfortable, so he quickly pulled the door shut.

"Don't worry. We have a room for everyone. Apparently, that wasn't your cup of tea," Regis said as he headed to the next door. He continued to talk to Saint as they made their way down the hall. "This is the place that every man dreams of. A buffet of whatever you like to do. Gambling, sex, drugs . . . They're all here. Whatever your twist is, there's a door for you."

"Y'all got some wild shit going on in this mu'fucka," Saint said, smiling, as he tried to wrap his mind around the whole experience.

"Trust me, the older you get and the more money you accumulate . . . your sexual pallet broadens. The more powerful you become, the bigger your appetite," Regis explained.

He stopped at the next door and opened it. Saint was hesitant about looking in, not knowing what he would see on the other side of the door. Regis stepped aside once again, making a clear path for Saint. Saint stepped in and saw a bed of women of mixed ethnic backgrounds in an all-out orgy. They looked like a pile of snakes how they were all intertwined with one another. Fake breasts, long hair, and different skin tones were everywhere. They were all in the bed, sucking each other and tribbing. "Tribbing" was a term used when two women rubbed their clitoris against each other while scissoring. Masturbation, moaning, and strap-on dildos were all in the human gumbo.

Saint couldn't focus on one particular thing because so much was going on. Sweaty bodies were thrusting against one another, and wet noises were rampant. Seven different women touched and pleased each other, and Saint liked what he saw. However, he didn't want to indulge. Although it did look enticing, the thought of the dream that he experienced earlier had him encouraged to stay faithful to Ramina.

Cuba be on that bullshit, Saint thought, as he remembered the last time that he tried to get some pussy, he ended up in an ocean. *Won't get me this time,* he thought to himself and smiled at his own inside joke.

He was there to get a plug, not get off track. He wasn't searching for something new. He wanted a plug to the good life outside of the streets.

"I'm good," Saint said as he stepped out of the room. Regis looked in confusion as he stepped back, boggled. It was very rare that a man didn't give in to his sexual desires—especially when it was presented on a silver platter.

"Ooh, I see. You like what *I* like," Regis said as he smiled widely and pointed his finger at Saint as if he had him figured out.

Regis walked back to the main area where they were before. He then put two of his fingers in his mouth and whistled so loudly that it made Saint's ears ring. Saint looked in puzzlement, not knowing what Regis was doing. But he would soon find out.

A few seconds later, a door opened on the second floor. Then out walked a beautiful young girl with long, flowing hair and an olive skin-colored complexion.

Saint's eyes followed Regis's, and they both watched as the girl with lacy lingerie came down the stairs. As she got closer, Saint felt immoral. She looked extremely too young to be in the presence of grown men. As she stood before them, Saint was sure that the girl was underage. Her body hadn't even fully developed yet. Her breasts were only nubs, and they barely filled the lingerie. She basically didn't have any. Her small frame didn't make it any better. She looked like a baby. She hadn't even developed womanly hips yet. Saint instantly grew uncomfortable and looked away, not wanting to look at a young girl that way. From his estimate, she had to be around 14, and that was a no-go for him.

"Hey, sunshine," Regis said as he cupped her face and pecked her on the forehead.

"Hey, papi," she answered as she avoided eye contact with him.

"Tay, I want you to meet our friend," Regis said as he placed his hand on the small of her back.

Saint looked at her and noticed that she wore heavy makeup. But he could still see the bruises underneath, obviously trying to be concealed. He looked at the skinny girl, and instantly his heart dropped, feeling sorry for her. Tattoos covered her body, and it made her look tomboyish. However, she was still was a pretty girl. Her long, curly hair and captivating light eyes gave her an exotic island look. Saint immediately knew that she was of Cuban descent by her features. Regis didn't fly her in like he did the rest of the girls. This was his local guilty pleasure.

"Hello, mister," Tay said as she looked up at Saint. Saint nodded his head at her and gave a half grin. He instantly started to second-guess his new friendship with Regis.

"Nah, I don't like what you like," Saint said through his clenched teeth as he looked at Regis with a piercing glare. His anger was too much to hide, and it was spilling out.

"Don't knock it 'til you try it," Regis said, not catching on to Saint's disgust for his choice of sexual indulgence. He looked down at Tay and then grabbed his crotch, thinking about what he would do later.

"Go back up to the room. We will continue this after the dogfight," he said as he rubbed her bangs from her face.

"Yes, daddy," Tay said timidly as she smiled. Saint could tell that the youngster was terrified, and it really bothered him. He wasn't a saint, but he didn't believe in pedophilia in no way, shape, or form.

"I can get you one of those delivered like a package," Regis said with a grin on his face.

"What do you mean?" Saint asked, not fully understanding Regis's statement.

"I can have one of those straight to your door. A live-in nanny that's open and willing to do whatever, whenever you want. All of her papers and green card would be legit and taken care of by my connections. They're like little lapdogs. Will be indebted to you just for getting them out of this hellhole country. Trust me," Regis explained.

Saint's insides were burning up in anger. He had a soft spot for things like that because of his mother. She was a victim of human trafficking in her past. Her former drug addiction put her into situations that she regretted every day. The stories that she told him broke his heart, and he immediately recalled those talks with his mom. When he saw Tay, he saw his mother. He immediately thought about the rise of young girls being human trafficked and how he despised it.

He watched as Tay walked away and knew that he would have to bite his tongue in the presence of this circle. He was sharp enough to understand not to offend people in positions of power. Although he didn't say anything, he knew that would be the last time he visited Regis's resort.

Chapter Nine

God of Dog

It had been a few hours since Saint had seen the young girl, and it still bothered him. He followed the group of men who were all mostly drunk and belligerent as they headed toward the elevators at the end of the hall. More guests had come in via helicopter, and the stage was set. It was time for the dogfight.

Multiple elevators lined up at the end of the hall as the men waited their turn to pile in. Everyone was itching to get to the basement level. Regis explained to Saint that he had created an underground arena where the fights took place. Throughout the night, Regis had introduced Saint to so many men that were willing and open to connect with him when he returned home. Not to mention a federal judge, who told Saint that if he ever needed any favors not to hesitate and call Regis, so it could "get taken care of." Saint's mind was blown at the networks that were made. However, the sight of young children was something that he could not shake.

As the group of men piled into the elevator, Saint noticed that the tension was high, and excitement permeated the air. Everyone was eager to see the fight. Saint couldn't understand how a dogfight could be so electric. It was unlike anything that he had ever seen.

Regis stood next to Saint as they watched the elevator doors close. Moments later, the elevator descended. Once they reached the bottom floor, the doors opened, and when they parted, Saint's mind was overwhelmed at what he saw. The chaotic, roaring sound of people filled the air and felt like a zoo. People were yelling, bantering, and waving money in the air like they were in a sports stadium. The atmosphere reminded him of a World Cup soccer game only smaller. It was so intense. The ground wasn't finished and was made of brown dirt and dust. It looked as if they were in a supersized bomb shelter. Lanterns lined the red clay walls and provided lights for the grimy venue.

"What the fuck?" Saint said as he stepped into the underground fight club.

Everyone stood in a gigantic circle and were taking bets with one another, awaiting the event to start. Regis leaned over and explained to Saint what was going on. The hot, humid smell of musty men was pungent, and the air was thick.

"This event is open to the locals to come to watch and bet. I had a private elevator installed that connects my estate. As you can see, this arena runs through the entire downtown Havana. This is what everyone is here for. Millions are won or lost right here," Regis explained as they squeezed in and joined the crowd. Saint nodded his head as he listened carefully.

A bell rang, and a short, chubby Cuban man emerged from the middle of the crowd. The crowd cheered and raved when he stood with both of his hands in the air. He then stepped onto a soapbox that was in the midst of the gigantic circle of men. He fanned his hands in a downward motion, signaling for people to calm down so that he could speak.

"Welcome . . . welcome . . . welcome," he yelled with a heavy Spanish accent. The crowd went crazy in anticipation as he waved his hands, once again signaling for them to quiet down.

"Coming from Santiago de Cuba, Luca Bazooka," the short man yelled as he looked to the corner of the room. Saint's eyes shot to the corner as well so that he could see what type of dog was being brought out. However, he didn't see any animal. Instead, he saw a young boy coming out as his trainer followed him massaging his shoulders. As Saint looked closely, he saw that the boy looked familiar. It was the young boy that he had given his chain to when he first arrived. The young boy still had on the golden chain with the saint on the charm, so that confirmed it.

"What's going on?" he said under his breath as he watched the boy walk past him and into the middle of the people.

Luca shadowboxed as he stood there, shirtless and shoeless. He swung wildly. There was obviously no real skill there. Anyone with sense could see that Luca was untrained. He wore raggedy, stained, and soiled jean shorts. They were the same ones that he had on when Saint had seen him before. That's when Saint understood that the "dogs" that Regis mentioned were, in fact, kids. They were running an underground kids' fight club. While everyone was ranting and raving, Saint just watched, shaking his head. The next fighter was introduced, and he got a warm ovation as well. The young boy came out and was much bigger than Luca. They didn't waste any time. The fight began.

The older boy immediately pummeled Luca. He delivered crushing blows, one after another. His fist seemed to touch every part of Luca's skull. Luca didn't even attempt to dodge or block any of the punches. He just swung wildly, giving it his all trying to fight back. Nonetheless, it was no match. Saint cringed and jumped at every vicious punch thrown at Luca. To see kids brawling like that was sickening to his stomach. After the boy beat Luca into a fetal position, he started stomping on him. Saint looked at the short Cuban man, thinking that he would stop the fight because, surely, it was over. But nothing happened. The men just cheered and hollered like barbarians.

"Stop the fucking fight," Saint said as he looked at the Cuban. The larger boy continued to stump on Luca's head, and blood oozed out of his mouth. "Stop the fight, mu'fucka!" Saint yelled as he stepped forward. Regis grabbed Saint's arm and pulled him back.

"It's to the death, son. Relax," Regis said. Saint snatched his arm away from Regis and gave him a stern stare. Regis then looked at the Cuban man and gave him a signal. Regis motioned his hand across his neck, signaling him to stop the fight. The short Cuban man instantly grabbed the bigger fighter and waved his arm, indicating that it was over. The crowd erupted as the Cuban raised the right hand of the boy, crowning him the victor.

Immediately, a man came, assisting Luca, and dragged him to the back. Saint watched as he shook his head in repulsion. He looked at the ground and saw that his chain had fallen off of Luca during the fight, so he quickly picked it up and examined it. He flipped it over and saw his initials on it.

They treated li'l homie like he was a dog. This ain't right, man, Saint thought to himself. He looked around and noticed that no one seemed to be bothered by the child abuse that was going on. They traded money. Some were cheering. Others were mad because of their loss. Saint stepped back next to Regis as he was conversing with an older Asian man that Saint hadn't noticed before. He listened closely as they exchanged words.

"Okay, so put your money where your mouth is," Regis yelled at the man. He then proceeded to light a cigar that was in between his index finger and thumb. He took a deep pull, and a bright orange ring of fire formed at the tip. Regis was very confident with his words as he didn't give the man the respect of looking at him as he spoke. The Asian man calmly whispered something to Regis. Regis nodded his head and said simply, "Bet."

The bell rang once again, and the crowd became antsy. The man stepped onto the soapbox once more and announced the second set of fighters.

"Next, we have Big Papi . . . the Spanish Bruiser," the short Cuban man said as he threw his hand in the direction of the fighter who emerged from the crowd. Saint looked at the young boy who was nearly six feet tall and seemed to be in his early teens. He was a full-blooded Cuban and had strong facial features. His bulging muscles didn't match his innocent, adolescent, baby face. The crowd erupted in jeers as the bruiser cracked his neck by stretching it from side to side. He then flexed his muscles, making each one of his pectorals bounce up and down. He was a beast.

Regis grabbed Saint and whispered in his ear. "Here comes my champion. Watch this," he said. On cue, the Cuban man introduced the next contender.

"Now, we have the fighter who everyone has been waiting on. The lady of the night . . . Tay . . . the Cubana."

The crowd erupted and chanted in unison . . .

"Cubana!"

"Cubana!"

"Cubana!"

The bell for the elevator chimed, and all eyes shot in its direction. Out came Tay, the same underage girl that Saint saw earlier wearing the sexy lingerie. This time, she wore shorts and a sports bra, exposing her tattooed body. Tay had different animals tatted on her body, which blended flawlessly. Lions, snakes, beautiful birds, and bears were all a part of her colorful collage. Her small frame was without any fat. The only thing that had any meat was her plump buttocks. Her breasts were nonexistent, and her long hair was pulled back neatly, showing her soft baby hairs that rested on her edges.

"That's my li'l bitch I was telling you about," Regis said proudly as she walked into the circle of men.

"Wait—she's about to fight that big mu'fucka?" Saint asked in confusion as he noticed the drastic difference in size.

"Don't let the size fool you. Tay is a boy at heart. She has a fire inside of her. She's a fucking animal. Watch this," Regis said confidently. Saint watched as Tay squared up and never took her eyes off of her opponent. Her fists were up, protecting her face as she shifted her weight from left to right, slowly rocking. Tay was laser-focused as she sized him up.

Saint couldn't believe what he was seeing. *I know they're not about to let this little girl fight this big-ass nigga,* Saint thought as he remained quiet and observed. He clenched his jaws down tightly and tried his best to bite his tongue and not speak up. With people feverishly placing bets with one another, it resembled the New York Stock Exchange.

Another bell rang, and the fight commenced. Tay strategically circled the bruiser, who was twice her size, slowly stalking him. The bruiser let out a roaring yell as he tried to attack her with a bear hug.

"Aaargh," he yelled as he lunged at her.

Tay swiftly ducked, and he missed terribly, catching nothing but the air in his attempt. Saint instantly realized that she was light and quick on her feet. Her footwork was amazing. It was a far cry from what he saw with Luca. The bruiser got noticeably frustrated and tried again. But this time, Tay stepped to the side and held out her foot, tripping him. He instantly fell flat on his face. A cloud of dust rose as he crashed on the ground. As he tried to get up, Tay caught him with a hard right fist to the jaw. Her ferociousness surprised Saint, and he watched the blood trickle from the bruiser's mouth. She then followed up with another one that sent him flying back onto the dust flat on his back. The crowd praised her. Tay stepped back and let him get up. When he stood, he staggered slightly. It was evident that he was disorientated.

Tay quickly ran up to him and threw a quick uppercut to the gut, making him double over in pain. She promptly caught him with a knee to the face, sending him flying onto his back once again. The audience went into a frenzy. Hoots and hollers filled the air as Tay stood over him and breathed deeply. Her chest moved up and down rapidly. It looked as if she had a baboon was in her chest cavity, trying to get out.

"That's right. That's Daddy's girl," Regis yelled and clapped his hands.

Tay looked over at Regis, and it was the first time that Saint had seen her smile. Tay immediately lit up, knowing that she had made Regis proud. She was so into Regis

clapping for her that she didn't see her opponent rise.
Regis's smile quickly turned upside down as he looked
past her, seeing the bruiser raise his fist. Tay saw the
change of expression on Regis's face and turned around.
But by then, it was too late. The boy came hard down
across her temple with a fierce elbow, causing her to fall
on the ground. The crowd gasped in harmony as the loud
thud echoed throughout the place. Tay tried to get up but
was quickly met with a fierce kick to her head. It didn't
stop there. The boy repeatedly kicked her in the stomach,
face, and then back. He stumped her out, beating her to a
pulp, and Saint grew uncomfortable seeing the girl being
abused like that. He looked at Regis and urged him to
stop the fight.

"Stop this, man," he calmly said as he couldn't stand
the sight anymore.

Regis was so infuriated that he would lose the million-dollar bet that he just gritted his teeth and remained
silent.

"Stop the fucking fight," Saint said again, this time
with more anger and aggression.

Regis looked at the short Cuban and made a gesture,
angrily waving his hand across his neck. Immediately,
the Cuban grabbed the bruiser, and just like that, the bout
was over. Some people were cheering, while others were
sulking in defeat. After a few moments of bickering, the
place cleared out. Regis watched as the people walked
past him and shook their heads in disbelief. Saint stood
there alongside him until it was mostly empty. Tay was
still on the ground, trying to gather herself. Regis looked
at her with hatred and shook his head just before storm-
ing out toward the elevators. Saint watched as he exited
and then focused his attention on Tay. He went over to

help her up, seeing that she needed assistance. It seemed like no one cared that a girl just got her ass handed to her.

"Let me help you up," he said as he kneeled and assisted her to her feet.

"Thank you," she said as she wiped the blood from her mouth. To Saint, it started to make sense about why she had bruises under her makeup. She was a street fighter.

"Are you okay?" he asked.

"Yes, I'm good. He just caught me with a lucky punch. It was my fault," she said in disappointment as she dropped her head in defeat.

"He was twice your size. You shouldn't have been fighting him, to begin with. That was some bullshit. Shouldn't even be fighting a dude. You're a fuckin' girl. Doesn't make sense," Saint said, not understanding how the men could be so cold.

"You don't understand this world," Tay said while looking Saint in the eyes. She realized that it was his first time in this underground thing of theirs. Most wouldn't understand the inner workings of that realm.

"How old are you?" Saint asked as he helped her to the stool in the far corner.

"I'm 17," she answered.

"You look like a baby. Didn't even think you were that old," he said, looking at her undeveloped body. His eyes wandered to her arms, and that's when he noticed the many track marks. He had been in the heroin game for a long time, and he knew what needle marks looked like when he saw them. He immediately understood that she did dope. "You're still too young to be involved in shit like this," he said, not wanting to believe her strife.

"Yeah, but I have been fighting all of my life. Nothing new," she answered.

"Why do you do this? Where are your parents?" he asked, trying to get a better understanding of how she ended up in a predicament like the one she was in.

"I don't have parents. Never have."

"Damn—"

Before Saint could say anything else, another Cuban girl emerged from the elevator and yelled something to Tay in Spanish. Tay instantly replied to her and then looked at Saint.

"Listen, I have to go get dressed and get ready for tonight." With that, she hurried to meet the girl and left Saint in the cave alone.

The current trip to Cuba had been crazy, and he was ready to get out of Dodge to get back to some type of normalcy.

Chapter Ten

Straight Flush

It was nearing four a.m., and guests were still at Regis's place. Everyone was in the estate's poker room, sitting at various tables gambling. Things had died down since the dogfight earlier that night. Regis and a few of his closest friends, including Morris Fillman, were at one table playing Texas Hold'em at $50,000 a hand. Cuban dealers sat at different tables, conducting the high-stakes poker games. Regis had it set up like a real casino—only it was in his place. Saint had never seen anything like it before.

Half-naked women walked around in lingerie, serving them cocktails, drugs, and blow jobs on command. Saint played the back and watched as the billionaires freaked off, going in and out of the random rooms. They would gamble and then go get their freak on . . . gamble . . . then freak. That cycle was ongoing all night. Saint only sipped Cognac and observed, deciding not to indulge. He played a few hands of poker on and off but didn't go overboard. He only played enough not to look like an outsider and blend in more easily. He sat and watched Regis lose north of $300,000 during that one sitting. Saint instantly realized that Regis had a bad gambling problem. Saint was sitting behind Regis, so he saw the hands that were played. Saint witnessed Regis go all-in on hands that he had no business doing so on. Regis was a reckless risk taker, and it was easy to see. Saint witnessed him lose hand after hand, just being frivolous with his money. Saint also noticed something else. The dealer was dealing from the bottom of the deck, always being in favor of Morris Fillman. They were cheating, but Saint minded his own business on that matter.

Saint's mind was elsewhere. The underage kids fighting was weighing heavy on him, and he couldn't shake the guilt of knowing and not doing anything about it. Also, the sight of needle tracks on the young girl's arm was constantly replaying in his thoughts. Saint's mother battled with addiction, and she explained how her pimp would use the drug to control her and to keep her needing him. He knew Tay was in a similar situation.

He looked around and couldn't understand how these grown men just overlooked the bullshit that was taking place on their watches. He wanted to speak his mind and leave, but he knew it was chess and not checkers. He couldn't look down on a room full of billionaires and not expect to make powerful enemies. Enemies in that room could be dangerous. Very dangerous, indeed. That was something he did not need in the line of work that he was in. So, he decided to play it cool and leave when everyone else did. But by the way things were looking, they would be there until the sun rose. The cocaine had everyone up and lively as if it were in the middle of the afternoon.

Saint saw Tay enter the room wearing a skimpy red nightgown and had a face full of makeup, attempting to cover her war wounds from earlier that night. He watched as she walked over to Regis while he continued to play cards. He had a fat Cuban cigar sticking out of the right side of his mouth.

"Hey, daddy," Tay said as she smiled and approached him. She placed her hand on his shoulder.

"You lost me one million dollars. Do you know that?" he said, not even giving her the respect of looking at her.

"I'm so sorry, daddy. I should—" Tay said in a shaky voice. It was evident that she was terrified because it was written all over her face. Regis put his hand up to signal her to hush, and she did immediately midsentence.

"I don't want to hear your fuckin' excuses," Regis responded as he studied his cards. The disappointment was all over Tay's face as the words killed her softly.

"I won't lose again. I'm so sorry," Tay pleaded as her eyes watered. She had a lot at stake when dealing with Regis. He provided her with a roof over her head. The thought of her being homeless and walking the streets of Havana again was terrifying. She had been staying at the estate for a while. It was her only home. Going back to the streets was an unbearable thought. Fear set in, and Tay's tears started to flow. Being desperate, she got down on her knees and clasped her hands in a begging position. She sat at his feet with her head down, like she was a small dog. Saint looked around and couldn't believe no one else was bothered by this.

"You know how to make this better?" he said as he looked down at her.

"Anything . . ." she said as she looked up with optimistic eyes.

"Blow every single person at this table," he instructed as he pointed to the four others around the table.

"Okay, I'll do anything," she said without hesitation as she wiped the tears away.

Regis looked down at her and forcefully grabbed her face. "At the same time," he added with a sick smile. He was getting enjoyment out of treating her like a filthy animal, and it was evident. Regis looked at his poker hand and tossed the cards into the center of the table, losing again.

"Fuck," he said under his breath. "This bitch is bad luck." He stood up and said, "Go in the red room and wait for everyone. They'll show you not to showboat while fighting again." Tay nodded her head in agreement and hurried out. Saint was disgusted as his eyes followed Tay as she walked away.

The men laughed and talked about the nasty things that they were going to do with her. Saint had seen enough. He had to do something.

"Hey, I want that dirty bitch," he said as he grabbed his crotch and rubbed himself through his pants. Saint ran his tongue over his perfect teeth and stood at the table.

"Excuse me?" Regis said as he looked at Saint in confusion. Saint was mostly quiet through the night, so it was a big surprise to everyone that he had said what he said.

"You heard me. I want the li'l dirty bitch," Saint repeated as he stood at the table.

"That's my boy. I *knew* you would come around. I was starting to think something was wrong with you," Regis lightheartedly said just before he puffed his cigar. Everyone at the table laughed. Saint put on a fake smile, but his blood was boiling on the inside. He hated to even talk in that manner, but he had to. He couldn't see the abuse go any further. He had to play their game.

"Cool, well, you can go in with everyone else. She can handle one more. Trust me," Regis responded.

"Nah, I want that bitch to myself. I want that nanny situation," Saint said, going with the flow, climbing deeper into the belly of the beast. It was as if the words flowed out without him wanting them to. For some reason, he just felt like he was supposed to save her. He felt the responsibility of making sure that she was okay. It was like nothing else that he ever felt before.

"You freaky motherfucker," Regis said as he pointed his finger at Saint and waved it while smiling widely.

"I knew it," Morris Fillman said as he smiled from ear to ear, seemingly being relieved that Saint was a part of their pedophilia ring.

"She's damaged goods anyway. The bitch is bad luck. So, if you want her . . . you got her. Papers and birth certificate saying she's 21. Green card. All of that will be taken care of. She can fly back with you on the private. No TSA . . . no trouble. Easy breezy," Regis said as if he had done it hundreds of times before. That was because he had.

"Play for her—one hand. A million," Saint said boldly as he looked directly in Regis's eyes. Regis paused and stared at Saint to see if he was serious. He studied him closely. It seemed like something clicked, and he was instantly game.

"Easy. Let's do it," Regis responded as he rubbed his hands together. The adrenaline rush of high-stakes gambling excited him to his core.

Saint grabbed Morris on his shoulder and gave him a very firm squeeze and said sternly, "I want this seat. I like the luck this spot has," he said as he stared a hole through Morris's eyes while keeping a firm squeeze. Saint then looked at the dealer with the same gaze, letting him know that he was up on their deceitful hustle. Saint didn't say anything to them verbally about it, but they both understood that their underhandedness had been exposed. Their hands were tied. They knew that they had to play along or potentially get outed as cheaters. Morris stood up, and Saint sat down, taking his place. Saint rubbed his hands together and clapped twice.

"Let's get it," he said excitedly.

"Okay, so the bet is one hand. One million, correct?" Regis confirmed.

"That's right. I want to take the bitch home," Saint said with fake excitement.

"Before we start . . . You know what you're getting, right? I just want to be clear," Regis said. Saint instantly knew that Regis was referring to the girl's age, which was illegal. He assumed Regis was just giving him a warning before he stepped into the ring of pedophilia. Once a member . . . always a member.

"Yeah, I know," Saint answered.

They were dealt their hand, and needless to say, Saint easily won with a straight flush. He had won the rights to Tay. However, Saint didn't know what he was getting himself into. But after that night, his life would *never* be the same.

Never.

Saint walked into the red room and saw Tay sitting on the bed with her head down. He closed the door behind him and locked it so that no one would come in. He walked over to her, and she immediately attempted to drop to her knees to give him a blow job. Saint caught her by her elbows and lifted her.

"No . . . no. Stop. You don't have to do that," he said as he stood her to her feet. He took a deep breath and shook his head, feeling sorry for her.

"What do you mean?" she said, not understanding why Saint denied her.

"I mean, you don't have to do any of this anymore. I'm getting you out of here."

"What are you talking about? I belong to Regis."

"No, not anymore. You don't belong to him or any of them other mu'fuckas. You're getting out of here," Saint said as he reached into his pockets and pulled out a wad of money. "Here, take this and get yourself together."

Tay took the money and looked at it. "Regis will have me killed. I don't think you understand how things work in this country."

"Listen, li'l mama, this isn't normal. This isn't the way it's supposed to be. Them mu'fuckas up there are sick. I can't make you leave, but I can give you a way out," he explained. Tay's eyes watered. She had never met any man that hadn't tried to use or abuse her. Her parents abandoned her, and Regis was the only person that had ever shown her any interest. She didn't know there was another way, and now this complete stranger was trying to help her. She was confused, overwhelmed, and grateful, all at the same time.

"I used to be on the streets selling my body. Regis came and saved me," Tay admitted, beginning to feel bad and ungrateful. A classic case of Stockholm syndrome.

"He didn't save you. He preyed on you. Why don't you understand that? You're a child still. Your mind hasn't even fully developed yet," Saint said, shaking his head. "Fuck that . . . You're coming with me," he said. His heart wouldn't let her stay.

"Okay . . . okay," she said as she cried. Somehow, she could see in Saint's eyes that he had good intentions.

"But how? Regis will come after me."

"No . . . No, he won't. You're free. I made sure of that. He thinks you're coming with me back home," Saint explained.

"Home, with you?"

"Well, I'm not taking you. I just said that so I could get you away from him."

"Are you serious? He let me go?" Tay asked.

"Yeah, dead-ass serious. You're not his property anymore. You got to get the fuck out of here. Can't you just go home? Where's the rest of your family?" Saint quizzed.

"Cuba is different. They disowned and threw me away. You wouldn't understand," Tay said as the tears welled up in her eyes.

"Fuck . . ." Saint said under his breath after realizing he didn't have a plan. His heart made him react, and now, he might have put her in a worse position than she already was. "You can just come with me. We can figure something out. But this . . . this ain't it."

"I can go with you?" Tay asked as she looked up at Saint. Saint nodded yes, not knowing what he was getting himself into. He just followed his heart, and his heart led him straight back to the bayou . . . with Tay.

Chapter Eleven

Wolves

"Y'all mu'fuckas better line up, or ain't shit moving," Zoo said as he sat on the stoop eating a bag of sunflower seeds.

Dope fiends were scattered around the house as they waited for the shop to open. A few of the wolves were standing behind Zoo. "Wolves" are what he called his street crew and the young hustlers who ran the dope houses. As soon Zoo made the announcement, the fiends got in line, anxiously waiting on their turn to get served.

"Gunner, open up shop," Zoo instructed as he looked back at the young hustler who wore short dreadlocks that were wild all over his head.

Gunner stood just under six feet and was chiseled. He was a young man but moved with an old soul. He had a caramel complexion and broad shoulders. He was one of the few that spoke to Saint personally. Zoo had taken him under his wing, and he knew that he would be the next one up. The only thing stopping him was his young age. But everyone knew that when Gunner got older, he would be strong in the streets. The work that he had put in for Zoo was legendary. Gunner had a long scar on his face that was barely noticeable. It ran from his earlobe to his chin and had a very dark story behind it. As Gunner

served the fiends their morning fix, a white Rover pulled
up on to the block. He immediately knew it was Saint.

Saint would always pull up but never get out to the
spots. Zoo looked over at him and nodded his head,
acknowledging him. Saint flashed his lights in response.
Zoo got back to business and watched their money
getting made. He pulled out a bag of weed and placed
it on a book that was on the porch. Then he broke down
the buds.

As the fiends came and copped their packs one by one,
Gunner took the money. Then he sent them two houses
down where another worker was distributing packs.
Their operation was a well-oiled machine and intricate.
Fiends would give Gunner the money, and he would hold
up his hand to signal how many packs they bought. The
lookout across the street would then signal to the worker
two houses down. After that, the fiends would walk down
to get served. The money and the dope were completely
separated.

Gunner looked at the young man who had a small Afro
and raggedy clothes who was up next in line. Gunner
always felt bad when he saw him because he was too
young to be a dope fiend. He didn't look a day older than
18, and he walked with a feminine bop. His eyebrows
were arched, and his nails were always painted. His hand
gestures were feminine. He couldn't help it. It was just
who he was. The humble young man went by the name
of Cooda.

"Cooda, I thought you were done with this shit, man.
Didn't you just get out of rehab?" Gunner playfully said
as Cooda held out a wrinkled twenty-dollar bill.

"Man, you know that shit doesn't work. I did that to
complete my drug program," he admitted as he showed
his gap-toothed smile.

"Oh yeah, you did get picked up the other week, didn't you?"

"Stealing copper out of them HUD homes," one of the wolves said, making some of the others burst out in laughter.

"Ol' zesty ass," another small-framed wolf added. They all got a good laugh off of Cooda's feminine ways. Zoo listened without saying anything but figured he'd heard enough. He saw that Cooda looked uncomfortable and embarrassed.

"All right, y'all better leave Cooda alone. Didn't he whoop off in yo' ass last summer for talking shit about him being gay? Better chill out before he gives yo' ass a round two," Zoo said with a smirk on his face.

"Ooh yeah, I forgot about that," somebody said as they laughed even louder, remembering when Cooda had enough of the bullying and put hands on the small-framed hustler.

The small hustler didn't like the fact that everyone was laughing at him. Cooda smiled and shook his head, not wanting to stir up old stuff. The smirk was too much for the wolf, so he went over to Cooda and shoved him off of the porch, sending him flying backward. The back of Cooda's head hit the grass as he dropped hard. The wolf then pulled out his gun and hopped off the porch. He walked over to Cooda, stood over him, and pointed his gun at the boy's head.

"Fuck you laughing at, faggot-ass nigga?" he asked, feeling humiliated.

Saint quickly hit his horn, and everyone's attention went toward his car.

"A'ight, that's enough," Zoo said as he licked the leaf that his weed was rolled in. He stood up and brushed the weed remnants off his fresh gray jogging suit. He put the rolled blunt in his mouth and reached out his hand and helped Cooda up. Cooda grabbed his hand and stood up. He then brushed the grass off the back of his head.

"Yo, Cooda, you still know how to hook up cable?" Zoo said, feeling bad for him.

"Yeah, big homie. I can do it," Cooda answered.

"Bet. Stop by the shop sometime this week and hook me up. I be needing to watch SportsCenter while I'm in that mu'fucka late at night," Zoo said.

"Bet," Cooda replied as he smiled through the pain that was in his lower back from the fall. Zoo looked over to Gunner and said, "This one's on me." Gunner nodded and held up a signal to the guy across the street.

"Gon' 'head and get right. Don't forget to stop by the shop later," Zoo reminded Cooda as he lit his weed.

"Thanks, Zoo," Cooda said as his face lit up. He stuffed the twenty in his pocket and headed down to cop his drugs.

Zoo looked down the block and blew out weed smoke. "Y'all niggas hold it down. I'll be back later to check the count," he said before heading over to Saint's car.

"Peace, beloved," Saint said as Zoo took a seat on his passenger side.

"Peace," Zoo said as he reached over and slapped hands with his right-hand man.

"How we looking?" Saint asked.

"Just opened up shop for the day. But yesterday, we killed 'em. Ran through the whole thang at this spot. Had to go uptown and take from that pack just to make sure we didn't run out again," Zoo explained.

"Good. Good," Saint said as he checked his rearview mirror.

Cubana 157

"Ever since you switched up the name and put that Cubana stamp on it, the business been booming. We got the whole city coming to the bayou to get our shit," Zoo said.

"Yeah, Tay is my good luck charm. Ever since I brought her here, we been running through them joints twice as fast. There's something about her," Saint said, not truly understanding how the business had nearly doubled since she'd been in the bayou. It had been almost a year since she came back with him.

"Yeah, li'l sis got that voodoo shit on her," Zoo said jokingly.

Saint half-grinned and shook his head at Zoo's crazy explanation. "Nah, she just got a good vibe, bro. Took her from that bullshit, and the Trap God's blessing a nigga, ya hear me?" They burst out into laughter.

"Damn, Tay is legal now, huh?" Zoo said, thinking about how she was now on the market.

"Yeah, she legal, beloved," Saint answered.

"Can't lie, she a bad Cuban mu'fucka. Pretty as hell. That long hair and pretty eyes be having them boys going crazy. The young wolves around the way say she don't be giving niggas any play. Tell the truth . . . You hitting that?" Zoo asked, trying to get the real from Saint.

"On God, I have never touched her. I don't mess with young girls. I don't deal with no one. I'm serious about settling down with Mi," Saint said, giving him a serious look. "But check this out. I'm thinking about asking Mi to marry me tonight after Tay's birthday party," Saint said as he reached into the side center console and pulled out a small black box. He popped it open, and a shiny ring emerged. A huge diamond rock sat on a platinum band, and it sparkled brilliantly.

"Oh shit. You going to do it, huh?" Zoo asked as he examined the jewelry.

"Yeah, man. I think she's the one. She's been holding me down for so long and kept it G all the way through," Saint admitted.

"Yeah, Ramina is a real one, for sure. Plus, she let you bring a whole chick from Cuba and said nothing. Man, had that been one of my bitches and me, they would've been tried to cut me," Zoo said, only half-joking.

"Nah, Tay is like my little sister, man. That's my li'l baby," Saint said, meaning every word. They had established a little sister/big brother bond that was unlike any relationship that he ever had. Ramina had given her a job at her salon and accepted her with open arms after Saint broke down everything that happened to her. Tay's story broke Ramina's heart.

Ramina wasn't too happy at first, but once she met the girl and got to know her, Tay became like her protégé. Ramina had a love for Tay, and the little resentment that was there, in the beginning, was gone. They had agreed to let Tay stay in the upstairs loft above the salon, which Ramina had remodeled. So, it was more than comfortable. Tay would wash her clients' hair and sweep up the floor in return for money at the end of each week. The only stipulation was that she had to stay out of their way after hours when Zoo and Saint would count up in the back room of the shop.

Tay was slowly but surely getting her life together, and she owed it all to Saint. She adored him and looked at him as her savior. And that's precisely what he did. He saved her.

Chapter Twelve

Li'l Baby

Tay had a broom in hand sweeping up the floor as Ramina and her friends sat in the salon's chairs drinking wine. Music was lightly playing in the background. It was after hours in the shop. They were having a good time and partaking in girl talk, and, as usual, Tay didn't join in. She just listened, not being able to relate, so she remained quiet. She never had a real relationship, so the majority of their topics she couldn't add to. Ramina and her two best friends, Brittany and Vera, sat there talking away.

"And I swear I be so horny while I'm on my period. It never fails. Nigga look like chop liver when I'm off. Soon as my monthly comes—*Boom!* Nigga turns into Idris Elba," Brittany said as she gulped her wine. The girls laughed at Brittany's joke as they thought about their own situations.

"Betta tell that nigga to put a towel down," Vera added.

"Girl, I wish. He ain't 'bout that life," Brittany responded. They were having a good time, and Brittany felt sorry for Tay. She never joined in on their gossip, so she decided to open the floor to her.

"And what about you, Tay? I know yo' li'l ass be fuckin'," Brittany said as she waved her glass in her direction. Tay smiled and blushed. She giggled and shook her head in embarrassment.

"I know that smile from anywhere. You can tell us shit. We can be like yo' aunties. Gon', spill it. You ever gave one of these li'l niggas some pussy while you were bleeding? It be soooo good," Vera admitted. Brittany doubled over laughing and went over to Vera to high-five her.

"I don't have periods," Tay responded, embarrassed. It was obvious that she was ashamed and felt out of place. Ramina noticed her get uncomfortable and shot her friend a look that said, "That's enough, bitch."

"Hey, Tay, can you go upstairs and grab a bottle of wine for me? I left some in the cabinet," Ramina said, trying to break up the awkward tension.

"Sure," Tay said, giving a nervous smile.

Ramina watched her until she disappeared into the back. Once she saw that Tay exited the room, she shot a look at Brittany.

"Bitch, you talk too much. I told you she had it rough back in Cuba. The man she used to be with used to fight her like a damn dog. She was a full-blown athlete. You know athletes don't start getting their periods until they're twenty sometimes."

"Oh yeah. I heard that. Those female Olympians don't get their period until late too," Vera added.

"I'm so sorry," Brittany said as she put her hand on her chest, knowing that she was insensitive to Tay's early childhood abuse.

"On her damn birthday," Ramina said, adding fire to the flame. They had agreed to celebrate her birthday on the date that she arrived in America. On that day, it marked an entire year since she had been there.

"I ain't shit," Brittany playfully said as she downed the rest of her wine.

"You sure ain't shit," Vera said jokingly. Ramina smiled.

Then they heard Tay's footsteps as she returned to the room. They all ceased talking and tried to act normal. Almost at the same time, Zoo and Saint walked through the front door. Saint had a birthday cake in his hand, and lit candles were on top of it. Ramina and the girls immediately started to sing "Happy Birthday" to Tay. It took Tay a second to figure out what was going on, but all the attention was on her, and she caught on quickly.

Happy Birthday to you,
Happy Birthday to you,
Happy Birthday to Tay,
Happy Birthday to you.

Tay was so surprised and happy to be celebrated. She put her hands over her mouth and was filled with joy. She couldn't remember the last time someone had done something for her birthday. She hadn't even realized that it had been a year already. She was just so happy to be free from Regis, she never thought twice about it. Saint walked right in front of her with the candle-filled cake. Tay closed her eyes and blew hard, blowing out all of the flames. A small cloud of smoke filled the air from the candles, and everyone clapped and crowded around her.

"Thank you so much, everyone. I appreciate this. I've never had anyone do something like this for me," Tay said as she enjoyed the moment.

"Let's get this party started," Brittany said as she turned up the music. They partied and had a good time all in honor of Tay. She was locked in as family.

***

It was approaching midnight, and Ramina hugged her friends as they headed out. Zoo had brought some tequila out, so they all were feeling good, including Saint. They even gave Tay a shot of liquor to celebrate her day. As the girls were leaving, Zoo leaned over to Saint and reminded him that they needed to count up before the night was over. He had the cash from all of their spots in his trunk and needed to make sure they were on point for the next re-up.

"But before we get into that, you gon' ask her?" Zoo asked, referring to the marriage proposal that Saint mentioned to him earlier.

"Nah, not tonight. I'm going to wait for a better time. Don't want to do it like this. I gotta put more thought into it for her," Saint explained.

"I feel that," Zoo whispered as they stood there conversing with each other.

Tay crept up behind them, coming from the bathroom. She hugged Saint from the back, slightly startling him. She hugged him so tightly, and her head was pressed tightly against his back. Saint smiled and patted her hand that was clasped snugly around his stomach. She slid around, and her tiny frame was tucked under his right arm.

"Thank you so much, big bro. This means a lot to me," she said while smiling. Zoo smiled and looked at her as well.

"No problem, Tay. That's what family does," he said, smiling as Ramina approached beaming. She felt good that Tay was in a good space.

"Yo, I'm going to the car and grab the bags," Zoo said. Saint nodded and watched him slip out the back. Ramina had a glass of wine in her hand and was noticeably tipsy. She slid under Saint's other arm. Now, he held them both and squeezed, giving them both a hug. He kissed Ramina on the lips and then pecked Tay on her forehead.

"I want to give you something," Ramina said as she moved from under Saint and grabbed Tay's hand.

Saint smiled as he watched Tay's eyes light up. They walked away, and Saint immediately looked at Ramina's huge backside.

"My big baby and my li'l baby," Saint said as he addressed them both. He would always play with Ramina and tell her she was a big baby because of how he had her spoiled. Ramina looked back and winked at Saint's comment. Saint smiled and watched them walk off into the corner to talk. He faded to the back so he could set up the money machine and begin the count up.

"I wanted to give you something," Ramina said as she looked down at Tay, who sat in the salon chair. Ramina reached into one of the drawers under the vanity mirror that lined the back wall and pulled out a book. It was a Bible.

"My grandmother gave me this when I turned 18 and told me that in life, whatever hurdles or demons I have, that I can find the remedy to them in here," Ramina said as she looked at Tay. A sticky note was on the front of it with Psalm 46:5 handwritten. "That was the first psalm she told me to look at."

Tay grabbed the book and hugged it tightly. It was the first gift she had ever gotten, and it meant a lot to her. Ramina wasn't heavy in religion at all, but she knew that Tay needed someone to do that for her. Her grandmother did it for her, so she would do the same for Tay. Ramina wasn't an angel, but she had a pure heart, and that was one of the reasons why Saint loved her so much. Tay got up and hugged Ramina and thanked her for the kind gesture.

"And tomorrow, I have us a spa day set up. Just me and you. No talkative-ass bitches tagging along," Ramina joked as they both shared a laugh.

Ramina grabbed the bottle of tequila off the counter and two red cups. "Okay, one shot for the birthday girl before I call it a night. I have to go home and get ready to put this pussy on Saint," Ramina said as she winked and stuck her tongue out of the side of her mouth.

"Aye," Tay said as Ramina did a halfhearted dance, moving her butt in circles. They took a shot together, and instantly, Tay felt it. After a few moments of small talk, Ramina called it a night and told Saint that she would meet him at home.

"All right, love, see you at home," Saint said as he sat at the table with no shirt on because the small room got hot. They would be there awhile. While he stuffed money into the top of the money machine, Ramina stuck her head inside the door of the back room and smiled. She told him that she was about to head out. She flicked her tongue at him in a freaky way, letting him know she wanted to taste him later. Saint knew that gesture well. They had been around each other long enough to talk without actually speaking. He knew that she was ready to get freaky that night. After the count up, he would head home to give her that masterful stroke, for sure. He smiled back, raised his eyebrows, and nodded his head, letting her know he was with it. She left, and he then focused on Tay. He watched as Tay walked past him and up the stairs that led to the upper loft.

"Good night, Tay," Saint said.

"'Night," Tay responded.

Zoo had on a wife beater as he paced the room and stretched his arms out. The table was full of money as the scattered bills almost covered the entire wooden table . . . so much that you couldn't even see the wood. Money was flowing in, and the Cuban dope was moving through the bayou like a plague.

"Yo, Li'l Cooda supposed to be hooking up some cable back here this week. We need to be watching SportsCenter while counting up this shit."

"Cooda? Li'l Cooda?" Saint asked, instantly knowing who he was talking about.

"Sharon's boy."

"Yeah . . . I remember Sharon. She died a few years back, right?"

"Right. She OD'd, remember?" Zoo reminded him.

"Yeah. Cooda is her son's name? That used to be my li'l partner," Saint said.

"Yessir. Li'l nigga out here bad on that shit, just like his mama," Zoo said as he shook his head.

"A shame . . ." Saint said as he stood up and watched the money flip through the machine.

Two hours later, they were at the end of the bag. The count was finally complete. They sat there and counted a little over two hundred thousand dollars, straight dope money. Saint sat back. The money felt good, but the smile on Tay's face felt better. That truly was the highlight of his night. As he rubber-banded the money, Zoo lit a blunt and wanted to run something by Saint.

"Yo, Tay was looking all right today. She a bad li'l one," Zoo said as he was feeling her style. "She reminds me of a baby Jhené Aiko," he said, referring to a famous singer as he took a deep pull of his weed.

"Oh yeah," Saint said as he handled the money. He shot a look at Zoo, and it was piercing.

"What's that, bro?" Zoo asked as he frowned and held his hands out, confused.

"What was what?" Saint said as he instantly knew what Zoo was referring to. He felt a type of way by Zoo's words, and he surprised even himself with his reaction. There was something that bothered him about Zoo addressing her like that, but he instantly shook that notion, knowing he was out of bounds.

"Nigga, I know you better than anybody. You soft on that girl," Zoo said with a huge smile.

"Nah, beloved. You off on that one," Saint replied as he shook his head and focused on the last stack of money in front of him.

"Yeah, whatever, nigga. I know you," Zoo said as he took the stacks off the table and stuffed them in the safe that was hidden behind a painting.

"You're bugging," Saint said as he smiled and took another shot of tequila.

"So, I'm about to head out. I got something on deck waiting at the room for me," Zoo told him as he slid on his hoodie and the jacket. He closed the safe and then placed the picture over it, concealing it. Afterward, he slapped hands with Saint.

"Love you, bro," Zoo said.

"Love you, beloved," Saint said as he took another shot, thinking about Ramina's phat ass and what he was going to do with it when he got home. He loved waking her up by way of his mouth, and he couldn't wait to taste his woman. He watched as Zoo headed out the back, and then he heard the door slam. His cell phone buzzed, and he saw that it was a text from Ramina.

You still at the shop?

Yeah.

Zoo there with you?

He just left. I'm on my way home now.

Saint smiled at his text thread with Ramina, and the thought of sexing her made his dick begin to thump. He couldn't wait to get home and get to her. He wanted to show her how much he had missed her. He stood up and slightly staggered. That's when he knew he had had one too many drinks. *I gotta get home,* he thought to himself as he reached for his shirt and then his coat. Just as he was about to put them both on, he saw Tay come in.

"Hey, I thought you were asleep," he said as he looked a bit surprised. She wore pajama pants and an oversized hoodie that she slept in.

"Oh . . . yeah. I heard the door close, and I was coming down to make sure it was locked before I went to bed," she answered.

"Cool. I'll make sure to lock up. Don't worry about it," Saint assured her.

"What you guys did for me today was really nice. I just wanted to say thank you again," Tay said as she walked over to him and hugged him. "Since I been here with you, I haven't touched any drugs and feel like a new person. I have you to thank for that," she said.

Saint wrapped his arms around her and kissed the top of her head. She hugged him so tightly, and he felt her brush up against his semi-erect penis. She slowly pulled back and looked up at him. Their eyes connected, and something urged Tay to kiss him. Saint kissed her back slowly, and she reached down to grab his rod and rub it. They continued kissing, and before you knew it, Tay was on her knees. Saint slightly stumbled, so he widened his stance to remain balanced. She pulled out his thickness and took him into her mouth.

"Wait . . . you can't . . ." Saint said, but it felt so good and warm. He threw his head back in pleasure and licked his lips, loving the warm sensation around his pipe. Tay slowly circled her tongue around his tool and bobbed on it. Saint felt kind of dizzy and then looked down at her, realizing what was happening. He instantly snapped out of it and regretted what he was letting happen. *What the fuck am I doing?* he thought to himself. Quickly, he looked over at the door, and his heart dropped. Ramina was standing there in her lingerie and a bottle of champagne with tears in her eyes.

"How could you!" she yelled as her heart broke into a million tiny pieces. He quickly stepped back and pushed Tay away as his hard dick popped out of her mouth.

"I'm so sorry," Tay said as she wiped her mouth and stood up.

"Baby, it's not what it looked like. I took too many shots and—" Saint tried to explain, but a flying champagne bottle came at him. It barely missed him as he leaned to the side. The bottle crashed against the back wall, causing shattered glass and champagne to spray everywhere.

"Fuck both of y'all. Y'all can have each other. What type of shit is this? After all we been through? Huh, Saint?" she screamed as her tears flowed. She then focused on Tay and tried to rush her, but Saint grabbed her as she lunged at Tay. Ramina kicked and screamed as she lost all control. She just saw red at that point. She was boiling.

"You dirty little whore. All I tried to do is help you. I want you to get yo' shit and get the fuck out of my shop. Get the fuck out now!" Ramina shouted as she pointed at the door. "If I see you around here again, I'll fucking kill you! Leave!"

Tay cried profusely, hyperventilating. She couldn't even respond. She just kept apologizing, but none of that mattered to Ramina. "Get out!" she yelled again, feeling that Tay wasn't moving fast enough.

Tay rushed to the door and out of the shop. She ran down the block to get away from the madness and didn't know what to do or where to go. She leaned against the wall of a building and slowly slid onto her bottom. She buried her head in her lap and cried like a baby. "What did I do?" she asked aloud as the tears streamed down.

"Are you okay?" a young man riding a bike said to her as he headed in the direction of the shop. He stopped right in front of her and placed one of his dirty shoes on the sidewalk pavement to balance himself. Tay looked up and saw the gap-toothed young boy. She hadn't seen him before.

"Hey, it's okay. It's okay. What happened?" the boy asked. "Are you hurt?" he said out of concern, thinking she had been raped or something like that.

"I just fucked up my life . . ." Tay said as she looked past the young boy, not focusing on anything in particular. She was talking to herself more so than to him.

"What's your name? I'm Cooda."

Chapter Thirteen

Three Months Later . . .

A furry brown rat ran across the wooden floor, but it didn't bother Tay. Although she hated rodents and was terrified of them, it didn't seem to matter. She focused on the task in front of her. The trash-littered home was filled with drug paraphernalia and empty bottles that had been used and tossed aside without a care. A rusty gun sat on the table as well. The owner of the house left it there, and Cooda toted it everywhere since the day that he discovered it.

The vintage couches were soiled and stained from years of careless use. The carpet matched its griminess, and the walls were covered in outdated wallpaper. The stench of body odor filled the spot. It looked as if a hurricane had blown through the living room. Tay and Cooda had been in this abandoned house that Cooda had illegally connected electricity to. He had stolen it from the next-door neighbor. The abandoned house acted as their crash house for the past few weeks. Cooda was on the couch with one thing on his mind, and that was getting high. A belt was wrapped tightly around his right arm as he rested his elbow on his knee.

Tay impatiently waited as she pulled the belt tight, trying to help Cooda find a suitable vein. She carefully watched as he smacked his arm repeatedly, attempting to make a vein bulge. As he eyed his arm, he saw a fat, greenish vein form and knew he was ready to indulge. His mouth watered, and an orgasmic feeling approached. The pure anticipation of the drug made him high without it even being in his system.

"Pull a little tighter. Shit . . . Come on now, Tay," he begged as he smacked his arm one more time. "Yeah, there it go," he said as his vein was to his liking. It looked like a fat gummy worm lying under his skin. It was the perfect candidate for injection.

He reached over and grabbed the syringe that was on the table and slowly pushed out the water that danced on top of the heroin. He carefully injected the needle into his bulging vein and slowly emptied the syringe. When he pushed all the dope into his vein, he pulled the needle out and placed it on the table. Then he sluggishly leaned back on the couch and closed his eyes. He smiled as he felt the warm sensation creep up his arm. He slowly grabbed his crotch area and squeezed as the drug worked its magic.

He opened one eye and watched as Tay hurriedly set herself up for her hit. She held a lighter under the spoon and waved it slowly, wanting to distribute the fire equally. She watched closely as the heroin liquefied. Then she grabbed the syringe and sucked up all the dope. The anticipation was killing her, and sweat beads formed on her nose as she anxiously prepped for her trip to cloud nine.

She reached over and unwrapped the belt from around Cooda's arm. She placed it on hers, prepping for her turn. She tightened the belt, placing it in between her teeth. As she clenched down, her jawbone flexed. Slobber dripped out of the side of her mouth as she anxiously searched for a good spot to poke. She jerked her head back violently, making it even snugger. She waited until a big vein formed and grabbed the needle with her free hand. Then she cautiously slid the needle in and let it flow.

"Ooh. Oooh shit," she crooned as she slowly slumped on the couch. Her body relaxed. To her, it felt like she were melting. It felt so good. She was shoulder to shoulder with Cooda, and they were experiencing forbidden heaven together. The drug felt so good as it traveled into her bloodstream and worked its undeniable magic.

This had become an everyday thing for the pair. Ever since the big fight with Ramina, Tay had been in the streets with Cooda. She didn't have anywhere else to go, so the streets were her only option. Cooda had pulled her into the downward spiral of being a junkie.

"This feels soooo good," Tay said as she closed her eyes and smiled.

"This that good shit," Cooda responded.

"Uh-huh," she hummed in agreement.

"They loved you on the strip. We gotta go back," Cooda said as he referred to the downtown area that was known as the ho stroll. After Cooda begged her, she eventually gave in and agreed to turn a few tricks. She told him that she would only give head, though . . . That was her stipulation. Somehow, that made her feel better about what she was doing. From the johns, they got a lot of nos, but the yeses they did get were enough to make a few bucks. She earned enough for them to score the drugs and stay high all day.

As Tay slipped in and out of her nod, she thought of Saint and how things had panned out. She lost track

of time since the last time seeing him. She missed him
so much and didn't know how much she depended on
him until he wasn't there. The big blowup that caused
her to leave was too much to recover from. She wished
that drunken night had never happened. There was so
much about herself that Saint didn't know, and she felt
guilty that she never would be able to tell him. As she
nodded, water formed in the corner of her eyes. As the
warm tears ran down her cheeks, she slowly drifted into
a drug-infused sleep . . . thinking about the good times.

Zoo and Saint sat in the back of the shop, counting
up the money from the month. It was their ghetto ritual
that they did every first Sunday, a day that the shop was
closed as well. Zoo, as usual, picked up all the money
from around the bayou and brought it back to the shop.
They had been there for a few hours, and it was now
approaching three a.m.

"It's getting late as hell," Zoo said as he pulled on
the marijuana-filled joint and slowly blew it out. Saint
quickly waved the smoke away from his face as it drifted
over to him.

"My bad, brody," Zoo said, not meaning to send the
smoke in his direction. Saint had just wrapped a rubber
band around the stack and placed it neatly in the bag that
was below him.

"That's a half right there," he confirmed as he zipped
up the bag. He was referring to the half a million dollars
that he would be taking to Alexandro.

"Bet. When are you headed back?" Zoo asked.

"Next week. We are going to Dubai for a weekend, and
I'm going to leave from there," Saint explained.

"Damn, bro. Y'all stay taking trips. Must be nice," Zoo teased as he counted the money. The joint dangled from the left side of his mouth.

"The trips aren't for me. They're for her. That's the key," Saint explained.

"The key?" Zoo asked.

"Absolutely, beloved," Saint said as he stood up and stretched. He then continued. "The key to keeping a woman happy is making sure she has something to look forward to. That's all a woman really wants. She wants something to get dressed up for and look forward to."

"Damn . . . That's deep. Maybe that's why I can't keep one," Zoo said as he paused his counting and nodded in approval.

"Might have a point," Saint responded.

"Yo . . . speaking of, peep this shit," Zoo said as he jumped up and went over to the TV screen that was on the corner of the wall. "So last week, I installed cameras in the shop. A few nights ago, I had shorty come through, and she brought her friend." Zoo pushed a button on the DVR, and an image popped on the screen. It was Zoo having a threesome right in the middle of the main floor of the barbershop. One thick, chocolate woman was riding his face, while another slim girl was bouncing on his shaft. The moans and slurping noises sounded through the speaker as they were caught on the hidden cameras.

"Peep how she working that ass," Zoo said in excitement as he smiled and pointed at the screen. He bounced his hand along with the girl's ass that was riding him. "*Bam . . . bam . . . bam,*" he said playfully as they both watched the peep show.

"You crazy than a mu'fucka, beloved," Saint joked as he shook his head and looked away. He grabbed his jacket and then picked up the duffle bag from the floor. "I got to get out of here. Hold it down while I'm gone. Remember to put seven thousand in the bank each night at the nightly deposit box," Saint said, reminding him of their strategy to wash their money.

"Go and enjoy yourself. I'll take care of everything here," Zoo assured him as he walked over and slapped hands with Saint.

"In a minute," Saint said as he always did. He walked out and headed home to his woman.

"He's just different," Ramina admitted as she sat on the couch with her legs tucked under her butt. The girls sat in Saint's home right in the middle of the living room. An oversized bearskin rug was their pallet, and the lights were dimmed. They all crowded in front of the fireplace as the flickering fire illuminated the room. The smooth sounds of Summer Walker's ballads provided the soundtrack for their girls' night in. Vera and Brittany accompanied Ramina, sharing wine and laughter, having a great time. The midnight oil burned, filling the room with the sweet almond aroma. They had been there for the past three hours laughing, talking shit, and getting tipsy. Ramina was trying to explain the difference between Saint and her past lovers.

"OK, bitch, you have to explain. What's so different? Spill the beans," Vera stated as she downed the last of her Merlot and wiggled in her chair, excited about the tale ready to be revealed.

"I know, girl, tell it," Brittany said as she clapped her hands, egging her friend to go on with the steamy details.

"Okay . . . okay," Ramina said as she blushed. She put her hand on her face, hiding it. Her cheekbones became apple red, and her light brown skin exposed her discomfiture. "Pour me another drink, first," she said as she stretched out her glass and waited for Brittany to give her a refill. As Ramina watched her wine getting poured, she spoke.

"It's different. It's hard to explain but . . . It's like a massage," Ramina said as she closed her eyes, getting flashbacks of her encounters with her man. She felt a tingle in her love button and crossed her legs to feel the friction.

"A massage? Y'all be on that tantric kick?" Brittany asked. She was well invested in the details.

"No, not like a massage with his hands. He massages me with his dick," Ramina said as she smiled widely. "Okay, so . . . he has this thing he does . . ." she said, just before pausing. Her girls were attentive and oozing off her every word. Ramina continued as she closed her eyes to reflect.

"So, this nigga rubs your body with his dick. Like with baby oil and all?" Vera said, trying to understand what Ramina was getting at.

"No, girl. Listen, it's like he massages my insides. He slowly goes in deep. I mean deep . . . deep. Then he just slowly rocks and goes in small circles. Whew, child," Ramina said as she placed her hand on her chest and took a sip of her wine.

"Okay, Saint massaging the coochie, huh? I heard that," Brittany said while laughing.

"These other men need to take notes. Especially the young ones," Vera exclaimed.

"Girl, yes. These young niggas be trying to beat my shit up. I mean, damn. I be sore for the entire next day."

"Y'all are too crazy," Ramina said, not being able to relate. They all burst into laughter, having a good time enjoying girl talk. All the sex talk had Ramina thinking about her man. She looked at her phone and noticed that he had texted her.

Be home in an hour, love.

Ramina's mind instantly drifted to him stroking her, which made her squirm in anticipation. She decided that she should do something special for him before their trip to Dubai. She had put him on pussy punishment for the past three months because of the incident with Tay. She felt betrayed. However, Saint had been a good sport about it and didn't complain once. They had been on four trips since it happened, and she could tell that he was really remorseful. So, at that moment, she decided that she would put it on him good that night. She texted back, deciding to cook something up special for him when he came home.

Dinner will be on the table . . .

Ramina took the bottle and downed the remaining wine. She wiped her mouth and looked at her girls. "It's time for y'all to go. My man is on his way," she said as she headed toward the stairs. "Y'all can let yourselves out," she said, while not even turning back around to look at them. She only had an hour to prepare Saint's special meal.

Chapter Fourteen

Medusa's Snake

The midnight chill was swirling in the air, and the hawk was out. It was an unusually cold night for the bayou, but that didn't stop the streetwalkers from going up and down the block selling sex. Men with short shorts, heavy makeup, and bad wigs roamed the small back street. Their muscular builds and wide shoulders made it clear what their true gender was.

Most of the streetlights had been shot out, so the full moon acted as the only illumination. On this particular back street was a small community of society's outcasts and the freaks who sought them. It was an area that was taboo, and the district was looked down upon by the locals. This was the part of New Orleans people never spoke of, which is why Tay stuck out like a sore thumb there. This wasn't her world; yet, she had to do what she had to do. After no luck on the main strip where the ladies turned tricks, Cooda suggested they visit there to try their hand with the freaks. At first, Tay was against it, but the insatiable pull of the drug and her desire to feel it in her veins overruled all. She wasn't the boss of her life anymore. . . the dope was. Cooda convinced her, saying, "A freak is a freak. At the end of the day, they want their dick wet. Let's just try it." Tay eventually gave in, and there they were . . . trying to feed their addiction on the backstreet.

Cooda stood against the brick wall and watched Tay closely. He observed intensely in hopes that she could get the customer. They desperately needed money, and Cooda had no other ideas. He was even open to trading his body and services for a score. That night, it seemed like the tricks weren't looking for what he was offering, so Tay was their only hope. They had been chasing for the past few hours since they had awoken from their her-oin-induced nod from earlier that day. Cooda knew that time was ticking before the stomach pains would kick in from withdrawal. At that point, they were just des-perate. He stared at Tay, feeling like he was standing on pins and needles. She was leaned over into the pas-senger-side window, and the bottom of her small cheeks hung from the bottom of her short skirt. A black Lincoln pulled to the curb, and a middle-aged white man was be-hind the steering wheel. Cooda shifted his weight from his left foot to his right as he frantically scratched him-self on his arms.

"What is he saying?" Cooda whispered harshly, trying to figure out what was going on. Tay looked back at Cooda in irritation and quickly held up her finger, signa-ling for him to hold tight. As she turned her head toward the car, the sound of tires screeching erupted. The abrupt sound startled Tay, making her jump back. The car peeled off while leaving a cloud of smoke. Tay stormed back toward Cooda, rubbing her hands together and blowing on them, trying to stay warm.

"Damn, Cooda, you scared him away," she said while shaking her head in disappointment.

"Sorry, Tay," he said, knowing that he messed up.

"It's okay. He didn't want what I had anyway," Tay said, not wanting to be too down on her only friend. She saw him sulking and tried to crack a joke to lighten the mood.

"He wanted one of the linebacker dudes walking down there . . . not me," she said as she looked down the block at the two muscular men that stood on the corner. They both got a good laugh out of it and cackled together.

"Let's get out of the cold for a second. I still have some change in my purse. We can get some hot chocolate from McDonald's until we figure out our next move. Standing out here ain't going to get us nowhere," she admitted.

"OK, cool, because I'm freezing my balls off," Cooda joked as he shook his shoulders playfully.

"Mines too," Tay added jokingly, which sent them into a fit of laughter. Cooda loved how funny Tay was, and he adored her. He never had a friend like her before. She was the only person in his life who didn't judge him for who he was. She understood him, and he loved her for it. Seeing her laugh brightened up his day.

"I love you, BFF," Cooda said as he threw his arm around Tay's small shoulders.

"I love you too, best friend," she replied, and with that, they headed around the corner to the restaurant to game plan how to get the monkey off.

"Aye, didn't you say they used to count money in the back of the shop on Sundays?" Cooda asked.

Saint grabbed the duffle bag from his trunk and slammed the door shut. He took a deep breath and patted his stomach. He had been so busy that he hadn't eaten all day, so the text that Ramina had sent him about dinner was just what he needed. He entered his home and saw that the light was dim, and he could smell oil burning. He also heard music lightly playing from upstairs. He automatically assumed that Ramina had company over earlier. He was used to the burning oil on their girls' night, so the smell was very familiar to him. He opened the closet by the front door and set the duffle bag in before making his way toward the kitchen.

"Mi, I'm home, love," he yelled upstairs to let her know he had arrived. As he made his way to the kitchen, he pulled off his jacket. He wanted to get comfortable so that he could eat dinner and get some much-needed rest. They had an early flight, and he hated traveling groggy. As he pulled his shirt over his head, he steadily walked toward the kitchen. He yelled loudly for Ramina again. "Love, what you cook?" He thought she could hear him from downstairs.

As he reached the kitchen with his shirt off, he saw a beautiful presentation. Ramina wore a full-bodied fishnet suit with red stilettos on. As she sat on the edge of the table, her legs were propped up, giving him a clear viewpoint of her glazed lips. Her freshly shaven vagina was on full display, and it was a sight to behold. Her bright red lipstick matched her shoe color exactly, and she was au naturel under the net. Her thick body filled out the suit. In fact, it seemed as if she would burst out of it at any moment.

"Come get your dinner," she seductively said as she put two fingers in her mouth to wet them. She ran her tongue around her fingers and pulled them out, letting spit sloppily drip from them. Next, she took those same two fingers and let them fall to her love box. She seductively spanked her clitoris, making a loud, wet sound resonate throughout the house.

Smack!
Smack!
Smack!

The sound of her hand smacking against her skin instantly aroused Saint, and he gripped his member through his jeans, slowly stroking it for preparation. Ramina kept direct eye contact with him, never looking away. The faint sounds of music by DVSN played in the background, and the mood was set.

She softly caressed her erect button, applying light pressure to it, then moaned while slowly moving her hips in circles. She was slow winding the lower half of her body like a snake, and her movement was in perfect unison with her two twirling fingers. As she masturbated, Saint stood there in awe, watching the erotic show in front of him.

"Damn, baby," he said in amazement as his eyes were fixated on her plump vagina. It started to drip onto the marble tabletop. She spread her legs a tad bit wider, exposing her pinkness. Saint felt his member harden to its fullest potential. It had been so long since he made love to his woman, and he was patient. He understood that he had been wrong, so he didn't want to rush the healing process by forcing sex on a broken heart. But from what he was seeing, he knew that it had been worth the wait. His tool was as hard as a missile. He slowly walked over to his woman, who was steadily playing with herself. He dropped down to his knees, and just so happened, his face lined up perfectly with her love below. He could smell the sweet musk coming from his woman, and it turned him on even more.

He moved Ramina's hand away from her love box and replaced it with his mouth. He carefully French kissed her clitoris, gently sucking it while unhurriedly flicking his tongue from left to right, then up and down. He knew how she liked it, so he was extra soft and tender as he kissed it. He took his time, looking at it and making sure he was perfectly lined up before he went back in. He put both of his hands on her inner thighs and used his two thumbs to open her lips for better access.

He pulled his head back and admired her hard button sticking out. He kissed it repeatedly and carefully worked on her with slow, wet pecks making a loud, smooching noise every time he did it. It was getting good to Ramina, so she grabbed the back of his bald head and plunged his head into her box with every peck. She stretched her neck, looking down so that she could see the magic happening. She noticed that her juices got caught in his beard, dripping off of it and onto the floor. The visuals drove her crazy, and she coached him.

"Suck it harder, baby," she whispered as she squirmed and continued to bob his head, but this time with force. She gradually slammed his face harder and harder into her wetness, causing a splashing noise with each slam. She stared intensely, and a crazed look formed on her face as she was in a trance of pure pleasure. Seeing his face, white teeth, and gold row turned her on to the fullest. She was in complete bliss and opened her mouth, panting heavily. Her eyes slowly rolled in the back of her head, and her body got stiff. She momentarily made an ugly and confused face as she groaned. She felt all of her tension building up, and the lack of sex had her anxiety built up to the max.

She continued to crash his head into her love box. It seemed as if she were trying to stick his whole head inside of her. Her feet went into the air, and her moaning became screams as she felt a huge orgasm approaching. One of her eyes involuntarily closed, and she felt her toes curl. Saint moaned, feeling it was getting good to her, and that sound alone sent him over the top.

"I love you! Oh God . . . I love you. Shit, boy," she yelled as her body shook. That's when liquid shot out of her and splashed against Saint's face like a tsunami. She squirted all over his face and chest as her body quivered uncontrollably. Saint wiped off his face and dropped his pants, showing his rock-hard member. He smoothly slid inside of her as he placed his thumb directly on her clitoris. Taking his tool, he went as deeply inside of her as possible and then slowly applied pressure to her button with his thumb. He expertly worked his thumb in circular motions. With his free hand, he lifted one of her legs and ran his hand down it, until he reached her heel. He popped off her shoe so that her bare foot was in his hand and close to his face. He slowly brought her foot to his mouth, skillfully licking her toes. He did this while still rubbing her button, keeping the pressure intact. He gradually worked his hips, moving his hard rod subtlety inside of her.

They made love that night all over the house, and it was long overdue on both of their behalves. They desperately needed to catch and release, and that's exactly what they did. The two reconnected that night, and what Saint had done with Tay was just an afterthought not worth a mention.

Just before the sun came up, Saint had gotten calls back to back to back. He finally got around to answering them, knowing it had to be urgent. It was Gunner, telling him that Zoo had been shot and robbed. Saint got up and rushed out of the house, heading to the hospital. He had to get to the bottom of what had happened.

Chapter Fifteen

Deceitful Intentions

Zoo watched Saint closely as he stood next to him. They were in the back of the shop. Saint kept rewinding the tape and pausing it on certain parts that displayed the shooter's tattooed arms. They were in the back room of the store, watching the playback of the recent robbery. Zoo had studied the tape for what seemed to be a hundred times before he had called Saint to notify him. Saint shook his head, not believing Tay's audacity. Zoo had on an arm sling and was bandaged on his shoulder. He had gone to the hospital and got looked at after the robbery. Luckily, the bullet went in and out, not hitting anything vital.

"I helped her in so many ways, and look, beloved," Saint said. He seemed as if he were in a daze. "*This* how she repays me, huh? I brought her over here from Cuba to have a better life, and she does *this* bullshit?" Saint said, talking more to himself than Zoo. Zoo had never seen Saint so angry. It was out of his character. Not until that very moment did he understand the hold Tay had on Saint.

He watched closely as the robbery went down. They had Zoo on the floor at gunpoint. Saint's heart was broken into pieces knowing that Tay would stoop that low and commit the ultimate betrayal. He watched as the scene played out, and Zoo ultimately ended up getting shot.

"That's Li'l Cooda from the block. Li'l sweet nigga," Zoo said, pointing him out on the screen monitor. Tay had on a ski mask, but her tattoos and petite build were a dead giveaway.

"The li'l dude that be hooking up the cable?" Saint asked to confirm.

"Yeah, that's him. Had a weak, rusty-ass gun. That's prolly the only reason I'm still here," Zoo replied.

"How much did they get?" Saint asked.

"The whole week's take."

Saint calculated in his mind and knew that it was over 200k. That wasn't little enough to let slide.

"Fuck!" he yelled as he put his hands on his belt buckle and slowly paced the room.

"I know where he be at, though. The wolves already got the drop on him for me. They're in an old bando on the East Side," Zoo explained.

"Say no more. Call the wolves off. I'm going," Saint said with fire in his eyes.

Cooda and Tay were lying on the soiled couch, both in the middle of a nod. They had just shot five hundred dollars' worth of heroin into their veins over the past forty-eight hours. They robbed Zoo, and this was the fruit of their labor. They coped some dope away from Saint and Zoo's territory and spent the past two days getting high as the moon. They didn't even notice the new visitors. Saint crept through the unlocked front door along with Zoo. He quietly walked up on the two sleeping beauties with a chrome .45 in his hands. The drug-induced duo slowly bobbed up and down, repeatedly jerking their heads up when their chins touched their chests. They made this same motion for the past hour. Saint looked on the floor and saw a familiar duffle bag, which confirmed what he didn't want to believe. He pressed the cold steel of his gun to Cooda's forehead, making him jump up.

"Wake up, youngin'. Let me talk to you," Saint said calmly. Cooda took a good look at him and stared for a second. He then closed his eyes and tried to go back into his nod. However, Saint gently tapped his temple with the gun. "Wake up," he said this time with more bass in his voice. This made Cooda jump up and look around again. He looked at Zoo and then at Saint, knowing what time it was.

"Hey, man. What's going on?" Cooda asked as he sat upright and backed away as far as he could, almost crawling up the couch to get away from the barrel of the pistol.

"You robbed me?" Saint asked calmly as he smoothly crossed his arms in front of him, letting the pistol dangle by his crotch area.

"Nah . . . You got the wrong one, man. I would never do that," Cooda said as he started to shake like a leaf.

"What's that by your feet?" Saint asked as he looked over at the bag. Cooda's eyes followed Saint's, and he trembled even harder. Tears formed in his eyes as he tried to gather himself to speak. Saint bent down and grabbed the bag. He tossed it to Zoo, who was standing by the door. Zoo caught it with his one good arm and placed it on the floor. Then he immediately opened it up and saw that not too much was missing.

"Most of it's here," Zoo said calmly.

"How much you shoot up?" Saint asked as he put his gun in his waist. Cooda instantly cried, knowing that he had fucked up.

"I'm sorry, man. This shit got a hold of me, man. I'm so sorry." Cooda pleaded as he buried his face in his open hands. The sobbing made Tay wake up, and she quickly realized the situation and froze with fear.

"Again, how much of my money did you shoot up?" Saint asked with more aggression in his voice this time.

"About two hundred today and three hundred yesterday," Cooda admitted.

"So, you traded your life for five hundred dollars' worth of dope," Saint said as he couldn't wrap his mind around their audacity. He quickly pulled out his gun, and Cooda tried to put his hands up to block the bullet, but Saint was too fast. He shot two bullets in Cooda's dome, sending him flying back onto the couch with double wounds to his skull. Tay screamed and panicked as the brain splatter from Cooda's head was all over his face. Blood was everywhere as Cooda's eyes were open, and he stared into space as blood oozed from the bullet holes.

"They say if you die with your eyes opened, you deserved it . . ." Zoo said as he stepped forward. He leaned over and whispered to Saint, "Want me to take care of her?" he asked, knowing that would be a harder task for Saint.

"Nah, I'ma let her live," Saint said as he stared at her with clenched jaws. He pointed his gun at her head as she held her hands up and hyperventilated. "I want you to leave this city. If I ever see you again. I'm going to do you just like I did your friend. You hear me?" Saint said boldly with no emotion. Tay nodded swiftly with her hands still held up.

"Now, get the fuck outta here," Saint as he stepped to the side and watched her leave with a heavy heart and guilty conscious. Their bond would forever be broken.

Epilogue

Ramina cried as she slipped the packet of bad dope into the Bible. She had it from when it fell from Saint's pocket the night before. She went back and forth about putting it in the book. However, her rage was as deep as the ocean, and she knew that this would be the only way to even the odds. For some reason, Tay had a hold on her man.

Matthew 27:3–4, that's what she wrote on the sticky note. She placed the bad dope on the same page as the verse, so Tay would find it and hopefully put it to use. Ramina was tired—tired of loving a man that never picked her. Even when she gave him a second chance, he didn't choose her. All she wanted was Saint to love her, and that was something that he refused to do. What was supposed to be the best day of her life, which was her wedding day . . . turned out to be one that she wished never happened. She placed a note on their bed, hoping Saint would find it. She requested that he urged Tay to read the verse that she quoted "for her own good."

"Lord, forgive me," she whispered as she stood up and left the room. Before she left, she peeked into the guest room and saw her man sleeping, sitting bedside of Tay. With that . . . she quietly left.

Ramina cried a cascade of tears as she sped down the highway, pushing nearly eighty miles per hour. The top was dropped as she glided in and out of lanes on the interstate. She needed to feel the force of the wind. She wanted to *feel* it. She had to feel something . . . something other than what she was feeling on that early morning. Everything was just so heavy on her soul, heavier than anything had ever been. Her entire being was shaken, and everything that she knew was for certain somehow was now unreliable. The picture-perfect life that she finally thought she had seemed to be snatched from under her. The only man that she truly loved was in love with someone else. She could tell. She just knew. There was something about seeing those tears in Saint's eyes that told her the truth. Not his words or his actions, but those tears told her everything that she *didn't* want to know. She had been with him for years and never once saw tears from that man.

Ramina had no makeup on her face, and her natural brown skin glowed in the sunlight. Being in public like this was a rarity for her. She hadn't walked out of the house in years without being dolled up. But on this day, she just had to get away from the anguish that was back home.

She slightly raised her oversized sunglasses with her index finger and wiped tears away as she wept. She cried uncontrollably as she thought about how her husband was at home tending to that dope-sick woman, rather than celebrating their new marriage with her. The loud purr from her silver Porsche Panamera ripped through the airwaves. She neared one hundred miles per hour. The sounds of Lauryn Hill knocked through her sound system as her long, jet-black hair blew wildly in the air.

She was supposed to be on an airplane on her way to Italy for her honeymoon. Instead, she was in still in the bayou . . . heartbroken. She was there wondering if she had made a mistake by marrying Saint. *How can he be trying to put her together, while I'm fucking falling apart?* she thought as the tears continued to flow. She had loved Saint with every morsel in her body, and she knew he was a good man. The problem was that he was being a good man to someone else. Anxiety crept in. Although she tried to breathe slowly, the heartache was overweighing it all.

"Why does he love her? I fucking hate her! I *hate* that bitch. I wish she would just die," Ramina cried as she smashed the accelerator to the floor, pushing the luxury vehicle to the limit. She was now nearing one hundred twenty miles per hour. Somehow, the speed seemed to help her release the unwanted tension that had built up inside of her.

Ramina's disappointment and frustration had reached its boiling point. She felt like she was being robbed— robbed of the life that she had deserved. She stood by Saint's side and played her position the right way throughout the years. The pain slowly started to become rage. She possessed a massive flame that burned deep within her soul, all behind the man that the streets feared, and the ladies lusted after. She was drawn to his quiet power. She was addicted to him, and she wasn't going to let him go.

"Fuck that!" she yelled as she squeezed the steering wheel as tightly as her grips would allow. She let out a roar of passion that she never knew she had.

"Aaaagh!" she screamed, which turned into a gut-wrench-ing sob. She angrily hit her steering wheel. She wasn't a hateful person, but over that man, she would become the worst. He was her trigger. *He was her trigger*.

She felt something in the pit of her stomach rumble as nausea set in. Suddenly, the urge to throw up overwhelmed her. She was sweating profusely and dry heaving while becoming dizzy. Vomit came up in her mouth. She leaned over to spit the vomit out in her passenger seat. Her eyes grew as big as golf balls when she saw all the clear secretions that she had thrown up. But it wasn't the spit and secretions that alerted her. It was the small green frog hopping around in it, struggling to escape the thick liquid . . .

What the fuck? she thought as she tried to refocus her fuzzy vision. Her heart raced rapidly. She was confused and frightened at the same time. She shook her head and focused on the road . . . but it was too late.

The sound of a thunderous crash resonated in the air, followed by screeching tires and crushing metal. Ramina crashed her car into the back of an eighteen-wheeler semitruck, instantly propelling her body into the air like a rag doll. She was launched about fifty yards and crashed violently onto the pavement. Her body rolled over a dozen times against the concrete, ripping her flesh with each flip. It all happened so fast . . . She never saw it coming.

Saint received an urgent call from the paramedics saying that Ramina had been in a bad car accident. Without hesitation, he dropped everything and stormed out. He left Tay at his home alone without hesitation. Guilt lay on his heart, and he knew that he had neglected the love of his life, Ramina, for another woman. Mixed emotions were running through his mind as he worried immensely. His white Range Rover sped at over 100 miles per hour en route to New Orleans East Hospital. He made it a point for Ramina to keep his name in her emergency contacts, inside her wallet. So, they prepared for something like this. However, he never imagined it would happen.

"Please, God, make sure my baby is okay. Please . . . please, God," he pleaded as he gripped his steering wheel so tightly that it hurt his hands. After a fifteen-minute high-speed drive, he violently pulled into the hospital and hopped out. He didn't care about anything or anyone at that point. He left his car running and door open as he ran full speed into the emergency room. He approached the emergency desk desperately, asking for help. He still had on his same pants and dress shirt from his wedding the previous night.

"Ramina Scott . . . I mean Ramina Cole. I need to know where Ramina Cole is. She's my wife," he said as his heart beat rapidly, and worry was heavy in his eyes. A short, pudgy African American woman sat at the front desk while typing on a computer. She ran her finger down a list and stopped at a name. She read aloud.

"Psalm 34:18," she said. Well, that was what Saint heard.

"Excuse me?" he asked, not understanding what she meant by that.

"I said room 3418, sir," the lady said, looking at Saint as if he were crazy. Saint rushed toward the ICU where Ramina was, hoping like hell that she was okay. As he reached the room, something came over him. His body froze before his hand touched the doorknob, not knowing what would be on the other side.

As he opened the door, he saw Ramina lying on the bed with tubes coming out of her nose and mouth. The sight alone made his knees buckle, and he instantly started to cry. He cried a river, and his eyes were glued on the love of his life. She didn't even look like herself. To see her that way was agonizing.

"No . . . No, baby," he whispered while breaking down. He stood over her and gently rubbed her head. His hand shook so badly that he couldn't even properly comfort her. He snatched his hand back and covered his mouth to stop his involuntary cries from seeing her swollen mouth, eyes, and lips. Her two front teeth were knocked out, and her head looked twice as large as it regularly did. He had never felt this weak in his life. He felt powerless that there was nothing he could do to help her. He wondered, *What happened? How? Who hit her? Who or what did she hit? Is she going to be OK?* There were so many things going on in his mind, and he couldn't understand what she did to deserve that. She was the purest soul that he had ever met. Little did he know, Karma seemed to have visited her.

Tay sat there and looked at the pack of dope that sat on the Bible page. Her high had come down, but that gigantic monkey was still climbing her back. She needed to get it off in the worst way. Her skin crawled, and the pains inside of her stomach were close to unbearable. She was living through hell, literally. She stared at the dope pack as tears welled up in her eyes. She wanted to flush it down the toilet, but her urge wouldn't let her do it. She couldn't understand why Ramina would have left something for her like this. *Maybe she didn't want me to fight the pains of withdrawal,* she thought to try to justify her self-destructing habit. She let that be the reason and grabbed her jacket, frantically looking for her shooter and lighter. Once she found them, she raced downstairs, rushing to the kitchen. She grabbed a spoon from the kitchen drawer and headed to the bathroom. Then she closed the door behind her and sat on the floor as she put her works together. She grabbed one of Saint's belts that hung on the back of the door and quickly wrapped it around her upper arm and made sure it was tight. She repeatedly smacked her arm with two fingers, causing a nice vein to form. She melted the drug down and liquefied it. Tears rolled as she filled her syringe with the poison.

Tay reflected on everything in her life and how difficult it had played out. She thought about how her parents disowned her, forcing her to the streets to prostitute herself. She thought about Regis picking her up and making her fight and sex his friends like she was a dog. She thought about how she crossed the line with Saint. She betrayed him in so many ways that he would never know. She thought about finally finding someone who understood her pain and secrets as Cooda did. He knew exactly how she felt and related to her on so many levels. Then she thought about how her actions got him killed. Thinking about all of those things . . . made her fill the needle. She slowly injected the heroin into her vein.

She smiled and noticed rain fall outside of the window and thumbed the windowpane. Lightning flashed in the sky, making her smile. Any other day, it would have looked like bad weather, but at that moment, it seemed so pretty, so beautiful. It seemed as if God were snapping pictures of the rain. Tay smiled as her eyes slowly rolled to the back of her head. Suddenly, her body started

jerking violently. Foam bubbled out of her mouth as she
slid onto her back . . .

   Tears filled Saint's eyes as he walked into the room
where the coroner waited. Saint walked over to him
and took a deep breath and blew it out slowly. He was
there to identify the body. His heart was broken into
pieces, and he wished that he could turn back the hands
of time and make things so much different from what
they were. The elderly white man put his hand on the
sheet and peeled it back. Saint looked down and saw
Tay's purplish face as she lay there naked on the cold
steel. He took a deep breath and gave the coroner a quick
nod to confirm. Next, the coroner pulled the sheet back,
so it exposed her entire body. Saint's eyes drifted down,
and his heart dropped when he saw a small penis on Tay.
   His knees got weak, and he almost fainted, wondering
what the fuck was going on. His whole world was turned
upside down. He was confused. However, the truth was
there all the time. He just never noticed. Neither did you . . .

The End

A teaser . . . for what's to come!

The Streets Have No Queen

by

JaQuavis Coleman

This isn't a sequel, but a well thought out puzzle.
Everything connects. It always does . . .

—JaQuavis Coleman

Prologue

A man lay comfortably on a brown leather couch, intensely staring at the ceiling. He had little to no movement as his eyes fixated on a small imperfection on the surface. His head was slightly propped up by a small pillow. The room was quiet . . . well, almost. Nothing but the constant sound of the steel balls clinking as they swung back and forth on the pendulum filled the air. Most people called this Newton's cradle. It caused a constant ticking echo throughout the dim room. A brown hue from the desk lamp hovered over the office, and the faint smell of vanilla danced around. Hundreds of books lined the bookshelves against the walls. A woman sat off in a corner with a notepad in hand, studying the man on the couch. She watched his every move.

"At first . . ." the man said in a low tone just before pausing. He took a deep breath, cleared his throat, and clenched his jaw firmly. He was trying his hardest to fight off tears and took a hard swallow. He inhaled deeply and slowly exhaled, almost as if he could release some of the pain he had built up in his chest by merely blowing it out. He closed his eyes and spoke. "At first, she asked if we could jump with no plan. I said, 'Fuck it, I'm with it.' I was all in," the man said, choosing his words wisely as they came out.

"They say love is exactly like skydiving. If you really think about it, that's some real shit. Love is a fucking free fall. You truly don't have any control of the outcome once you've committed to love someone. Shit's crazy, right? Just think about it. You don't 'walk in love,' and you don't 'run in love.' You fucking '*fall* in love' . . . that's what her love was like. It always felt like I was falling. No control. No foundation. I was just falling. It was the greatest feeling in the world to me." As he lay there, a single tear slipped down his face, traveling down to the rim of his ear. The man quickly sat up and shook his head in grief.

"Bless, please continue," the doctor said as she gently tapped her pen on her notebook. The beautiful Dr. Celeste Ose was a Haitian-born psychiatrist. She had perfect ebony skin and high cheekbones. Her natural kinky hair was pulled neatly into a bun on top of her head. She was slightly intrigued by Bless. He was so mysterious, and he was a man she couldn't quite understand. She repeated herself eagerly, wanting him to resume.

"Please . . . continue," Doctor Ose said. Again, he said nothing. She had been seeing him for months, and he had never talked about *her* for more than a sentence. She saw progress, and she wanted him to keep going to enable her to dig deeper. Doctor Ose paused and waited for a response. He remained quiet and seemed as if he were in deep thought, searching for the right thing to say.

"I can't. I just see red when I think about her. All I can see is red," Bless said as he shook his head in grief.

"I know it's upsetting and hurtful to lose a spouse, but the first step to healing is to—" The doctor said, but before she could finish her sentence, the man stood up and grabbed his blazer.

"I'm sorry, Doc, I have to go," he said as he gave her a forced grin. "I appreciate your time."

"I understand. I'll see you next week for our next session, correct?" Doctor Ose asked as she smiled back with understanding eyes.

"Yeah, sure. I'll be back," Bless said in a low tone just before exiting the office, leaving her sitting there puzzled. In all her years, she had never had a patient so complicated and so hard for her to get a breakthrough. Doctor Ose reached over to her desktop and stopped Newton's cradle. She contemplated referring him to a different doctor to see if someone else could help him, but she chose to keep trying.

Bless had been coming to the doctor for six months straight, and their sessions never went more than ten minutes because of his unwillingness to talk about his deceased wife. He would start and then just abruptly leave. Every. Single. Time. However, on that day, he spoke longer than he ever had before, and because of that, she knew he was making progress. Doctor Ose's professional integrity wanted to refer him elsewhere, but her greed stopped her. You see, Bless was a high-profile client. He paid in cash every week and always paid triple the invoice. His only request was that his files would be kept secret, and he came after hours. It was evident that he was a very private patient. She didn't know exactly what Bless did for a living, but by the way he paid . . . she knew he did it very well.

Bless got into the back seat of his luxury Maybach and instructed his driver to go to the cemetery. He want-ed to talk to Queen, his deceased wife. He needed a release. He needed to speak to his best friend to try to find some sort of clarity. On that day, her death weighed heavily on his spirit, and he felt himself breaking down. Bless knew that death was a part of life, but the way she left him was something that he couldn't accept. He watched aimlessly out of his window as they maneuvered through the Detroit traffic. Although cars, nature, and pedestrians were in his eyeshot, the only thing he could see was the face of the love of his life. Her smile is what he missed the most. The way her dimples were deep always made him smile. Queen had dimples so deep that you could securely place nickels in them. Her chubby cheeks and her sweet smell was something that he would never forget.

Scattered pictures of Queen flashed in his mind, causing him to smile from ear to ear and randomly chuckle when he thought about the way she laughed. Her laugh could make any room a happy one.

The twenty-minute ride only seemed like a minute or two because of his extended daydream. As the vehicle entered the cemetery, the pain slowly crept back into Bless's chest. He grabbed a small briefcase from the next seat and exited the car. The closer he got to her grave, the more Bless could feel his wife's presence. It was a bittersweet feeling because he could always feel his heart get heavier with each step when he made his way to his baby. The harsh reality that she was buried six feet underground plagued his thoughts.

Bless finally approached where she rested and took a deep breath. He looked at the three-foot tombstone and examined the wording. It read, *My Earth. My Isis. My Queen. Fall 1990–Rise 2018.* The cemetery staff and tomb makers pleaded with Bless when they got the tombstone wording request. They tried to convince him that he had it backward. Every time, Bless would laugh and simply answer, "If you knew her . . . you would know it's 100 percent correct." He and his wife would always talk about how loving each other was like falling, and he laughed at their inside joke that the world didn't seem to get. Leaves covered the cemetery lawn since it was the middle of autumn. The trees were almost bare, and the light wind made small, beautiful tornados in various parts of the walkway.

Bless approached the grave and rubbed his hand over her name. "My Queen . . . my Queen," he whispered as his eyes teared up. He had married his dream girl and found the love of his life. Not too many people live without regrets, but up until her death, Bless had none. He was happy, content, and free when he was with her. Queen understood him, and he got her. They had been childhood classmates, and as they grew, so did their love. By high school, they had already vowed to each other that they would spend the rest of their lives together. The word *soul mate* didn't do their union any justice. Their bond was spiritual. Their bond was unbreakable. Their bond was no more. Bless pulled off his jacket and laid it on the grass. He sat down and opened his briefcase.

"Hey, pretty girl. I had a rough day today. Wanna hear about it?" he whispered as he wiped a tear away. He dug into the bag and pulled out a small blank canvas and a few paintbrushes. He started his routine as he prepared to do a small painting while talking to her. This was something that they did while she was alive, and it brought him peace then, and it seemed to do the same thing now.

An hour passed as Bless painted a picture while casually talking to his wife as if she were sitting there with him. He laughed, cried, and reminisced, all while re-creating the cemetery scenery. The speckled orange and red leaves were scattered throughout the canvas with so much detail that you could see the veins within the leaves. Bless even added a small fox in the background to complement the esthetics of his creation. He smiled, knowing that Queen loved the way he always strategically did things and painted with precision. She would tell him he was like a mad scientist with his paintbrush. She had always been his number one fan.

Bless continued to paint until the sun set and then headed back to the car to go home. It was a rough day for him. His days were up and down, and this particular day was a down one. He just wanted to go home and sleep the pain away. Sometimes, you have to sleep and give your pain to God, and that's what his plans were for that evening.

The driver returned Bless to his home, and he immediately poured himself a glass of Cognac and put on some jazz. The smooth and soothing sounds played throughout the house, and Bless started to unwind. He loosened his shirt and kicked off his shoes as he went to the back window that overlooked a pond. The moonlight bounced off the water, and he stood there, admiring the scene. Bless took a small sip of the aged Cognac and closed his eyes as he savored the taste and the excellent music. He heard thunder, and shortly after, the rain came down. He smiled, remembering how Queen liked to make love when it rained. For some reason, the sound of water crashing against the ground made her love flow. The spacious home always seemed cold to him after Queen left. It never really seemed like home without her being there with him.

The smooth sounds of trumpets soothed his soul. Bless swayed back and forth, enjoying the moment . . . until an unexpected bell chimed. He instantly shot his eyes toward his door. *Who is that?* he thought to himself. He never had guests, so he wasn't expecting anyone.

Bless was confused as he set his drink down and made his way to the front door. He opened the door, and to his surprise, a stranger was standing on his doorstep. It was a young lady that looked to be no older than 25. The rain was pouring down, and she was completely soaked. He looked into the woman's face in confusion, wondering if she was at the wrong house because he had never seen her a day in his life. She had kind, big brown welcoming eyes, and her hair was soaked and stringy. It hung past her shoulders. The young lady had a bundle in her arms and what sounded like a screaming baby. She had it wrapped loosely in a pink blanket. She rocked her baby as she whispered to it, trying to keep it calm. She tried her best to cover the baby's face from the rain as she rocked it, trying to keep it quiet. The loud crying was as if the baby was in pain and immediately tugged at Bless's heart. A child was something that Queen always wanted, so he thought of her instantly.

"Hello, sir, so sorry to bother you, but my car broke down just up the road. My phone is dead, and I didn't know what to do," she said as tears filled her eyes.

"Sure. Sure. Come in, sweetheart," Bless said as he instantly wanted to help. His heart couldn't let him leave a crying baby and distressed woman outside in the thunder and rain. He looked at her frame and noticed that she had a similar build to his Queen and immediately thought about grabbing an old hoodie for her. "Let me grab my phone for you. Also, my wife was about your size. Let me see if I can find you some dry clothes."

"Bless your heart. God is good. Thank you so much," the woman said, as she continued to rock the baby, trying her best to keep it calm. However, the crying just got louder and more frantic. "I'm sorry. She's terrified," the woman said as she looked down at the baby and whispered to it again. Bless turned around to head to his coffee table where his phone was.

"It's okay. You can use my phone to call who you need while—" Bless said as he headed to the next room, but he stopped midsentence when an iron bar crashed against the back of his head. Bless fell forward and lost consciousness before he even hit the ground. He was out cold. A man with a bright skin tone and multiple scars on his face stood above him. He had snuck in right behind the woman when Bless turned his back.

"Let's get it," the man said, as he looked back at the woman whose face was once innocent, but now had a sinister look on it. She dropped the blanket that was in her hand, letting her "bundle of joy" drop on the ground. The sinister woman smiled as she carelessly dropped the small speaker box that she had wrapped up. The recording of the baby crying sounded through the speaker box even louder now that it was exposed.

"Turn that bullshit off. Grab the ropes from outside. Let's get this nigga tied up before he wakes up," the man said as he dropped the crowbar and scanned the house.

"I'm on it, daddy," the woman said as she quickly did as she was told. Bless had let the devil in, and that's when the game began.

Chapter One

Bless woke up groggily and in a compromising position. He was sitting upright in a chair, and his hands were bound by rope, tied behind his back. He realized that he was in his own living room and tried to make sense of what had got him there. The last thing Bless remembered was answering the door and nothing much after that. The back of his head throbbed, and when he saw the unfamiliar man standing in front of him, he looked in confusion.

The fair-skinned intruder was light bright and seemed to be the next step above albino. His eyes had red circles around them, and his lips were so pink that it looked as if he had a touch of lipstick on them. This was an unusual-looking man. He had a weathered face. Scars were all over his cheeks and forehead as if he came directly out of a comic book. He definitely looked like a villain—the evilest type.

"What's going on? Why am I tied up?" Bless asked with a shaking voice. Fear was obviously present inside of him. It was all in his demeanor and tone.

"Rise and shine, sweetheart," the man said sarcastically. He circled Bless and scrutinized him. He smiled and noticed that Bless was just as his partner described him . . . a four-eyed, soft-spoken man. An easy target, to say the least.

"I think you might have made a mistake," Bless pleaded.

"No, we have the right house. Believe that," the man
said as he looked around the house and admire the
paintings on the wall.

Bless looked confused as he sat there. While being
bound to a chair, Bless looked around and tried to get a
grasp on who was in his home. He looked at the young
lady who had been at his front door, asking for help. She
was now sitting on his counter, eating a bag potato chips,
as if she didn't have a care in the world. The man stopped
directly in front of Bless and looked down on him.

"I'm not even going to play with you, my nigga. We
know what's going on, and you do too. This is a stickup.
We came for the paper," Red said with confidence as he
rubbed both of his hands together. He had a stern look in
his eyes, and Bless stared directly into them. Bless felt
like he was looking at the devil directly in the face. The
man didn't blink once, and he had a look of not giving a
fuck. Bless instantly knew that the man didn't have it all
and was legit crazy. It was written all over his face.

"A stickup? Paper?" Bless asked while frowning up.
The man grew enraged and was not in the mood to play
games. He gave Bless a swift and powerful punch to his
midsection. Bless folded over like a lawn chair as he let
out a grunt from the thunderous blow.

"Okay, let's try this thing again," the man said as he
aggressively placed his hand on the back of Bless's neck
and pulled him slightly. He kneeled so they could be
face-to-face. The man wanted Bless to look directly into
his eyes and see that he wasn't with any type of game.
He wanted to be firm and clear in his intentions. "I'm
going to be blunt with you," the man said as he intensely

gazed at Bless. Without breaking eye contact with Bless, the man reached out his hand and wiggled his fingers, signaling his woman to hand him the gun.

The woman hopped off the counter and grabbed the gun from the countertop. She quickly walked it over to her man and placed it in his hand. The man, in a single sweeping motion, placed the pistol directly against Bless's forehead. The cold steel against his skin made Bless realize that it was a real situation.

"Okay . . . I get it. Please don't hurt me," Bless conceded.

"Now, we're getting somewhere," the man responded while smiling. He stood up, but not before pushing Bless's head forcefully, causing him to jerk back violently. "I know that you have that delivery this evening, and I need that bag. Understand me?" Red instructed. Bless instantly dropped his head in defeat, knowing that he had gotten caught slipping.

"Damn, man," Bless whispered to himself as he shook his head in disbelief. He had moved so cautiously and low-key. He had dotted all his i's and crossed his t's. How did this happen?

"I know, right? It's kinda fucked-up, playboy," the man said playfully as he slowly circled Bless. "You opened your door to a woman in distress and a crying baby and got much more. Life is fucked-up, man. Tell me about it. I know more than anyone how cold this world can be. But dig this . . . I don't even want to kill you, my nigga. I just need that paper," the man said.

"It's not coming tonight," Bless admitted as he avoided eye contact with Red.

"What the fuck did you just say?" the man quizzed as he grabbed the back of Bless's neck again.

"I said, it's not coming tonight. My mule got stuck in Denver on a layover. He won't be here until tomorrow night," Bless admitted.

"Don't fucking play with me!" the man yelled as frustration set in.

"I'm telling the truth. He texted me about an hour ago, letting me know that his plane was delayed. Check my phone and verify it. It's right in the messages. My phone is in my pocket," Bless suggested as he looked in the direction of his right pocket.

The man immediately grabbed for Bless's pocket to retrieve the phone. He pulled it out and read through the message threads. The most recent message was one from Watson. The man instantly clicked on the name. He knew the name because of the intel he got on his mark. Watson was the moneyman and was the person who delivered the cash to Bless. He read the message, and it confirmed what Bless had alleged. Watson had informed him that he would be over the following night when his new flight landed in Detroit.

"Fuck!" the man yelled in frustration as reality set in.

"What, baby?" the woman said as she hopped off the counter and walked over to her man, whose eyes were still fixated on the message. The man showed her the text on the phone, and her joy was also taken.

"Well, what are we going to do, Red?" she asked, panicking.

"Bitch, what did you just say?" Red harshly whispered as he used his free hand to wrap around her neck. The woman put her hands up, conceding, as she gasped for air. Red was squeezing her throat so hard that it blocked her airway, and veins formed on her temples and forehead. He lifted her, causing her to stand on her tiptoes as he looked at her with disgust. "You said my name, you birdbrain bitch."

"I'm sorry . . . I'm sorry," she managed to whisper, knowing that she had slipped up and made a big mistake by saying his name. Red slightly eased up on his grasp, then released her, letting her fall to the ground. She held her neck and violently coughed as she tried to catch her breath.

"Dumb ass," he said as he shook his head in disbelief while looking down at her beneath him. Bless just looked on, feeling sorry for the woman. Then Red refocused his attention back on Bless.

"Well, it looks like we're going to be here for a while. Ain't that right, *Shawna?*" Red said, making sure her name was yelled out in the open as well. He didn't care either way at that point because he had already decided to kill Bless after they got the money.

Red knelt and rubbed Shawna's hair away from her face, exposing her wet cheeks. "Sorry, baby," he whispered in her ear as he cradled the back of her neck and awkwardly kissed her. "You just have to be smarter, OK?" Red instructed. Shawna nodded her head in agreement as her tears still flowed, causing her mascara to streak down her face.

"Well, sir, I guess we're going to have a little sleepover. Time to get comfortable," Red said with a demented facial expression. He was going to wait until the money got there, and then he would murder Bless. Red's mind was set.

Chapter Two

A man in his late 20s sat patiently in a mint-conditioned vehicle. He looked around in awe, admiring his surroundings. He gripped the woodgrain circle that was in front of him and tightened his grip on the mint leather. He slowly cracked a smile as he stared at the world-renowned symbol that rested square in the middle of the steering wheel. He couldn't believe that he was in the driver's seat of a Bentley—the same car that he used to dream about having while staring at a cutout of it on a cement wall. Just three months earlier, he was sitting in a federal penitentiary in the Upper Peninsula of Michigan. He shook his head in disbelief as he checked his rearview mirror. He saw the sign that read, *Arrivals,* as he sat curbside at Detroit Metropolitan Airport.

"One day . . . one day," the man said to himself under his breath as he imagined whipping the vehicle through his old neighborhood. He slowly traced the outer steering wheel with his right hand. He was determined that soon he would enjoy it as an owner rather than his current position as a chauffeur.

Luck had been on his side, getting a great job through a work-release program. Initially, Fonz wanted to return to the street game so that he could get back on his feet, but instead, Fonz felt this job was a blessing sent from above to steer him in the right direction. He vowed to fly straight for as long as he could, and this route seemed to be the best option. Also, he loved the position's perks. It wasn't bad for an alternative to a life of crime. The job was simple. Every other Sunday, he picked up his boss and took him to the airport. Then twelve hours later, he picked him up to return him home. The best part of the job was that it paid in cash, which was helpful because between Fonz's three kids and their two mothers, child support drained any check that came through his pipeline, not to mention an ill mother that he cared for.

Fonz was working the current gig along with a third-shift job as a security guard. It didn't pay much, but he was doing the best he could with the opportunities placed in front of him. It was a far cry from his past life, and he had switched his lifestyle tremendously since he'd been out. No matter how hard Fonz tried to convince himself that he could get used to living below the poverty line, he knew that it wouldn't last long. He was accustomed to having money since his early teenage years, and his current situation wasn't cutting it for him. Fonz needed more.

Alfonzo Coolidge was the name of the driver, but in the streets, he went by the moniker, Fonz. He was an ex-convict who had a reputation for robbery. He was pretty good at it too. As far as he was concerned, he would have never gotten caught if it wasn't for him taking on a partner who eventually snitched on him, landing him in front of a judge. He spent six years in jail for a simple in-and-out job at a local check-cashing joint. Fonz vowed never to go back.

Fonz checked his wristwatch and then over to his right. He focused on the double doors, looking for his client to emerge from the airport. Just like clockwork, his client came walking out of the building.

A tall, lean, dark man with a cell phone to his ear headed toward the car. He looked to be in his mid- to late thirties and had a shiny bald head. The man wore a well-tailored charcoal suit, looking as if he stepped off the pages of the latest *GQ* magazine. His perfectly straight white teeth sparkled as he moved his mouth while talking on the phone. They seemed even brighter against his deep chocolate complexion. The man wore reading glasses, and his posture didn't match his appearance. He walked with a sense of insecurity and seemed to be an introverted soul, avoiding eye contact with people as he maneuvered through the sea of travelers. The man walked with a certain bashfulness that screamed "insecure." He carried a leather briefcase and swiftly made his way over to the car after spotting it at the curb.

Fonz noticed Mr. Brigante awkwardly weaving through the crowd and making his way over to the car. He quickly checked his mirror to glance at himself and straightened his tie. He pulled up his collar, trying to hide his big neck tattoo that read "*Linwood,*" paying homage to his neighborhood in the inner city of Detroit. Fonz quickly exited the car and went to the passenger side, reaching for the handle. He opened the rear door, timing it perfectly with his boss's stride.

Mr. Brigante ducked his head and slid in smoothly, never breaking stride or even acknowledging Fonz. Fonz closed the door behind him and made his way back into the driver's seat. Not wanting to interrupt his boss's conversation, Fonz nodded to greet him. Mr. Brigante casually waved his hand as he continued his business call. Fonz strapped on his seat belt and merged into the lane heading out of the airport.

Fonz listened carefully as he always did when the man discussed his business, hoping he could learn something by eavesdropping. Fonz always wondered what the hell his boss was involved in. He knew that it was something illegal, just because the boss always dealt in cash and moved with a certain mystique. He didn't peg him as a drug dealer. He was much too timid for that. However, he did get the referral from a known drug dealer, and he knew that birds of a feather usually flocked together.

Maybe he sells black market organs or funds illegal heists. What type of time is this nigga on? Fonz thought to himself as he merged onto the freeway.

For months, Fonz always wondered what line of work his boss was in but never had the balls to spark up a conversation to dig deeper. The one thing Fonz knew for certain was that it was something that he wanted to keep from the government, which, nine times out of ten, was always an illegal endeavor. No one knew much about his boss.

"These art units were beautiful. Not one flaw in them. They will sell quickly for sure. The flakes in the picture looked like fish scales," Mr. Brigante said to the other person on the phone. Fonz listened and smirked slightly, knowing that Mr. Brigante was speaking in code. Fonz was much too slick for that disguised lingo to go over his head. To the untrained ear, one would think Mr. Brigante was talking about a painting. However, the way Fonz heard it, he was describing a batch of drugs coming in. Hence, the code word "units." Also, Fonz heard him say there were "no flaws," which wasn't referring to actual flaws. He was referring to the units being pure and unstepped on.

Who this nigga think I am? An amateur? I can decipher homie whole convo, he thought to himself while continuing to listen.

"Great, so once it's done, text me the final number. Good job, Watson. See you tomorrow evening," Mr. Brigante said just before he ended the phone call and focused on Fonz. "It's Alfonzo, right?"

"Uh, yes, Mr. Brigante," Fonz said, not expecting his boss to talk to him.

"Mr. Brigante is my father. Call me Bless," he said as he smiled and loosened his tie.

"Bless?" Fonz asked, making sure he heard it right.

"Yeah, I know . . . It's uncommon, right? My mom had a vivid imagination. She always said there's power in one's name, so she decided to name me Bless," he said, cracking a small smile.

"Well, sir, if you don't mind me saying . . . She was telling the truth. You are definitely blessed," Fonz said as he rubbed the dashboard in appreciation. Bless chuckled lightly.

"You can say that, I guess. Moms always know best," Bless said as he unbuttoned his cuff links, getting more comfortable. Bless stared at Fonz for a second and then said, "What about your mom? Is she still living?" he asked.

"Yeah, she's a trooper. She's battling cancer and taking it day by day," Fonz replied.

"Sorry to hear that. Do you see her a lot?" Bless questioned.

"I work two jobs, and I try to get over there to take care of her as much as I can. The plan is to save up enough to eventually get her a nurse a few times out of the week. Ya know, to help her out a bit while I'm away," Fonz said.

"I lost someone special to me not too long ago. It's tough. You should spend as much time as you can with her because time is the only thing you can't get back. It's the most valuable thing on this earth," Bless said as he looked forward as if he were staring into space, not particularly looking at anything.

Fonz nodded in agreement but didn't respond. He appreciated the advice knowing that Bless was telling the truth. Fonz wanted to keep the conversation going because his employer had never said more than two words to him during the three months that he had worked for him. He wanted to figure out what exactly Bless did for a living. The mystery was killing him, and since the ice was broken, he thought that was his way in.

"So, what line of work are you in?" Fonz asked as he checked his mirror and switched lanes.

"I'm a painter and an art dealer," Bless responded.

"Business must be good," Fonz said as he cracked a smile involuntarily.

"It's booming," Bless said with a smirk. He looked at Fonz, and they made eye contact through the rearview mirror. Fonz knew at that moment that Bless was into some illegal shit. Fonz had doubts before, but he knew a criminal grin when he saw one. He nodded, knowing nothing more needed to be said.

"Turn that up for me, please," Bless said as the faint sounds of jazz pumped through the speakers.

Fonz quickly dialed up the music and continued to cruise down Interstate 75, heading to the quiet, secluded suburbs of Auburn Hills. Fonz remained silent the rest of the way to Bless's residence. However, his mind unremittingly started to churn. He had been raised in the streets, and the prize position is either a plug or a wealthy target. Either way, Fonz wanted to learn more.

Half an hour later, the luxury car was pulling into the long driveway that led to the extravagant home. Just as usual, a modest Honda Accord was sitting there parked. It was Fonz's mom's car and what he was using to get around until he got on his feet. He always parked his car there and switched vehicles before coming to pick up Bless.

When Fonz parked, he quickly hopped out and skipped over to the back passenger side to open the door for Bless. Bless stepped out and nodded to Fonz before picking up his ringing cell phone. Fonz closed the door behind him with his mind running a thousand miles per minute. He wanted to take advantage of the opportunity to build with Bless, so he went for it.

"Excuse me," Fonz said, as he held up one finger trying to catch Bless's attention.

Bless, still engaged in his phone conversation, turned slightly, and looked at Fonz to see what he wanted.

"Sorry to bother you, but may I use the restroom?" Fonz requested, trying to gain access to Bless's home as an attempt to get in good with him. Bless paused as if he was thinking hard about it and then nodded in agreement.

"Sure, I guess. Come on in," Bless said as he headed to the door.

Fonz quickly closed the door and followed Bless up the walkway. Fonz didn't show it physically, but he was beaming on the inside. He could spot people like Bless from a mile away. The brains behind an operation, but he had no street in him. In a world of sharks, Bless was something that you called *food*. Fonz could tell Bless didn't have any toughness. It was all in his demeanor. Bless lacked self-confidence, which usually meant a man was weak.

Fonz admired the property's immaculate landscaping as he followed close behind. He observed as Bless approach the door. Rather than pull out a set of house keys, Bless placed a thumb on a sensor and held it there for a second. Then the sounds of a few deadbolts clicking erupted. Bless ended his phone conversation and pushed the big steel door open. Fonz was amazed at the technology. It was something that he had never before witnessed. The sophisticated entry method blew his mind, and Fonz watched as he stepped over the threshold, entering the home. Marble floors lined the house, and a gush of cool air hit Fonz's face as he trailed behind. The smell of lavender filled his nostrils. Bless stepped to the side to give Fonz a pathway to walk.

"The bathroom is down the hall and to the right," Bless said, as he looked at Fonz skeptically.

"Thanks," Fonz responded as he walked down the long corridor and admired the remarkable paintings that lined the wall. The abundance of radiant colors and abstract objects were stunning to the naked eye. The lights had a trickle effect, so each step he took, the area of the hall would light up. Fonz looked around in disbelief as the seemingly futuristic home amazed him. Then he spotted the bathroom to the right and stepped in.

Bless took off his suit jacket and got settled in his home. He walked into his marble kitchen and placed his briefcase on top of the counter. He then rested his hands over the sink and took a deep breath. He looked over at the life-sized, hand-painted portrait of his wife and smiled, admiring her beauty. The smile instantly turned into grief as he closed his eyes, remembering the only true love of his life.

***

Queen sat naked in the chair. Her shoulders were pulled back, and her posture was immaculate. Her body glowed radiantly as her smooth, cocoa complexion was on full display. Her big, long legs were crossed, and her extra serving of loveliness was hanging over the sides of the stool. Queen wasn't a small lady by any means, but she was well put together. Her plump, smooth baby skin was moisturized with natural oils, and it was as if she were shining. Her sides had small rolls where her ribs were, and her wide hips were on full display. She slowly bopped her foot to the smooth music as Badu played in the background.

The smell of sage burned throughout the home, mixed with the scent of marijuana. Queen subtly took a pull of the joint as she bopped her head to the music. Her breasts were perky, sitting high, and her full, dark areolas were on exhibit. Her natural hair was wrapped in a multicolored head wrap, and only the soft baby hairs that rested on the edge of her scalp were visible. Queen smiled as she caught the eyes of her man studying her intensely.

Bless's piercing stare contained extreme passion and admiration as he crossed his arms, squinting his eyes. He was covered in paint and was shirtless with snug-fitting khakis. Different specks of paint were all over his body from his hours of creating, using different shades, trying desperately to re-create Queen's honey-brown complexion. He stood barefoot in the middle of his garage with his paintbrush in his hand. He was painting what he considered one of his most important pieces ever.

"I'm almost finished, my love. Thanks for being patient with me," he said in a low, baritone voice.

*"Patience is mandatory when you're in love with a man.
What would I ever rush anything for? We have an entire
lifetime to experience together. Patience is—"*

"A virtue . . ." Bless cut in, finishing her sentence as
he stood before her, examining her facial features. Bless
froze as he looked into her big brown eyes, and the urge
to cry overcame him. His soul was connected to hers.
There was no mistaking that. He understood that love like
hers came once in a lifetime, and that, alone, gave him
tears of joy every time he thought about it. She was gentle.
She was kind. She was patient. Most importantly, she
was his woman. They had been together since they were
teenagers. Queen put the marijuana-filled joint to her
lips, taking a deep pull of smoke into her lungs. Then she
slowly puckered her lips and blew out a stream of creamy
smoke. The smoke drifted into Bless's face as he squinted
and smoothly turned his head.

"I'm sorry, daddy," Queen said while smirking at his
cuteness. She rubbed the side of his face and giggled. She
frequently blew trees to relax and get her in a familiar
vibe. However, she felt guilty, knowing that Bless wasn't
a smoker. *"I'm going to stop smoking one day,"* she said.
She watched as he turned back to her with a small grin.

*"No worries. Do what makes you happy, love. Everyone
has an addiction. Mine just happens to be you."* Bless
stated it with sincerity while he stared at her in admiration. He leaned in and kissed her deep right dimple, then
her left dimple, and followed it with a gentle kiss to her
forehead. Bless held the kiss on her forehead and whispered, *"My pretty girl."* That move of his always sent
sparks through her spine. It never failed. While most men
thought that women had a cord connecting their clitoris
to their heart, the real "hot spot" was their foreheads.

That's where women truly felt love at. For that is the spot where women usually experience their first kisses.

A parent usually shows their love for an infant by kissing them on their forehead. It is subconsciously embedded in a woman's anatomy to feel real love by this type of kiss. Only a man that paid attention to detail understood this. Queen closed her eyes and swayed back and forth as if music were playing. There was no music playing, but their vibration was real and on the same accord. She could feel it moving her.

"I love you," she whispered.

"I love you too, pretty girl," he responded, as he stepped back and went directly to his large canvas mounted on the wall. He swiftly stroked his paintbrush and continued crafting his chocolate Mona Lisa.

Fonz exited the bathroom and headed down the corridor to the kitchen area where Bless was. The hallway walls were full of paintings, and splashes of red were throughout each one. Fonz looked closely and admired the works of art. The attention to detail was stellar, and thick cedar oak wood frames outlined all of them. The high ceilings in the house seemed to make his footsteps echo even louder throughout the quiet home. The technology blew his mind as Fonz, once again, looked down at the floors as they lit up with each new step.

He studied each painting as he went past them and noticed a recurring theme in each one. They all had a fox as the main focal point. Fonz even saw a painting that had a man posing in a suit; however, his head was that of a fox. Every painting was different with the fox being the common denominator. Surprisingly, the fox made it all come together. The color clashes and intricate pallets were visually stunning. *This looks amazing!* Fonz thought as he looked on in admiration. He reached the kitchen and saw that Bless had taken off his shirt and only wore a beater. He was already engaged in painting when Fonz walked in.

"Uh . . . Thanks for letting me use your restroom, sir," Fonz said, as he walked up on him. Bless was so locked in on his painting that he didn't even look back at Fonz. Fonz stood there awkwardly and waited to see if Bless was going to acknowledge him, but he didn't. Bless was beginning to paint on the canvas that was propped on the wall. "I'll just let myself out," Fonz said unsurely.

"Sorry about that. I didn't want to lose this vision I had for my new piece," Bless said as he used his index finger to balance his glasses on the bridge of his nose. He then set down the paintbrush and wiped his hands on a towel that laid nearby. "You want a beer?" Bless hesitantly asked as he walked over to the refrigerator and opened the door.

"Hell yeah," Fonz said. He couldn't control his eagerness, and the words just slipped out of his mouth.

"Great." Bless pulled out two longneck bottles. "Here ya go," Bless said. He tossed one over, and Fonz quickly caught it. Bless popped open the bottle and began making his way over to where Fonz was standing.

"Cheers," Bless said, as he raised his bottle and pointed at Fonz. Fonz then popped his open and followed suit, clinking his bottle's neck with Bless's.

Clink!

Both men took a swallow, and Fonz nodded his head in approval at the taste. "This is some good stuff," Fonz said, as he examined the foreign-looking bottle.

"Yeah, it's Irish beer. I get it shipped directly to me. Only kind of beer I drink," Bless said, smiling as he took another swallow. "You play chess?" Bless asked as he threw his head in the direction of the table that was off in the corner.

"Chess? Hell yeah, I can play a little," Fonz said, as he nodded his head. Fonz's gamble had worked, and he had gotten Bless to open up a bit. Fonz knew that he was one step closer to see exactly what type of business Bless was in. He knew that selling those paintings had not gotten him the house and the lifestyle that he was living. Fonz was determined to find out Bless's game. He didn't know exactly how, but he did know one thing: he wanted in.

"This is a nice-ass house, bruh. The floors, the lights . . . Everything is so futuristic. Some real fly shit," Fonz said, as he sat at the table and looked around.

"Thanks. I love new technology. I have the most modern systems installed throughout the house," Bless answered.

They sat down and played. Fonz carefully watched the man across from him, trying to figure him out. Bless's timid nature and the way his shoulders would always hunch over were a dead giveaway of his meekness. As they played, Fonz noticed that Bless would occasionally check his phone as if he were waiting for something. Fonz tried to eye hustle and see what was on his screen, but he couldn't get a good look from where he was sitting across the table. Bless studied the board strategically and remained quiet as he made his moves against Fonz. It was obvious that Bless was much more advanced than Fonz, as he quickly removed his pieces on the board, knocking them off one by one.

"I'm kind of rusty. Haven't played since I been home from Upstate," Fonz shamefully said as he moved his queen piece across the board.

"I can see that," Bless said calmly as he looked at his phone again. A text had just come through. He slightly grinned, then set his phone down. He refocused on the board and then looked up at Fonz. Bless used his index finger to prop his glasses up on the bridge of his nose and smiled nervously. "Check," he said.

"Damn," Fonz said as he studied the board, seeing that he had no way out. He was trapped. He knew the game was about to be over.

"See? You play fast and without a plan. Chess is a thinking man's game," Bless stated.

"You got me. You got me," Fonz admitted as he pretended like he cared. However, inside his mind, chess was the last thing he was thinking of. He didn't give a fuck about the game they were playing. He just was trying to make a connection, so if losing a few chess games helped Fonz do that, he was all for it.

"You're not so bad. You just rush. I can see it all in your game. I was baiting you with every step," Bless said in a matter-of-fact tone.

"Baiting?" Fonz asked, trying to understand what Bless was talking about.

"Yeah, bait. One of the laws of power is 'use bait, if necessary.' This works well in chess too. I did it on you all game," Bless said, breaking down his tactics for Fonz to understand clearly.

Bless's phone buzzed, and he glanced at it and nodded his head in approval.

"Checkmate," Bless said, as he took down Fonz's king. He then looked at Fonz, smiled, and took the last swallow of his beer. "Give me a sec. I have to take a leak," Bless said as he stood up and hurried to the back of the house where the bathroom was located.

Fonz stared at the board and saw that he really had no chance of winning that game. Bless had trapped his king from all angles. However, Fonz noticed that Bless's phone was still on the table. Just so happened, it buzzed as Fonz was looking at it. Fonz looked across the room and made sure that Bless was nowhere in sight and then quickly grabbed it. He looked at the text message that was across the screen. It was a message from a person named Watson. Fonz immediately knew it was the person that he was speaking to on the phone earlier.

The message read: **350k. I'll be by tonight to drop off. Talk soon.**

Fonz heard the footsteps of Bless returning and quickly put the phone back in its original position on the table. Bless returned while drying his hands on his shirt.

"Another game?" Bless asked as he sat down at the table.

"I wish. I got a call from my mother while you were away. I have to check on her. She isn't feeling too well," Fonz lied as he abruptly stood.

"Oh yeah. Okay. Take care of your mother, for sure," Bless said as he stood up and reached out to shake Fonz's hand.

"No doubt. Thanks for the beer, homie," Fonz said with a fake smile.

"Maybe we can play again soon. I don't have too many friends, so a good game does good for my mental, ya know?" Bless said as he awkwardly shook Fonz's hand.

Fonz nodded his head in agreement, but cringed on the inside, knowing that Bless was *not* his type of company.

Fonz couldn't imagine becoming friends with a square like him. Fonz would much rather rob Bless. And from what Fonz just saw, he knew that there was a very high probability of that happening in the near future.

The seed was planted, and the greed consumed Fonz's thoughts. He wanted to take what Bless had, and his mind had already been set. Fonz was about to put a play down on his boss. He saw a sucker in Bless, so he was about to hit the lick. Fonz had been waiting for a moment like this since he got out. He had been searching for a plan or a sense of where he was going. Fonz had finally got that. He had a plan now. It had been a long time coming.

Let's take a stroll down memory lane to see how Fonz got to this point . . .

BODY SCISSORS

JEROME DOOLITTLE

POCKET BOOKS

New York   London   Toronto   Sydney   Tokyo   Singapore

POCKET BOOKS, a division of Simon & Schuster Inc.
1230 Avenue of the Americas, New York, NY 10020

ISBN: 0-671-70753-1

First Pocket Books paperback printing November 1991

10 9 8 7 6 5 4 3 2 1

Cover art by Robert Grace

Printed in the U.S.A.

To D.

BODY
SCISSORS

1

ON A PARCEL OF LAND ALONG MASSACHUSETTS AVE-
nue between Dunster and Holyoke streets in Cambridge,
just across from Harvard Yard, is an office building
called Holyoke Center. It is a ten-story concrete block
that gives the appearance of having been built on the
cheap, in some marginal commercial block of a city like
Bangkok or Rabat. Harvard owns the ugly building. Harvard owns most of the real estate in sight. Harvard is
the largest landowner in Cambridge.

One of the ground-floor tenants of Holyoke Center is
a sort of bakery-café called Au Bon Pain, which pays for
the use of a large, tree-shaded terrace out front. To sit
there, you're supposed to be nursing a croissant or whatever. But other identical, cast-iron tables and chairs
stand on the brick-cobbled plaza next to the terrace,
along with three concrete tables with inlaid chess
boards. And all these are for public use.

1

I was using one of the cast-iron tables one Friday morning in August, cool and breezy for a change, when a man stopped on the sidewalk and spotted me after a while. It was Arthur Kleber. I hadn't seen Arthur since the 1982 Democratic miniconvention in Philadelphia, where I was guarding the body of a would-be president who was then—and still was—a long way from rating Secret Service protection. Since back then in 1982, I hadn't missed Arthur Kleber even one time. And yet here he was, taking the free chair at my table just as if I had invited him to.

"Most guys, you don't have to track them down on the streets like a bag lady," he said. "Most guys got phones."

"I got a phone, too."

"Information doesn't know about it."

"It's unlisted."

"Information doesn't say, 'Sorry, sir, that party has an unlisted number.' Information never heard of you."

"It's unlisted under another name, Arthur."

"So what's the number?"

"Think about why I would have an unlisted phone under another name. Could it maybe be because I don't want people to call me? What do you think?"

"What the hell use is a phone, then?"

"It calls out okay."

"Jesus, Bethany . . ."

"Shut up a minute, Arthur, okay? Maybe we got a fight going here."

Kleber looked where I was, out at the architecturally advanced public space that Harvard Square had become since they rebuilt the old T-stop. Now there were stone benches and swooping ramps that probably the architect hadn't envisioned any practical use for, but the skateboarders quickly had. There was a kind of overgrown conversation pit, too, this side of the subway entrance.

2

At the moment the conversation was between two large freaks, who were shouting and shoving each other. Both of them bore tribal disfigurements, like the tiger tattooed on George Shultz's Princeton ass. One freak had a center strip of green hair growing on his otherwise shaven head; the other was a skinhead with a half dozen or so gold rings, or gold-colored rings anyway, hanging from the ear I could see. He wore leathers; black, of course, and studded. (I myself wore a J. Press jacket of khaki gabardine, summer-weight gray flannel slacks, and cordovan loafers polished to a soft shine with Meltonian Cream. Different tribe.)

"Fuck you," hollered the one with the green Mohawk.

"Fuck you, too," shouted the skinhead. But they had stopped shoving.

"Aw, hell," I said to Kleber. "They're starting to talk things out."

"You got a nice life, Bethany," Arthur said. "This is it, huh? You just sit around all day waiting for the freaks to fight?"

"At least I don't have to wait four years for the next one."

"Hey, there's midterms, too. And referendums. And special elections. Nowadays, politics is forever."

"What are you, with Markham now?"

"Yeah. Phil wants to see you."

"Jeffers?"

Kleber nodded. I looked over at the two freaks. Their hands were down; they were talking loud, but not shouting.

"Does he want to give me any money?" I asked.

"What my understanding is, yes, he does."

"Okay," I said. "Let's go."

*   *   *

3

Headquarters was just off Milk Street in Boston. Everything else around was high-rent: a jewelry store, two expense-account restaurants, a gentlemen's outfitters with bolts of British woolens gracefully draped in the window. In the middle of all this, strung pretty nearly halfway along the block, a banner sagged from its supporting ropes. It read MARKHAM FOR PRESIDENT NATIONAL CAMPAIGN HEADQUARTERS in big, sloppy, red letters, hand-painted.

"Nice location," I said to Kleber. "Somebody go bankrupt?" He didn't have to ask what I meant. We both knew that campaigns search out troubled real estate.

"Even better," Kleber said. "Axel, Shearman moved to smaller offices and the lease here had four months to run."

"Nice they moved out early, out of their nice location," I said. "People that nice, I think I'll put my money with them, I ever get any."

Plainly Axel, Shearman was putting its own money with Senator Dan Markham. The investment banking firm had been indicted two months before on seventy-two federal charges. One of their flacks had written an op-ed piece in *The New York Times* the day before, whining that the government prosecutors shouldn't use the racketeering laws against financial statesmen whose nonexistent offenses were civil, not criminal. The flack's point seemed to be that his bosses had stolen too much money to be racketeers.

"Hey, we're paying rent for the place," Arthur said. "The going rate, too."

"Hey, I can fly with my arms. You believe that, Arthur?"

"Fuck you, Bethany," he said, unoffended.

The headquarters was like all campaign headquarters, busy and inefficient. Four years ago, when I was doing some security work for the last campaign, I came across

4

sixty-three thousand dollars in uncashed checks the day after we lost the election—donations that had got mislaid in somebody's desk while we were canceling TV ads for lack of money. Campaigns are a lot like real wars: disorganized messes that don't get won because anybody running things on either side is smart. They get lost because one side is even stupider than the other.

Meanwhile, they use up a lot of enthusiastic and idealistic young people, and these were what was providing the high energy level of the Markham headquarters. No one sat doing nothing. Everyone in sight was on the phone or waiting for the copier, or typing or running around with papers. Out of sight the professionals would be meeting, muddling through to the decisions that would make most of this effort useless. Boss of those professionals this time was Phil Jeffers, who had earned the job of campaign manager by being deputy campaign manager in the Democratic party's last overwhelming defeat. The man who had been campaign manager that time was now getting rich with his own consulting firm, which had Senator Markham's campaign as its principal client. Failing upward is an established route to the top in politics; take a look at Bush's résumé.

Kleber stuck his head into a door and said something I couldn't hear. After listening a moment he pulled his head back out and said, "Phil's tied up in a meeting. We'll go see Billy Fuller."

"Who's he?"

"Phil's deputy. The administrative guy."

"Let's see Markham instead."

"Come on, Bethany. The senator isn't even in town."

"Okay, so long."

"What do you mean, so long?"

"You came looking for me, Arthur, remember? Not the

5

other way around. Phil isn't talking to me and I'm not talking to the administrative guy, so it's so long."

"Jesus, Tom . . ." Now it was Tom.

I looked at Kleber until he stuck his head back inside the door. In a minute Phil Jeffers came out. Nearly as he let me know from his big smile and hearty handclasp, his meeting had turned out to be a terrible waste of time and he was glad to get out of it. He took me to a little room down the hall that had probably been a closet back when Axel, Shearman was floating junk bonds and swindling its clients from these offices. He gave me the only chair in the room, and himself sat on the desk. Not only was this polite, it also gave him the height advantage. People like Jeffers think things like that are important.

"The campaign needs you, Tom," he started out.

"Well, I don't need the campaign. Frankly, I don't give a damn if Tweedledum wins in November or Tweedledee does."

Jeffers smiled, as if I had said something lovable. "Same old Tom," he said. He even shook his head in mock exasperation. "Same old pain in the ass."

"You knew that when you sent Kleber to find me. So a pain in the ass has got to be what you're looking for."

"It is. Let me tell you where the senator is headed."

It turned out that Senator Markham wanted to kick off his campaign on Labor Day, four weeks away, by announcing his choice for secretary of state. I figured this would mean that every other plausible candidate for the job would immediately bail out of the campaign and start sniping from the sidelines, if he didn't go over to the other side entirely. But I probably hadn't been called in for my political advice, and so I didn't offer it.

"Of course the big risk is we could wind up dragging an Eagleton or a Ferraro behind us for the rest of the campaign," Jeffers went on. "That's where you come in."

"Why me? Use your lawyers to woodshed the guy."

"Yeah, right. The way McGovern and Mondale did. No, this time we want somebody objective, from outside. Somebody with a different kind of mentality."

"What kind of mentality?"

"An investigative mentality."

"Is that the way Markham put it?"

"What difference does it make how he put it?"

"Not a bit. Five thousand dollars a week, payable in advance each Monday in a cashier's check made out to Infotek." I spelled it for him. "Plus expenses. I'll trust you over the weekend for the expenses. I'll put in for them every Friday for the previous week and you can add them to Monday's check."

"That's ridiculous. I could hire Ellison or Futterman and his guys for a quarter of that."

"Hire them, then."

"Come on, Tom. The campaign can't afford that kind of money."

"Why not? You pay that kind of money every day to political con men that couldn't find their ass with both hands. The difference between them and me is I know what I'm doing. And you know I do, or you wouldn't be trying to hire somebody that you don't like a goddamn bit more than I like you."

"Now that right there. That's the mentality we want."

"I know. Who's your guy?"

"Kellicott."

"Does he know you want him?"

"He knows he's under consideration."

"Call him and tell him you're aiming me at him."

"All right."

"Today's Friday. If I've got the money Monday I'll go over and see him, get started."

"Where do we send the check?"

"Messenger it over to Charles at the Tasty. He works six A.M. to four."

"The fuck is the Tasty?"

"Just send your guy to Harvard Square and tell him to look around till he sees a sign says Tasty. It's a lunch counter."

We didn't shake hands when I left, which was a sign that our new professional relationship was starting out on a realistic footing. Another sign was that Jeffers hadn't even bothered to sound offended when I insisted on prepayment. We both knew that only a fool lets a preacher or a politician run a tab.

Monday at nine, an hour when honest people are at work, I was at the Tasty having breakfast. The Tasty isn't much to look at, but it's durable. The most modern thing about it is the neon sign in the window saying the place was established in 1916. The equipment and furnishings suggest that this is true. The chromed stools along the counter have worn oak tops. The pattern on the yellow countertop has been mostly rubbed off. Here and there the dark brown stuff underneath shows through the yellow.

Along the counter are five steel struts, the chrome long since pitted, that support circular platforms a little bigger than pie plates. Each has three tiers, probably meant for three pies, but now the racks hold doughnuts and various pastries. Plastic covers protect them from flies and customers. Underneath all this, on the counter itself, are glass cookie jars full of bagels and muffins. In whatever room is left, you arrange your own food the best way you can.

The Tasty is laid out on the same general lines as a

U-boat, except not quite as wide and only eleven stools long. Along the left wall are a cigarette machine, a Coke machine, a glass-covered case displaying a T-shirt that says "Tasty College" on it, and four more stools with a shelf for your food in front of them. And back there in the rear was a pay phone and a stamp machine, which fully met my office needs most of the time. The rest of the time, there was the Au Bon Pain terrace, Widener Library, the Harvard faculty club, and the various waiting rooms in the Harvard University health services, a few steps away. The Tasty, though, was the only one of these places where they knew my name.

"Is there a Charles here?" asked a kid with an ROTC crew cut. What goes around comes around. When I was his age, the hard hats were cleanshaven and short-haired. Now it's the college kids, and the truck drivers wear the beards.

"This is your lucky day," the counterman answered the kid. "I'm Charles."

"Oh, good. I've got something for a Mr. Tom Bethany."

"You still lucky, then. That's him down at the end."

The kid looked at me and nodded politely. "I'm supposed to deliver it to Charles," he said to Charles. "In your hand."

"I see your point," Charles said. "I wouldn't trust him neither." He took the kid's envelope and handed it to me.

"I'm sorry," the kid said to me. "But Mr. Jeffers specifically said Charles, in his hand." Jeffers was still terrorizing the troops, apparently.

"No problem," I said, and the kid left happy.

After breakfast I managed to cash the cashier's check from the Markham for President campaign at a branch of the bank that had issued it, with no more than the usual amount of hassle that banks give you over parting with money they owe you. Then I deposited the five thousand dollars cash in another bank, in one of the several accounts I'm always opening and closing in several names and in different places. Cash leaves no paper trail, or not much.

And then I went back to my room to dress for the meeting I had scheduled with Professor Kellicott. Phil Jeffers, a small man, tries always to occupy the high ground. Tom Bethany, a man to the polyester born, makes it a point to be at least as well-dressed as anyone he goes up against. And so I picked out a blue cord suit tailored by Southwick, twenty dollars secondhand from Keezer's and another thirty-five for slight alterations. Shirts and ties I buy new, but from Filene's basement. Dress shoes they've got you on, though. You can't cut corners on shoes. I bought mine from Lobb's of London, when I was coming back from the war in 1974, flush with money for the first time in my life. I had them make me four pairs, two black and two brown, and if they ever wear out, my lasts are on file.

On the way out I stopped to clear the occupant ads out of my mailbox, which had the name Tom Carpenter on it. The only nonadvertising mail that ever came was Tom Carpenter's phone bill, and it wasn't that time of month. Carpenter was the name my phone was unlisted under, and the name my neighbors and landlord knew me by. The best security isn't bars and alarms; it's when people who don't like you can't look up your address.

The weather had turned hot over the weekend, and I strolled down Harvard Street, in the shade wherever I could manage it. The trick to dealing with heat is to keep your movements slow and smooth, as if you were underwater. Professor Kellicott probably didn't have to worry about these things, since his station in life and his wife's money made it pretty certain that he would be air-conditioned most of the time.

I didn't start out entirely neutral about J. Alden Kellicott, Phillips Professor of Political Economy at the John F. Kennedy School of Government. For one thing, he parted his name on the left like my old high school principal, C. Darwin Feuerbach. You had to ask yourself what was wrong with Charles. Or John, in Kellicott's case, since he was presumably descended from the Mayflower's youngest Puritan. The second problem I had with the professor was that his brilliant career in academia and government had brought him to the top of America's foreign policy establishment. And for a good many years in Laos, I had been on the receiving end of America's foreign policy.

Kellicott's office wasn't air-conditioned and he was in shirt sleeves. His tie, still knotted, hung from the back of a chair. The tie blew in the wind from a floor fan as tall as a man, the kind you still see now and then in barbershops old enough to have a striped pole outside.

"Here, sit where you can catch some of the breeze," he said. "Take off your coat."

And so I took it off. I didn't want to be any worse-dressed than him, either.

"I used to have a sore throat all summer from the damned air-conditioning," he went on, taking my coat from me and hanging it on the chair by his tie. "This spring I found out that Harvard has a whole basement full of these old fans. Sorry to make you suffer for my sore throat."

"The fan's fine, Professor Kellicott."

"Call me Alden. My parents christened me Jephthah, as if I didn't have enough trouble as it was. Jesus, I was already a skinny little kid with glasses."

I nodded, but I certainly wasn't going to call him

Alden. I would call him nothing. "Phil Jeffers told you what I'm up to, I guess," I said.

"You're my official biographer. I'm supposed to open my soul to you."

"I'll get most of it elsewhere. For now, the main thing I'll need from you is access."

"Whatever I can do."

"I need a blanket letter on letterhead stationery, authorizing whoever it may concern to talk to me fully and frankly."

"Won't that get around? Dan doesn't want news of all this to leak before he's ready to announce it, I'm sure."

"Introduce me in the letter as a free-lance writer, working on a profile of you. With your full cooperation and support."

"All right. What else?"

"I need letters to all your old schools back to first grade. Giving them permission to release your records to me."

"Will they do that?"

"Maybe, maybe not. They certainly won't without a letter of authorization. I'll need one for your doctor or doctors, too. Psychiatrists, psychologists, or counselors, if any. And for your accountant."

Kellicott was making notes. "No problem," he said. "If you want to wait around after we're through, I'll have my girl do all this up. Well, we don't say 'girl' anymore, do we?" He was completely matter-of-fact about it all, as if strangers pawed over his life as a regular thing. No reluctance at all; not even curiosity over what I expected to find in, for example, his first-grade report cards. I expected to find nothing, actually, but my way of working is to rake together as big a pile of facts as I can. Then I look for patterns, incongruities, relationships between this thing and that. Whatever. If I knew exactly

12

what I was looking for, I wouldn't have to look. I'd go straight to it.

"And I'd like a copy of your most recent Standard Form Eighty-six," I said. "That's the biographical form you filled out for your government security clearance. Also your financial disclosure forms from when you were in the State Department and your income tax returns as far back as you've got them."

"Between my secretary and myself, we should be able to put together everything you need."

Kellicott had a wonderful voice. It was deep and warm and it carried well. If he had read out a list of the day's ten most active stocks in that voice, you'd have thought he was saying something grave and wise. I've seen stuff about the advantages that height and good looks and slimness give to the people who happen to be born with them, but nobody seems to study the role that voices play. In my basic training company there was a kid from Illinois with a voice you could hear from one end of the barracks to the other. That voice was enough to convince the dummy noncoms to make him a platoon leader, wearing an armband with temporary sergeant stripes on it. With this head start he became a real squad leader in Vietnam, and a sniper aimed for his real stripes. So maybe that voice was enough to make him dead, too.

Kellicott's voice would probably have made him a general, just as William Westmoreland's looks had made him one. But all Westmoreland had was the looks, whereas Kellicott had brains along with his command voice. For looks the professor was average, a slightly gawky six-foot ectomorph with a pleasant, homely face.

"You know about my daughter, don't you?" he asked—a statement more than a question.

"Not much. I read the papers at the time. If they ever caught the guy, I missed it."

"They never caught him. It seems to me they should have, but the Cambridge police aren't the FBI."

"Why should they have caught him?"

"It wasn't in the papers, but there were initials on her."

"On her?"

"Carved." His voice wavered a little on the word, and he stopped talking till he could get a hold of himself. "It doesn't matter," he went on, still with a hint of unsteadiness. "We don't really want to know who did it, anymore. We've tried to move on. You have to."

Kellicott got up and looked out the window, his back to me, for a long moment. Then his posture straightened slightly, and he turned away and sat back down.

"I'm sorry," he said. "I think I can talk about it after all this time, and mostly I can. But sometimes it comes back on me."

"I know," I said. "There are things in Southeast Asia that I thought I'd be over by now, but they come back on me, too."

Kellicott jumped at the change of subject. "Vietnam?"

"A few klicks into it sometimes, but mostly Laos."

"Were you with the military or the embassy?"

"First with the military, then sort of with the embassy."

"You don't look like someone who was sort of with the embassy. Of course, you don't look like my idea of a private detective, either. Maybe it's the glasses."

"I'm not a private detective. I'm sort of a researcher, sort of a security consultant."

Kellicott smiled. "I bet you are. Phil Jeffers says you're sort of a wrestler, too. You don't look like my idea of a wrestler, either."

"Real wrestlers don't look like anything special. Not

14

like Hulk Hogan. He may know how to wrestle, for all I know, but that isn't what he does for a living."

"Well, I hope I'm sort of a teacher the way you're sort of a wrestler. Phil says you made the Olympic team in 1980. The team that wasn't."

"Yeah, well, Carter and I wanted to send a signal to the Russians. We were pretty pissed off over Afghanistan."

"I argued as strongly as I could against it, but you see how far I got," Kellicott said. "The boycott was a totally futile gesture."

"I don't know. It just took a while to work."

"Eight years is a while, all right," Kellicott said. He shook his head, over the folly of Jimmy Carter and Olympic boycotts. "You take it well, I've got to say. I can't imagine what it must have felt like to train at that level for what? Years at least. And then have it all snatched away from you."

"You don't have to imagine. Just remember what you felt when Reagan beat Carter."

Kellicott smiled again. "I guess that's right," he said. "Of course, what the papers were saying might not have happened. I didn't know for sure that I would have been secretary of state in a second term."

"I didn't know for sure that I'd win a medal, either."

"I suppose the point is that neither of us got the chance to compete," Kellicott said. He paused for a moment, looking down almost as if he were shy. "I wonder if Dan Markham appreciates what he's got in you," he said at last.

It was unlikely that Senator Markham did; I was just a sharp instrument to be used for special jobs. I waited to see where Kellicott was going with this.

"Have you ever considered going back into the government?" he asked.

"Not really."

"The State Department's security operation has gotten a lot bigger over the past decade, but it hasn't gotten a lot better. If everything comes together, I'll be looking for somebody ..." His voice trailed off, and then he came firmly out of his reverie. "Well, let me take you out to Mrs. Weintraub so you can explain to her exactly what you need."

And so he took me out to Mrs. Weintraub, and pretty soon I was back at one of the black cast-iron tables outside Holyoke Center, thinking about running the State Department's security office for Secretary of State Kellicott. But thinking about it was as close as I would ever come, since my style of life depends on escaping bureaucratic notice at all levels, from the federal government down to Harvard University.

I took out of my briefcase the fat, three-subject spiral notebook I had just bought and began to set down my conversation with Professor Kellicott. I don't use tape recorders for routine interviews, because people talk differently when they know the recorder is going. But I can re-create even a long conversation pretty nearly word-for-word if I can get at the job soon afterward. I know, because I used to check myself against the tape, until I decided that hidden recorders were a waste of time.

When I had finished setting the conversation down, I read it through twice. I saw nothing to change the impression I had formed of Kellicott during the interview. He was good the way Peggy Lee is good: so good you have to listen hard to tell how good she is.

Then I crossed the street, entered Harvard Yard, and headed for the stacks to fill up as much as I could of my new, 150-page notebook. I started out in the reference room at Widener Library, which is pretty nearly the size of two basketball courts laid end to end. It's a public facility, and so a lot of the readers, like me, have no connection with Harvard. God knows what sad and curious notions, manias, obsessions, mad delusions they pursue all day. Which one will end up in tomorrow's Texas Book Depository? Which is Karl Marx? And who is this peculiar stray, this mesomorph with reading glasses? Why has he spent so many thousands of hours in this building over the years? At least this time I was getting paid, though. I only left, as reluctantly as the other stack rats, when they closed the joint at quarter till ten.

Next morning, Tuesday, I was there at nine when the government documents section opened. All day and Wednesday as well, I spent going through transcripts of congressional hearings and the microfilmed files of *The Washington Post*, *The New York Times*, the *Los Angeles Times*, *The Boston Globe*, and *The Wall Street Journal*. J. Alden Kellicott had left a considerable paper trail behind him during his three years as assistant secretary of state for Latin American affairs, and he had done nearly as well before and after his stint in Washington. Whenever Kellicott had a few minutes to spare, it seemed, he would knock out another op-ed piece or magazine article or contribution to a scholarly journal. Or get himself interviewed on television. Or give a speech. Or write a book.

He had written five altogether, mostly on something he called global interlock. Interlock seemed an odd word, but the books were familiar enough. What they offered was the same old insecure self-doubt, alternately bragging and whimpering, wrapped for sales purposes in red, white, and blue, that Kissinger and Brzezinski had been peddling to the suckers all along. Only those two had already laid claim to the respective brand

17

names of global architecture and global mosaic, leaving
Kellicott stuck with global interlock.

Kellicott, the public man, presented himself to the
world this way:

> **Kellicott, J. Alden,** educator, former government
> official; b. Sharon, Conn., March 19, 1938; m. Susan
> Leffingwell Milton, June 20, 1960; children: Emily,
> Phyllis. B.A., Yale, 1959; M.A., Harvard, 1961; lectr.
> government, 1961; asst. prof., 1962; Ph.D., Harvard,
> 1964; Inst. de Science Politique, U. of Paris, 1964–
> 65; assoc. prof. Harvard, 1966; assoc. dir. Harvard's
> Center for Internat. Affairs, 1967; prof. government,
> Harvard, 1968; Asst. Sec. of State, Latin American
> affairs, 1977–80; Phillips prof. pol. econ., JFK
> School of Govt., 1981—. Author: Politics of Paucity:
> Political Stability in the Sahel, 1965; Deterring
> Doomsday: The Nuclear Interlock, 1968; Recon-
> structing Interlock: The Challenge of the Post-Carter
> Years, 1982; Rim of Revolution: Asia's Technologi-
> cal Challenge, 1984; The Non-nuclear Umbrella:
> Beyond Disarmament, 1987.

As Who's Who entries go, that was nicely stripped
down. A man with less self-confidence wouldn't have
left it at B.A., Yale, 1959, for instance. Kellicott could
have added "summa cum laude, Phi Beta Kappa, Scroll
and Key, winner of the Snow scholarship, and of the de
Forest Prize for public speaking." He could have mentioned that his doctoral dissertation at Harvard won the
Sumner Prize. He could have listed the learned societies
he belonged to, the journals and magazines he had written for, his trusteeships and directorships and honorary
degrees. And his clubs, the Metropolitan in Washington
and the River in New York.

I found all these things out in other reference books, and in various articles I dug out of the newspaper microfilms and the Widener Library's collection of magazine back files. But there was one omission from Kellicott's *Who's Who* entry that I couldn't fill in. Between their own names and the names of their spouses, most respondents listed the names of their parents. Since the format of the entries was standard, presumably the compilers worked from a form that the subjects filled out. Kellicott must have failed to fill in that particular blank. A little break in the pattern, then, and anomalies are one of the things I look for. The closest I could come to filling in the blank was a sentence in an old *New York Times* profile of the then-new assistant secretary of state: "Professor Kellicott grew up in the little town of Sharon, Connecticut, where his father operated a local transportation firm."

The rest of the biographical stuff that I got out of the library's back files just fleshed out the entry in *Who's Who*. If Kellicott had ever faltered on his way up the university and government ladder, no evidence of it appeared. Fresh out of Yale he had married a Milton, one of the steamship, chemicals, and mining Miltons. Full professor at thirty. The promising young scholar had found himself a powerful patron in the foreign policy field, Orville Plummer (of the railroad Plummers). Rain just never seemed to fall on Kellicott's parade, until the early morning hours of a March day two years before.

PROFESSOR'S DAUGHTER SLAIN, the *Globe*'s headline read.

The body of Emily Kellicott, 26, was found early yesterday under a pile of snow in the parking lot of a mall on Lowell Parkway, Cambridge police said.

The victim, daughter of Harvard professor J. Alden Kellicott and his heiress wife, the former Susan Milton, had
apparently been strangled to death. Her clothes were
found in the snow beside the body, which bore lacerations.

Det. Sgt. Ray Harrigan said that there were preliminary
indications of sexual assault, although final determination
would not be possible until completion of the autopsy.

Harrigan said that while there were no suspects at present, investigations were continuing and Cambridge police
had several promising leads. The dead woman was a
Wellesley dropout who was said to have led a troubled life.

Her address was given as 37 Standish Lane, Cambridge, which was her parents' address. The president
of Harvard, I happened to know, lived on the next block.

The story in the *Boston Herald* added nothing substantial to the account, although the tabloid made a good
deal more of the beautiful-heiress angle and had dug
up her yearbook portrait from Buckingham, Browne &
Nichols School. Emily had been a pleasant-looking girl,
if you could judge by the photograph, but not a beauty.

Plenty was missing from the stories. What was she
doing in the parking lot at that hour? What was troubled
about her life? What kind of lacerations did her body
bear? Where? From what kind of instrument? Was her
purse found? Was anything gone from it? Did she have
a car? Where was it? Were bloodstains found in it? What
were "preliminary indications of sexual assault"? What
kind of assault? How long had she been dead? Had she
been missing from home? How long?

Very likely the police didn't have the answers to some
of those questions. Another cop had pointed out Sergeant Harrigan to me once; the joke was that he had
been promoted to detective because he wasn't bright
enough to fill out a parking ticket. But the reporters
ought to have tried to plug the holes in their stories,

particularly the *Herald*'s man. When you worked for Rupert Murdoch, you didn't let go of a murdered "socialite beauty" until you had milked the last line of copy out of her. And yet the second-day stories added little to the first ones. A "sexual assault" of some unspecified type had indeed occurred; the wounds to some unspecified part of her body appeared to have been made with a knife; the medical examiner estimated the body had been lying unnoticed in its snowbank for twenty-four hours or so.

The third-day stories added only that services would be private, and the useful information that investigations were continuing. There were no stories on the fourth or fifth days, or after that. Their absence was hardly surprising. I could almost see Professor Kellicott running into the *Globe*'s publisher at the St. Botolph Club, and the two of them agreeing on how painful all this was to the poor girl's mother. The *Herald* might have been a little tougher to reach through the old boys' network, but at Kellicott's level everybody is acquainted with everybody else, or knows someone who is. In consequence we were for once spared the normal rooting around in the victim's "troubled" past, and the pop-sociological analyses of rebellious youth or whatever she had been, and the stories prodding the police for inaction, and the anniversary pieces every year until all involved got tired of the mystery.

And so my days of poking around in the library had brought nothing to the surface but two anomalies, two breaks in the pattern of a phenomenally successful life. Kellicott had left his parents out of his *Who's Who* entry, and his older daughter had been murdered. Neither avenue looked terribly promising, but one of them led to Sharon, which is in the Berkshire Mountains of northwest Connecticut. And the weather in Cambridge was so hot that the asphalt gave under your weight. And Hope Edwards would be attending a conference in Stockbridge, which is in the Berkshire Mountains of southwestern Massachusetts. Hope Edwards is my lady and my love, even if I have to share her. Today was Wednesday and tomorrow was Thursday, the first day of the conference.

2

ONE OF MY FEW EXTRAVAGANCES IS MY CAR. IT'S AN eight-year-old tan-colored Datsun that looks right at home in Cambridge. Eight years of Cambridge residential parking permits, the mark of the old-timer, clutter up the left-hand side of the rear window. Rust is rotting away the rocker panels and the bottoms of the doors. A crack runs along the bottom of the windshield. The fenders are chipped, bent, and dented. The upholstery used to be sort of reddish, but the sun has long since bleached it to a pale, unhealthy pink. Paper napkins, discarded notebooks, old books, and nonbiodegradable trash from Burger King and McDonald's cover the seats and floors. Most of this optional equipment was left in place by the car's previous owner, a divinity school student who sold it to me for four hundred dollars three years ago, after the steering gave out. He also left me his bumper stickers, which identified me as a friend of whales and an enemy of war. This may have overstated the case slightly, but it was close enough for government work.

No thief was likely to bother hot-wiring the old junker, even though Greater Boston is the car-theft capital of America. After all, how could he know that the motor and the drivetrain and everything else you couldn't see were either new or rebuilt or perfectly maintained by the guys at MacKinnon Motors? That the aging clunker with the bad case of body cancer would keep on going at nearly forty miles to the gallon as long as you wanted it to? That the old AM radio with one knob missing was camouflage for a hidden CD player? The only thieves that ever bothered me were the worst ones of all, the ones with a license to steal, the companies that write auto insurance in Massachusetts.

Thursday afternoon the car started at the first touch, as always, and I headed toward the Mass Pike. For the first fifty miles or so going west from Boston, the pike goes through scenery that is about as dull as you can find in New England. The solution is to run up the windows, switch on the air-conditioning, turn Julie London on barely loud enough to hear, settle the speed at sixty, and, honey, as the song says, "let your mind roll on." What it mostly rolled on about was Hope Edwards, who was giving the keynote speech as well as leading several workshops at the annual meeting of the Massachusetts Bar Association. We were both card-carrying members of the American Civil Liberties Union, but she was also director of its Washington office. A lobbyist for criminals, as Ed Meese used to say. You would have thought he'd be grateful that somebody as smart as Hope was looking out for him and his pals.

Hope was as good-looking as she was smart, which seemed an unfair helping of blessings for one person to have, but that was only the beginning. She made good money herself, and was married to a Washington lawyer who made even more, and had two handsome small boys and a beautiful twelve-year-old daughter, and a big town house overlooking Rock Creek Park, and she was a champion sculler for the Potomac Boat Club, and she had an easy, outgoing way that made everybody either like or love her. And why she wasted as much as two minutes of her life on me, God knows, but there it was. Maybe she needed a dark side; certainly I needed a light one.

The farther west I drove on the pike, the prettier the countryside got. In the heavy heat each leaf and blade of grass and cow and high, white cloud stood still. Only the cars moved, roaring through the sun-stunned landscape. And one of them was carrying Dumb Tom Bethany to his sole and only true love, as I would admit to myself but never aloud.

"Oh, that's right, that's right, yes," I was saying when the phone rang, making it no longer right.

Hope reached out for the phone and answered it the best she could. "Uh-huh," she said. "Uh-huh, uh-huh. Uhn-uhn, huhn-uhn." Then she arranged matters so that she could broaden her vocabulary and said, "I'm afraid I'm bushed, Larry. I'll have to talk to you tomorrow." The instant she hung up she burst out laughing.

"What's so funny?" I said.

"Just something he said."

"What?"

"Nothing."

"Tell me or I'll hold my breath until I die."

"He wanted to know what I was eating."

Before I could deal with that properly, Hope attacked with the speed of a mongoose, tickling me till I could do nothing but laugh, and so I tickled her back, and there we were, rolling to escape each other like a pair of nine-year-olds. The odd thing is that I'm not ticklish with anyone else and neither is she. We are too dignified, to use a word no longer used. Too uptight, people say now. After a while we lay back on the pillows, laughed out. I reached for the phone and disconnected it.

"I looked in on your speech," I said. "When you were talking about *Arizona* vs. *Youngblood*."

"Mishandling evidence," she said. "Here, let me show you."

"I liked watching you."

"Hmm," she said into the side of my neck.

"Massachusetts bar. Whole roomful of men, hundreds. Made me feel good. You know why?"

"Mmm."

"Because I looked into their hearts, and every single male heterosexual in the room wanted to tickle you after the show. But none of them would except me, and they'd envy the shit out of me if they knew."

"I envy the shit out of you, too, and you know what I envy about you guys? Specifically?"

She made me forget for a while all about the sad part—that I had had to slip unobtrusively into the back of the hall instead of sitting in the front row as the guest of the featured speaker. Hope was a public lady, and it was public knowledge that she was married, or at least it was in a crowd of lawyers. So she had left a duplicate key to her room with me, and I had only looked in on the speech briefly. Then I went to her room and waited there for her. She would have made her excuses as soon after the talk as she gracefully could, and Larry, whoever he was, would have figured what the hell, why not wait a while and ring the room? All she can say is no.

Which she had to him, but not to me. After a long

and leisurely time we lay side by side, just touching along the length of our bodies.

"Driving down to Sharon and back tomorrow?" Hope asked.

"Ummh."

"Good. Two nights here, then."

And we lay there silent for a while more, until she said into the darkness, "Sharon is where Bill Buckley is from. Did you know that?"

"No, I didn't. Is there a shrine or something?"

"No, so you can't be going there for that. And you don't have any Republican friends. So why are you going?"

I was able to tell her everything, because she's the person I trust with everything. The only person.

"It's a dumb idea," Hope said when I told her about Markham's plan to name Kellicott. "All the Vance and Muskie people will be shooting at him because he was Brzezinski's mole at State."

"Sure it's dumb. But they're not paying me this outrageous price for political advice."

"When I get back to Washington I can ask around about Kellicott. If you want."

"Would you?"

And then, since Hope had a 7:30 breakfast meeting, we left a call for 6:00. That way, we figured, we would have time for a good long shower or something.

At 7:25 Hope was out the door, looking cool and businesslike and slightly remote, and not a bit the way she had looked a half an hour earlier. I took my time dressing, and only left the room after I had checked to be sure there were no ACLU lawyers hanging around the hall. Then I walked out of the inn, trying to look like an ACLU lawyer myself. It was the Red Lion Inn, a huge, sprawling hotel built in the days when trains brought

27

rich New Yorkers up to summer in the Berkshires of western Massachusetts. The coolness of the night still hung on at quarter till eight. The lawyers weren't around yet to enjoy it, but two old ladies were already seated in the rocking chairs that ran the length of the inn's veranda. The scene wouldn't have been much different a century before. The Mauve Decade was a miserable time to be poor, but a wonderful time to be rich. Maybe these things go in hundred-year cycles, and Reagan was nothing but a historical imperative.

My car was parked conspicuously in a line of Saabs and Mercedes-Benzes and Porsches, a mutt among show dogs. Fuck all of you, was my reaction, at least I didn't steal for mine. An illogical and possibly even an unfair reaction, I know, but I can't help that. I have met the enemy often enough, and generally he ain't us. Generally he drives a Mercedes and stops at places like the Red Lion.

To get away from the inn, and the thought that Hope was having breakfast there but not with me, I drove down Route 7 to the McDonald's outside Great Barrington. When on the road I give my breakfast business to McDonald's, as the most intellectual of the fast-food chains. Who else sets out free copies of the local paper? And in this case the local paper was the *Berkshire Eagle*, an honest, workmanlike product that the chains haven't got around to swallowing yet.

Below Great Barrington down to the Connecticut line, to judge by the signs, the principal local industry was people selling their antiques to one another. The locals had evidently discovered the economic equivalent of a perpetual motion machine. On into Connecticut the antique shops thinned out somewhat. Here and there were modest houses, for the support troops, but the trend was toward million-dollar estates sitting well back from the road, shaded by trees way too big to get your arms around. The owners had to be beyond the necessity of going to the office every day, since New York City was a hundred miles to the south. Presumably they were the kind of people, as Hope describes them, who get money in the mail.

Sharon, Kellicott's hometown, had almost the air of a New England village restored by the Rockefellers to its original appearance. But not even the Rockefellers could restore the giant trees that must have shaded the entire village green before the Dutch elm blight hit. One or two huge elms remained, but the rest of the green was planted with maples no more than forty years old. I knew about tree age because till I went away to college and never came back, I had to cut wood to help get us through the north-country winters.

The white houses that stood around the green dated from the late 1700s or early 1800s. I'm not as good on houses as I am on trees; house ages I could tell because a number of them had the dates above the front doors. The town hall, a one-story brick building, seemed to be of more recent manufacture. The woman behind the counter in the town clerk's office gave me directions to where the Kellicotts once lived, the two parents being now dead. Since the clerk was a woman of a certain age, as the French say, and it seemed to be about the same age as Kellicott's, I asked her if she had gone to school with him.

"Jeff was a couple of grades ahead of me," she said.

"Jeff?" I asked.

"That's what he called himself in those days. Stood for Jeffrey, I imagine, but I'm just guessing. None of us knew him too well. He only stayed at Sharon Center School for the first few grades and then he went to Indian Mountain."

29

"What's that?"

"School for the hilltoppers, over in Lakeville. Like the prep schools, only they start younger." I got directions from her to Indian Mountain School, too. Then I asked if I could have a look at the deed to the Kellicott property.

"There isn't any Kellicott property. They lived on the Milton place."

"Susan Milton?" I asked, remembering the maiden name of Kellicott's wife.

"Well, her father's really. Leffingwell Milton. Not Little Leffingwell, the son that has the place now. Big Leffingwell. The old man who died."

"How did it happen that the Kellicotts lived on the Milton place?"

She looked at me as if I had asked a dumb question. "He drove for the Miltons."

"Who did?"

"Mike Kellicott did. Jeff's dad."

"How about his mom?"

"Nobody ever knew her. From what I understand, she died in childbirth with Jeff."

I went next to the probate office, across the hall. There I learned that Michael Kellicott had left everything he had to his son, Jephthah Alden Kellicott. The will superseded an earlier will in which he had left everything to his beloved wife, Catherine Wynsocki Kellicott. The legal boilerplate gave no clue to the size of the estate; presumably nothing much was involved beyond furnishings, personal effects, and maybe a few bucks in a bank account somewhere.

Leffingwell Milton's will was another matter. It went on for sixteen pages of bequests, codicils, trusts, trustees, etc. It was the will of a man with vast and complex business interests, and firm opinions about his heirs. Big Leffingwell, it seemed, had regarded Little Leffingwell as an idiot—or at least as a man who was incompetent to handle money.

The junior Leffingwell got the two-hundred-acre family homestead in Sharon, true enough. But the will went on to read:

"All the rest, residue and remainder of my estate, both real and personal, of every nature and wherever situate, of which I may die seized or possessed, including without limitation, all property acquired by me or to which I may become entitled after the execution of this Will, and all property herein attempted to be disposed of, the disposition whereof by reason of lapse or other cause shall fail to take effect, I give, devise and bequeath to my Trustees hereinafter named, IN TRUST NEVERTHE-LESS, for the following uses and purposes hereinafter set forth."

These uses included the upkeep and operation of the Sharon estate. But the apparently unbreakable trust was administered by a Hartford law firm. Little Leffingwell, in effect, had been put on a lifelong allowance. The trust was also charged with taking care of his children, who would inherit equal portions of a third of the trust's principal as each turned thirty-five. If I had been Little Leffingwell, I would have interpreted this as meaning that the old son of a bitch trusted my little kids more than he trusted me.

His sister, Susan, and her husband, Alden Kellicott, came out a lot better. Her trust fund amounted to two thirds of the estate, as compared with her brother's untouchable one third. She had immediate limited access to her two thirds of the trust, and had gained total control of the money at the age of forty. She was now, I knew, forty-nine. Kellicott, for his part, had inherited outright "the sum of $2,000,000 (two million dollars) to dispose of as he may see fit." My guess was that the old man saw the income from two million as barely sufficient to raise his son-in-law above the poverty line and give him a measure of psychological independence.

My further guess, pretty nearly amounting to a certainty, was that Little Leffingwell would hate his brother-in-law's guts. So naturally I called him up to see about a meeting, but he turned out to be in the middle of a month's fishing at his lodge in northern Quebec. The lodge was phoneless. That's the way it goes, often enough.

But I drove out to the Milton house anyway, to have a look at the place where Kellicott grew up. Before turning into its driveway, I pulled up along the blacktop country road and inspected the estate. The main house was a three-story brick building, weathered to a soft red. The roof was slate. A four-car garage with a cupola on top stood off to one side, all four doors open. Two of the bays were empty. Another held a 1956 Ford pickup that looked to be in excellent shape for its years; in the last was a new and shiny Jeep-type vehicle from Japan.

Like the house, the trees and plantings had been in place a very long time. The fences were made of stones cleared from the fields. Along the road, a tangle of brambles and bushes almost hid the fences from view. Large maples grew between the fence line and the roadside. The fields behind were unmowed, a tangle of midsummer wildflowers. Far beyond were barns and other fields, with brown and white cattle resting in the shade of the large trees that stood here and there. A standard hardware-store mailbox stood by the side of the road, with no name on it. Presumably the mail carrier knew who lived there.

I drove down the graveled driveway and parked in front of the house. No one came to the door, although I could hear the bell ringing inside the house. I could see the front hall through the narrow windows that ran up both sides of the front door. The general impression was of brass and leather and waxed mahogany and expensive wallpaper and striped or flowered upholstery. I heard footsteps on the gravel drive and turned to see a man in his sixties, carrying an edging tool.

"All gone," he said. "Mrs. M's in the city. Mr. M's off fishing in Canada with the kids."

"No fishing around here?"

"Oh, sure. There's a good stream right on the property, just this side of that rise. I been known to take a dozen or more brookies out of it, after a good rain."

"Can you work a fly in all that brush?"

"Oh, hell, no. Only way to get 'em out of there is worms. Couple of split buckshot and let the high water carry your bait down into the holes under the bank. And even then the sons of bitches'll hang your line up on a root half the time."

He paused a moment. "Up there where he goes," he went on, "the fish practically jump in the canoe with you. According to what they say, anyway."

"Some life," I said. "Actually, I wasn't looking for the Miltons, anyway. Actually, they told me the Kellicott place was out around here. Mike Kellicott?"

"Kellicott? He died in '79."

"Yeah, well, I knew he was dead. I just wanted to see the house."

"Just past the bend on the road, on your left. Not much to see, and I ought to know. I live there now."

"Thanks."

"I wouldn't have thought anybody even remembered old Mike Kellicott after all this time."

"I was just going to drive by, get an idea. I'm doing a magazine story on Alden Kellicott."

"I still can't get used to that Alden. I know he calls himself that now, but he was always Jeff around here. He's the one told me about those fish up in Canada, long time back."

"He used to go up there?"

"Oh, yeah, sure. Big Leffingwell practically raised Jeff like his own son."

"Already had a son, didn't he?"

"Well, yeah. He had little Leffingwell, that's up in Canada now."

"But he liked Jeff better?"

"Jeff done all right for himself. Put it that way."

The gardener had started to wonder who I was and whether he should be talking to me. It was time to move along.

Kellicott's childhood home turned out to be a two-story stucco cottage. Its walls were the color of wet cement. The trim was dark green, almost black. The house stood in the shade of several large hemlocks, and it probably smelled perpetually of mildew inside. Grass tried to grow in the yard, but there wasn't enough sun for it to do well. Kellicott had had to go elsewhere to find his place in the sun.

I couldn't see that there was much more to be gained from looking at the dreary little cottage, and so I drove the few miles to the school that the town clerk had mentioned. The Indian Mountain School receptionist had me wait in a sort of living room outside the headmaster's office while he finished with a phone call. I was glancing over the various awards and trophies on the wall when I came across the name "Jephthah A. Kellicott" as the 1952 winner of something called the Triangle Prize.

"Mr. Bethany?" a voice behind me said. "Hi, I'm Judd Baxter."

I turned to find a surprisingly young man, probably

around thirty-five, dressed for tennis and tanned to match. He wanted to be helpful, but the school didn't keep records that old, as far as he or his secretary knew. Although this was only his second year in the job, actually. Maybe I should try old Mr. Dooley, who was headmaster back then and still lived right down the road, on Lake Wononscopomuc. Evan Dooley.

"What do you give the Triangle Prize for?" I asked.

"Academics, sports, and character," the young headmaster said. "By vote of the faculty. It's our top prize."

I found the retired headmaster splitting wood outside a small house on the shore of a large lake. He was working slowly and carefully, getting the job done little by little. He looked pretty good for a man in his eighties, which Baxter had told me he was. When I stated my business he set aside his splitting maul willingly enough and invited me inside. An old springer spaniel on a couch opened his eyes just long enough to dismiss me as uninteresting, and went back to sleep again. His old master looked over my all-purpose letter of authorization from Alden Kellicott, and seemed equally unimpressed.

"I don't know how much help I can be to you, Mr. Bethany," he said. "It's been a long time."

"You do remember Professor Kellicott?"

"Oh, yes. Jeff was one of the brightest boys we ever had. He did well at everything. Sports, extracurricular activities. A good many of the students looked up to him."

"Popular with the faculty, too?"

"We voted him the Triangle Prize."

"What was the vote?"

"The actual vote? You need that for your story?"

"Probably not. I just like to get a feel for my subjects."

"Well, I don't remember what the vote was."

"How did you vote, yourself?"

"I don't think I'll remember that, either." Mr. Dooley took a sip of the iced tea he had brought both of us before I had started asking my questions. Then he looked at me with the disapproving stare that had no doubt unsettled hundreds of schoolboys. It unsettled me.

"I was in the school business forty years," he said. "A good many of my boys have done quite well by themselves. Actors, politicians, champion athletes one or two of them, one fellow won the Nobel Prize in chemistry. The man who produces the boxing films, what are they called?"

I shrugged. I didn't know, either.

"Over the years I imagine I've read a couple of dozen magazine stories about former students of mine, and not one of those reporters ever came all the way up here to interview the headmaster the boys had in the ninth grade."

Neither of us was fooling the other, and I decided to stop trying. "Mr. Dooley," I said, "I'll bet you voted for Jeff Kellicott for the Triangle Prize and I'll bet you held your nose when you did it."

"I don't know why you'd think that."

"Let me tell you about a conversation we might've just had, but didn't. Here goes your part. I'd be delighted to help you, Mr. Bethany. I could never forget Jeff. He was one of the finest boys we ever had. A terrific athlete and scholar. A natural leader. The faculty voted him our top prize."

"I said all those things."

"But I had to drag them out of you, and you qualified every one."

Dooley remained stubbornly silent, and so I knew I was on solid ground. It was coming to me that he was something I didn't run across often: a man of uncompromising, old-fashioned integrity. No doubt I wouldn't agree with him on most things, any more than I'd agree with Barry Goldwater. But I could count on what they said being what they really thought. If, that is, they chose to say anything at all.

"Do you keep up with politics, Mr. Dooley?" I asked.

"I do. I was treasurer of the Republican Town Committee till I gave it up last year."

"Do you think Senator Markham's going to the White House?"

"I wouldn't want to see it, but that's the way the polls are running right now."

"Then let me tell you something I hope you'll want to keep confidential once you've heard it."

The old headmaster nodded, and I went on.

"Alden Kellicott is likely to be our next secretary of state."

"That would be a mistake," Mr. Dooley said.

"I thought you might think so," I said, and did something I've never done before. I told him exactly who I was working for, and what I had already found out, and what I hoped still to find out. I also told him how Phil Jeffers would feel if he knew I had leaked the name of Markham's candidate for secretary of state to a former Republican official. Mr. Dooley listened till I was done. Then he closed his eyes for such a long time that I thought he might have gone to sleep.

At last he opened them, and said, "What's the phone number of the Markham campaign headquarters?"

"Five-four-six, four-six hundred. Area code six-one-seven."

"What's the extension of this campaign-manager fellow, this Jeffers?"

"Six-oh-nine."

He picked up the phone, dialed Boston information, and asked for the number of the Markham campaign.

Cute old man. When that checked out, he dialed the campaign switchboard and asked for extension 609. In a moment he nodded, apparently satisfied with the way the extension had been answered. "Yes, you can help me," he said to whoever had answered the phone. "If I wanted to mail something to Mr. Jeffers, how would I address it?"

I admired the way he had worked out to get the address without actually saying he intended to send Jeffers anything. Which would have been a lie, of course. Mr. Dooley listened to the answer to his hypothetical question, said thank-you, and hung up.

"I don't remember the address," I said, before he could ask. "But it's off Milk Street, used to be Axel, Shearman's Boston office."

"I'm satisfied," Mr. Dooley said, and began to talk.

Jeff Kellicott and Leffingwell Milton II had come to Indian Mountain in 1947, when they were both nine. For the first two years they were day students; from then on young Leffingwell was a boarding student, while Kellicott remained a day student. The senior Milton had become worried about his son's poor grades, and thought the boy would do better as a boarder.

"Did he?" I asked.

"Not really. They seldom do."

"How were Kellicott's marks?"

"He was the first in the school right from the start, every year."

"Do you have school buses?"

"We didn't then."

"How did the two of them get to school?"

"In the Miltons' station wagon."

"Who drove them?"

"Sometimes Mrs. Milton, but she was generally sick in the mornings. Most of the time it was Jeff's father."

"What was the matter with Mrs. Milton?"

"Ginny liked her cocktails."

"Where would the boys ride?"

The old headmaster looked puzzled.

"Up front with Jeff's father or in the back?" I asked. "Or maybe Jeff up front and the other boy in the back?"

"Both up front, I imagine. I don't really remember, but any other way would have looked peculiar, wouldn't it?"

"I don't know, really. I don't move in those circles, so I'm just trying to get a sense of how things fit together. Did Mrs. Milton ever drive Jeff later on, when her own son was a boarder?"

"I don't really know. Actually I never saw who brought him to school after Leff became a boarder, now that you mention it. Jeff would show up every morning from the direction of the barns. I always assumed he had his father drop him off down the road."

"Ashamed of his father, you think?"

"Maybe. Boys that age get odd notions."

"Who paid his tuition?"

"Leff Milton Senior paid. One check for both boys."

"How did they get along?"

"The boys? They got along beautifully, as far as anyone could tell."

"Far as anyone could tell? You think there was maybe something else going on, though?"

"Just a feeling I had. Nothing solid to it."

"On the surface what did it look like? Did they hang around together?"

"Quite a bit, yes. Jeff was one of those boys who's very self-assured, old for his age. Always a little bit aloof and independent. Other boys are drawn to that. They wanted him to like them."

"Did he?"

"Not the way they wanted, no. He was always pleasant, always nice to everybody. But a little remote, you know. No real best friend, or even close friends. Although you'd see him more often with Little Leff than with anyone else."

"Was Little Leff popular?"

"Alone, Leff would have been in the middle of the pack. Not the most popular, not unpopular either. But being with Jeff made him popular. Leff and Jeff, the kids called them. Like Mutt and Jeff. I suppose nobody remembers Mutt and Jeff anymore."

I nodded to show that I did, at least. "Apparently Kellicott was good at sports," I said. "How about the Milton boy?"

"Potentially better than Jeff. You have to understand that neither of them was a great natural, the kind of athlete that only comes along now and then. In terms of ability they were probably in the middle, or a little above. But Leff didn't have the fire and Jeff did. Jeff made himself into a standout."

"That the way it was in the classroom, too?"

"Oh, no. Leff's aptitude was pretty well below the middle there, and Jeff was the best student we ever had. He was one of those people who can read something once and never forget it. One of those trick memories."

"Is memory enough?"

"At our level, it pretty much is. But we've had one or two other students with photographic memories and they didn't do as well as Jeff. He had an amazingly quick mind, too. He'd grasp a concept while you were still in the middle of explaining it."

"Well, you know, so far I can't see why you think it would be such a mistake to make him secretary of state."

"It was a mistake to give him our Triangle Prize, too,

but you couldn't not give it to him. I hope it won't be like that this time."

"Why was it a mistake, though? He fulfilled all the requirements for the prize, didn't he?"

"That's it exactly. He fulfilled them. You felt he was doing all the things he was doing not because he wanted to, but because he knew you wanted him to. You felt he was using you. He was always respectful, always pleasant, always polite, and there was nothing you could ever put your finger on. But you always felt the way you do with a waiter, you know? That he's only smiling because he's learned you get bigger tips that way."

"And maybe because he knows he just spit in your soup, too," I said.

"Exactly," the old headmaster said. "That's exactly the way Jeff made you feel."

"He's better at it now," I said. "Or maybe he's changed."

"He may be better, but I doubt if he's changed. In my experience, the person you are at twelve is pretty much the person you're going to be, under the surface at least, for the rest of your life. That's why I'm telling you things I'd normally keep confidential. Like that old cheating business."

"You haven't told me about any cheating business."

"I haven't? Well, perhaps I haven't. Short-term memory loss. Fortunately, most of the things I want to remember call for long-term memory."

Mr. Dooley was silent for a moment.

"It's forty years ago now, and you'd think everybody would have forgotten it," he continued. "Unimportant schoolboy stuff. But every time I see Leff I think about it, and I'd bet you he does, too. Not that either of us would ever mention it. I'd bet Jeff remembers it too, although I haven't seen him since Honors Day when he walked off with all the prizes. Funny thing, Leff didn't do nearly so well here, but he went on to take quite an interest in the school over the years. Even served a term on the board of trustees. That's something you see more than you might think. You take a boy who must have had a miserable time in school, you'd think he'd put it all behind him. But just as often as not he'll wind up as class agent, active in alumni affairs, annual giving, going to all the reunions. It's almost like they're trying to give themselves a second crack at school, to make a go of it this time around . . ."

"I gather the Milton boy was the one who cheated?" I prompted.

"I don't know, damn it. Never will know. Officially, the Kellicott boy was the one who did."

"What happened?"

"Well, it was when they were both day boys, living at home. Leff turned in a paper that was much better than he usually did—got a B, as I recall. Jeff turned in a paper that was worse than he ever did. Also a B. Wasn't just the grades that were the same. Whole sections of the papers were, too. Jeff admitted that he had copied from Leff."

"Wait a minute, Mr. Dooley, am I getting this straight? The smarter one, Jeff, copied from the dumber one, Leff?"

"That's right."

"What would be the point of that?"

"Jeff said he did it because he just got behind."

"Had he ever got behind before?"

"Nope. Nor after."

"Didn't he know that the teacher would be bound to spot it?"

"They had different teachers. Jeff was in an advanced English section. Covered roughly the same material and

42

had the same writing assignments, but they read more in Jeff's section."

"How did the teacher spot it, then?"

"That was odd, too. Leff's teacher, in the regular section, was the one who caught it. Leff's paper mentioned a poem that Leff's teacher hadn't assigned, but Jeff's had. So the two teachers compared notes."

"What did the Milton boy say about it all?"

"Just that Jeff had helped him a lot with his paper, but hadn't really written it. It turned out they did their homework together a good deal of the time, with Jeff sort of being the teacher. That confused the whole thing even more, of course."

"But there's no confusion about Jeff turning in a paper that wasn't his?"

"Some confusion, yes. Jeff might have in effect written the paper Leff turned in. That's what Leffingwell Senior thought."

"Meaning that Jeff would have turned in a B paper that was essentially his and Leff would have turned in pretty much the same B paper as Jeff's. In which case Leff was the one who cheated, and Jeff tried to cover for him."

"But why would Jeff have done such a thing?" Mr. Dooley asked. "He could have written a much better paper for himself. That's what has always baffled me."

"Supposing he had written his own A paper and helped Leff write a B paper. Probably nobody would have suspected anything."

"Why didn't he do that, then?" the headmaster asked.

"What if he intended to be caught?"

"I find that hard to believe."

"Or at the very least didn't care if he was caught, because he would be in a no-lose situation."

"He could easily have been expelled for plagiarism. That would have been quite a loss."

"It didn't happen, though, did it? What happened was that nobody believed that Jeff cheated, and everybody believed Leff did."

"I had my doubts. But no evidence."

"Mr. Milton didn't have any doubts. He thought his son had copied from the chauffeur's son, didn't you say?"

"He ranted and raved about it for a while, yes. Big Leff could be a very forceful man."

"A bully?"

"Some might say so. He certainly reduced Little Leff to tears that day. Told the boy he was going to be a boarder from then on, so he'd be forced to do his own homework for a change."

"Was Jeff there, too?"

"Oh, yes, I had all three of them in my office, Leffingwell Milton and the two boys. Very unpleasant scene."

"Jeff Kellicott's father wasn't there?"

"I never really knew Mike Kellicott. Leff Milton paid the bills, and Jeff's father never really entered the picture."

"What did Jeff say during this meeting?"

"He took all the blame and did his best to clear Leff. Said he hadn't helped Leff hardly at all with his paper. Said he was sorry he cheated and was ready to accept whatever the punishment was."

"What was it?"

"Nothing. I had no real evidence that Jeff had written Leff's paper for him. And if he had, I couldn't very well punish Jeff for plagiarizing himself. To this day, I don't really know what happened. I just suspect."

"Suspect what?"

"That Jeff planned it all. What I don't know is why."

I didn't know why, either, although I had one or two notions about it. Freud tells us that the result achieved is apt to be the result intended, and even Freud can't be wrong all the time. In this case the results achieved had been to drive Big Leff and Little Leff apart, while at the same time bringing Big Leff and the Kellicott boy closer together. Would a schoolboy be capable of thinking up and then carrying out such a complicated, sophisticated scheme?

"Do you still see anything of Little Leff?" I asked the old man.

"Not really," he said. "While I was still at school I saw quite a bit of him at board meetings and so on. And then after my retirement I'd occasionally run across him at the little country club we have over in Sharon. But I gave up tennis a couple of years ago, when I turned eighty."

"Did he ever talk about Kellicott?"

"Constantly."

"In what terms?"

"Admiration. Gratitude."

"Gratitude for what?"

"What he's done for Susie."

"Is that Susan Milton?"

"Yes, Leff's sister. She was a handful when she was young, and I guess Jeff took her on and steadied her down. God knows her father couldn't do anything with her."

"What was the problem?"

"Partly the bottle, I gather. Like her mother, poor soul. She was always—Susie was, not her mother—getting fired from schools and disappearing with inappropriate people and attempting suicide. That sort of thing."

"Did Big Leff feel gratitude, too?"

"Oh, he was delighted over the marriage. He used to say that buying Jeff an education was the smartest investment he ever made."

"Did he admire Jeff, too?"

"I doubt if Big Leff ever admired anybody except himself. This is going to sound funny, but he wasn't really bright enough to understand that Jeff was brighter than him."

"Doesn't sound funny at all," I said, and it didn't. To think you're smart when you're not, you have to be really stupid or really rich. Big Leff seemed to have qualified on both counts.

I thanked Evan Dooley for his help, meaning every word of it, and headed a mile or so down the road for the next stop on Kellicott's path upward, Hotchkiss School. It turned out to be a collection of undistinguished-looking brick dormitories and halls that barely missed looking like the buildings at a state mental hospital. The place was maintained a little better, though. And the windows, while they lacked curtains, also lacked bars.

I asked directions from a group of summer students who seemed to be majoring in competitive dressing, and found my way to the administrative offices. The assistant headmaster who finally agreed to see me was totally unimpressed by Kellicott's letter authorizing Hotchkiss to show me his records and extend all other courtesies. The furthest he would go was to permit me to examine the yearbooks in the school library, and even then he took no chances. He escorted me there, and instructed the librarian to limit my browsing to the yearbook in question.

"I wish we could help you more, Mr. Bethany," he said in a friendly way that fooled neither the librarian nor me. "Fact is, though, the law is pretty darned strict on the privacy of student records. But I'm sure Harriet would be glad to show you the 1956 yearbook, not that we're a public library of course. That should be enough to give you a darned good overview of Dr. Kellicott's career at Hotchkiss." I thought of the young headmaster at Indian Mountain, who hadn't been any more helpful than this turkey, really. But two guys can say pretty much the same thing, and still you can tell right off which one is the asshole and which one isn't. Style is substance.

Actually, the yearbook probably did give as darned good an overview of Kellicott's Hotchkiss career as his records would have. He had won most of the available prizes. Although he didn't strike me as particularly well-constructed for contact sports, he had lettered in football and hockey, as well as tennis. He had been president of the student council, editor of the school newspaper, and a member of the cum laude society.

I returned the book to Harriet, who was in the process of closing up shop, and went back out into a day that remained hot. At a little after five the sun was still burning down strongly out of a blue sky, with high, white, puffy clouds here and there. I had parked in the shade, but the shade had moved. The car seat was so hot that I had to take my weight off it a time or two and let the air in under before I could sit down without hurting.

Hope's room at the Red Lion was air-conditioned, though, and cool enough to make you uncomfortable without clothes on. This forced us to stay under the covers until it was time for dinner. By then the heat had broken outside. We drove a few miles out of town and ate bad food at a restaurant called Trumbull's Taverne. The "e" should have tipped us off. The menus opened out to the size of a *Boston Globe* at full extension and the dishes had names like "Priscilla's Deep-Dish Apple Dowdy." All the esses were written as efs, but at least they had Baff Ale on tap.

Afterward we drove for miles on some county road until we found a lonely spot to park, and then we did something we did whenever we got the chance. Why, I don't know. I'm just reporting. We necked like teenagers for an hour or more under the crescent moon. We did everything you can do short of going all the way, and then we drove back to the inn and did that, too.

Next morning, Saturday, I drove Hope to Worcester, where she was catching a flight home. Along the way, I told her what I had learned about Kellicott.

"How old was he when this business with the plagiarized paper happened?" she asked.

"Ten, around in there."

"That young, you think he was capable of setting the Milton boy up so his father would send him away from home to be a boarder?"

"No, I don't think he could have predicted the boarder part. It was just a lucky accident that Little Leff got moved out of the way."

"So young Jeff could move in on the old man?"

"He seen his opportunities, and he took 'em."

"What part wasn't an accident, then?" Hope asked.

"The part that couldn't have been. Jeff turning in the same paper he had helped Little Leff write."

"Little Leff. Poor little rich kid."

"Sure, he was in a double bind. What was he supposed to say? My best friend helped me with my paper and then turned in the same paper himself? Certain drawbacks to that, but what other choice did he have? He was stuck with the truth."

"And the truth was unbelievable," Hope said.

"Right. The only conclusion that Big Leff could possibly draw, remembering here that it doesn't look like he was any brighter than Little Leff, was that his boy had copied from the chauffeur's boy."

"Do you really think a ten-year-old kid could have plotted all that out?"

"Not really, no. Maybe he just thought it was a joke. Maybe he just got tired of helping his dumb pal with his homework. But I think he thought it through enough to know there was no real downside for him."

"And no upside for Little Leff?"

"That part I doubt. I'd bet that part was unconscious or subconscious, whatever. Just a kind of an underlying understanding that anything that made Little Leff look bad would probably make Jeff look good."

"I imagine you're right," Hope said. "Guys like Kellicott seem more conniving than they really are, because their hearts are pure."

"That's deep, very deep. What does it mean?"

"Means that somebody like you looks at somebody like Kellicott and says, boy, is that a smart son of a bitch. He figures life out like a chess game, three or four moves ahead all the time."

"Doesn't he?"

"Not in quite such a calculating way, no. All it is, Kellicott only has one thing in his head. Getting to be secretary of state. So he looks at the entire world, everything, through that particular lens. Which socks should he wear? Where should he go to college? Who should he marry? No problem. He just checks off the boxes that will get him to the seventh floor of State the fastest."

"Doesn't he need a brain to know which boxes to check?"

"Not much of one. Those aren't tough choices to make. Anybody could figure out that a Yale degree is better than a CCNY degree, for instance, if what you want to be is secretary of state. What's that place where the swallows go?"

"Capistrano?"

"Okay, every one of those swallows knows the best way to Capistrano. That's a no-brainer."

"Of course none of them could get into Yale," I said.

"I'm not saying Kellicott isn't smart," Hope said. "I'm just saying that guys like him can look a lot more brilliant and Machiavellian than they are. Same way those swallows look pretty bright, for birds. But they're just machines that are programmed to get to that bell tower by a certain date."

"Still, I couldn't do it."

"Sure you could, if you were a machine for becoming secretary of state. Look at Sully Shapiro and Robert Holton."

One was a Democratic congressman from Ohio, the other had been deputy to one of Reagan's parade of national security advisers.

"Are they as close to it as Kellicott?"

"My guess is any one of the three could wind up with the job. I don't know Kellicott, but I do know the other two. And you're smarter than either of them."

"I just lack that instinct for the bell tower, huh?"

"You have more interesting instincts, thank God. But you can be just as single-minded."

"I was about wrestling, for years."

"And other things. Whenever you get interested, you don't let go. You're interested in Kellicott, aren't you?"

"Yeah, I am. You know one of the things I found out in the library? Kellicott was one of the most active backers of the Olympic boycott."

"So it's payback time?"

"No, that isn't it. What it is, he told me he had argued against the boycott. He didn't have to say that. He didn't have to say anything at all. I don't think we ought to have a secretary of state who lies when he doesn't have to."

"Actually," Hope said, "I think it's in the job description."

"It shouldn't be."

"I know. Look, I'll ask around in Washington next week. And you go see the ACLU guy up here, the head of our Boston office. He used to carry Kellicott's briefcase at State."

3

I MET TOBY INGERSOLL AT HIS OFFICE MONDAY MORNING. He was a round-faced, round-bellied young man wearing round glasses that needed polishing. His shoes needed no polishing, being sneakers. But they could have done with a scrubbing, or whatever you do with sneakers that have turned gray. He wore dark blue cotton socks, falling down, with clocks on them. I wouldn't have thought it was still possible to buy socks with clocks on them; maybe they had been in the family for a long time. Maybe his baggy gray flannels had been, too. Lately pleated pants seem to be coming back, but Ingersoll's pair, loose-cut, low-crotched, cuffed and untapered, hadn't been in style since before he was born. The rest of his fashion statement was a rumpled, button-down blue cotton shirt with the sleeves rolled up, and a four-dollar haircut.

I liked him immediately. I got the same feeling from

"What kind of a secretary will Kellicott make?" I asked Ingersoll.

"I'd rather see somebody like Shapiro or Holton in there."

"Why?"

"Because Kellicott's a lot smarter than they are."

"That's bad, huh?"

"Sure. If a job's not worth doing, it's not worth doing well."

"Secretary of state's not worth doing?"

"Not under any president we've had in my lifetime. Well, maybe Carter for the first few months. Before Brzezinski had poured too much poison in his ear."

"Yeah, well, okay. I can put it in my report that Kellicott is twice as smart as all the other candidates. That ought to finish him off."

"I don't expect to finish him off."

"But you'd like to?"

"I suppose I would."

"Well, go ahead, then. Do your best."

As Ingersoll described it, special assistants are like valets in one sense: if they're going to be any use to the boss, he's got to let them get close enough to see him with his clothes off. Kellicott seemed to have had no qualms about dropping trou in front of his aide; in fact he apparently did it enthusiastically, as part of the younger man's education. Most of the things Ingersoll told me were the small, routine obscenities of a successful bureaucrat's life: taking credit for the work of your subordinates, suppressing bad news and punishing its bearers, grabbing turf from rivals while protecting your own, massaging the facts until they seemed to support the boss's preconceptions, making sure that the boss never spoke alone with any of your subordinates—or, insofar as possible, with any other human being but you.

All of this was routine stuff which he had probably absorbed as a graduate student at Harvard, watching the professors snap and snarl like starving razorbacks over what few crumbs came their way. One of Ingersoll's stories, though, showed a nastiness well beyond the normal.

It was during the Iranian hostage crisis, if anything lasting 444 days can be called a crisis. But life went on, and on that particular day the problem that had brought Kellicott and his young aide to the White House situation room was death squads in El Salvador. The President was there, and a bunch of other people, and the White House expert on Latin America, a man named Paul Lasker. Lasker was Kellicott's opposite number at the White House, and his greatest bureaucratic enemy.

"Kellicott had been trying to get Lasker fired for eighteen months," Ingersoll said, "but the guy kept hanging on. It was driving poor old Alden nuts. At the time of this particular meeting, the issue between them was aid to El Salvador. Lasker wanted to cut it off, and Kellicott wanted to continue it.

"Lasker had a plane waiting for him at Andrews to take him to Argentina or some damned place, but he kept it waiting and fought on till he got agreement to cut off aid. He finally asked for a show of hands and won it, six to two. And one of the six was the President. Lasker figured that locked it up, so he grabbed his bags and headed for Andrews.

"Alden hadn't had much to say up to that point," Ingersoll said. "But then he moved in. He never said a harsh word about Lasker. In fact you came away thinking Paul was a warm, woolly, huggy-bear kind of a guy. Except he should never have been allowed out of the nursery to play with the grown-ups.

"You've heard Alden talk, that great voice he has.

Deep, reassuring. Makes you want to be just as reasonable and sensible and pragmatic and practical as he himself is. It's the voice your father should have had.

"Took him twenty minutes, but he turned the thing around. The next show of hands was four to three for continuing aid, and the President was one of the ones who switched. So that was that, or so I thought in my youthful ignorance.

"On the way back to Foggy Bottom I congratulated Kellicott on his win. I still remember what he said. Said it was irrelevant, he had it fixed on the Hill so Congress wouldn't cut the aid anyway. The real victory would come tomorrow. And so it did.

"Next day Evans and Novak said in their column that the administration had decided to cut off aid to El Salvador. Lots of colorful and accurate details. Even had a rundown of the six–two vote. You see the beauty of it, of course?"

"Sure," I said. "Lasker had to be the leaker, since he was the only one who left early and didn't know that the final vote went the other way. I assume the real leaker was Kellicott?"

"Actually I was. Kellicott had me call them."

"How much longer did the poor guy last?"

"Lasker? A week after he got back from the Argentina trip he was named ambassador to Burkina Faso. You know what the capital of Burkina Faso is?"

"Ouagadougou."

"Vicar of Christ, now Ouagadougou," Ingersoll said. "What is this shit?"

"I'm like Kellicott. I've got a trick memory."

"Oh, yeah? I bet you don't know what the embassy staff does for excitement in Ouagadougou."

"That I don't know."

"Every Sunday they go over to the ambassador's residence and look down the well."

"Out of curiosity, what he had you do to Lasker, is that the kind of thing that made you leave the government?"

"Hell, no, I still do that kind of thing. What do you think I'm doing right now?"

"You got a point there."

"The point is who you do it to, and why. In government, a lot of the time you're doing it to the good guys, for bad reasons. Now I try to do it for good reasons, to the bad guys."

"You think what you've given me on Kellicott will do it to him?"

"Hell, no. It'll be a character recommendation."

"Well, if anything more comes to mind, call this number and leave a message for me, okay?" I scribbled the number of the Tasty on a piece of paper for him.

Ingersoll shoved it into a corner of the old blotter on his desk, along with a dozen other slips of paper. "The only other thing that comes to mind is nothing, really," he said. "But two or three years ago I saw him down in the Combat Zone, coming out of a dirty bookstore. Tell you the truth, I was kind of surprised."

"Which dirty bookstore?"

"The one across from the Black Cat Theater."

"You don't mind my asking, what were you doing in the Combat Zone?"

"I don't mind your asking. I was coming out of a suck-and-fuck flick, something with Georgina Spelvin. You know her?"

"Not personally. But I know her work."

It was only quarter till eleven, and so I headed from Ingersoll's cluttered office to the cluttered former office of Axel, Shearman to see if I could catch Phil Jeffers before he took off for a fancy lunch on somebody else's expense account. I found him in the fax room, shouting at a volunteer, a skinny kid who looked about eighteen.

"I'm sorry, Mr. Jeffers," the kid was saying. He was red and ashamed and embarrassed and about to cry. "I tried to follow the instructions Louise gave me but the machine just ate it."

"Don't try to blame Louise, you dumb shit. Jesus fucking H. Christ, do I have to do every fucking thing myself around this fucking place?"

"I'm sorry, Mr. Jeffers. I said I was sorry." Then the most awful thing the kid could probably imagine happened and his eyes overflowed in front of the four or five other staffers who were standing around, being glad they weren't him. He turned and ran from the room.

"Boy oh boy, are you a tough son of a bitch," I said, keeping my tone flat and my voice just loud enough so all the staffers could hear. "I would never dare mess with a tough son of a bitch like you, not in a million years."

"Oh, fuck you, Bethany," Jeffers said. "Let him go home to Mama. Politics ain't beanbag."

"Oh, no, politics is hardball. Politics is hot kitchens. If I was a newsmagazine you know what I would call you, Phil? I would call you hard-boiled. That's how they spell *bully*."

"Did you come over here to piss on my leg or to earn your goddamn money?"

"Both."

"Well, now you pissed on my leg. Come on into the office."

He was really mad when we got alone, not just the playact mad he had been with the kid. It showed in the way he closed the door behind us, slow and careful, testing that it was good and shut—overcompensating because he wanted to smash the son of a bitch home with all his strength. He sat down behind his desk without motioning me to sit down. I sat down anyway. When other people get mad I slow down instead of speed up, for some reason. I get cold instead of getting hot back at them. That's what had got Jeffers so mad out in the fax room, and it was what was getting him madder now. I waited patiently.

"I never met a pain in the ass as bad as you," he finally said. "What is this shit, you dump on me in front of my people?"

"Who were you dumping on the kid in front of?"

"Fuck the kid."

I sat and waited. Jeffers rubbed his jaw and looked at me, and looked out the window, and looked at me again. He picked up the phone. "Louise," he said, "send the Shure kid in, okay?"

Neither of us said anything else till the kid came in. His cheeks weren't wet anymore but his eyes were still red. "Jason," he said, "this is Tom Bethany. He's helping us out."

"How do you do, Mr. Bethany," the kid said, still sounding shaky. I nodded. Jeffers got up, went over to the kid, and put his arm around the boy's shoulders.

"Jason here is helping us out, too," he said, at first to me. Then he spoke to the boy. "I was a shit to you out there, Jason," he said. "You know it?"

"That's all right, Mr. Jeffers."

"I could say I'm under a lot of pressure and all kinds of shit like that, but that would be shit, too. I didn't have to be a shit and I didn't have to say what I did to you, and I'm sorry."

"Really, Mr. Jeffers, it's okay."

"Phil." The boy stood silent. "Come on, say it," Jeffers said. "Phil."

"Phil."

Jeffers smiled. He took his arm from around the boy's shoulders. He shook the boy's hand with his right hand while his left hand gripped the boy's thin forearm. "Friends?" he asked.

"Friends," said the boy. Now he was smiling, too.

Jeffers took him out the door, patted him on the shoulders, and loud enough for a couple of nearby people to hear, said, "Hey, I just had the rag on, okay? I'm sorry."

When we were alone again, I said, "What can I say? I was wrong. Actually you're a really nice guy."

"Bullshit to that, too. But I'm not a stupid guy. I don't stay mad. Now I got a friend instead of an enemy, cost me two minutes."

I sat there. I wasn't the friend he had. Let him come to me.

"What've you got on the professor?" he said after a minute.

I gave him the biographical stuff, all of which he knew except for the nature of Kellicott's original relationship to the Miltons.

"That's just stuff from old clippings," he said when I wound down. "That's all you got?"

"Well, he told me the 'J.' in his name stands for Jephthah," I said, pronouncing it as Kellicott had during our interview, with the "p" hard.

"Yeah?" he said, so I spelled it for him.

"It's 'p, h,' " I said. "Pronounced 'f.' When he was a kid he called himself Jeff."

"So?"

"So Jep might sound weird and you might want to go by your middle name, but what's wrong with Jeff?"

"Stop jerking me around. What else have you got?"

"He's a prick, Phil. He's a knife artist."

"Literally?"

"Not literally, no. Literally he's not a prick, either. Only the part of him that made him rich."

"That's no crime."

"I've been talking to a few people, Phil. The guy is a compulsive liar and he's paranoid and he's completely amoral. Probably a very smooth borderline sociopath, or maybe not so borderline."

"Hey, we're not looking for Mother Teresa here. We're looking for a secretary of state."

"Well, I just thought you'd be glad to know you're on the right track. Only bad thing I could come up with is he likes dirty books."

"Dirty books?"

"I got a guy saw him coming out of a dirty bookstore in the Zone."

"So? Jacking off's no crime."

"I guess it depends what you jack off to." And I set right off to the Combat Zone to find out.

The Black Cat Theater was playing a pirate movie called *Jolly Rogered*, starring Jolly. The bookstore across the street had no name, unless its name was XXX ADULT BOOKS VIDEOS XXX. The shop window had been painted over so that you couldn't see inside. I went in, hoping it was air-conditioned, and it was.

To the right of the door was a sort of cubicle, raised up so that the enormously fat man sitting in it could overlook the racks. He was doing paperwork at his desk, and barely bothered to glance up when I came in. The three or four customers didn't even do that much. Each man pretended he was alone, kept quiet, and minded his own business. Dirty bookstores are the last public places in America where good manners survive. Or almost.

"This ain't a library," the fat man brayed. Even then the customers remained polite, pretending that no one had rudely raised his voice. And in fact the fat man had sounded bored, not angry. Like everybody else, I continued to paw through the picture books. Where I was, they had names like *Bottoms Up* and *Hershey Highways*. Other sections were devoted to cunnilingus, pregnant women, bondage and sadomasochism, overdeveloped mammaries, pedophilia, homosexuality, obese women, biracial couples, and fellatio. There was even a small section that catered to the unweaned, as far as I could tell. Who else would pay twelve bucks to look at breasts dribbling milk?

After I had checked the stock out pretty thoroughly, I went up to the fat man on his enclosed platform. "Got anything with kangaroos?" I asked.

"Huh?"

"Kangaroos."

"Kangaroos?"

"Right. You know, with pouches. I like pouches."

"Nah, we don't carry it. I doubt they make it. I never heard of it."

Once again, I was missing connections somehow. When I'm serious, people think I'm trying to be funny. And when I'm trying to be funny, they take it seriously.

"Just a little joke," I said.

"This is a bookstore, Jack," the fat man said.

"Oh, right. Well, actually, what I wanted was something else anyway. I wanted to ask, are you the manager?"

"Yeah, I'm the manager. Why?"

"Well, I was looking for this certain item I saw in here maybe three years ago."

"What item?"

"Probably you wouldn't recognize it from my description unless you were here then."

"Six years I been here, all right? Every book goes in and out of here, I know it."

"Well, it's not a book, that's the thing. It's this guy. Ever see him in here?"

The fat man looked at the photograph of Kellicott I had handed him and said, "What is this shit? You a cop or what?"

I slid a folded twenty-dollar bill across the raised counter toward him, keeping my hand firmly on it. That let him know I wasn't a cop; in his line of work the cash flow was to cops, not from them. His manner changed from uncertain confusion to hostility.

"You're not here to buy books, you better get out," he said.

"I don't want to know who he is," I said. "Just what kind of books he buys."

"Out."

A good idea came to me. "See, I already know who he is," I said. "He's a rich guy. You tell me what he reads, I'll give you his name." But the fat man was too stupid to see the blackmail possibilities in my good idea, which was probably why he was the manager of a porno bookstore instead of something higher in the organization, like a drug dealer or a loan shark.

"All right, asshole," he said. "You asked for it."

He reached under the counter to press a button. I heard it ring in the back, where you paid a quarter to watch a few seconds of a dirty movie in a dirty booth. A short, wide, strong black man with a lot of scar tissue around his eyes came out.

"Lou?" he asked the fat man.

"Asshole here won't leave," Lou said.

The man put his hand on my shoulder, which is a move that a wrestler deals with thousands of times over the years. I forced him to his knees and leaned into his wrist joint enough to make him scream. Now my fellow customers were paying attention. So was Lou.

I made the man turn over onto his face on the floor and ran my free hand over him. Once I had taken away the balisong butterfly knife he carried, I set him loose.

"I know a lot of shit like that," I told him. "Try me again and I'll break both your thumbs."

The man said nothing. Lou said nothing. I said to Lou, "You, you fat fuck, you sicced him on me."

Without giving Lou time to think that over, I grabbed a handful of the belly that strained his dingy T-shirt. I squeezed the fat as hard as I could and twisted it, like turning off a faucet. Another thing you develop in wrestling is a really strong grip. Now Lou screamed, too, which seemed only fair.

The sudden summer daylight was blinding when the Red Line train first came up out of the ground on its way over to Cambridge. Several convicts were leaning against the grid work of bars that covers the windows of the Charles Street Jail. One flashed a finger at the train as it rolled along the trestle nearly level with his third-floor window. Only a few sailboats were out in the boat basin, and those were under power, with their sails slack. There was no breath of wind. The air was heavy with lightning to come. But for the moment the sky was bright blue, except for a line of dark clouds off to the northwest. The train went underground again, once it had crossed the river over to the Cambridge side. I thought about what I had learned at the bookstore, which was absolutely nothing. Even more discouraging, what if Lou had taken my money and told me that the customer in my photo liked to look at wet shots in the privacy of his own home, or at pictures of Oriental transvestites? When you came right down to it, so what?

When I surfaced from the Harvard Square T-stop, the weather was no more threatening, and no less. The storm seemed likely to hold off till the evening. From the pay phone in the Tasty, I called the direct number Kellicott had given me.

"Tom Bethany," I said when he answered. "Any chance of seeing you for a half hour or so this afternoon?"

"Pretty tough, today. Is it something we could do over the phone?"

"Well, I need to know about a couple or three things maybe we shouldn't talk about over the phone."

"All right. Listen, I'll be tied up for probably another half hour," he said when I asked if I could see him again. "Can we make it for then?"

I said we could, and ordered some coffee. The Red Sox were on the radio. When the action in wrestling reaches the level of baseball's most exciting moments, the ref calls you for stalling. So instead of listening to the game, I got to thinking about something equally motionless, my background investigation of Kellicott. Gossip from the old headmaster and the young civil rights lawyer were the high points so far, but as Karl Marx said about John Stuart Mill, they drew their eminence from the general flatness of the terrain. The dozen or so other people I had talked to had nothing but praise for Kellicott. He was brilliant, patriotic, a devoted husband and father, a tireless public servant, a scholar of world renown, a generous, kindly, sensitive, thoughtful, and so on and so forth human being. But when the vote gets unanimous or close to it, I can't help remembering that the Tonkin Gulf resolution passed the Senate 88 to 2. And the only senators who managed to get it right were the two, Morse and Gruening.

They lost, though, and it looked like I would, too. I still had a credit check to run, and Kellicott's home life to look into. But if those wells turned out to be dry, as it seemed likely that they would, candidate Markham could announce his selection of Kellicott to be secretary of state. Still, like Morse, I would give it my best shot. After a second cup of coffee, I headed down JFK Street to the JFK School, which is just this side of JFK Park. All are located in JFK's old congressional district, which was now represented by JFK's nephew.

The windows to Kellicott's office were open, and he had the big floor fan trained on him. The clutter on his desk was weighted down with staplers, books, coffee cups, whatever was handy and heavy. Papers fluttered in the hot wind. Kellicott waved me to a chair and hauled the fan around so that it blew in my direction. Then he left his desk and took a seat beside me, in the breeze.

"How's it coming along?" he said. "Everybody cooperating with you?"

"Oh, yes," I said, leaving fat Lou and his punch-drunk swamper out of it.

"Good. I was afraid that various misguided souls might think they were doing me a favor by not talking with you." I noticed that he was calling me nothing—not Tom, or Bethany, or Mr. Bethany. He must have filed away my failure to pick up on his earlier invitation to call him Alden, and decided reciprocity was the polite and tactful course of action.

"No, pretty near everybody thinks you're great stuff, and they didn't mind telling me about it."

"Well, they probably want jobs."

I smiled. Whenever I saw Kellicott in person I felt less

hostile toward him. Like lawyers. In the abstract I hate them, but I like most of the ones I know. One of them I even love. And for most people, to know Kellicott seemed to be to love him. The only exceptions were his old headmaster and his old gofer at the State Department. If his gofer didn't like him, I wondered what his various secretaries through the years had thought of him; but my Labor Day deadline probably wouldn't leave me enough time to find out. First things first.

"One or two things," I said. "Do you have somebody to handle your business affairs or do you do it yourself?"

"Fellow named Harvey Atkins, at Atkins Sherrold Fitch & Bursley. I'll tell him you're coming. The main thing you'll find out is that I've got more money than any one person deserves to have. I made it the old-fashioned way, too. Married it."

Again I smiled back at him. "Any potential trouble with your investment portfolio?" I asked.

"Take a look, but there shouldn't be. When I first went down to Washington, I had Harvey clean it out, much against his better judgment. Sold Nestlé because of the baby formula flap. Sold all my stuff from companies that did business in South Africa. Don't eat grapes, don't drink Coors. Well, I don't go quite that far, although it's true I don't drink Coors. But that's because it's watery."

"What about your real estate? Deeds clean?"

"By clean I imagine you mean restrictive covenants. Actually, there was one on our property out on the Vineyard. Unenforceable, of course, but I wouldn't buy the place till they took it off. Which they did. Harvey can show you the papers."

"Ever had electroshock therapy?"

"Nope."

"Been to a psychiatrist or psychologist or anything at all along those lines?"

"Nope." Kellicott paused. "But maybe you should know that my wife had a pretty rough time psychologically when she was younger. I could put you in touch with her various doctors if you think it's necessary."

"Not unless it's still a problem."

"No, it's all behind her, thank God. Just an unusually stormy passage through adolescence."

"Ever been prescribed any medication for depression, insomnia, hyperactivity, or any other emotional or behavioral disorder? You, I mean, not her."

"Not insomnia, really. I've taken sleeping pills now and then, to help beat jet lag problems. I take Valium as a muscle relaxant when my back goes out, which happens once or twice a year."

"Do you take any other drugs at all?"

"Actually I don't. Except for the damned back, my health is perfect."

"Benzedrine, amphetamines, diet pills, Quaaludes, cocaine, marijuana, heroin, any drug at all that you can't buy over the counter?"

"Alcohol, but you can buy that over the counter."

"How much alcohol?"

"Sometimes I take a drink before dinner. Most times, I guess, although it isn't quite a daily habit. Wine is. We always have wine with dinner."

"Do you ever have severe hangovers?"

"Once in college."

"Any disciplinary action taken against you in college or graduate school?"

"Nope."

"Plagiarism, cheating?"

"Like poor old Joe Biden? No. Wait a minute, I take that back. When I was nine or ten I copied a paper from my best friend. My future brother-in-law, in fact."

"I imagine the Senate would let that one slide."

"I imagine so, yes."

"Anything in your past that might disturb a red-blooded he-man like Lee Atwater?"

"Am I homosexual, do you mean?"

"I have to ask."

"I know. The answer is no. Not even a schoolboy experience."

"What about rampant heterosexuality, then?"

"Like poor old Gary? No, I'm pretty well settled in at home. Actually, though, maybe there is something along those lines you ought to know about."

"What's that?"

"There was a time when I used to make the rounds of pretty nearly every strip joint and topless bar in the Boston area. I wouldn't imagine anybody would know that, but it would certainly look odd if it ever came out."

"What did you do it for, then?"

"My daughter Emily, who died. Didn't you say on the phone you were interested in her? Or was it my other daughter, Phyllis?"

"Both, I imagine. Emily at the moment, I guess. She was why you were making the rounds, you say?"

"Yes, she was why. I'd go out nights looking for her, try to get her to come home whenever I found her. Those are the kinds of places I had to look."

"Would she be a customer or working?"

"Working. Waitressing at first. Then on to the other things. Finally, of course, she got herself killed."

"You think that's what she was trying to do all along?"

"I sometimes think so, but who can say?"

"I guess you should tell me about her."

"All right, if you think it's necessary." Kellicott was still for a long moment, composing himself perhaps, or getting his thoughts together.

"Emily was a difficult child," he started out. "Right from the start, right from kindergarten, she had trouble with authority. She was so smart that school bored her. Well, it bored me, too, till I got to the postgraduate level. But I used school in a rational way. I didn't fight back against it the way she did.

"The first time she ran away she was only seven. She walked two miles to a school friend's house and asked to stay there. The friend's parents called us, naturally. Wasn't the last time we'd get calls like that, I'm afraid to say. By the time she was in the eighth grade, she had started to cut school and hang out at the malls. Sometimes she'd stay out all night, too, God knows where. When she was fourteen, she had an abortion . . . This isn't too easy to talk about . . ."

That was plain from his voice. I didn't offer him any encouragement; he'd have to decide for himself if he wanted to go on. He did.

". . . Do you know Buckingham, Browne and Nichols? They start them out in kindergarten, you know. Right up to college. All through the elementary years, she at least did well in her schoolwork, but then it changed. Drugs, I'm sure, even though the school never actually caught her. The worst boys she could find. The only reason she got into a decent college was because I got after her at the beginning of her junior year about her grades. Not that getting after her had ever worked before, but that year she took a few minutes off to get straight A's. I presume the idea was to show her contempt for the whole process, probably for me, too, by demonstrating how easy it was. It was enough to get her into Wellesley, though, just barely. That and the fact that she was a development case."

"What's that?" I asked.

"That's the delicate way that deans of admission refer

to a kid whose parents are in a position to build the place a new gym. Not that we ever got around to building one, or would have. Anyway, Emily managed to stick it out for a while without going to hardly any classes, but then she dropped out entirely in May of her freshman year. From then on she just drifted further and further away from us, just sank down and down . . ."

"Did she keep in touch?"

"Not directly, but I think she wanted us to know roughly what she was up to. She'd tell friends, and they'd tell us. Never exactly where she was, but in general what she was up to. And I'd go looking. Pretty tough stuff, to be sitting there in the dark in some sleazy dump, and see your daughter come out on the runway and take it off for a bunch of drunken sailors."

"Would you go backstage afterward?"

"If I could. Or wait for her outside. She'd laugh at me if she was sober, or scream at me if she was drunk or on drugs, or whatever she did. I never told her mother when I found her, or even that I was looking for her."

"Did she use her own name?"

"I don't know, actually. If part of the idea was to humiliate me, us, she may have used the family name. And made it clear to everybody just what family it was. I just don't know. I don't even know where she was living all those years, or who she was with, or what name she used. Not sure I want to know."

"Well, did they announce her by her right name when she danced?"

"I never really saw her dance. I don't think I could have stood that. I left before she came on."

"Then I suppose there's at least a chance that none of her new pals knew her real name," I said. "In any event, as long as Markham's people know about the situation in advance, I can't imagine it causing any trouble if it does come up. Hell, even the Eagleton thing could have been contained if he had been honorable enough to tell McGovern about it beforehand."

"That was my thought at the time, too. Very poor behavior."

"Do you remember the names of the places Emily worked?"

"Do you really need ... Well, if you do, you do."

Kellicott reeled off from memory the names and addresses of the topless bars and strip joints where he had run across his daughter, and I just nodded instead of writing them down. We were two teenagers showing off our grips.

"I'm going to need to talk to your wife and your other daughter, too," I said. "What time would work out?"

"Let's see. Today's Monday. Friday they're taking off for the Vineyard. I'm going with them and coming back Sunday night, but they're going to stay on through Labor Day. So we should do it this week. I'll let you know when I set it up. That number you gave me at the Tasty is still the only way to reach you?"

"The quickest way, yes."

On the way out of the JFK School I spotted an untended phone on a receptionist's desk. Dialing nine got me an outside line, and I called the Boston office of the ACLU. It was after five, but Toby Ingersoll was still there.

"This is the guy you were talking to earlier," I said. "I've just come from talking to our buddy."

"Hello, guy I was talking to earlier. Are you calling from a bugged phone?"

"I doubt it. It's a phone right outside his office. I figured maybe I was calling to a bugged phone, though. Meese said you were a lobby for criminals."

"Sometimes we are, I guess. What can I do for you?"

"The time you saw our guy in the Zone, was it day or night?"

"Night. Eleven, maybe."

"Are you sure he was coming out of the bookstore?"

"Pretty sure."

"I mean, could he have just been walking by? Maybe just stopped in front of it to tie his shoelace or peek in or something?"

"It's possible."

"You don't have any specific memory of him coming out of the door?"

"Not really, no."

"Was he carrying anything?"

"In a plain brown wrapper? I don't remember. Probably I didn't notice. I was about to come out of the theater when I spotted him. Tell you the truth, I turned around right away so he wouldn't see me. When I looked again, he was gone."

"So he was in the Zone, but you can't actually connect him with the bookstore."

"Except that he was in front of it, no. I should have made that clear."

As I hung up, the receptionist came back to her desk. "Sorry to steal your phone," I said, hoping I looked like a visiting dignitary. "There was a number I had to leave for Professor Kellicott."

The woman smiled, just as if this made perfect sense. As it would have made perfect sense for Kellicott to be wandering the Zone at night, searching for his daughter.

4

I ATE AN EARLY SUPPER MONDAY IN EMACK & BOLIO'S ICE cream parlor—an Oreo cookie cone. For dessert I had a French vanilla cone. Then I spent the evening in the reference room of Widener Library, putting my notes together in some sort of preliminary order for the report I'd probably have to submit to Markham's people.

Throughout the evening, a storm threatened but never hit. The air was heavy, waiting. Tuesday was like Monday, hazy, humid, hot. I spent it running down more loose ends in the library. None of them seemed to lead anywhere interesting. Toward the end of the afternoon, physically and mentally stale, I gave it up.

Outside the weather had changed. Thunder rumbled a long way off. The sky was beginning to darken, and the light had the strange, clear quality it gets just before all hell breaks loose. I hurried toward my car so I could go out to Fresh Pond and run around it. I like to run in storms, even electrical storms. G. Gordon Liddy used to climb on top of haystacks when he was a kid, to conquer his fear of lightning. Presumably nobody ever told him that fear of lightning is a mark of sanity. Personally, I try to believe that I run in storms not because of the lightning, but in spite of it. The proof is that when there's lightning around, I abandon my usual treeless route along the Charles. Instead I run around the reservoir out at Fresh Pond, where the trees make better lightning targets than I do. And I'm willing to run a certain reasonable risk for the pleasure of being sluiced cool after a steaming day. And, face it, for the sensation of facing down the Furies. Come right down to it, maybe I'm as crazy as Liddy.

The weird, greenish light held till I got to Ellery Street, where my car was parked, and most of the way out to Fresh Pond. Then fat drops of rain began to splat on the windshield, making craters in the dust that covered it. In less than a minute water was sheeting down the glass faster than the wipers could throw it aside. The cars on Memorial Drive slowed down, headlights went on, traffic poked along at twenty-five or thirty, each car sending out plumes of water to both sides.

When I pulled off the road into the small public parking lot provided by the Cambridge Water Board, the rain was still driving and the wind was threshing the trees. Inside the car it was steamy and stifling. My clothes came off reluctantly, sticking to my sweaty skin. To run naked would have been best; a poor second best were the nylon shorts and Nike training flats I put on before getting out of the car.

I am alive by accident.

The first of my prerun stretches is a squat and I was just dropping into it at the last second that would have saved me. An instant earlier and the man running unheard at me in the storm would have killed me standing; an instant later and he would have had time to adjust his strike downward.

As it was, something made me aware of a presence behind me. I hesitate to get mystical about these things, but a good many years spent dealing with fast-moving, hostile opponents either develops more than five senses or sharpens the way the five work. A pressure in the air, a scent? In any event, I turned my head and caught movement on the periphery, and I spun right as I dropped. I swung my right foot like a scythe into his ankle so that his momentum pitched him forward. He somersaulted and came up to face me, a pale shape in the storm with the glitter of a knife in its hand.

To do his job he had to come in on me, but to do mine, all I had to do was wait until he came into reach. When he did, stabbing down with his right hand, I caught his wrist and pulled his arm across my chest. There was no calculation in this, just an automatic continuation of the hundreds of hours I had spent back in Iowa working on the Russian two-on-one till it took no more thought than breathing. With my left hand I took him under the right arm, crossed in front of him, and tossed him over my hip to the ground.

Causing pain is at the heart of wrestling as a sport. Pain is a tool you use to move your opponent the way you want him to move. He does it because the pain is talking to him, and what it is telling him is that his body is about to be torn or broken if he doesn't move to relieve the pressure. But the referee is there to keep you from breaking his body, when wrestling is a sport. Now it was no sport. Now I put my left knee into his back and deliberately popped his right arm out of the shoulder socket. He grunted and dropped the knife.

I held onto the dislocated arm while I made sure he

had no more weapons on him, and then let him loose. When he turned to run, I got him by his trailing ankle and brought him down heavily before he could take the second step. He couldn't break the fall with his useless arm, and so he came down with his full weight on that shoulder. This time he screamed with the pain, but just once, and then he lay there defiant. His lips were open in a grimace of pain, but his teeth were clamped shut. They were square, yellow, horselike teeth. He looked Hispanic, with a trace of Indian in his features. I dropped down to my knees beside him.

"Who sent you?" I asked. He said nothing.

"What's your name?" Still nothing.

"¿Como se llama?"

This time he spoke. "Chinga tu madre," he said. Between us we had now exhausted most of the Spanish I knew.

I looked for the knife he had dropped, but it was lost in the mud somewhere. I had another one, though, the balisong knife I had taken off the black pug earlier. In all my life I had never taken a knife from anyone, and now, in a single day, I had done it to two men. I went to the car and took the pug's knife from the glove compartment where I had tossed it.

"Come on, Pedro," I said, gesturing for him to get up. "We're going into the woods where we can talk without bothering anybody."

He didn't get up, and so I took him by the bad arm and he followed it the way a bull follows his nose ring. All that held his arm to the rest of him was skin, nerves, blood vessels, and the complicated system of muscles that previously rotated the arm in its socket. At the very least he would have to sleep on one side for the rest of his life.

I led him off to the right of the parking lot, past a

jumble of cables, cast-iron pipe, broken hydrants, and other Water Board debris. Once we were into a little patch of woods, hidden from the jogging path and the highway, I had him stop. All fight was out of him now. The shock had passed off and the pain made his face gray under its natural olive. The rain plastered his long black hair flat to his forehead. The strands hung down below his cheekbones, and drops ran off them. I shook the blade out of the butterfly knife, and he began to chant what I took to be a prayer. I wondered how many murderous bastards had ended their lives with a prayer to the God who was about to burn them in eternal fire if their beliefs were correct. He prayed faster as I approached him with the knife.

I took hold of his light jacket and carefully, slowly, sliced the sleeve off. My idea was to have a look at his shoulder. Once he saw what I was doing, he stopped praying, from the tone of him, and started cursing. It took me a moment to figure out why he was all of a sudden mad instead of scared. Then I understood.

I had paid no attention to what he was wearing, except for registering in a general way that he looked like a prisoner escaped from some Latin American jail, dressed in third-world surplus fatigues. Looking closer, though, I saw that he was wearing an Ellesse cotton outfit—what they call running suits, although I've never seen one worn for running. It probably cost a couple weeks' wages for an honest man. On his feet were a pair of Nike Air Balance shoes with bright blue patches that made his toes seem to glow. My man was a sharp dresser, and that was why he had abandoned prayer for curses. He cared more for his "Miami Vice" threads than he did for his soul, or even his skin.

Noting his concern, I sliced his sodden Don Johnson outfit to ribbons and left him standing naked except for

a pair of ridiculous purple bikini undies and a gold
Rolex. I took the gold watch; somebody I liked might
find a use for it someday. Nobody I liked would ever
find a use for a purple bikini, though, and so I sliced
that off his body, too. By now the rain was slowing, but
it still came down hard enough so that water ran from
the end of his penis as if he were pissing. Maybe he
was. I would have been.

Dislocations look much more serious than they are.
The knob on the end of the humerus, now out of its
socket, made a lump the size of a jumbo egg on the front
of his shoulder. The lump was a dark, angry red that
would soon turn black. It is a common enough injury in
wrestling, and I knew from people who had been there
that the pain was terrible. I also knew that a lot of the
pain would go away, almost from one second to the
next, once the bone was reseated. And I was pretty sure
I knew how to do that, since I had twice watched team
doctors do it.

I tried to get all this across to the man, talking slowly
and simply and using sign language in case his English
was shaky. He didn't say whether he understood. He
didn't say anything. But I figured he must know some
English, if he was functioning enough in this country to
get a job as a murderer. I made it as clear as I could that
I would put his shoulder back together and make the
pain go away if he answered my questions.

"Where's the car?" I said. "¿Donde está automobile
usted? Car?" I held up his keys, which were the only
things I had found in his pocket. "¿Donde?"

He had to have followed me out there in a car, and
its registration might tell me who he was. But there were
plenty of cars parked in walking distance, and the storm
was lifting, and I didn't want to risk leaving my captive
while I wandered around trying doors like a car thief. I

had to get finished with him in a hurry, in fact, since joggers and dog walkers and motorists would come drifting back into the neighborhood as soon as the evening sun came out. Already the sky was getting lighter and steam was rising from the soaked ground. The thunder was far in the distance as the storm moved out to sea.

My catch said nothing. He wouldn't give his name, he wouldn't say who sent him, and he wouldn't tell me which car was his. He just stood there, furious, scared, stubborn, and naked. And in agony. I felt as sorry for him as he would have felt for me, after stabbing me to death. I herded him back to the car, where I opened the trunk and took what I needed from the jumble of tools, implements, and equipment in it. Back in the shelter of the woods, I twisted a length of wire around the wrist of his functioning arm, and tied it above his head to the limb of a maple tree. Probably the circulation to his hand would be cut off after a while. I thought about that and couldn't work up much concern. With the old pawnshop Polaroid I kept in the trunk, I took a picture of his face. It probably wouldn't do me much good, but without a photograph I'd stand no chance at all of ever finding out who the man was.

After taking a few steps back toward the car, I turned around to give him a last chance. I told him I'd let him loose and give him back his keys and kiss his boo-boo and make it well if he decided to talk. He talked.

"Tu madre," he said again, and so I threw his keys over the Cyclone link fence, into Fresh Pond.

It would still be hours till nightfall, and the sun after the storm was bright as I drove back down along the Charles. I parked on Plympton Street and set out on my delayed run. My plan out by Fresh Pond had been to do intervals, but now I set out at an easy, steady seven miles to the hour. The loop up to Arsenal Street Bridge and back was a few yards over five miles, which ought to take me five sevenths of sixty minutes, which I tried to figure out for a while but then gave up on. Easier to run it and see what my throwaway Casio said at the end.

The footing was a little soggy, but not too bad. The pace was enough below what I could do if I pushed myself so that I was able to think about something other than my lungs and legs as I went along the riverbank. It occurred to me, too late, that I should have left the man loose and left him his keys. Then I could have driven out of sight, sneaked back, and followed him to whichever car was his. At least that way I would have had his registration number, and might even have been able to trail him home.

No question but that there was a certain lack of brilliance in walking away from a man who had just tried to kill you, with nothing but a snapshot to find him by. Why had he tried, though? Think it out. Could it have anything to do with the unpleasantness at XXX ADULT BOOKS VIDEOS XXX? Unlikely on the face of it, but barely possible. The man could have followed me from the store easily enough, although it was hard to figure out why he would have done such a thing.

Or he could have nothing to do with the bookstore; could have had my car staked out for some entirely different reason. This would probably mean he had tracked me home at some point, which was a very disturbing thought. It meant that he could find me again, and that I would have to move. On the other hand he could have picked me up at the Tasty, which wasn't so disturbing. Plenty of people knew that I was in and out of there every day. From there he could have followed me to the library and then to my car—in which case he wouldn't necessarily know where I lived.

Those were the only two answers I could see to the question of how, but they didn't get me anywhere with why. No random maniac follows you in a driving thunderstorm, tries to kill you, and then, through the pain of a dislocated arm, keeps his mouth shut except to tell you what to do with your mother. But I couldn't think of why anyone but a random maniac would want to murder me. Although lots of people had reason to dislike me, I didn't think I was unpopular to quite that extent. At least not with anybody who was out of jail at the moment. It had been a long time since I had worked on anything that even involved a murderer.

And then it came to me I was involved, even though at a considerable remove, in just such a business right now. Somebody, after all, had murdered Kellicott's daughter. For there to be any connection, though, whoever wanted me dead would have to be somebody who knew that I was stirring around in Kellicott's past life. That narrowed it down to Senator Markham, Phil Jeffers, Arthur Kleber, and anyone else in the campaign that they might have informed; to Kellicott and, presumably, his family; to the Miltons' gardener and the past and present headmasters of Indian Mountain School and the assistant headmaster and librarian of Hotchkiss School; to Hope and Toby Ingersoll and the fat man at the bookstore, if he knew who Kellicott was; to the dozen or more colleagues and associates of Kellicott's that I had interviewed; and to anybody that any of those people had happened to talk to since. It wasn't a crowd that would fill Shea Stadium, but it was big enough.

And it was even a little bit bigger, now that I thought about it. A few days back I had telephoned my only cop connection, Jackie Carr, to ask him to find out about whatever dealings the Cambridge Police Department might have had with Kellicott over the years. Jackie had left a message with Ralph at the Tasty for me to call him back, which I hadn't done yet. Right now he'd be off duty, but I'd probably be able to catch him at the VFW. Why he did his drinking at the VFW was because his lieutenant had warned him to go light on the booze, and nobody from the cops that might snitch on him hung out at the VFW. Why he drank at all, or one of the reasons, was so he could face up to going home to his responsibilities. Jackie had a lot of trouble with being a grown-up.

I found Jackie Carr playing darts with a couple of other gentlemen of our generation. Baby-boom vets hitting the wall at forty, down at the VFW hall. After his pals had beat him, he brought his beer over and joined me.

"Fucking darts, you imagine?" he said. "Not like the old days, huh?"

Well, he was right about that. In the old days we would have been sitting around the bar in the USAID compound in Vientiane after work, wondering whether to get our ashes hauled at Loulou's, the White Rose, or the Bamboo Forest. I had known Jackie for about three weeks back then, before he was rotated out of the air attaché's office in Laos. I was just beginning my tour with the army attaché's office. We hadn't been real buddies even for those three weeks, but you wouldn't have thought it when we ran into each other in Kendall Square more than a decade later. I had forgotten he was from Cambridge, if I ever knew it. He had just gotten married and joined the police department. I had just come to town to see if I could get a Harvard education without going to Harvard. Naturally we went off to have a few beers together, three or four for me and maybe twelve or fifteen for him. I took him home staggering drunk and his wife never forgave me. She figured I was a bad influence on her Jackie. I knew about that. I had a wife once, too, and back then I was a drunk like Jackie. My wife always blamed my friends, too.

"Not like the old days," I agreed.

"Remember the meat rack?" Jackie asked. I remembered. It was a bar in the Somboun Hotel that stayed open later than the other bars in town, so that all the hookers who hadn't connected yet came by to make one last stab at finding a customer for the night.

"Those were the days," Jackie said, ". . . my friend . . ."

"We thought they'd never end," I finished. And so we didn't. In our young lives, the war seemed to have been going on forever. But we had all come a long ways since then, and Jackie and I hadn't really been friends then anyway, and some son of a bitch had tried to kill me a few hours back. Back to business.

"How's it going, Jackie?" I asked. "Still busting heads?"

"Shit, it's all paper work. Might as well be a fuckin' clerk, tell you the fuckin' truth."

"How's Catherine and the kids?"

"Ah, she's okay. Busts my balls a lot. Sometimes I think I ought to walk away. You had the right idea, Tom, you know it?"

"I didn't walk away. She did."

"Whatever."

"I got your message from Ralphie. Have anything on my guy?"

"Professor whatisit? Kelly something?"

"Kellicott."

"Fuck kind of a name is that? Anyway, he filed his daughter as a runaway with Juvenile a couple of times, way the fuck back in the seventies. Both times she showed up back home after a few days. Last year some asshole sideswiped his car in Inman Square and split. Got him pretty good, sixteen hundred bucks' damage."

"That's it, huh?"

"That's it. Except for his daughter got wasted, you heard about that, I guess. But you wanted him, not her."

"No, I want her, too. You know anything about it?"

"Only that we never got the asshole."

"Can you get me a look at the file?"

"Maybe. I guess I could. Over lunch I could take it out, maybe, something like that."

"Tomorrow?"

"I could see. Call me, okay?"

We talked about Laos for a while and what a good time we had had there, mostly him talking. He was envious because he had only done six months in-country, whereas I did two years with the ARMA office and then three more with Air America after I got out of the army.

"It was like being rich, you know it?" Jackie said. "On a sergeant's pay, it was like being a fuckin' millionaire. *Bo pin nyang*, have yourself a good time, who gives a shit? You're rich. Here I get hassled at the fuckin' VFW, I get a few bucks behind on my tab."

"How much you running?"

"Hundred sixty, hundred seventy, like that."

"Shit, let my client take care of it. I'm on expenses."

"Oh, yeah? What are you working on?"

"Background check for employment." I put four fifties, folded, under my coaster and slid it over to him. "Buy us both a beer with this," I said. "It's a big outfit. If we don't take their money, somebody else will."

I didn't need to pay his tab, since he had already agreed to get me the file for the price of a free lunch. But I wanted to get him in the habit of taking money from me, in case I ever needed something tough. Besides, it wasn't my money.

By 8:30, Jackie was laying a solid foundation for a brand-new tab at the VFW and I had broken loose from him. Not knowing where else to start, I decided to show the Polaroid of my Hispanic attacker around in every bar, restaurant, and hotel where I was acquainted. Since this meant mostly in the Harvard Square area, I started there. The night manager of the Sheraton Commander had hired hundreds of Hispanics over the years, but not mine. The owner of the Greenhouse Coffee Shop didn't know him, and I had no better luck across the street at the Wursthaus. Moving right along, I found Chris Catchick behind the bar at the One Potato, Two Potato.

"What makes you think he's from Cambridge?" Chris said. He was an old friend and I had told him the whole story of the attack.

"Nothing except he was here and I'm here now and I've got to start some place."

"And when you think immigrant you think of the food service industry?"

"Actually I do, yeah. If a guy ran into the kitchen hollering, 'Green cards!' he'd shut down any restaurant in Cambridge."

"Actually you're probably right, but that's a lot of restaurants. Why don't you just buy me a Sam Adams and take your picture down to the union hall tomorrow morning?"

"Why is it I suddenly feel like such an idiot? Bring me one, too."

By the time I had finished breakfast Wednesday morning—which was a microwaved portion of the stew I make and freeze every Sunday—I had worked out a story to tell when I got to the Berkeley Street office of Local 26, Hotel Restaurant Institutional Employees & Bartenders Union. My story involved a former employee of my fictional restaurant who had left some valuable stuff in his locker, and so forth. It struck me as a pretty good story, but I never got a chance to find out if it would have worked. Instead, I got lucky.

On my way to catch the T into Boston I got to thinking about the empty lot I was passing, where Mass. Ave. and Harvard Street come together. Till not too long ago the lot had held a funky, beat-up, 1930s Gulf station with a blue cupola on top. But the building disappeared over Christmas vacation, when most of the local landmark lovers would be off work, out of town, or not paying attention. The station had been bulldozed flat by its greed-crazed landlord, Harvard University. Harvard figured a hotel on the property would make more money than an old Gulf station would, and the hell with whether the old station was a wonderful piece of period kitsch or not.

Also the hell with whether a hotel would overshadow, literally and architecturally, the historic church next door. The Old Cambridge Baptist Church was a large, awkward, but oddly attractive pile of black stones. It wasn't the kind of place you'd go to for that old-time religion, from a pastor in a powder blue double-knit polyester suit, hollering hellfire sermons against the pope and the perils of the big city. Macon, for instance, or Lubbock.

In the Baptist house are many mansions, apparently, because Old Cambridge Baptist catered to an entirely different crowd. Its parishioners drove old VW beetles, carried books and babies around in backpacks, and ate tasteless stuff like tofu instead of tasteless stuff like grits. They let their nave be used for union rallies. Their basement was a warren of offices that promoted various liberal causes. Among other things, Old Cambridge Baptist was a principal way station on the underground railroad that carried refugees from Central America to extralegal political asylum in this country.

With nothing much more in mind than that a lot of Hispanics must hang around the place, I found the basement entrance and went in. A cramped corridor led from one end of the church to the other, with tiny offices on both sides. On the doors were signs, often two or three to a door, for committees for this and that, mostly justice, freedom, liberty, equality, fair play, and equally subversive things. I picked the Committee for the Brotherhood of the Americas more or less at random. Inside I found two college-age girls stuffing envelopes, and a thin young man only a few years older. A sign on his desk said he was Jeff Lichtenberg.

The young man listened to me politely as I told him the story I had dreamed up in the hall. This maid working in my motel in New Hampshire, an illegal from one of those countries down in Central America, heard that her cousin had beat it out of the country before the secret police, and on and on. Anyway, his name was Ricardo Sanchez, and . . .

"Ricardo Sanchez is about as common a name down there as Bill Jones or Jim Smith or something," the young man said.

"That's what Rosita said. She figured a picture would help." I hoped it wouldn't occur to Lichtenberg to wonder how come Rosita would be carrying around a picture of her long-lost cousin wringing wet. At least I had cropped the photo at the neck, so the dislocated arm didn't show.

"That's Jose Soto," Lichtenberg said.

"You sure? She wrote down Sanchez."

"Sure I'm sure. We helped him out with clothes and a place to stay when he first came here from El Salvador. A long time ago, probably four or five years. He couldn't even speak English then."

"Can he now?"

"Oh, now he's practically fluent."

"My understanding, she said he just got here a little while back and can hardly speak at all. Maybe it's a bad picture?"

"It's him or his twin brother. I couldn't possibly be wrong. He's here two or three days a week, helping out the various committees. He's the most dependable volunteer worker we've got. Although I haven't seen him for a few days, come to think of it."

"Got to be the same guy, then," I said. "About five-eight, five-nine, maybe a hundred and sixty? Sharp dresser, kind of California style?"

"Jose? I think he's still wearing the same Salvation Army clothes we got him when he came. Looks like it anyway."

"Can't be the same guy. Rosita says every buck he gets, he puts it on his back."

"Well, we'll soon find out," Lichtenberg said. He dialed a number, spoke in Spanish to someone, and then put his hand over the phone. "Jose's asleep," he said. "He hurt his shoulder and they gave him some stuff at the hospital that makes him sleep." Lichtenberg turned his attention back to the phone, listened and talked a little, and then hung up. I could see we were no longer pals.

"Jose was viciously attacked in the street last night," he said. "He was seriously injured and the use of his shoulder and arm may be permanently impaired. Are you satisfied?"

I made a gesture with my own unimpaired shoulders,

meant to convey that I didn't know what the hell he was talking about. It failed.

"And Jose doesn't have any cousin Rosita, according to his cousin Juanita. I thought all the publicity we put out about the break-ins scared you guys off, but I guess I was wrong."

"What guys, what publicity?"

"Give me a break, Special Agent Whatever Your Name Is. You send people to burglarize the offices down here eight or nine times I think it's been, over the years. Nothing ever missing except stuff from the files. Now you cripple one of the finest human beings I've ever worked with. A decent, humble, gentle man. Let me tell you something, mister, that man you hurt was worth a hundred of J. Edgar Hoover's cossacks."

"Hoover's dead."

"His cossacks aren't." This was true enough, so I ceded him the point.

"I think you'd better leave," Lichtenberg said. "I have nothing more to tell you."

"Fair enough," I said, getting up. "But there's something I guess I ought to tell you. Your boy Jose tried to kill me with a knife late yesterday afternoon, for no reason I've been able to figure out. He pretended not to talk English, and he was wearing probably five, six hundred bucks' worth of casual clothes. If you want to find out who's FBI, you might start there."

"I don't believe you."

"I didn't think you would."

It was early yet, and nothing useful to do till lunch. I walked on down to the Square and checked at the Tasty for messages. Detective Carr, it turned out, was free for lunch today and had suggested that I meet him at 12:30 at the Singha House, 1105 Massachusetts Avenue, if that was convenient. That was the substance of the message at any rate, although not exactly its style. What the counterman actually said was, "You just missed that asshole Jackie Carr. He says tell you half past twelve at the new Thai joint next to where the old Food Shak burned down. Call him you can't make it. Tell me something, Tom, how come you're hanging out with a prick like that? Fuckin' lush, you know he puked in here one night? I shit you not. Right where you're sitting, practically. What'll you have?"

"I was thinking maybe a western omelette."

"Ten, twelve years you been coming in here, I never knew you to order a western."

"It was the puke made me think of it."

We settled on a cup of hot water with a generic tea bag in it, and a sliver of lemon on the side. After a while the water changed color, and I drank it. When it was gone I wandered out to the public tables outside Holyoke Center and tried to watch the passing show. But instead I kept picking away at the puzzle of Jose Soto, who was still out there somewhere. Whatever had made him want to kill me yesterday would probably make him want to try again, and this time he would take a personal interest in the project. I would probably be able to find him, now that I had his name. But then what was I supposed to do? Reason with him? He had been tough enough or loyal enough or scared enough to keep his mouth shut through the pain of a dislocated arm; he wouldn't be easy to reason with.

And who was he loyal to or scared of, or both? It seemed likely to me that he was an FBI plant in the sanctuary movement, but it didn't seem likely that the bureau had ordered him to kill me. The FBI was too cowardly an outfit to go in for murder; slander, character assassination, and malicious prosecution were more its style.

Besides, the FBI would have no reason—or way—to be aware of my existence. A Tom Bethany had existed on paper from birth until 1980. School records, army records, Air America employment records, GI bill, social security, income tax at a very modest level, pilot's license, marriage license, divorce papers, a few stories on the sports pages. But the only part of this that would have involved the FBI was an outdated full-field security investigation in connection with my job flying for Air America, which was a CIA proprietary.

And anyway that Tom Bethany had disappeared at the age of thirty-two, as far as any bureaucracy was concerned. He moved out of his Allston apartment, leaving no forwarding address. His credit cards, all paid up, were never used again. His driver's license expired. His car was sold and his auto insurance was canceled. His phone was disconnected. He stopped filing state and federal income tax returns.

What had happened was that we pulled out of the Olympic Games way back in 1980. If Reagan can blame all his problems on Jimmy Carter, so can I. Maybe it's even partly true. Certainly I was focused for the first time in my life back then, and certainly the Olympic boycott threw me badly out of focus.

After Southeast Asia—not because of the war, but after it—I went through a long black patch. I got married, I went up to Alaska as a bush pilot, I had a daughter, I got drunk for years, I got divorced and broke. Then one night I vomited all over a pool table, and I began to get better.

During those years I was a bully. I wasn't generally the biggest person in the bar, but I had my little trick. I could wrestle and they couldn't. I only had to play my trick a few times before even the prototype Alaskan males—bearded, 250-pound six-footers—came to understand that I could make them cry from pain. And I would, too, and did, and that made me a bully no matter how much bigger they were than me.

One night, in an Anchorage saloon full of drunks wearing six-hundred-dollar parkas and white Mickey Mouse thermal boots, I went up against one of these bearded bears. He knew some of the same tricks I did, as I learned the moment we touched. An untrained man grabs you; a trained wrestler lays his hands on you light as a priest so that he won't have to release the muscular tension before he can make his next move. The big man's next move was a pretty good one, nearly unsignaled, and it nearly got me.

But I was enough better than him so that after a couple of minutes in which it could have gone either way, I had him helpless on top of the pool table, lying on top of three or four balls that couldn't have felt good. But my muscles felt rubbery and weak and they had already begun to stop doing what I wanted them to do. And then I vomited, all over him and the table. Neither of us wanted to go on.

Next day, I hardly wanted to go on with anything at all. There was the hangover. I was humiliated from having puked in front of all the world like a stumble-drunk Eskimo. Worse, I had unarguable proof that I had turned soft and fat: a two-minute workout had taken my strength away. I might still make an impressive show for the ignorant, tying up nonwrestlers in a few explosive seconds. But any of a dozen wrestlers I had beaten in my high school days would no longer have any trouble with me. Furthermore, I had lost my wife and my daughter long since. And I had lost my last two jobs because of unreliability and sloppy flying.

My hangover disappeared the way hangovers do, unnoticed. At some point in the late afternoon it just occurred to me that the pain wasn't there any longer. The shaking was, though, and so was the desire to start in on the beer that filled two shelves of my refrigerator. But I didn't do it, then or for years after.

Instead I went back to the lower 48 and got myself into the University of Iowa with the help of the wrestling coach. I did well by him, although not so well by my professors. But I was graduated, just barely, with a degree in political science. And next year I made the Olympic wrestling team.

It had taken five years of daily discipline and self-punishment, never letting go, never slowing down or even coasting, always whipping the shrieking machinery past old breaking points, on toward new ones. Only one goal was left, five years spent winning the chance to try for it. And then Carter made a schoolboy gesture that dumped those five years down the toilet. It was January of 1980, caucus time, and I was already in Iowa. I went to work for Teddy Kennedy.

Two things made me useful. I could fly, and I didn't look like a bodyguard. In both capacities, I wound up spending a lot of time next to the candidate. Well before the end, it had become plain that Kennedy was in a perfect double bind that would keep him out of the White House forever: he couldn't get elected if he didn't tell the truth about Chappaquiddick, and he couldn't get elected if he did. Along the way, though, I learned a good deal more about politics than I had at the University of Iowa.

During the general election I worked for the Carter campaign, which was just as educational, but less fun. Most of the Kennedy people had really wanted their man to win; the Carter people didn't seem to care much one way or another, except as it affected their employment. For a while I couldn't figure it out, since neither candidate was terribly exciting up close. Then I thought of Mae West's advice on choosing between two evils: "Always pick the one you haven't tried yet."

After the old actor won, I followed two or three Democratic policy advisers back east, where they planned on hanging out at the JFK School of Government till the weather in Washington changed. My idea was that there might be something to be learned at Harvard, something that would make sense of all the things I had seen in Asia and in America. But I had no money left, and an academic record that wouldn't impress a graduate school admissions committee. And so I settled into a house in Allston, across the river from Cambridge, with a shifting population of graduate students. My idea was to steal an education, since I couldn't buy one.

I stayed alive with one odd job of research or another, many of them coming to me from my political friends. From the graduate students I learned how to live on practically no money, and how to get as much education as I wanted for no money at all. There's nothing much to this, actually. It's easy enough to get into the lectures and the library, and what else is there about a university that matters?

One day, doing a little research at the JFK School library, I came across a Department of Transportation manual that told motor vehicle enforcement officers how to spot phony credentials. What it amounted to, if you wanted to read it that way, was a manual on how to create a false identity. Telling myself it was just for fun, I followed the instructions. Before long a fully documented Tom Carpenter existed, and it seemed like a shame not to let him out for a little run. So I moved out of my communal house in Allston, and Tom Carpenter

rented a one-bedroom apartment in a converted residence on Ware Street in Cambridge. He had a brand-
new passport. He had a Social Security number, too,
although his account was empty. But he put the number
on his applications for a driver's license, car registration
and insurance, and various short-lived bank accounts.
This Carpenter paid his rent and his phone bill by postal
money order. He had no credit cards and had never
applied for credit, and therefore had no credit rating
that anybody could check. The tenants of the three other
apartments in his house knew only that he was some
vague sort of a consultant, and that he kept politely to
himself. Tom Carpenter had an active official existence—an ongoing file, so to speak—only with the Massachusetts Department of Motor Vehicles.

At the time I saw shedding my skin as a project to
pass the time, an amusing stunt to pull off. Maybe. But
maybe I had it in mind that the last time I was on the
government's list it got me drafted. Or maybe I was still
hiding from my dead father, who used to make it home
one way or another after closing time at a roadhouse
called the Round Tuit, and then beat the shit out of me.
He died, driving drunk, before I got big enough to beat
the shit out of him.

Or maybe I just didn't like my old skin that much, and
made a sensible decision to leave it behind in Allston.
Whatever. In any event, the thing worked. I felt a lot
better with a hidey-hole not many people knew about,
and a name that the computers had forgotten. I liked the
feeling so well that I even went to the trouble of building
myself a third identity: a fully documented Alan W.
Bowen was in one of my safe-deposit boxes, ready in
case of need.

Maybe the need had come, since Jose Soto had been
able to find me somehow. But even if the FBI had hired

him to murder me, the bureau only knew what it had on file. I couldn't think of any way to locate the present Tom Bethany from the traces left in old files by the old Tom Bethany. Unless you knew me personally, that Bethany was long missing and presumed dead. And therefore nobody from his former life, in Southeast Asia, Alaska, elsewhere, was likely to have been behind yesterday's attack.

That limited it some, if not much. The new Tom Bethany had been hanging around Cambridge fairly visibly for a long time. Even if his address was a box number in the Brattle Street post office and his place of business was the terrace in front of Holyoke Center and his phone was the pay phone in the Tasty, anyone who cared enough could track me down eventually. But why would anyone care?

I crossed the street to the sidewalk phone kiosks, skirting a loose circle of Harvard Square freaks. They were kicking a ball back and forth, trying to keep it from touching the ground. I dialed Kellicott's private number. He answered on the first ring, and I put my question to him.

"Jose Soto?" he repeated. "No, I don't know him. Who is he?"

"I think he's probably an FBI informant," I said. "More to the point, he tried to kill me with a knife yesterday afternoon."

"Kill you! What for?"

"I don't know. We had a talk after I dislocated his arm, but he wouldn't tell me."

"Shouldn't you go to the FBI, if you think he's connected with them?"

"Eventually I may have to, but I'll stay away from them as long as I can."

"Well, you know your own business, but I shouldn't

think it would be very pleasant to know somebody is out there who wants to kill you. Or did you have him locked up?"

"No, I let him go. I try to stay away from the police, too. First I'll try to work it out for myself, who sent him."

"Well, I hope you do, and I'm sorry I can't help you. Oh, by the way, while I've got you, would Friday night be convenient to come by and meet my wife and Phyllis? Phyllis being my daughter."

"Friday's fine."

"About seven, then. Do you know where it is?"

"Actually, I do. I drove by on Sunday to have a look."

"Did you really? You're very thorough."

He sounded impressed, not offended. For a minute we talked about how hot it was, which everybody tended to talk about that August, and then I went back to my table. The sun would get up over Holyoke Center before long and make the terrace untenable, but for the moment it was all right. I opened my soft leather briefcase and took out one of Professor Davis's books on slavery. At the moment I was interested in the influence of Christianity on abolition. My unreached aim for the past fifteen years or so has been to find out why the people who govern the world generally act like idiots whether they are or not. Right now I was collecting exceptions to the rule, like the abolition of slavery. After all, here and there society got it right now and then. I thought these aberrations might help me understand the larger question, in the same way that madness helps us define sanity.

Everybody needs a hobby.

5

THE THAI WAITRESSES IN THE SINGHA HOUSE OPENED THE sewer gates of memory for Detective Jackie Carr. "The guys you had to get in with were the TCNs," he said, meaning the Third Country Nationals who worked for the embassy in Laos. "We had this Filipino guy over at AIRA, Tony Maldonado. Janome by any chance?"

"Nah, I never noom."

"Anyways, one night he takes a bunch of us to this place they called it the Turkey Farm, know why they called it the Turkey Farm? Account of all the girls gobbled. So anyways, they come out with this girl she was probly fourteen . . ."

"Jesus, Jackie, fourteen?"

"Hey, I know what you're thinking. No problem, though. She had the body of an eight-year-old . . . Anyways, the point I'm making here is after we come back, the cunt and me, Maldonado says . . ."

I left Jackie at the table, working on his fourth Amarit beer at $3.50 a pop. A few doors up was a copy shop, where the kid behind the counter agreed to do my job while I waited. "Police stuff?" he said, when he spotted the departmental heading on the Emily Kellicott homicide file.

"Naturally," I said, hoping I looked like Captain Furillo. I kept an eye on him while he ran the pages through, so that he wouldn't stop to read them.

Back at the restaurant, Jackie had had a chance to think things over and get cranky. "I don't know how hot an idea it is, you having copies," he said.

"Jackie, come on," I said. "How often do we get together, shoot the shit, huh? How was I even supposed to eat, if I'm reading all this shit at the table?"

"I could get my ass in a crack, is all."

"Nobody sees the file but me, Jackie. My word."

Just then the check came, and he forgot all about his problems in the pleasure of watching me fork over three twenties to the waitress. Once he had driven off to fight crime, I walked over to the Harvard faculty club. It was too late for a free cup of the coffee they set out at lunchtime in the reading room, but on the other hand the place was generally deserted after the waiters cleared the coffee things away. And nobody bothered you if you looked like you belonged. And the air-conditioning sort of worked. I sat down on one of the tufted leather sofas in the paneled reading room, to work my way through the thick police file. It began like this:

"Car 23 responded to report of a possible dead body 0634 hours 13 March 1986, Lowell Mall. Officers Flannery and Tedesco discovered apparent female hand visible in snowbank which witness showed them. Witness identified as Bobby Schmertz DOB unknown as he is a WM retard who is employed as a night watchman by the mall owners. Call to police was made by Schmertz who discovered alleged body. Scene of incident was secured by Officers Flannery and Tedesco pending arrival of undersigned. Arrival was effectuated at approximately 0720 hours accompanied by Medical Examiner A. M. Karpegis and Crime Lab technicians G. L. Williams and O. W. Moskow and photographer L. L. Lumpkin. Deceased was determined to be Emily Milton Kellicot, DOB 14 Jan 1960, of 37 Standish Lane, Cambridge, daughter of J. A. Kellicot also of that address. Victim was employed at Personal Leisure World in Lowell Mall. Cause of death determined by Medical Examiner Karpegis was strangulation and time of death was estimated at 48 to 60 hours previously (see attached coroner's report). Knife lacerations of the letters 'P' and 'L' were noted on the victim's breasts as well as semen in her vagina . . ."

It went on and on, for pages of tortured sentences, typos, crossed-out words, and misspellings. In this respect it was probably no different from most literary efforts by most lower-middle-level bureaucrats in any American bureaucracy, corporate or public. The only difference was that detectives weren't lucky enough to have secretaries to clean up their prose. My objections weren't stylistic, but substantive. Sergeant Harrigan just hadn't collected enough information, or the right information, or both. Nearly every sentence of the report raised questions that needed answers. I had hoped to be able to limit my contacts with the Cambridge Police Department to Jackie Carr, who already knew I was around. But that wouldn't be possible. I went to the pay phone off the faculty club lobby, dialed campaign headquarters, and got Phil Jeffers on the line after only a few minutes.

"You got anything?" he said.

"A lot of little things that haven't come together yet," I said. "Maybe they never will."

"Good."

"I need you for something, nothing much. I've got to talk to a guy named Sergeant Ray Harrigan, a Cambridge detective."

"What about?"

"He investigated the murder of Kellicott's daughter. I need to look at the paper work on it and talk to him. Can you have somebody tell him I'm coming?"

"Is this important? I mean, I'm not asking because it's hard. It's not. It's easy. I'm asking because it doesn't sound important."

"I know it doesn't, but I think it is."

"All right, I'll make a call or two. Get right back."

"Literally right back?"

"Should be." So I gave him the number of the pay phone, sat down nearby, and started to make notes to myself in the margins of the report that Harrigan, when and if I talked to him, wouldn't know I had already read. Phil Jeffers called back, sure enough, in less than ten minutes.

"Your guy, Harrigan," he said. "He knows you're on your way."

"Doesn't know why I'm looking into Kellicott, does he?"

"Come on, Bethany."

"Just checking. Who talked to him?"

"Nobody talks to sergeants. Baby Joe's AA talked to the chief." This meant the administrative assistant to Joseph P. Kennedy II, boy congressman from the Eighth District.

"That should work."

"Listen, how are you coming, Bethany? Number one,

your meter's running, and number two, we've got to get this thing on the track or off it by Labor Day."

"Shouldn't be long. Maybe another week. I'm going to meet the family for dinner Friday."

"Meet the family? What are you, marrying the guy?"

"Markham's the one that wants to marry him."

Sergeant Ray Harrigan's office in the Cambridge detective bureau was a cubicle with chest-high walls made of painted plywood topped with glass. On his desk he had one of those aluminum and Formica nameplates you can get made for you in the stores surrounding any military base. It read, "Lance Cpl. Ray Harrigan, USMC." A U.S. flag was to the left of his name, and a Marine Corps seal to the right. The display impressed me neither with his patriotism nor his toughness. Your typical Marine is a perennial adolescent with something to prove and very little to prove it with. The former lance corporal gestured me in when I knocked, and came out from behind his desk to shake my hand.

"Real good to meet you, Mr. Bethany," he said, with a hearty deference that seemed to me appropriate for an ex-jarhead in the presence of an ex–army grunt. Probably those weren't his sentiments, though. Probably he just figured I outranked him, since his boss had told him to see me. Marines are taught to grovel in a manly way before rank.

"Good to meet *you!*" I said, exaggerating the heartiness a little to see if he would notice. He didn't. He was about as sensitive to sarcasm as an Apple IIg. "Understand you're the man to see about the Kellicott girl."

"Sure am, Mr. Bethany. I've got the file for you right here. Why don't you just take a seat right here, and take your time looking it over? I'll just step out for a cup of coffee so I won't be in your way."

And so there I was, trapped into a second reading of the Kellicott file. Actually it worked out fine, because I thought of another couple of questions in the half hour before Harrigan came back.

"So what do you think?" the sergeant said.

"It's interesting," I said. "I never saw a police report before."

"Oh, yeah? I don't know why, but I had the idea you did security work for the campaign."

"No, nothing like that. I'm kind of on the personnel side."

He wrestled with that for a few seconds and then gave it up as none of his business. "Anyway," he said, "what can I do you for?"

"What this is all about," I said, "is this girl's father. He volunteered to do some stuff for the campaign. What do you think? Is there any potential embarrassment for the senator in this girl's murder?"

"I tell you the truth, I don't see how. I mean, it's already been in the papers already, you know?"

"Not where she worked," I said. "That wasn't in the papers."

"Well, yeah, that part . . ."

"Or the other places she worked, or this man Wales."

"Wales?"

"Lloyd Wales."

"Oh. Pink Lloyd, her pimp. Sure, all that stuff, we kept it out of the papers."

"How come?"

"I don't know. It came from high up. Higher than the chief, even."

"All that stuff could come out now, though," I said. "That's what happens in a campaign."

"Hey, what's the difference?" Harrigan said. "It's only his daughter, right? I mean, who gives a shit what the guy's daughter did and besides she's dead anyway, am I right?''

"Right," I said. "Only thing is, in politics you never know how the voters are going to react."

Harrigan thought over this bit of wisdom and found it good. "You got something there," he said. "What I was getting at, though, I don't know how long you been in the area, but back in the sixties, around in there, they had a case kind of like this, maybe you remember it?"

"A murder like this one?"

"No, it was this MDC captain, police captain, you know? He was cousin to a guy I knew actually. Anyway his daughter, the captain's daughter, she used to call herself the Plaster Caster, maybe you heard of her?"

"I guess I missed it. I was over in Asia for a lot of that time."

"Yeah, well, she was in all the papers with those plaster casts, and the point I'm making is everybody and his brother knew she was his daughter but it never hurt the captain none."

"Plaster casts of what?"

"Rock stars. She had a whole collection."

"Of rock stars?"

"Yeah, she'd make these plaster casts of their dicks."

There was a lot more I wanted to know about this, to tell the truth; during those years in Laos I had missed a good deal of American cultural history. But it didn't seem fair to the campaign to catch up now, so I hoisted our conversation back on the rails.

"Probably you're right it wouldn't make any difference," I said. "But you know how it is." I shrugged my shoulders to suggest that we were both in this together, doing the best we could to satisfy superiors who weren't as bright as they might be.

"We may as well get this over with, Sarge," I went

on. "Mostly your report looks pretty straightforward to me, but one or two points occurred to me as I was reading it . . ."

"Shoot."

"How did Emily get to work at this massage parlor?"

"Drove, I guess."

"Was there something in the report about a car? Did I miss it?"

"We didn't know about the car till after that report you got. The way we heard about it was a towing company pulled it away a few days later and nobody showed at the lot to pick it up. They ran the plates through the computer and somebody remembered the girl's name."

"When did they tow it off?"

"Couple days after the retard watchman found the girl, as I recall."

"How long did the towing company have it?"

"I don't exactly remember. Ten days, two weeks, in there."

"Anything show up in the car? Bloodstains, signs of a struggle?"

"I guess her father would have said."

"I don't follow you, Sarge. Her father?"

"He got the car, near as I can remember. From the company. I mean, she died intestate, so it was his car."

"Is there a chance she was killed in her own car, you think?"

"I wouldn't think, no."

"Where was she killed?"

"My guess would be she was killed in the guy's car."

"The murderer's?"

"Right. Pink Lloyd. Her pimp."

"It doesn't say he was the murderer."

"Official reports, you can't put down everything you know sometimes."

"You mean if you can't prove it?"

"Right."

"Was there any blood in Pink Lloyd's car?"

"She was strangled."

"She was cut, too, right?"

"Both tits, yeah. With Pink Lloyd's initials. 'P' on the left tit and 'L' on the right."

"The coroner's report said it was the other way around. 'P' on the right and 'L' on the left."

"They must've got it wrong. Let me see."

The sergeant puzzled over the report, moving his finger under the relevant words once he had located them on the page. His lips moved, too.

"I'll be goddamned," he said. "I could have sworn."

I had just wanted to see if he would get it, but he hadn't. And so we moved on.

"Maybe the coroner was looking at it from the girl's point of view," I said.

"Huh?"

"Probably what she'd think of as her left tit, we'd think of as her right tit. You see what I mean?"

Sergeant Harrigan frowned for a moment, and then his whole face lightened as the concept came clear. "Jeez," he said, "all the autopsy reports he's done, you wouldn't think he'd fuck up like that. Jeez."

"Well, there you go," I said. "Anyway, there would have been some blood from the cuts, right? That was why I was asking if there was any blood in Pink Lloyd's car. I mean, you know, if that's where he killed her."

"He would have washed it out, probably."

"Did you look?"

"You gotta understand we didn't come up with Pink Lloyd's name until maybe a week into the investigation."

"Plenty of time for him to get rid of evidence like that?"

"Right."

"The girl's clothes were under her in the snowbank . . ."

"Under her and kind of around. Here and there, you might say."

"But nothing missing?"

"No."

"Any cuts in her clothing?"

"No."

"Says here her clothes were bloodstained. A lot of blood?"

"I think there was a little on her hat. Not too much. The lab would have it on file."

"Why her hat?"

"Who knows?"

"So when she was cut she must have had her blouse and her bra and so forth, most of her clothes off. Otherwise they'd have blood on them."

"I would think."

"Why would she take her clothes off?"

"He was her pimp. He wanted to fuck her."

"Why not drive on home where it's warm?"

"He wanted to kill her, too."

"He wanted to fuck her *and* kill her?"

"I guess. That's what he did."

"Why?"

"Maybe she was holding out on him and he carved his initials on her so his other whores would stay in line. Niggers, who knows why they do anything?"

"What did he say when you asked him?"

"He said he was in Boston that night, and a couple of his whores said he was, too. Plus the bartenders in the place where he said he was."

"But he wasn't?"

"Shit, those people lie for each other all the time. You gotta understand, they're not like us. Give you an idea

109

what kind of a liar this guy is, he swore up and down he was never even her pimp. Said he lived with her for a while the summer before but he never turned her out."

"That couldn't be true?"

"No way. You gotta know these people."

"He say anything else that isn't down here?"

"Not a fucking thing. I mean, not word one. We were talking along, you know, and I was getting to where I knew he did it, and so I read him his rights. That was it, far as him telling us anything. Fucking Supreme Court. Let me try to explain it to you how it works. We had him downstairs, all right? Just questioning him nice. So I read him his rights and he shuts up. Well, it just so happens at that point it turns out it's gonna be a pretty long time before he can get to a phone for a lawyer, you follow me? So a couple of us are trying really hard to convince him to talk to us, okay? Pink says nothing. Zilch. Not even fuck you, honkie motherfucker, like a lot of 'em say every time you ask them a question. Which only makes it worse for 'em, the dumb shits."

"Let me ask you something unrelated," I said, to cut short the seminar on advanced interrogation techniques. "All the people you talked to in the investigation, were any of them Spanish-speaking?"

"Maybe they could have spoke Spanish. To be honest with you, I wouldn't know."

"What I mean, did any of the hookers, bartenders, anybody that was involved at all, look or sound Puerto Rican, Mexican, Central American, that kind of thing?"

"No, none of them. That I would have remembered."

Next I had Sergeant Harrigan take me downstairs and introduce me to the chief lab technician. She turned out to be a tough, cheerful woman of around thirty named Gladys Williams. Probably you had to be tough and cheerful if you were a Gladys in a world of Jessicas and Tiffanys.

"Sure I remember the Kellicott homicide," she said. "Another feather in your cap, huh, Ray?"

"Get off my ass, will you, Gladys," he said. "Hadn't been for the Supreme Court, I would have closed that case two years ago. Fuckers Mirandized him right back on the streets."

"Sure, Ray."

"I don't want to take up any more of your time, Sergeant," I said, truthfully enough. "Can I call you if any more questions come up?"

"Absolutely, absolutely," he said. He seemed happy to leave; I got the impression that Gladys made him feel uneasy. She got out her files on Emily Kellicott as Harrigan left, babbling about how welcome I was to call him anytime, day or night.

"I think he likes you," Gladys said. "You must be important."

"No, I'm not."

"To Ray you are. The way Ray is, he's either at your throat or at your feet."

"You think he's wrong about the Kellicott case?"

"That the pimp did it? I don't know, maybe he did. But I've gotta tell you one thing. The way Harrigan works, he looks around until he comes across the first black, and then he stops looking."

"You were at the crime scene, weren't you? There was a G. L. Williams in Harrigan's report."

"That was me, yes."

"You remember it pretty clearly? Reason I ask is because Harrigan was shaky on a lot of stuff."

"I remember it like it was yesterday, as the man says. It was the first homicide I went out on."

"No fun if you're not used to bodies, I guess."

"Oh, I was used to bodies. Before this I was an assistant in the pathology lab at Mass General for three years. Bodies were my life, you might say. No, the thing was the girl herself. We had the same birthday, I saw from her driver's license. I was two years older, but still. There she was in a snowbank and there I was ... Well, you see what I mean. And she was gorgeous."

"She was?"

"You're going by the police photos, right? Forget that. Everybody looks like shit in those photos. Face it, they're dead."

"She looked pretty in her graduation photo, but nothing spectacular."

"You can't tell from photos, period. But if you've been around bodies enough, you can tell what they looked like alive. She had a dancer's build. Legs I'd kill for. Perfect muscle tone, she would have looked just as good in a bathing suit when she was fifty. Not a beautiful face exactly, but lively, you know?"

"You could tell all this from looking at a body in a snowbank?"

"I went to the autopsy. I told you, I took an interest."

"Tell me about the cuts."

"Right on her breast, here." She indicated the locations on her own breasts. "That was another thing. She wasn't anything like me otherwise, but her breasts looked just like mine. I mean, exactly. I've worked with cadavers a long time, but a thing like that still shakes you. You think, Jesus, that's *exactly* what *I'd* look like if some fruitcake carved on me."

"The cuts were pretty shallow, as I understand?"

"Right. Superficial."

"What I'm wondering here, it doesn't sound like some weirdo like Jack the Ripper, slashing her all to pieces."

"No. The idea seemed to be just to leave his mark."

"Or somebody's mark."

Gladys showed interest. "Speaking of ideas, you've got one, don't you?"

"Not yet. I just don't like Harrigan's. Tell me, is there any way of telling whether she was raped or she consented?"

"Not really. There were no marks or bruises on her body, apart from the cuts. Penetration occurred, because there was semen in her vagina. I combed her pubic area and recovered a few hairs that weren't hers. In case we ever catch anybody to match them up with. But none of that proves rape."

"Can you tell sex from the hair?" I asked.

"No. It's not even too useful for general coloring. Pubic hair is sometimes a different color from the hair on your head."

"You can tell race, though, can't you?"

"Oh, sure. From looking at a cross-section under the microscope. But it doesn't get you very far, knowing he was white."

"It wasn't in Harrigan's report that he was white."

"The son of a bitch left it out? Well, I'll be damned. Now you see what I mean about him and blacks?"

"Still, what does it prove?" I asked. "A white person, not even necessarily a man, right?"

"Well, you've got the semen, of course, but I see what you mean. The hairs could have come from a woman, a customer in the massage parlor, or anybody. They wouldn't have to be from the guy that killed her."

"What happens to that stuff?" I asked. "The hairs, I mean. Semen."

"In homicide cases I keep it till the case is closed, which could be forever. The semen specimens are in little plastic envelopes in the property room, locked in a refrigerator we've got in there. The hair is in little envelopes, too. Just tossed in with her clothes and all, all the stuff we took from the scene. In wire evidence baskets with the case numbers on them."

"Could I take a look?"

"Sure."

The property room was down the hall, guarded by a fat corporal who wouldn't let me in on Gladys's say-so. He had to call Sergeant Harrigan before he would unlock the grillwork door for us. Basket A128 held mostly clothing: a raspberry-colored down winter coat, a white wool beret, soft deerskin gloves the color of cordovan, panties with a Filene's label, zippered boots, a light gray wool skirt, and a beige blouse of some silky-feeling material. The clothes were dirty and discolored and crumpled, as if they had come from a ragbag.

"Neatness counts here in the property room, huh?" I said, trying to straighten the garments out enough to inspect them.

"Take a look at him," Gladys said, gesturing toward the front of the room, where the corporal sat oblivious, watching the soaps on a miniature TV. "He look like the kind of guy who folds things up? He's too busy leading the life of the mind."

On the beret I found a small, faint, brownish mark, shaped something like an arrowhead. Next to it a square had been cut from the fabric.

"There were two of those bloodstains," Gladys said. "I cut the best one out for my tests."

I couldn't find any other cuts or tears in the clothing. Nor did I see any other bloodstains.

"He must have cleaned his knife on her beret," Gladys said. "A small knife, from the marks. Apart from that, no blood anywhere."

"What do you figure from that?"

"I figure she had her clothes off, or there would have

been cuts in them. I also figure she was already dead when he marked her up."

"That part I don't follow."

"Because there was very little blood on her body, or in the snowbank. It struck me at the time."

"That's not in Harrigan's report."

"I didn't tell it to him because I can't prove it. It's only a guess, but it's a good guess."

"Things don't fit together very neatly here, do they, Gladys?"

"They don't, do they?"

I opened a small brown envelope, the type jewelers use for repaired watches, and tapped its contents out onto my palm. There were four pubic hairs, black or possibly dark brown. I tapped them back into their envelope.

"That narrows it down," I said. "A male or female Caucasian may have been intimate with her sometime in the . . . when?"

"Last few days before she died," Gladys said. "Or longer. Depends on how often she washed, how carefully. I mean, most days you don't have somebody like me come along, comb you out."

"And I suppose the hairs don't have to come from the same person the semen does?"

"Not necessarily, no. You might be able to tell with DNA testing, but we're not equipped for that."

"I get the feeling we're closing in on the son of a bitch, Gladys. What do you think?"

"Oh, yeah," she said, deadpan. "He's dogmeat now."

I opened the dead woman's large purse, but it was empty. Gladys fished another brown envelope, stuffed full, from under the rumpled clothes.

"This is the contents," she said.

"I know what's inside without looking," I said.

"What's that?"

"Used Kleenex all rolled up into little wads. Women just can't grasp the basic concept of the disposable tissue."

I emptied the envelope—and separated out the dozens of little Kleenex balls. The other contents were ballpoint pens, keys, various buttons fastened together with a safety pin, a pocket sewing kit, coins, MTA tokens, an emery board, a couple of restaurant toothpicks still wrapped in plastic, a checkbook, credit card receipts, a comb and a brush, an envelope full of discount coupons, a Chapstick, a dispenser for birth control pills, and four Life Savers twisted up in their wrapper.

"See what's missing?" Gladys Williams said. I shook my head. "I didn't notice it at first, either. No makeup. No perfume, no compact, no eyebrow pencil, none of that stuff."

"Is that unusual?" I asked, before I thought. Of course it was unusual, particularly for someone who worked in a massage parlor. And I found something else unusual when I emptied out a soft leather clutch, itself the size of a small purse. It held a small bound sketchbook, a half dozen needle-sharp pencils of varying lengths, a sharpener, and two kneaded erasers. The sketchbook was almost full with what seemed to have been visual notes to herself: details of a nose or an eye, fluid sketches of people in various poses and postures, the folds and wrinkles in clothing, quick lines suggesting how clasped fingers slotted into one another, or how glasses perched on a woman's hair. Many of the impressions seemed to have been of people on the subway; most of the rest must have been done at work.

"Are these any good?" I asked Gladys.

"I don't know. They look good to me."

They looked good to me, too. In a few lines that

looked easy but probably weren't, she had suggested movement, character, whole scenes. Often the movement was suggestive—the flinging and thrusting of pelvises and breasts. The faces I took to be the faces of topless dancers, B-girls, johns, emcees, whores. In one scene, four women were sitting in a sort of waiting room dressed in what looked like nurse's uniforms. Their attitudes suggested boredom; their expressions were a queer mixture of passivity and discontent. Presumably these were her colleagues at Personal Leisure World. There was turning out to be more to Emily Kellicott than had met Sergeant Harrigan's eye—or, as a matter of fact, her father's eye.

Her wallet held several credit cards, a driver's license, a Cool Cash card from the Coolidge Bank, and a student member card from the Museum of Fine Arts. The card had been two years out of date when she died. "Harvard" was on the line marked "School or College." Probably this meant she had taken courses at Harvard's extension school. I had done the same thing when I first came to town, before I had made my discovery that you didn't have to pay to take courses at Harvard. Not as long as you stuck to large lecture courses and didn't fool around with nonessentials like registration, grades, exams, and credits.

I put the dead woman's effects back into the big wire basket, somewhat more neatly than I had found them, and headed back to the police lab with Gladys Williams.

"What was she like?" I asked Gladys. "Judging from her stuff."

"Confident, self-assured," she said.

"Because she didn't use makeup?"

"That, and her clothes. She wore what she liked, not what the other women in that massage parlor must have worn. Good stuff, nothing fancy or showy. Functional.

And she was neat. I carry a hairbrush, too, but mine is all full of hairs. Hers was clean."

She reflected for a moment, and went on. "Probably kind of a go-to-hell person. I mean, think of her sitting in those dumps with a sketch pad. I've never been in topless bars or strip joints, but would most of the people there want you drawing pictures of them?"

"I doubt it."

"She had to be tough, then. And together. Look in my purse, it'd be full of trash, useless junk. Old ticket stubs, grocery lists, cash register slips, gum wrappers. She kept hers shaped up. Nothing much in there she didn't need, except the old MFA membership card."

"What about that?" I said. "Would you mind making a call or two for me? It'd have to be a woman's voice."

I explained what I was after, and she agreed to help. Gladys turned out to be an accomplished liar over the phone, and it only took her two phone calls to make sense of the expired museum pass. The first was to Harvard's extension school and the second to the Museum of Fine Arts. Then I made a third call—to the painter who had taught Emily Kellicott's advanced drawing workshop two years before her death. Gladys had gotten the name out of the course director of the museum's art school. By now it had been four years, but Gregory Emmett remembered Emily well.

"She didn't really need me," the painter said. "Emily was a first-rate draftsman already. In fact I hate to admit it, but she was better than me. Most of my own work is nonrepresentational, and my drawing has gotten pretty rusty. Emily had a wonderful line. You know Ellsworth Kelly's work?"

I didn't.

"Anyway, her line reminded me a lot of Kelly's. Very pure, very spare. I encouraged her to take life classes."

"Meaning nude models?"

"Right. There's nothing like it for building fluency."

"Well, from her sketchbook she took your advice."

"It was terrible what happened to her. I felt so bad when I read it in the paper. All that life. All that energy. All that determination."

"What kind of determination?"

"To make an artist of herself. Her portfolio must have been two inches thick at the end of the course. She'd just take the assignments as a place to start, and then go on from there. She must have spent most of her waking hours sketching."

"Do you happen to know what she did for a living?"

"Anything to make ends meet, I'd imagine. Like most art students. Come to think of it, I think she said she was a cocktail waitress."

Emily Kellicott was starting to look very different from the coked-up wreck that her father described, or the whore murdered by her pimp that Harrigan saw.

"Tell me something, Gladys," I said after I hung up. "I've met three members of your department. A detective named Jackie Carr, and Sergeant Harrigan, and Corporal Whatever, the property room guy over there. Would you say they were typical?"

"Put it this way, there's a lot like them. It's the bell curve."

"Bell curve?"

"Face it, half of the world is below average."

"Yeah, but there's different averages. There's your average lawyer, your average stockbroker . . ."

"I don't know how much difference that makes. For instance I've seen plenty of doctors and plenty of cops. Maybe the doctors are better educated, but I can't see that they're much smarter, on average."

I thought about this and it seemed probable, all right,

if a little depressing. The army was the only organization I had done much time in, and certainly officers, as a group, were no brighter than enlisted men. Nor did it seem to take much brains to make rank, as I told Gladys.

"Same way in the department," she said. "In fact, the smartest people are mostly pretty well down in the chain of command."

"Who's the highest smart guy in the chain of command?"

"Billy Curtin. Deputy chief of detectives."

"I may not need to talk to him. But if I ever do, will you introduce me?"

"Sure."

"Okay, fine. One more thing. Will you go out to dinner with me tonight?"

"Actually, no. You're too much better-looking than I am."

"Help me back on board here. What are you talking about?"

"Well, people that go out together ought to sort of balance, you know? For example, we're both smart, so that balances. But you're kind of low-incredible handsome and I'm kind of bottom-third-of-the-class plain except for my tits, so that puts us out of balance, see what I mean? Now if you were sweet but really stupid, for instance, or if I were really rich . . ."

"What about if I were just asking you out to dinner?"

"My experience, men don't just ask women out to dinner."

"I do. The thing is, Gladys, I'm sort of a one-woman dog. Only the woman is married to somebody else and lives some place else, so I don't see her much. Anyway, the long and the short of it is that I don't give a shit for most men and they don't seem too crazy about me either, so most of my friends are women. And they're just friends, and she knows all about them. In fact she's met most of them. They range in age from seventy-four to nineteen going on twenty."

"That's some of the weirdest shit I ever heard. You're kind of a heterosexual walker?"

"What's a walker?"

"It's like that guy that used to escort Nancy Reagan to openings and stuff, what was his name?"

"I never kept tabs. Tell you the truth, it was almost like I didn't care."

"Anyway, a walker is a gay guy that makes his living going out with rich ladies while their husbands are off stealing more money."

"That's me, a heterosexual walker. Want me to walk you to dinner?"

"I've got to be the one who pays, then. That's the way it works, with walkers."

6

I HAD DRIVEN PAST LOWELL MALL DOZENS OF TIMES WITH-
out particularly noticing it. Mall was much too grand a
name. It was one of those small, dingy, suburban shopping centers that had preceded the giant malls. Its
ground-floor tenants were a cut-rate drugstore, a liquor
store, an electronics store, a video rental, an ice-cream
parlor, a tanning salon, and a shop for the full-figured
woman. All the shops were still open when I drove up,
just before five, but there was no problem parking. The
pavement was cracked, and weeds grew wherever they
could put down roots. I parked next to a large dumpster
that smelled of garbage.

I looked around the lot, trying to imagine how it
would have looked on the night of Emily's death. Cars
going by regularly on the parkway, but their lights not
reaching far into the parking area. The shops would have
been closed at that hour. Two streetlights, one at either

end, but no way of knowing if they were both working. Piles of dirty snow here and there, where the plows had pushed them. And coming out of one of them, a hand.

At first I didn't spot Personal Leisure World. Its sign was on the second floor, which was the top floor of the low, adjoining buildings that made up the complex. The entrance at first seemed to be through the neighboring drugstore, but after I struck out there, I discovered an unmarked glass door nearby that opened on to an unmarked concrete stairway. At the top was a cheap door, the hollow-core kind made of veneered plywood so flimsy you could put your fist through it without much trouble. A Formica sign said PERSONAL LEISURE WORLD, SAUNA AND MASSAGE.

Nobody seemed to be home when I opened the door, but I heard the noise of a TV somewhere. In front of me was a shelf sticking out of the wall, with an open photo album on it. The pockets in the Plasticine pages held color Polaroid shots of women wearing bikinis. The four I could see were called Wendy and Terri and Toni and Donna. To my right, an opening in the hall at waist height seemed to lead to an inner office. I caught a flash of movement behind it, and then a woman wearing a terry cloth bathrobe and slippers came from around the corner.

"Oh, hello," she said. "I didn't hear you come in. Anybody special you wanted to see?" She was older than the women in the album, and was just starting to become matronly. Her voice was deep and pleasant.

"I saw you had saunas," I said. "How much for just a sauna?"

"Thirty dollars," she said.

"Thirty dollars," I repeated, in a tone that perhaps conveyed a certain sticker shock.

"But a massage is only fifty dollars," she said, "including use of the facilities."

"What are the facilities?"

"The sauna."

"All right," I said. "Fine." Actually, it wasn't particularly fine. I hadn't been to a massage parlor since leaving Southeast Asia, and hadn't really felt the urge, either. But the prospect of sticking the Markham campaign for a fifty-dollar massage was an attractive one. The woman showed me to a cubicle down the hall with a sink and a massage table in it. She gave me a towel and a little bar of hotel soap. "The showers and sauna are just around the corner," she said. "When you're ready, just ring this button right here. Toni will be your masseuse." I tried and failed to remember which one of the photos had been Toni's.

The sauna was clean and newer-looking than the rest of the place, and so I suspected it didn't get much use. But it wasn't a bad unit. No one seemed to be in charge of the operation, so I ducked out and scrounged around till I found an empty soda can in a wastebasket and a scrub brush in a broom closet. I filled the can with water to pour on the hot rocks, and sat down to wait till a good sweat broke. After three cold showers and nearly an hour, scrubbed raw with the brush, mottled pink from the heat, I had had enough. I went back to my cubicle, lay down on the massage table with the damp towel draped over my middle, and rang the buzzer. I nearly fell asleep in the few minutes it took Toni to arrive.

She was a young woman, maybe no more than twenty, who was at that awkward stage when baby fat hasn't quite turned to the solid, permanent, adult fat soon to come. We must have the only civilization in the history of the world where the poorer you are, the fatter you are. We ought to send our entire production of potato chips, Twinkies, and Coke to Ethiopia, and keep the whole grains and powdered milk here for the Tonis.

It didn't seem likely she would have been here for two years, but I asked anyway as she kneaded inexpertly at my shoulders. "You ever know a girl called Emily, used to work here?"

"I never knew anybody named Emily at all," she said. "Probably it was before my time. I only started here a couple months ago, actually."

"No, this was a couple years back."

"Couple *years?*" she said, as if I had brought up some impossibly remote historical period, like the reign of Queen Victoria or the Carter presidency. "I don't think any of the girls was around that long ago, except probably Wanda."

"Is Wanda around today?"

"Oh, sure. Wanda's the manager."

I shut up and tried to enjoy the massage, but failed. My massage standards had been established nearly twenty years before on Bangkok's Patpong Road, where the massage parlors are the size of hotels and the masseuses the size of Girl Scouts. They were generally light-hearted, laughing and giggling a lot as if there were something irresistibly comic about sex. As of course there is. But Toni didn't seem as if she knew how to laugh by herself, without a sound track to show her when to do it and how hard. The Thai girls would walk up and down your spine with bare feet, which you'd figure would cripple you but it never did. With Toni it would. She would go, I guessed, 165 or 170 pounds. And, for all her size, she had hands that were weak and hesitant instead of strong and sure.

When she had finished and I lay on my back, the

towel still keeping me decent, Toni said, "How about a special, honey?"

The words were charged with romance. I was reminded of the summer when I was fifteen and visiting relatives downstate. My older cousin took me to a whorehouse in Hudson, New York, where he paid for our two whores to put on a show before I lost my virginity. The only line I remember was when the naked woman doing the memorized voice-over sat on the other woman's lap. "This is the way the boss gives dictation," she said. "More dick than tation."

Instead of walking out, we both went ahead with the awful business. But now and then, here and there, we pick up a little sense as we grow older.

"Not today," I said to Toni.

"Regular special is only a twenty-buck tip, honey," she said. "Special special's whatever you feel like giving."

"What's a special special?" I asked.

She ran her tongue over her lips, the way models do in the TV ads that show lipsticks sliding out of gleaming plastic foreskins.

"Do you take dictation?" I asked.

"Huh?" she replied.

"Never mind about the specials," I said. "You can have the twenty, though. I hit the numbers yesterday."

"Oh, wow," she said, coming to life at last. "Every day I play and my girlfriend, like she never plays and last winter she hits for five hundred bucks. I'm like Debbie give me a break, okay?"

"Huh?" Wanda asked. I had spoken clearly enough, but she must have figured she misheard. It probably wasn't a request the manager got every day.

"A receipt. I'm on expenses."

Wanda got a block of forms out of her desk and leaned forward as she began to fill one in. This let her terry cloth robe gape open so that I could see her breasts, which were still good. The receipt forms were the standard ones you can buy in any stationery store. Probably she used them mostly for tradesmen delivering supplies. At the top, in a neat, parochial-school script, she wrote out "Personal Leisure World."

" 'Received by,' " she read off the form. "What name you want me to put?"

"Tom Bethany. B, E . . ."

"Oh, I know how to spell it. It's where Jesus stole a horse."

That was certainly the way a D.A. would have looked at the matter, although it isn't exactly the slant St. Luke gives to the story.

"Not too many people know that," I said.

"You didn't know that stuff cold, you got a whack with a steel ruler from Sister Margaret," Wanda said. "I see nuns on the street to this day, I feel like hiding my hands behind me."

Wanda wrote down my name, and looked up at me again. "Mostly, what I use these for, it's for janitor supplies or laundry or something. What do you want me to put on it that it's for?"

"Just say 'massage.' "

"Your boss not going to mind?"

"I don't have an actual boss. I'm kind of a consultant."

"Yeah, but still . . ." She was signing the form. Wanda Vollmer.

"Well, this is kind of what I'm consulting on."

"On massages?" Wanda said. She had torn the receipt off the pad, but now held on to it.

"I'm working with Emily Kellicott's family."

"What are you, insurance?"

"No."

"A lawyer? We're gonna get sued, that's it?"

"No."

"Well, what?"

I gave her a card identifying me as vice president for research of Infotek, Inc. She inspected it and said, "I don't get it."

"Well, the thing is, the Kellicotts were never happy with the police investigation. So they asked us to go over the same ground and make sure everything was done that could be done, you know?"

"You're a private investigator?"

"No, no. Tell you the truth, this is pretty much out of our line. Mostly we do library research, computer research, that kind of thing."

"I told everything I know to the police."

"I know you did. Sergeant Harrigan gave me a copy of the report."

To establish how official I was, I took the report out of my briefcase and let her look it over. Wanda skimmed a few pages. She gave it back, along with my receipt for the fifty dollars.

"Well, everything must be in here, then," she said. "I told that dumb son of a bitch . . ."

"Harrigan."

"Whatever. I told him everything I knew about it. Which was nothing."

"I know you did. But I was wondering about other stuff, about the girl herself. For instance, I was wondering about the pictures she drew."

"How'd you know about them?"

"She had some of them in her purse."

"They were something, you know it? She did 'em just like that." Wanda made rapid scribbling motions in the air. "They didn't exactly look like the person, not like a photo, but you could always tell who they were. I could never figure out how. A few lines, but you could always tell."

"She ever do customers?"

"Mostly the other girls. Maybe once in a while one of her regulars."

"Do most girls have regulars?"

"Well, you take a girl like Toni, she won't have no regulars to speak of. Nelda, though, regulars is practically all she had."

"Who's Nelda?"

"Nelda was like her stage name, I guess. I never knew it was really Emily, until the police said it."

"Okay if I sit down?" I asked, doing so. "How come was it that Nelda had so many regulars? Because she was so pretty?"

"Only partly. You got to understand what sort of person Nelda was. Normally girls that do this kind of work, to be honest with you they're not real bright. And mostly they're lazy. It's work for lazy people. Nelda was different."

"How was she different?"

"I don't even know where to start. She was always moving, always doing something, for one thing. And she dressed different, like a college girl. She never wore makeup, kept her fingernails short, hair short. She talked different. In fact, I was surprised to find out she was even from around here at all, the accent she had."

"She never mentioned about her family, then?"

"Never a word. I remember once one of the girls says something about Father's Day was coming up or something, you know, and Nelda goes, 'They got a day for those bastards now?' So dumb me, I ask her what's the matter, you don't get along with your dad? 'My father's dead,' she goes. 'He died when I was thirteen.' "

"Which wasn't so," I said.

"I saw in the papers, yeah. But she never said another word about her family."

"Why did she work here, Wanda? What's your idea?"

"I don't have to give you my idea. I asked her once and she told me. She was here for the drawing."

"So she could use the other girls for models?"

"Partly that. A lot of the time, like I said, there's not much to do and she'd get out her big pad. But mostly it was the hours. She came on at four and so she had most of the daylight hours to work outdoors. From what she told me, the light at various times of day is important."

"When do you close?"

"Ten, and that's another thing. You're talking money, I got no doubt she probably did better in the clubs. But with the clubs, you're not out of there till three, four in the morning, maybe five, and you wind up sleeping most of the day."

"What did she do in the clubs?"

"Topless. She did some stripping in a couple clubs in the Zone, too. You don't see too many bodies like hers down there, I'll tell you."

"Dancing, was it?"

"Did she turn tricks, you mean? I'd be amazed."

"What about here?"

"Nobody turns tricks here. Why? Did that dumb cow try to make a date with you?"

"Toni? No, she just wanted to sell me a regular special or a special special."

"Yeah, well that's not tricking. That's a handjob or a blowjob."

"Did Emily do specials? Nelda, I mean."

"Handjobs is all. Anybody'd ask her about blowjobs, she'd always tell him she was saving that for when she was married."

"They didn't mind?"

"No, she said it so's they'd laugh. I'll tell you the truth, most of them would have gone to Nelda even without the handjob."

"How come?"

"Just for the massage, would you believe it? She read a couple books about it and she used to know this girl that was Chinese or Vietnamese, some kind of Asian anyway, and she taught her a lot of stuff they do over there. Plus Nelda had a personality. Guys liked her. Some of them liked her a lot. She handled them just right, a friend but always professional, if you see what I mean."

"The ones who liked her a lot, did any of them come by the night she was killed?"

"Only Pink Lloyd."

"The pimp?"

"That's the only Pink Lloyd there is."

"To get money or what?"

"He wasn't her pimp."

"The police say he was."

"Well, he wasn't. I told that to that guy, that Harrigan. He wasn't ever her pimp."

"What was he, then?"

"He was an ex-boyfriend."

"Why would a pimp have a girlfriend?"

"You'd have to ask him."

"You ever ask her about it?"

"Not in so many words, no. But my impression was they were together for a while when she first worked in the clubs, and it pissed off his regular girls, the working girls. Whether it was that or what, I don't know, but from what I understand, recent years, she'd only see him now and then. Like she was sneaking around with a married man, you know?"

"I know, all right."

"My impression was it was okay with her that way. From stuff she'd say."

"What kind of stuff?"

"Once she said he was like custard cream pie à la mode. You might want to duck out for some now and then but you wouldn't want it as a steady diet. If that makes sense."

"I can see where it might," I said. "Tough if you're the pie, maybe."

"Personally I could see her point," Wanda went on. "But plenty of girls wouldn't mind Lloyd for a steady diet."

"What's the attraction?"

"Well, you know, people say 'pimp' like it's a dirty word. But there's pimps and pimps. I'd have to say Pink Lloyd isn't too bad a guy, as far as pimps go. Plus which, they tell me you can't look at him without wondering what it'd be like with him."

"They tell you? I thought you knew him."

"I do, but I'm not them."

"There's women like that, too," I said, thinking of Hope and the roomful of lawyers.

"And Nelda was one of them," Wanda said. "I guess you never knew her, huh?"

"I'm just starting to. Did the other girls resent her?"

"Why would they?"

"My experience is that if men really like a woman, she generally doesn't have many women friends."

Wanda considered this. "Generally, I guess that's right," she said at last. "But even if Nelda had a lot going for her, you couldn't feel jealous of her. She'd never take a man away from another girl. In fact she didn't even have any men that I knew of, except sometimes Pink Lloyd. You just kind of felt good around her, somehow. She dressed her own way, talked her own way. Never tried to hide that she was different. Better, really, and we all knew it. But you didn't feel like she knew it. She was what she was, that's all. Like it wasn't specially good or bad, but just what she was. I don't know, it's hard to put it into words."

"You're doing fine."

"Well, she was just real nice to be around, that's all. If she'd have had a real funeral, I bet everybody she ever worked with would have been there."

"What kind of funeral did she have?"

"Some kind of private service just with family and then they cremated her. She would have looked real pretty in makeup, too."

Wanda paused, as if seeing the funeral that might have been. With Nelda looking real pretty, in the makeup she never wore alive.

"I'd like to get my hands on the prick that killed her," she said. "The son of a bitch would be singing soprano."

"You sound like you'd really do it."

"Bet your ass I'd do it."

"What if it was Pink Lloyd?"

"It wasn't."

"The police think it was."

"The police don't know shit."

"His initials were carved on her."

"Not by him."

"Why not?"

"Look, I've had two different girls worked here, they went on to work for Lloyd. So I know how he does his business. Plenty of pimps, they beat up on their girls, but not him. A girl keeps getting out of line, all he does is he tells her to take off, don't come around no more. So the only ones that get out of line are the ones so fucked up you wouldn't want 'em around anyway.

Everybody else in the life knows what a good deal they got with Pink Lloyd. He takes care of 'em, treats 'em good, lets 'em keep a fair share."

"That's how he treats his working girls, okay. But she wasn't one of his working girls."

"I hear what you're saying. You mean if he loved her, who knows what the hell he might do? You're wrong, though."

"Somebody carved his initials on her."

"Not him."

"How do you know?"

"Because she had her clothes off."

"That's what I thought, too," I said. "Somebody you've known for years, why would you do it with him in the parking lot?"

"Particularly in the cold."

"Right. So who, then?"

"The guy that walked out on her."

"What guy was that?"

It turned out that a man had come into Personal Leisure World the night of Emily Kellicott's death. He wasn't a memorable man, at least not to Wanda. Nothing particular about him that remained in her recollection: she couldn't say if he was thin or fat, short or tall, young or old, handsome or homely. She couldn't remember the color of his hair or of his eyes; she couldn't recall how he was dressed or whether he was fair-skinned or dark, except that he was a white man. This ruled out the extremes—he wasn't Abbott and he wasn't Costello, for example. But it probably left hundreds of thousands of possibilities, just in the Boston area.

"Did he have an accent?" I asked. "Mexican, South American, like that?"

"No, no accent. Nothing special about him."

This nobody man had showed up sometime around eight or nine. That was the last Wanda saw of him.

"I was in and out of the office," Wanda said, "and I must have missed him when he left. Fact I didn't even know he was gone till Nelda come out and said the guy took off without his massage."

"Does that happen much?"

"Now and then a guy loses his nerve, changes his mind, whatever. It don't make shit to me, long as he doesn't want his money back."

"What if he does?"

"Fuck him," Wanda said. "Anyway, I wouldn't have paid any attention at all, except Nelda sounded funny when she told me the guy split. I asked her did he try anything weird or what, but she said no, it was nothing. And that was it. I wouldn't have ever thought of it again except for what happened."

"He's not in the police report, this guy. Did you tell Sergeant Harrigan about him?"

"I told him, but he said it didn't mean nothing. What did the cop care? He already had it figured out. Sure he did."

"What about Pink Lloyd? Did he show up before or after this guy?"

"After. The next customer, in fact, except he wasn't a customer. He just came to say hello or something, which was okay because she was between guys. So he did. Said hello."

"How long did he stay?"

"Maybe twenty minutes, maybe a little longer. Nobody else came in for a while, so she was free. They talked in the little kind of room we have for the girls in the back. I buzzed back when I finally needed her."

"Did he leave then?"

"Nelda came out with him and walked him downstairs. I guess he left."

"He could have hung around, though?"

"He could have."

Wanda and I talked for another ten minutes or so, until a couple of clients showed up, one right after another. It seemed like time for me to take off, too. But I waited till she had taken care of her business and then asked her one more thing that was on my mind.

"You yourself," I said, "would you say you liked Nelda a lot?"

"Sure I liked her a lot."

"Did she handle you just right?"

"How do you mean?"

"The way she handled men who liked her a lot. A friend but always professional?"

Now she saw what I meant. "I don't know why I should answer that," Wanda said.

"I don't know why either."

"You know something, Bethany?" she said, and I shrugged my shoulders a tiny bit to show I didn't. "You're pretty goddamned sharp, for a man."

7

GLADYS WILLIAMS HAD SAID TO MEET HER BY THE statue in Harvard Square, and I had asked what statue? Look around till you see a statue, she said. It'll be right next to the Out-of-Town Newsstand. And that's where the statue was—an ugly, graceless construction that jabbed into the air in an ugly, graceless way. How come there's never a Jesse Helms around when you really need one?

This hideous misuse of public funds must have been in my field of vision ten thousand times, and yet I didn't remember ever seeing it before. The mind protects us by airbrushing out power lines, street signs, telephone poles, and modern sculptures that would otherwise spoil our enjoyment of familiar scenes. I said as much to Gladys, who was waiting at our rendezvous.

"That's real deep," she said. "And real weird."

"Well, shit, Gladys, now I'm going to sulk all night."

"Okay, where we going to do it?"

"How about the Harvest?" I said. The Harvest was an overpriced yuppie joint, but it had a courtyard and I thought she might like it.

"How about the Bow and Arrow?" she said. "They got the same beer for half the price and nobody talks about real estate."

The Bow and Arrow is as downscale as you can get in the Harvard Square area. We took a table about halfway down the room, at a point equally distant from the jukebox and the TV.

"So listen, what should we talk about?" Gladys said when the waitress had our order for a pitcher of beer. "For instance, I saw this terrific show on Channel Two about otters. Want to talk about that?"

"Actually, no. I want to talk about how come you quit a good job cutting up corpses to comb out pubic hairs for the police department."

"You want to talk about me, is that it? My hopes, my fears, my dreams?"

"Sure. You show me yours, then I'll show you mine."

Gladys turned out to have been graduated from Lesley College after six years of combining study with work. Her job for the last two of those years had been as an assistant in Harvard's biology department, by which time it was too late to change her Lesley major in office administration or something. But a Harvard biology professor gave her free textbooks from his shelves full of publishers' samples, and let her sneak into lectures. By the time she had her bachelor's degree, he was willing to recommend her for a job in the pathology lab at Beth Israel. During her three years there and her two subsequent years with the Cambridge police, she had taken Harvard extension school courses in biochemistry, genetics, microbiology, immunology, neurobiology, endocrinology, and metabolism. Now she figured she was about ready for medical school.

"A Ph.D. is just as good for the kind of research I want to do," she said. "Or better. But with the M.D., you get twice the salary for doing the same research. So I'm laying out six hundred dollars for the Stanley Kaplan course this winter and I'll take the MCATs in February."

"Think you'll get into med school?"

"Why not? Look at all the assholes who did."

The reasoning she employed in her personal life was also impeccable. She lived alone, in a small apartment just off Kirkland Street. Most of the time she managed to have two boyfriends, each of whom she told about the other's existence. "First thing is it gives me a backup if one of them takes off or gets to be a pain in the ass," she said. "Also it keeps them on their toes if they know there's competition. They try just that little bit harder."

"How come everybody else has got to advertise for men in the *Phoenix* classifieds and you've got 'em two at a time?"

"You go after the shy ones. That's the easy part, finding them. They're grateful to be found. The trick, though, is knowing what to do with them once you've found them."

"Well, what?"

"Hey, I can't tell *you*. You're the wrong sex. You introduce your ladyfriend to me sometime and maybe I'll tell her."

By then we were on our third pitcher of beer. Pretty soon it would occur to Gladys that she was doing all the talking, at which point she might start asking all kinds of questions about me that I wasn't ready to answer yet. Not at this early stage of our acquaintanceship. To head this off, I told her about my conversation with the manager of Personal Leisure World.

"The thing that struck me," I said when I was done, "was that there seemed to be two totally different Emily Kellicotts. The one her father described to me was a pathetic, rebellious, undisciplined mess. The impression I got was she spent her whole life trying to embarrass her father."

"Well?" Gladys said. "Working at a massage parlor isn't exactly going to impress the shit out of his buddies at the faculty club, is it?"

"No, but nobody knew about her at the faculty club, either. She danced under another name, and she never talked about her folks, stoned or sober."

"She was a druggie, huh?"

"Actually, no. Wanda said maybe a line now and then if one of the girls offered her some, but nothing regular or serious."

"She drink?"

"Wanda said no, but her father said she was a lush and a druggie, both. Said every time he tracked her down she was either hammered or high. Screaming and hollering awful things at him. Very painful scenes."

"Maybe it made him more comfortable to think she was out of her head when she said the awful things."

"Maybe, but even shouting awful things doesn't sound like the Nelda they knew at the massage parlor. That woman was hardworking, reliable, pleasant, calm, popular with everybody, disciplined, in control of her life."

"Sounds like me, except for the pleasant and the popular."

"Actually it kind of does. Even to running the men in her life instead of letting them run her."

"You going to talk to this Pink Lloyd?"

"If I can find him."

"Pink Lloyd, Jesus. What's his last name?"

"Wales."

"Close enough."

"What do you mean?"

"You really don't know?" she said. "You never heard of Pink Floyd and the Wall? The rock group?"

"No."

"Hey, welcome aboard. This is the 1980s."

"Harrigan said the guy always wore pink shirts. I figured that was how he got the name."

"You must be in a time warp."

"Gladys, I feel so ashamed."

"You should." She topped off my beer and filled her own glass. She was keeping right up.

"Tell me more about this Wanda," she said.

"Lesbian in her early forties," I said. "Going to fat a little, but still not too bad a figure. She went to parochial school but didn't like it much. Probably dropped out young, ran away from home, something like that. Basically uneducated, but smart and perceptive. My guess is that she runs the place pretty well."

"Is it her place?"

"I doubt it very much. There'd be somebody else behind it, almost certainly."

"The mob?"

"Possibly. Not necessarily."

"Did you like her?"

"I kind of did, yeah. But then I don't have to work for her. My impression was that she wouldn't put up with much shit from the help."

"Tough, huh."

"Pretty tough."

"Tough enough to strangle a girl who held out on her?"

"And carve her male rival's initials into the girl as a little hint to the cops?" I said.

"For instance."

"I thought of that, but I don't like it much. The fact that she was naked. The semen. The hair you found."

"What do you like, then?"

"I don't have anything I like, really. Just questions."

"Here's another one for you, then," Gladys said. "How come she said her father died when she was thirteen?"

"To avoid talking about her family."

"Sure, maybe. But why thirteen?"

"Instead of twelve, or fifteen, or twenty-one? Where are you going with this?"

"I don't know, either. It's just another question. I thought of it because of my mother."

"She died when you were a kid?"

"She died, but only last year. I hadn't seen her in years, didn't want to, but I had to take care of getting her buried. I came across a medical history form she had filled out for the insurance company years ago, and she put down that she was hospitalized in 1960 for severe depression.

"Well, she was basically crazy and she had been put away three different times that I knew of, which she didn't list on the form at all. But I never heard of one in 1960. So I called my dad up in Portland, and sure enough, he said it never happened. That was one of her good years. She was locked up before and after, but not even close to 1960."

"The question being why she put down 1960 instead of 1957 or 1962?" I said. "Okay, what happened in 1960?"

"Her first child was born. Me."

"I get your point. I'll try to find out what happened when Emily was thirteen. I'm having dinner with her family tomorrow."

Meanwhile, though, the night was ahead of us. "What do you think?" I said. "Want to move on?"

"To where?"

"The Top Hat Lounge."

"You're still in that time warp, Bethany. There hasn't been a Top Hat Lounge in America since what? Maybe 1955?"

"It's a strip joint on Boylston Street. Emily used to work there. And Pink Lloyd hangs out there, according to Harrigan."

It turned out that the Top Hat, too, was in a time warp, just like Boston's whole Combat Zone. Chinatown was taking over the Zone, along with developers. I hadn't been down there for years, except for my visit to the dirty bookstore. Now, at night, it looked like a sad, near-deserted movie set. At the corner of Washington and Boylston was the China Trade Center, a shabby office building. A handful of pimps and petty thieves sprawled and slouched in the little open space in front of it.

"Whatever you want, man, I got it," offered one of them as we went by, but he seemed to be speaking his line by rote, like a telephone canvasser, without much hope of success. I didn't believe he really had it, any more than he did, and so we went on by. Video Peeps was closed and boarded up. Movies-Nude Photos was closed. Boston Bunnies was closed. Club 66, which had been sort of renowned in the old days, was closed. In the doorway lay two Cossack Vodka bottles, a bottle of Wild Irish Rose wine, a 7-Up can, and three paper napkins that had been used to blot up blood.

But down Boylston Street the Top Hat still hung on, no doubt preyed on by such minor parasites as cops, health inspectors, liquor inspectors, and bottom-rung mafiosi. The Top Hat's real enemies, and Chinatown's as well, were likely to be the politicians, bankers, developers, and lawyers who root for slops in the city's real estate market. Between them, they steal more on a slow

day than the entire city bureaucracy does in a year. Soon
enough they would gentrify the last of the hookers and
sailors and Chinese waiters right out of the old Zone.
Let Lowell or Quincy or some place take care of them;
here, though, the yuppies are coming. With the eighteen-
hundred-dollar-a-month condo payments that will leave
nine tenths of them homeless and bankrupt when the
national bill comes due. In ten years it will be hard to
figure out how Reagan ever got elected by two land-
slides, since not a one of the busted baby boomers will
confess to voting for the man. Admitted Reaganauts will
be found only in a handful of country clubs, protected
from extinction by heavily armed bartenders, ball boys,
and caddies. To the *pock, pock, pock* of the tennis balls,
they will nap on the terrace and dream of the gone Gip-
per, as their grandfathers dreamed of Warren Gamaliel
Harding.

"Probably you're right," Gladys said when I finished
explaining all this to her. "But right now, let's go on in.
I've got to take a leak."

When you entered the Top Hat you were met right
away by a wall—a baffle to keep the sidewalk traffic
from getting a free peek at the show. Past this obstacle,
a large man met us. "Table for two?" he said, like a real
maitre d'.

"Maybe," I said. "We're looking for someone. Pink
Lloyd?"

"Probably be in sometime," the large man said. "Probably late."

"Any way to reach him?" I asked. "I got this girl here
that wants to talk to him about a job. Only right now
she's got to take a leak."

The large man looked Gladys up and down and gestured toward the rear.

"Okay tits," he said when she had gone. "Where'd you find her?"

"She's waitressing for me, I got a place over in Allston. She wants to make a little more money, you know?"

"There's somebody here that might know where Pink Lloyd is. Who should I tell him?"

"Tom Bethany. Just say Tom. Tom from Allston."

The big man took me to a table and disappeared out back. While he was gone, Gladys returned and a waitress came and took our order.

"I told him you were a waitress just like her," I said to Gladys as the woman left. "Only now you want to go for the big bucks, with Pink Lloyd."

"I don't know," Gladys said. "Would I have to go all the way?"

"I don't think so. My understanding is that most of them just want to talk."

"The hell with it then."

Our drinks came. Gladys had stuck with beer; I had broken my beer-only rule and ordered rye and Coca-Cola, out of a vague idea that rye and Coke was the thing to drink in a time warp. It was revolting.

The stage was a runway down the middle of the horseshoe-shaped bar. A light-skinned black girl, if such a thing can be, had just finished. The emcee invited us to give her a great big hand. Then we all settled down to a brief intermission, during which we were expected to drink our overpriced drinks and buy overpriced drinks for the bar girls.

"That would be the hard part, I'd think," Gladys said. "Look at that slimeball at the table over there. Can you imagine going up and talking to him?"

"I'd think the hard part would be getting up there naked."

"It would be for me. Not for her."

"How come?"

"I've got a fat ass and she didn't. Look, one of the police photographers is this repulsive creep that likes to take nude photos of girls. I asked him one time, I was curious, why would any girl take off her clothes for a repulsive creep like you? My exact words."

"Oh, I believe it."

"He didn't mind. Assholes like him, they think you're kidding. Anyway, what he told me he'd do is he'd walk up to the girls with the best bods on the beach and give them his card. The better the bod, the more likely she'd call him up."

"Makes sense, I guess."

"Sure it does. Look at you, the build on you. You telling me you'd be embarrassed to get up there in a male strip club? Let the girls stuff money in your jock?"

"I'd probably never do it, but you're right. I wouldn't feel embarrassed if I did."

"Naturally not. If you've got it, flaunt it."

"What about at the massage parlor? You think that'd be hard?"

"Why? You'd massage women, wouldn't you?"

"Some women I would."

"You'd do them all if it was your business. It only feels funny the first time or two. Ask a nurse or a hairdresser, anybody that handles other people."

"They're not giving handjobs, though."

"Get a clue, Bethany. How big a deal do you think a handjob is?"

"Well . . ."

"Look, probably you never handled another man, so it seems weird. Doesn't seem so weird to us, though. You've got to bear in mind we've been doing it since ninth grade."

"Not with strangers."

"Everybody's a stranger at first. Besides, a handjob isn't really too personal, you know? In fact, it's what you do to a guy when you don't *want* to get too personal with him."

I was thinking that this seemed to make sense, too, when Pink Lloyd came up to our table. He wore a pink shirt and a pink handkerchief in his breast pocket. His jacket and pants were the color of coffee, very heavy on the cream. They were cut loose and floppy, in a fashion tradition dating all the way back to the early days of the Banana Republic. And on Pink Lloyd, to be honest about the thing, the look worked. He was slim, wide-shouldered, just short of six feet tall, and moved in the loose, bone-less, graceful way of a good tap dancer. He was the color that we whites spend the summer at the beach trying to reach, but never quite get to.

"Hey, how you doing?" he said, taking possession of the chair I waved him into. "Manny say this young lady looking around."

"Yeah, you could say."

"What's your name, honey?"

"Gladys."

"Well, we have to do something about that."

"Bullshit we do," said Gladys.

"Probably I ought to explain," I said. "The fact is, she's not looking for work. We're looking into the Kelli-cott murder."

Pink Lloyd looked at me without speaking for a moment. His eyes narrowed a trifle and the lines of his face hardened up. He reached into his mouth, tugged at something, and then laid a portable bridge down on the table, sharply enough to make a little click. Two teeth, attached to a device made of metal bands and pink plastic.

"I talked to you people already," he said. "Now I got to wear this."

"This is nothing to do with the police," I said. "We're working with the family on this." I passed him one of my Infotek cards. When he had looked it over, and looked me over some more, he handed the card back and put the bridge back in his mouth.

"Still it don't matter," he said. "Everything I said, you can get it from the police. I told the fuckers everything I know, can't help it if they didn't believe it."

"Well, they didn't," I said. "But I do."

"Then what do you want with me?"

"I want to find out about Emily herself."

"Emily?"

"Emily, Nelda. Where did she get Nelda from?"

"I guess 'cause it rhymed. The way she made Tony say, it was Nubile Nelda from Needham."

"Tony being?"

"The greaseball was just up there. The emcee."

"Nubile Nelda, huh?"

"Nubile meant like young stuff, way she told me."

"She wasn't from Needham, though."

"That was 'cause it rhymed, too. I axt her one time and she said it was just for fun, the whole name."

"But she used Nelda offstage, too?"

"Oh, yeah. Nobody knew no Emily. I didn't even know that myself till it come out in the papers."

"And you were pretty close to her, right?"

"Close as anyone."

"Which wasn't that close? Is that what you're saying?"

"It was and it wasn't. I'd see her sometimes and far as I know I was the only one that did. So that's why I say close as anyone."

"She didn't work for you, though? It wasn't that?"

"You knew her, you wouldn't even ask that question.

Even when I only saw her dancing here the first time, before I ever met her, it never even crossed my mind."

"Why not?"

"Shit, who knows? It's like when you're a kid, you know, when you go to robbing people on the street? You just get a feeling which ones ain't gonna fight back, which ones are. The way they move. Something."

"How did she move?"

"Like she was going somewhere all the time, and she was late."

"Somebody you could turn out, how would she move?"

"Different ways, but not like that. Lazy. You take your whore, mostly she's a lazy bitch. Move lazy, you know? Last thing you could say about Nelda."

"She worked at Leisure World, though."

"Not turning tricks."

"Pretty close, from what her boss says."

"Then her boss is giving you shit. Nelda done massages and that's it. She got through with you, it was like she took you apart and put you back together again. She didn't have to give you no more than a massage, and you got your money's worth."

"The manager said she gave handjobs to regular customers."

"Well, that could be, if she liked somebody and happened to feel like it." Pink Lloyd looked at Gladys, and said, "Any woman would do that, am I right?"

"If she liked somebody and felt like it?" Gladys said. "Sure, why not?"

"Sure. Don't make her a whore."

"You think there's any chance the manager could have killed her?" I asked.

"You know Wanda was hitting on Nelda?" I nodded. "Then you know she didn't get no place, either. If they had something going, maybe Wanda would have done it. Except it don't make sense."

"Why not?"

"Just don't. Nelda would have been too strong for Wanda. Besides, she had her clothes off."

And there it was again. What sense did it make for a woman to take her clothes off in a parking lot on a cold night?

"Did Nelda know anybody, any man, with a Spanish accent?" I asked.

"Not that I know of, unless it was somebody at work. Why? You think some spic did her?"

"Probably not, but a guy named Jose Soto came at me with a knife a few days ago and he wouldn't tell me why."

"I never heard that name, but that don't mean nothing. She knew plenty of people I didn't know."

"You didn't see that much of her?"

"Now and then is it. Used to be more when I first met her, but my bitches got jealous."

"You met her here, you said?"

"She was dancing, yeah. Sometimes she'd come over and sit with me between dancing so nobody wouldn't bother her, you know? The thing is, she wouldn't hustle drinks, told 'em that from the start."

"They didn't mind?" I asked.

"Don't matter if they minded. The body she had, they wanted her to dance more than they minded. Shit, Tony and them, they wanted to keep her picture outside even though she was dead."

"Why didn't they?"

"I told 'em. 'You sick fuckers,' I said, 'the girl's *dead*. You keep that picture out there, I bet you that guy Barnicle at the *Globe* would like to hear about it, put it in the paper.' I told them sick fuckers."

"Would they still have the picture?"

"I got it, you want to look at it. She had pictures of me, but I didn't have none of her. In fact that's how we happen to get it on, her pictures."

"How was that?"

"What happened, one night we was talking right at this table and she asked me would I model for her. I figured she was just coming on to me, you know, but it wasn't that. I went over to her place five or six afternoons before she finished the picture. Just sitting there while she would draw. But all the time we were talking, getting friendly, you know?"

"None of my business, but how long was it before you did get it on?"

"I'd say maybe a couple months."

"But it didn't last long because of your girls?"

"I wouldn't say it didn't *last* long. It lasted more or less up till she died, you know? Only there was a couple weeks there at first when we was seeing a lot of each other, and after it was whenever we could manage it, you understand what I'm saying?"

"I understand," I said, and actually I probably understood better than he wanted me to. It was looking to me as if Wanda had been right—that Emily had kept him on a string, for whenever she felt like a little custard cream pie à la mode.

"What happened to the pictures she made of you?" I asked.

"I guess her daddy took them when he cleared her place out."

"You ever meet him?"

"Not exactly. I seen him once."

"Where was that?"

"Right here. This dude came in and as soon as she spotted him she goes, 'Why, that fucker!' and runs up to him. She's hollering and the guy on the door comes over to see what's the trouble. You couldn't hear what she was saying on account of the music but then it stops and she's hollering, 'Get this son of a bitch out of here or I'm not going on!' Everybody's looking at the guy by now."

"He goes, does he?"

"Oh, yeah, he goes. She was pissed off you wouldn't believe. I never saw her like that, before or since."

"Was she drunk?"

"Sheeit. Know what she drank? Cream soda with a scoop of ice cream in it."

"How about drugs?"

"Somebody offer her some good coke she might take it or she might not. Mostly not."

"She tell you who the guy was after he left?"

"She had to dance first. Then she come back, told me it was her daddy wanting her to come home."

"She say why she didn't want to?"

"Wouldn't say another word about him. Till it come out in the paper I didn't know she was from around here, had a family, went to college, nothing. She didn't want to talk about it and you hadn't better ask her, neither."

The music came up so loud that we couldn't hear ourselves talking—a record or tape of some generic-brand bump-and-grind music. A girl with enormous breasts and thin legs came out, moving in vague relation to the beat. Except for the breasts, there was no point in watching her. We waited it out until it was time to clap, which I did loudly, out of pity rather than enthusiasm.

"Good tits on her anyway," Pink Lloyd said when the girl had bowed herself off the runway. "Can't dance for shit, though."

"How was Nelda?" I asked.

"She like something on the TV. She could *dance*. She'd put on this weird music, but she made it work, I'll say that for her."

"What kind of music?"

"From shows. She had this one about umbrellas and Rockefellers."

" 'Puttin' on the Ritz,' " Gladys said.

"Something," Pink Lloyd said. "She'd end up with this bow tie and a top hat on, like the Top Hat Lounge. Another one she'd come out with this miniskirt on and a kind of a round hat, came down over her ears. Song called the 'Viper Rag.' "

I didn't know that one; from her smile, Gladys did.

"She could've done real good as a dancer, no question," Pink Lloyd said. "I told her she ought to go to school for it. But couldn't nobody make her let go of that art shit."

We left before the next stripper came on. I drove conservatively, knowing that I wouldn't have a chance against a Breathalyzer. Nor would Gladys by now, so she wasn't much use as a designated driver.

"Fats Waller," she said. "That's who wrote 'Viper Rag.' Imagine playing stuff from *Easter Parade* and *Ain't Misbehavin'* for that crowd."

"I'm liking her more and more as we go along," I said.

"Me too. It must have tickled the shit out of her, dancing to those numbers. I'm surprised she didn't do 'Miss Otis Regrets.' "

"I got the distinct impression Pink Lloyd found his match when he met Emily, didn't you?"

"Lot more than his match," Gladys said. "I wonder what happened when he went out to Personal Leisure World that night. Suppose he was asking her for a date?"

"Probably close to it," I said. "I keep thinking of how it had to be that night, in the lot. Cold, raw, shitty."

"How do you know that?"

"I checked the weather in the papers for that day. Inside it's a regular night down at the massage parlor. Nothing special except a guy loses his nerve and walks out on Emily. Pink Lloyd comes in. He shoots the shit for a while. She walks him downstairs, says good night. How? Would she kiss him good night?"

"Might. Why didn't you ask him?"

"Hey, nobody's perfect. Okay, Pink Lloyd takes off. Emily goes back up. Joint closes. Emily leaves. Her car was found locked later on, so she never got to it."

"Probably."

"Okay, probably. Probably she got in somebody else's car, the weather the way it was."

"Or went back inside after Wanda closed up. Did Emily have a key?"

"She did, actually. She kind of ran things for Wanda whenever Wanda had to step out or took time off. But if it happened that way, why not just leave her body inside?"

"Or why not carry it outside and dump it in a snow-bank so nobody would find it for a while? Makes as much sense as anything else."

"Not as much sense as if the guy dragged her into his car and raped her there."

"On the other hand, she doesn't sound like she would have been real easy to drag, does she?" Gladys said.

"No, definitely not too draggable."

"Not too undressable, either," Gladys said. It kept coming back to that.

I drove Gladys to her house and there was that awkward moment when each of you wonders what the other expects you to do. I was just drunk enough to want to, but just sober enough to know how dumb it would be. She must have been about the same, because we both looked at each other, and both started to laugh at about the same time.

She opened her door, got out, closed it, and looked in at me through the window. "I like you and I feel like it," she said. "You understand that, don't you?"

"Sure, I do. I like you and I feel like it, too."

"But we've each got our custard cream pie à la mode," Gladys said. She smiled and went up the walk to her door. Once she was safe inside I drove off—a little bit frustrated but mostly happy and relieved. Pieces of pie are everywhere, but it isn't every day you find a friend.

Thursday morning I woke up with a hangover, which used to happen to me a lot but doesn't so much anymore. I took a long, hot shower and then turned the cold on. Cold water in Cambridge in August is a long way short of icy, and it was a while till the top of my skull started to hurt from it. Then I repeated the hot-cold cycle twice. Sometimes, in mild cases, this takes care of a hangover. This wasn't one of those cases. I decided to run down to the corner for a *Globe* and then lie around in my air-conditioned bedroom until my head felt better. Which would have been around noon fifteen years ago, but would be more like four o'clock now.

And I would certainly have followed this program if I hadn't turned on the radio to catch the weather while I was shaving. It was going to be hot again—and police were trying to identify a corpse pulled from the Charles just after dawn. A sculler navigating through the fog downstream from the Weeks footbridge had bumped into what he at first thought was a floating log. The cause of the man's death was unknown pending results of an autopsy. "Police say the dead man may have been in a recent accident," the announcer said, "as his right arm was in a sling." I thought about that while I finished shaving, and then picked up the phone.

"This is your old pal, Tom," I said when the switchboard had finally put me through to Gladys Williams. "How do you feel?"

"I feel like shit, old pal. Which is exactly the way I hope you feel."

"Well, you get your wish. Listen, I'm sorry to bother you, but what do you know about the floater they pulled out of the river this morning?"

"That's part of why I feel so good. He was waiting when I got in this morning."

"Which arm was in the sling?"

"Right one."

"Had it been recently dislocated?"

"Could have been. There was edema, discoloration."

"What does he look like?"

"Late twenties, early thirties. White male, about five-nine, 160 or 165. Probably Hispanic."

"Shit."

"You know him?"

"I hope not, but I bet I do. Can I look at him?"

"Why not?"

His body cavity had been sewed back up after the autopsy with big, sloppy stitches. He looked a good deal like the man who had attacked me at Fresh Pond, although I could have been wrong. A corpse sometimes looks considerably different from the living person.

"The FBI should have his prints from the Immigration Service," I said. "If he's who I'm pretty sure he is, he's an immigrant from El Salvador named Jose Soto."

"Who is this guy, Tom?"

"He's the asshole who tried to kill me during the storm Tuesday. What happened to him?"

Gladys showed me the pathologist's report and interpreted where necessary. Death had been caused by drowning, but there was evidence of trauma to the trachea as well. He might have been choked into unconsciousness, and then revived enough in the water to gasp his lungs full of water. Or the choking might have had nothing to do with his drowning. His injured arm had been taped into immobility, and he could have panicked on hitting the water. Or maybe he just didn't know how to swim.

"Choked like Emily," Gladys said. "Shouldn't you talk to somebody here? They're not all like Harrigan. I can get you with Billy Curtin, the guy I told you about."

"I can call his office and tip them anonymously who this guy is," I said. "That'll keep you out of it. But I'd like to keep myself out of it, too. If I ever figure out what's going on, though, I'll find a way to let Curtin know."

"Yeah, well, be careful, Tom. It could be your neck. Literally."

"I do some wrestling," I said. "A lot of pretty good guys have had a crack at my neck."

" 'I do some wrestling,' " she mimicked. "Jesus, Tom, do men realize what assholes you sometimes sound like?"

"Some of us do," I said. "But we can't always help it."

8

OR IF TONIGHT ISN'T CONVENIENT, I COULD DRIVE OUT
to the Vineyard next week," I said. It was Friday night
at the Kellicotts'. "Either way is fine."

"Lot of trouble for you," he said. "Might as well talk
to them tonight while you're here. Save you the drive."

Kellicott raised his voice slightly, to include his wife
and daughter in the conversation. They were across the
large living room; Kellicott and I were at the bar, where
he was fixing predinner drinks. "At some point Tom
needs to talk to you ladies," he said.

"Yes, dear," said Susan Kellicott.

"Yes, Papa," said her daughter, Phyllis. I had never
heard anyone call her father Papa before.

Phyllis needed a second glance. At first glance you got
no clear impression of her. She was indistinct, like a
half-erased drawing. You had to look again to see that
she was one of those pretty girls who don't know that

they're pretty. Her mother, on the other hand, had never been pretty and probably knew it all too well. She would have stood nearly as tall as her husband, but she stooped and her shoulders were hunched. She was bulky without having any definite shape. I tried to imagine what the Kellicotts had looked like as a young couple, in the light of Gladys's theory on couples balancing out.

Kellicott turned his attention back to me. "You're right to want to be sure," he said. "Teddy's wife, Gerry Ferraro's husband. You don't want these things coming up during a campaign."

That was certainly a reasonable, sophisticated reaction to a stranger's request for private interviews with your wife and your daughter. Personally I would have been irritated as hell and shown it. That was just another one of the reasons Kellicott was up for secretary of state and I wasn't. He didn't show it.

We joined the two women and talked for a few minutes about how hot it had been and when the gypsy moth caterpillars were due back and how people watered their lawns too much when the reservoirs were down. I had no very strong positions on any of these things; all I paid attention to was Mrs. Kellicott's behavior with her bourbon and water. She didn't seem to be going at it in any great haste, but the drink was gone before the ice cubes had lost their squareness. She didn't bother her husband for a refill; she went over to the sideboard and took care of herself. I recognized the pattern, which had been mine for long enough and on occasion still was. A glass left empty, even momentarily, disrupted the proper order of things.

"When are we going in, dear?" Kellicott asked when his wife rejoined us.

"I told Bridget seven," she said, "but it doesn't really matter. Everything's cold."

"Twenty minutes or so till we sit down, then," Kelli-cott said to me. "Would that be time enough for you to get started?"

It probably would. I decided to talk with Phyllis first, on grounds that I would probably need more time with her mother. We went into a small study, lined with bookshelves, off the living room. Phyllis left half of her gin and tonic behind her on the sideboard. I took my drink in with me. It was straight tonic, not because I cared about keeping a clear head, but because Kellicott hadn't had any beer. Beer was all I usually drank, anymore.

I explained the kinds of things I had to ask her, and why, and then, when she seemed resigned enough, I set out. In a small voice, managing to sound cooperative and offended at the same time, she said she didn't very much like the taste of liquor, she had never experimented with drugs, had never been arrested, had never been under treatment for any psychological or emotional problem, never been expelled from school, been pregnant, hospitalized, ticketed for a moving violation, addicted to any substance, affiliated with any organization advocating the overthrow by force or violence of the United States, and so on and so forth.

"Well, that takes care of it," I said at last, and then went on to ask her about the only thing so far that really made me curious about her. "I notice you call your father Papa," I said.

"Isn't that all right?" she said.

"Oh, sure. I just never heard it before, is all."

"We called him Papa when we were little, and I guess I just kept on."

"Did Emily keep on?"

"Not once she got bigger, no. She called him A.K."

"Like the rifle."

160

"Rifle?"

"There's an assault rifle called the AK-47."

"No, it was his initials."

"Oh, right," I said, cutting my losses. It's tricky dealing with somebody who's totally humorless. "A kind of a nickname. I guess they were pretty close?"

"Papa loved her very much."

"And presumably she loved him?"

"Emily was a very cold person."

I waited, and waited. Until she felt she had to explain herself.

"It wasn't her fault. She was very young."

"Do I have it wrong? I thought she was your older sister."

"She was. I don't mean young in that way."

"Young in what way?"

"Always taking. Never giving. I shouldn't be saying these things. I don't want to talk about my sister. It's over for her, but we still have each other. Our family. We're alive and we have to take care of each other."

She stopped talking and sat there, her hands working and working at one another.

"Well," I said, "I guess we must be about ready to go in." I had never heard anyone use the expression "going in" before, in the sense that Papa had. "Incidentally," I asked, "what do you call your mother?"

"Mummy," Phyllis said.

Nobody I knew had ever called their mother Mummy, either.

Dinner was cold, as Susan Kellicott had warned us. But it wasn't just stuff out of the refrigerator. We started with vichyssoise so good it was obvious I had been served counterfeits up till then. "Oh, Bridget probably had some of that old duck stock still around," Mrs. Kellicott said. Duck soup.

Then we had a macédoine of vegetables, steamed, chilled to crispness, and dressed with olive oil and vinegar. The main course was cold lobster meat, tails and claws. To go with it, Bridget served each of us a small bowl of freshly made mayonnaise, bright yellow and glistening. Dessert was sliced peaches with whipped cream. It was the best meal I had eaten in a long time, perhaps ever, which I told Bridget as she was clearing away.

She jerked her head in the direction of the kitchen and said, "I'll tell Otto you liked it."

"Otto is Swiss," Mrs. Kellicott said when Bridget had gone. "The Swiss are beautifully trained."

Otto and Bridget could be a complication.

"Do they go with you to the Vineyard?" I asked.

"Oh, yes. We do a good deal of entertaining there, you know. Bridget and Otto will drive down tonight as a matter of fact, so they can go over first thing tomorrow and open the house." And so they wouldn't be a complication at all.

At dinner we had talked some more about the heat, and about the Vineyard, and parking problems in downtown Cambridge, and how the best way to keep silver looking good was to use it every day. The silver did look good, too: simple, graceful utensils with their monograms worn to soft illegibility by countless polishings.

My interest was in how the members of the little family acted around each other, and in how Emily might have fitted into those patterns. The Kellicotts gave few clues, though; perhaps they never did, with an outsider present. The father was polite and deferential toward the mother; the daughter was polite and respectful toward both parents; the mother was polite and slightly withdrawn. She carried along the conversation competently but absently, the way a person might drive one-handed on the interstate, her thoughts far away. Neither woman seemed stupid, although neither seemed particularly smart, either. This meant nothing, though, particularly where women were concerned. In America, for women even more than for men, intelligence is a weapon to be carried concealed.

After dinner I excused myself and went to the small bathroom off the entrance hall. There I set to work. With the few small things I had brought with me, I backed out the screws from the bottom half of the window latch, replacing them with screws that were a size too small for the holes. I cracked the screen just far enough open so that the latches on each side were unable to seat, and slid a broken twig under the screen to hold it up. Then I closed the window so that it appeared locked, and rejoined the company.

I would just as soon have gone on talking about the servant problem or something, since I wasn't looking forward to my interview with Susan Kellicott. Her background, unlike those of her daughter and her husband, actually did create problems for the Kellicott appointment. She knew it and I knew it and Kellicott knew it. Even Phyllis probably knew it, although her mother's psychiatric and medical history may have been kept from her. It was a dirty job but it had to be done, as Ted Bundy no doubt used to say to himself before squaring his shoulders and getting on with it. To Mrs. Kellicott, I said, "Well, shall we get it over with?"

We used the same room where Phyllis and I had talked. "I'm sorry about all this," I said. "It's no fun for me, and even less for you."

Susan Kellicott nodded. I remembered her daughter's nervously twisting hands. The mother's hands lay motionless in her lap. As far as appearances went, she was just waiting for her caller to get on with whatever he had on his mind. Fine.

"Your husband said you had a rough time when you were younger."

"That's true."

"Were drugs involved?"

"Drugs weren't such a big thing in those days."

"So the answer is no?"

"I smoked a marijuana cigarette in Paris with a boy I was seeing then. Or he said it was marijuana. It didn't seem to me that it did anything."

"And that's it, for drugs?"

"Except for prescription drugs, yes."

"Which prescription drugs?"

"I've had Librium prescribed. And Valium."

"Was that for depression?"

"Depression, yes."

"Would you have any objection if I talked to your doctors?"

"I thought they weren't supposed to do that."

"They're not, unless you give them permission. Even then, they might not."

"You could talk to Dr. Peterson, I suppose. Dr. Wiley and Dr. Milmine are dead."

"What kind of doctors are they? Were they, I guess?"

"Nervous disorders. Specialists in that sort of thing."

"Psychiatrists?"

"I don't know. Not with couches and things, certainly. Father would never have stood for that." I guessed he never would have stood for a Jew treating his daughter, either. Peterson, Wiley, and Milmine. It must have been tough finding three Gentile psychiatrists.

"Are you still Dr. Peterson's patient?"

"I see him occasionally. He's right here in Cambridge."

"What would he tell me if I talked to him?"

"I don't know what he'd say. How could I know?"

"Would he say that he currently writes you prescriptions for Librium and Valium?"

"Valium only."

"On a daily basis?"

"Oh, no, not nearly. Not for years. They don't think as highly of Valium as they used to, you know."

"I have to ask these things, you understand, Mrs. Kellicott . . ."

"Oh, I understand."

"The campaign has to be ready in case the Republicans get hold of it and put it out, the way they did with the Eagleton business. Senator Markham's people have to be able to say they knew all about it, it's ancient history, so on and so forth. Conceivably even put it out themselves as a preemptive strike. Your husband can tell you."

"He has."

"Then you know what I have to ask. Any electroshock?"

"Twice, when I was a girl."

"Suicide attempts?"

"The same thing. Twice. I took sleeping pills. Dr. Milmine said they weren't serious attempts."

"Cries for attention?"

"How did you know he called them that?"

"I didn't, but that's what they always call taking pills. Unless it works."

"Really? I thought it was a phrase he came up with himself. My feelings were hurt because he didn't take me seriously. Of course I was just a child."

"Maybe he did take you seriously. Were the two courses of electroshock therapy after the two attempts?"

"Not too long after. While I was ill."

"Maybe you stopped trying to kill yourself because you were afraid he'd shock you again if you did."

"I never thought of that."

"I doubt if he did, either. Shock treatment was just the fashion in those days, like tonsillectomies."

"Tonsillectomies?"

"Nothing. Just thinking aloud. Anyway, the most anybody could conceivably come up with, it would be these things years ago. Before your marriage?"

"Oh, yes. Both of them."

"Nothing since?"

"No, nothing. Sometimes I go away for a rest, sometimes."

"Where's that?"

"Different places. Cherry Plains. Hartford Retreat."

"When was the last time?"

"Oh, years. Maybe last year."

"Mrs. Kellicott, I want to tell you something. I drink now, to some extent. But I used to drink a lot. Day in and day out, a lot. So the people I'd be around, they'd mostly be drinkers, too. For years that's mostly who I knew, people who drank. What I'm saying is we understand each other."

"Maybe we do."

"How early do you start?"

"At lunch."

"I used to keep it in my bureau. You?"

"In the blanket chest."

"Do you ever get drunk?"

"I suppose it depends what you mean by that."

"Blackouts, passing out, throwing up, not making sense when you talk, stumbling or falling down."

"Heavens, no."

"So you're like me, a good drinker. Good drinkers don't do those things. You learn what your dose is and you keep yourself up to it. The dose goes up as you develop tolerance, so other people sometimes think you're a drunk. But that's because they'd be drunk if they took your dose."

"I never thought of it that way."

"I used to function just fine, whenever I wanted to. If I decided I didn't want to, I just went over my dose. You function fine, too. I was watching you. Nobody would know but another drinker."

"Will it hurt Alden that I drink?"

"I doubt it very much. Mrs. Eisenhower and Mrs. Ford drank, and it never hurt their husbands. It's just something the campaign needs to know, in case."

The easy part was over. Now for the hard part. "The other thing they need to know, Mrs. Kellicott, is about Emily."

"Emily? Why Emily?"

"It's just a loose end, is all."

"But that man did it. The man who was using her. They just couldn't prove it, Alden said, but they know."

"They could be right, but the thing is that officially it's still open. So I have to find out all I can. Did you see much of Emily after she dropped out of college?"

"I never saw her, not once. She called me every year on Mother's Day. If Alden answered, she'd hang up and call again until I was the one who picked up."

"What did she say?"

"Just that she was fine, and not to worry. To take care of Phyllis. They were short conversations, just a minute or two."

"Did you ask where she was, what she was doing?"

"Not after the first time, no. She made it very clear it wasn't any of my business."

"Was she hostile?"

"Not hostile, no. She couldn't be bothered to show that much emotion to a mere mother."

Susan Kellicott had been talking the way I had driven the night before—so practiced at being drunk that she mostly seemed sober. But let a child dart into my headlights and the liquor would have shown itself, no doubt of it. It had shown itself in Mrs. Kellicott just then, at the thought of Emily's calls on Mother's Day. I sat without saying anything, knowing she would go on. When she did, it was in the unsteady voice of someone trying to avoid tears.

"You don't know what to do, you just don't. You try to raise them the way everybody says you should raise them and they hate you. Not hate, hate would be better. Contempt. Pathetic. They think you're pathetic. Maybe they're right. How can we know why they think these things? How in God's name can we know?"

I made a gesture with my hands to show that I didn't have the answer, either. As indeed I didn't. To look at the question with uncomfortable honesty, contempt had certainly been part of what I felt for my own parents. Perhaps my distant daughter, off in Alaska, felt contempt for me. What had Kellicott felt for his father, the estate chauffeur?

"She was such a sweet, sunny child," Mrs. Kellicott said. Now her voice was frankly out of control, and her eyes were shining with tears. One ran down her cheek and she brushed at it, not bothering to hide it.

"She'd sit on Papa's lap and he'd pretend to pull her little braids and she'd pretend to be hurt, and then she'd laugh and laugh."

"This is your father?"

"Emily's father. Alden. When the children came, I got into the habit of calling him Papa."

"Was that what you called your father?"

"As a matter of fact it was, yes."

"When did she stop laughing?"

"I don't see ... Oh, Emily. It was the summer she went off to canoeing camp in Maine. They saw bears and moose, and she learned how to cook some kind of awful oatmeal bread they ate. There was never a clue in her letters that anything was wrong. She sounded like her same old self. All the counselors and the other campers wrapped right around her little finger, according to her. But Alden noticed right away that she was different, when he went up to drive her back."

"In what way?"

"Well, she was always a strong-willed, self-determined little thing, and God knows she still was. But it turned into a rebelliousness, almost a hatefulness. The sweetness was gone. The sunniness was gone. You read so much these days, those poor children on the milk cartons. Back then you didn't hear so much about it."

"You think she was abused or molested somehow at the camp?"

"Well, she wasn't that way before. The first time Alden noticed the change in her was when he was driving her back down."

"Did you ask her whether anything had happened?"

Her fingers got busy with the collar of her blouse. "I was away at the time," she said.

"Away ..."

"Hartford ... the Hartford Retreat."

"Did your husband ask her?"

"Alden tried. They had always been very close. But she told him nothing at all had happened."

"Were they close after that?"

"She wasn't close with anybody after that summer. She completely changed. She lost interest in school. She dropped her old friends and she didn't bring her new friends around the house, if she even had any. She had been a wonderful little field hockey player, but she gave it up entirely. The only thing she took any interest in was drawing."

"What did she draw?"

"She would never show anybody, but one time she left out something she had been working on. It was a meadow full of flowers, with a lawn mower up front. An old-fashioned hand mower, just standing there. Somebody had mowed part of the meadow, and the jonquils and daffodils were lying on the ground, all cut off and just lying there."

"How old was Emily?"

"Let's see, I came across the drawing when I was getting her things together for spring break. That was the year we went to Bermuda over the spring break ... Fifteen, going on sixteen."

"I meant when she went to the camp."

"Oh. That was the summer she was thirteen."

When I was a high school student in Port Henry, New York, we still wrestled on the old canvas mats. The mats were hard, but the worst was the canvas itself. All season you'd be covered with what the cyclists call road rash, big patches of cracking scab where the canvas had rubbed the skin off your elbows, your knees, your ears, your nose. If you wrestled long enough, you'd probably have been worn smooth like a stone in a stream.

Now it was better. The floor of Harvard's wrestling room was covered wall to wall with thick foam rubber with a smooth surface that went relatively easy on your skin. And the foam itself soaked up a lot of the impact when you smacked into it. The top of my head was socketed into the thick mat as comfortably as you could expect, considering that my skull was supporting half my body weight. The other half was on my feet. Everything else was arced into the air as I held my bridge. I was looking upside down at a sign running along one wall. It read EARNING THE RIGHT TO WIN BEGINS HERE.

I kept the strain on my neck muscles as long as I could and then rolled my weight forward until my body pivoted over my head in a sort of backward somersault with no hands. I wound up on my hands and knees, facing in the opposite direction. One drop of sweat followed another off the point of my chin, and made spots on the crimson mat. Soon the spots ran together into a wet blotch. No one bothered to air-condition the wrestling room during the summer. No one was expected to be in it, but I had a key and one of the duplicate staff ID cards I get every year from some underpaid teaching assistant in exchange for paying his gym fees. The privacy meant that I could perform bizarre drills—like the one I had just finished—without worrying whether non-wrestlers in the public exercise room thought I was showing off, or crazy. I had been at it since nine in the morning. Now it was close to eleven, and the sun was coming in strongly.

I stayed on my hands and knees for a few moments, letting my heart and my breathing slow down. Then, not bothering to get up, I crawled over to the two throwing dummies lying against the wall, one on top of the other. Their limbs ended in stumps, as if the hands and legs had been burned off. The arms stuck out stiffly in front, and somebody had jammed one dummy down on top of the other so that they were spending the summer locked in congress. I leaned back against them, folding my arms and closing my eyes while my system settled back to normal. I saw the Kellicotts at dinner, eating with their old and beautiful silver off new and beautiful bone china by Pfaltzgraff. There had been something at dinner that reminded me of something. What, though, and of what?

Three quarters of an hour later, the heat in the airless room woke me up. My T-shirt and shorts were still as sweat-soaked as they had been when I fell asleep. The top dummy was dark with sweat where my cheek had lain against it. I was still half in my dream, a dream from my time in Alaska. Judy Purvis was there, and her husband, Ham, who had had half the women in town sniffing around after him hopefully. Now and then their hopes were realized, too, which Judy probably knew. In the dream Ham was going out the door into a storm and she was looking after him the way she always did when he didn't know her eyes were on him. Beyond any possible misunderstanding, the look said I love you, and it said something terribly sad besides. It also said I know perfectly well you don't love me back, but after all, who could?

That was what I had been trying to remember about dinner at the Kellicotts': where I had seen that kind of look before, the look that Susan Kellicott gave her husband when she thought she was unobserved.

9

SATURDAY AFTERNOON PHIL JEFFERS WAS IN WITH THE senator and couldn't see me just yet. That's what Arthur Kleber told me, and so I told Arthur that Phil specifically said 2:00 P.M., and here it was 2:00 P.M.

"You want to bust in on the candidate, go ahead," Arthur said. "I can't stop you." He thought about that for a moment.

"I'd have to try though, wouldn't I?" he said. "Shit."

"Don't worry, Arthur," I said. "I won't bust in on the candidate. Him and Phil are probably having one of those top-level strategy sessions, right?"

Arthur shrugged. Maybe they were dissecting frogs in there, or saving the rain forest, or amending the constitution of South Dakota. He didn't care.

"You pick out your embassy yet, Arthur?"

"I should live so long."

"Things not going so good, huh?"

"Put it like this, okay? This guy, you kick him in the balls, he goes, 'Hey, listen, I'm sorry. Did my balls get in your way? Does your foot hurt?' "

"Are you saying he's a gentleman?"

"Well, it's not quite that bad. But I'd say he was in the wrong business, definitely yes."

Just then the man in the wrong business came out of Jeffers's office. He was closely followed by Jeffers and two other aides.

"You remember Tom Bethany," Jeffers said, on the assumption that the senator didn't.

"Certainly," Senator Markham said, sticking out his hand. He sounded as if I had never been far from his thoughts. "How have you been, Tom?"

I took his hand in mine and covered both our hands in a warm grip with my left hand, just firmly enough so that he wouldn't execute the rest of his maneuver. Which would have been to move on without a break in his stride, trailing a "Nice to see you again" behind him.

"Just fine, Senator," I said when I had brought him to a halt. "Coming up with some stuff you ought to know about."

"Good, wonderful," he said. "That's the way. Tell Phil about it, will you?"

And I let him go, having given it a try. "Nice to see you again," the senator said over his shoulder, moving on with his two aides. Phil Jeffers stayed behind and gestured me into his office.

"What was that shit all about?" he asked when we were alone. We both know what shit he meant. A courtier's main business is keeping anybody else from speaking directly to his prince.

"What shit?" I nevertheless said.

"What shit?" he mimicked. "You were covering your

ass in case it turns out later that Kellicott was butt-fuck-ing Mary Poppins or something."

He had lost me, but just for the instant it took to pre-tend I was him. Then I saw what he had seen. If I missed anything big on Kellicott and it later blew up in the campaign's face, Jeffers would be figuring I had just arranged matters so that I could claim I told him but he never passed it on.

"Actually, Phil, I just wanted to find out whether your guy has enough brains to reach past you for his information."

"Bullshit."

"And he doesn't."

"You tell me anything that amounts to shit, it'll get to him. What have you got?"

"That's just it. Nothing that you'd figure amounts to shit. That's why I wanted to give Markham a chance to hear it."

"Well, he blew his chance. So what have you got?"

"I had dinner at Kellicotts' last night."

"You told me you were going to. So what happened?"

"She's a lush, his wife."

"No crime, as long as she can carry it."

"Oh, she can carry it."

"So let her."

"His daughter, the one that died? She was a good kid. Had it all together."

"And?"

"And Kellicott says she was a mess."

"Plenty of people don't know their own kids."

He had me there. I didn't know my own kid, either.

"Usually they get it the other way around, though," I said. "They pretend a bad kid is a good kid."

"Sometimes yes, sometimes no." He had me there, too. As soon as I had said the words, I knew they were wrong. Plenty of parents think perfectly good kids are bad kids. Still, something smelled wrong to me about the murder of Kellicott's daughter and I was being paid to try to make Jeffers smell it, too. So I went on, without much hope.

"The point here, Phil, is that the case is still open."

"What are you telling me? Kellicott has to put his whole career on hold because the cops can't find out who killed his daughter?"

"It's just something that could come down on you someday, that's all."

"Like one of those pianos that fall on guys in the cartoons? You ever hear about a piano that actually fell on a guy?"

"There's a piano up there. That's all I'm telling you."

"Not enough. Tell me something else."

"A guy tried to kill me."

"A guy? What guy?"

"A guy named Jose Soto. From El Salvador. He wound up dead in the Charles, full of water."

"Oh, Jesus, no . . . Bethany, what kind of shit have you dumped us into?"

He must have been feeling the way Haldeman and Ehrlichman felt when E. Howard Hunt's name turned up in connection with a third-rate burglary in a place called the Watergate. Jeffers relaxed when I explained that I hadn't killed Soto; Soto had only tried to kill me.

"What's it got to do with anything?" Jeffers said when I had finished. "I mean a Hispanic tries to mug you, you see it in the papers all the time." Jeffers said Hispanic the way Billy Carter used to say Negro, so you knew what he'd rather say.

"I was wearing shorts and a twelve-dollar Casio," I said. "What was he mugging me for?"

"How do I know?"

"It was a jogging path and he followed me there in a thunderstorm," I said. "Get real, Phil."

"All right, let's get real. A guy you never saw before tries to kill you. Nobody else ever saw the guy before, either."

"The sanctuary guy saw him before."

"That's nobody. Nothing ties him to Kellicott, nothing ties him to you. He tried to kill you, I'm sorry. But it's your worry, not ours."

"You don't think he's got anything to do with that piano?"

"Give me a break with the pianos, okay?"

"Up to you. You're paying for it, I'm giving you what I've got."

"So far you've got just what we hoped you'd have, Bethany. Nothing."

"Will you tell Markham about it?"

"About nothing? Why?"

"I'll send you a report, then."

"Don't. Nothing on paper. You held the guy upside down and shook him and nothing came out. Fine. Now wrap it up."

"I hired on by the week, so you're still entitled to today and Sunday. There's one other thing I thought I'd look into."

Jeffers waved his hand to say go ahead and look, be my guest.

The night was so dark that only the outlines of the Kellicott house showed from the street. But from my invited visit the night before, I knew that it was a two-story clapboard house, painted white with black shutters. Enormous maples rose higher than the tall brick chimneys on the four corners of the Kellicott house. The grounds, big enough to hold three or four smaller houses, took up the middle of the short block. The property was enclosed by a six-foot picket fence with gates standing open at either end of a semicircular driveway. A mounting block stood in the middle of the semicircle, where carriages once discharged visitors. Four steps led from the cobblestoned driveway up to a small portico. There was a fanlight over the front door. The entrance was lit by a lamp that hung from the ceiling of the portico, giving an impression of occupancy. But in theory the family and the servants were safely on Martha's Vineyard.

In theory, too, I knew perfectly well that most burglars don't get caught. But in the here and now, I also knew perfectly well that unseen neighbors were wondering what I was doing on their quiet street. Certainly the people next door could see me from their windows, even though clouds covered the moon and I was creeping along the hedges that bordered the drive. Certainly their dogs could smell me and would bark any minute. The people across the street would see me now as I left the bushes and went out onto the open lawn quickly but casually, as if I belonged. They'd know, of course, that I didn't. They'd be dialing 911 right now. Reporting that I was in the shadows along the side of the house, raising the bathroom window . . . hoisting myself up to the sill . . . disappearing inside.

I slid the window shut behind me and listened to the dark house. Only a hum was in the air—and then it stopped. I thought of some sort of burglar alarm, before I got a grip and thought of the air-conditioning system shutting off. There's no better way to slow down time than to listen with every nerve for noises in somebody else's house at night. An hour or so passed in perhaps thirty seconds, but nothing broke the silence except the tiny sounds of internal housekeeping—my own breathing and my own pulse in my ears.

I began to move one slow foot in front of the other, picking up courage with each step that went unchallenged. In a minute or two it was hard to remember what all the fuss had been about, and I was making my way along with only the normal caution of somebody in a dark and unfamiliar place. When I had reached the hallway the moon came out from behind the clouds so that I could see well enough, my eyes having got used to the darkness by then. This was all to the good; I didn't dare turn on any lights for fear that the neighbors might know the house was supposed to be empty over the weekend. My plan, in fact, was to find some place to sleep upstairs and to go exploring seriously only when the sun came up. I was heading for the stairs when it happened.

A crash of music came from behind me—the discord of notes struck at random, followed by an awkward riffling of keys from the piano in the drawing room. Another time and another place, the sound would have been unremarkable. Just then it taught me that fight or flight aren't the only two options when danger explodes in the hunter-gatherer's face. He can also stand paralyzed, which was the choice my system made for me.

After that single harsh musical phrase came nothing, no whisper of noise, nothing at all. I stood forever, or so it seemed, without moving. Once before I had been frozen with fear like this, one time rock climbing in the Aleutian range. I had got myself in a kind of cup on the face of a cliff in the Valley of Ten Thousand Smokes, with a two-hundred-foot sheer drop before me and an unclimbable incline behind me. The same fear immobilized me then, until at last I worked it through my head that I had just climbed down the unclimbable incline after all. And now I would damned well have to make myself climb back up if I didn't want to die there on the rock face.

I didn't want to die with one foot on the bottom step of Kellicott's stairway, either, and so I had just about decided to head toward the drawing room when a cat came out of it.

"Fucking cat," I said aloud, sounding mean to myself. The cat, indifferent, padded off down the hall silently. Pretty nearly the only time you can hear a cat walking is when the damned thing jumps onto a keyboard.

Upstairs at last, and my heart slowed down somewhat, I examined the Kellicotts' living arrangements. There were four bedrooms on the second floor. The windows of the large master bedroom gave out on the gardens in back of the house. Under bright lights instead of dim moonlight, it would have looked like a boudoir display in a very expensive store. Flower patterns and puffy comforters and down pillows and ruffles were everywhere. Rugs and fabrics and wallpaper seemed to be in various shades of pale gray, but probably in daylight they would turn out to be pastel.

It reminded me of Hope's separate bedroom in Washington, which gave the same impression of overwhelming femininity. You felt like an intruder into some secret, perfumed place where no men, or few, had ever been allowed entrance before. I imagined Mrs. Kellicott lying propped up on these pillows, wearing a satin peignoir, watching the large TV that sat on a table at the foot of her bed. Did she have a remote control so that she wouldn't have to get out of bed except for bodily functions?

I left and moved down the hall.

The bedroom next door was that of a teenage girl, with school banners and posters of male rock stars on the wall. It had a look of unnatural and temporary order about it, like a room that will only stay neat until the occupant returns from freshman year in college. But the occupant would never return. On the wall was a framed diploma from Buckingham, Browne & Nichols School. I took it to the window and read the hand-lettered name in the moonlight: Emily Milton Kellicott.

Alden Kellicott's room was around the corner. It was part office and part bedroom. Bookcases ran around all four walls, interrupted only by the windows and the two doors. The door to my left stood half open, showing a bathroom sink with a mirror over it. A bed sat to my right, pushed up against the bookshelves. In front of the windows there was a massive desk of carved mahogany. The computer sitting on the antique desk should have clashed with it, but somehow didn't. Nor did the space-age telephone with the elaborate console. Another, smaller telephone was on a table next to an armchair opposite the bed. The room was also equipped with a bureau, a second armchair, a couple of low, two-drawer oak filing cabinets, and a small refrigerator camouflaged to look like another oak cabinet. An expensive German coffee machine sat on top of it.

The room seemed to have been assembled for utility rather than show. The carpeting underfoot felt like some durable indoor-outdoor stuff. The furniture seemed to have been plunked down wherever it would be handy. A portable TV sat on one of the filing cabinets. No photographs or anything of a personal or family nature stood on the bureau, or on the unused portions of the bookshelves. There was no closet in the room, which made me curious enough to poke around till I found sliding doors in the hallway outside; in them I felt his suits and jackets, hanger after hanger, dozens of them.

Back in the bedroom I opened the refrigerator, risking

the brief and slight illumination. Inside were two bottles of white wine, one full and one half gone, and a six-pack of club soda. Kellicott could have afforded Perrier by the shipload, but he seemed to have enough sense not to do it when he could get the same absence of flavor at a quarter of the price in a fine domestic water.

His bathroom had what looked like light-tight shutters on the windows. I closed them and turned on the light. The bathroom was huge, the size of a large bedroom. Perhaps that was what it had once been. Now it was where Kellicott kept his expensive toys. A sauna was built into one end. Next to it was a glass-enclosed shower stall with six shower heads installed at different heights and angles, from overhead down to knee level. Thick, fluffy towels, big enough to serve as sheets, hung from chrome racks along the wall. A bidet was next to the toilet. I wondered about that. Piles? A Nordictrack exerciser and a Concept II ergometer stood side by side on the black tile floor, and an exercising device with pulleys and chromed weights was folded up against the wall. The walls themselves were dark green with white trim; on them hung silver-framed prints of Victorian vintage. There was an alcove with mirrors on three sides, the sort they have in tailor's shops that lets you check the fit from all sides.

I might have added parallel bars for dips and a chinning bar, and perhaps a foam-rubber exercise mat instead of the deep-piled white throw rugs. Apart from those small additions, Kellicott's facilities struck me as just about perfect. He even had a set of straight razors, a shaving mug, a huge badger-hair brush, and a strop hanging by the sink. Learning to shave with a straight razor, like learning to play the trumpet, is one of those things I'll never do and always regret that I didn't.

The last bedroom was Phyllis's. It was less grand than

her mother's, but very much along the same lines. Delicate, costly, nondurable, decorative. Frills and femininity. The only sign that a child must once have lived there was a doll, which was perched not on the pillows but on a windowsill. For the rest it was a woman's room, not a girl's. There was even an old-fashioned ladies' writing desk, and a boudoir settee of the type that lets you lean against one end while your feet hang off the other. Or mine would, anyway.

Of the four bedrooms, Phyllis's struck me as the least uncomfortable, speaking psychologically rather than physically, for me to sleep in. I locked the door to avoid further surprises from the damned cat, got undressed, and slid under the light down comforter. It was just about the right degree of covering, with the air-conditioner maintaining a steady seventy or so.

I had established a line of retreat before turning in—out the window, onto the roof of a rear porch, and an easy drop into the geraniums. But the thought still stayed with me that I would be in very bad trouble in a number of ways if I got caught breaking and entering. I lay awake worrying about that, until my thoughts turned at last to the life that must be lived on this floor.

The upstairs rooms told a clear story. Mrs. Kellicott, the former Susan Milton, lived alone in what amounted to an elaborate private ward, self-medicating herself with alcohol and, perhaps, whatever drugs she could talk the doctors out of. Her husband had long since moved out of the sickroom and built a retreat of his own.

I imagined how evenings must be in the Kellicott home. Emily, the life and vibrancy of the family, gone for years and now dead. Mrs. Kellicott, disappearing upstairs after dinner to her drugs, booze, and television. Alden Kellicott disappearing to write or read in his bedroom-study, or to exercise in his miniature health club. I wondered if Mrs. Kellicott ever set foot in his territory, or he in hers.

Did Phyllis stay downstairs in the evenings or did she disappear, too, up to this room? I thought of Phyllis, pretty but not knowing it. Young, but old in her manner. Perhaps she was the mother in the house, and her mother the child? What did she do up here, in her grown-up's bedroom, with no books, no TV, no stereo? Did she sew? Knit? What?

I let the birds wake me, before the sun was up. I shaved and brushed my teeth in Phyllis's bathroom, and then I began my daylight search of the big house by climbing up to the attic. As attics go, the Kellicotts' seemed practically sterile: a few pieces of unused furniture, empty luggage, six new-looking footlockers full of blankets and linens and smelling of mothballs. The only clutter was in a corner set aside for the artifacts of childhood. It held field-hockey sticks, toys, picture books, dollhouses, and that sort of thing. Even all this had been somewhat organized. The rest of the huge expanse was as trim as a barracks waiting for inspection. No dust was on the floor, no cobwebs hung from the rafters, and the windowpanes were clear. Somebody—Phyllis, at a guess—must have made sure that it got a going-over once or twice a year.

From the attic I went downstairs to the kitchen and made myself a cup of instant coffee, washing up afterward and replacing everything carefully. I made a fast pass through the kitchen cabinets and drawers, and then began to search the rest of the ground floor. I didn't expect to find anything of much significance in this relatively public part of the house, where guests and servants were most likely to go poking into things. And I didn't. The only partial exception was in the study off the living room, where Kellicott kept various souvenirs of his travels—the equivalent, at his level, of plaster Eiffel towers and Disneyland bumper stickers.

On the wall was a glass-fronted case that held a collection of brilliant, iridescent rain-forest butterflies, arranged by someone with such an eye for color and composition that they almost amounted to art. A small god or devil that looked pre-Columbian sat on a shelf, and a stylized pendant from the same period hung from a nearly invisible filament inside a hand-blown bell jar. Both seemed to be solid gold, although perhaps they weren't. It was hardly likely that Kellicott would set that much temptation in the path of the help, or of burglars like me, for that matter.

A miniature bayonet sat on Kellicott's green blotter. It was an exact duplicate in sterling silver of a U.S. Army bayonet, down to the saw teeth on the back of the blade and the blood gutter down its length. The silversmith had even fashioned tiny silver rivets to hold the silver grips on the haft. The whole letter opener or ornament or whatever was about ten inches long. "A Alden con amistad, Roberto, San Salvador, 1979" was engraved on the blade. With friendship, from Roberto.

Roberto D'Aubuisson, the psychopathic death squad commander? It seemed possible. Carter's foreign policy by the time of Kellicott's appointment, after many months of listening to Brzezinski's cold war puerilities, was edging away from human rights and toward Jeane Kirkpatrick's worldly-wise tolerance of torturers and murderers.

I also found a cheap bronze casting of the Liberty Bell on Kellicott's desk. The small plaque on the base said "To Alden Kellicott, U.S. State Department, from the City of Philadelphia, Frank Rizzo, Mayor." Presumably he kept this around as a joke; maybe he kept the bayonet as a joke, too. Or maybe he kept it because the silver knife was such an elegant toy.

So was the chrome-plated Beretta semiautomatic pistol I found in his desk drawer, or at least the Soldier of Fortune set would have considered it a toy. Its .25-caliber bullets would have very little of what the gun freaks call stopping power. On the other hand, the weapon of choice used by Mafia killers is the .22. And their victims wind up just as dead, clinically, as a man whose head has been exploded by a .357 Magnum. Kellicott's more modest pistol was a gift of state. According to the engraved inscription it came from a prominent West Point graduate who went on to success as the ruling kleptocrat of Nicaragua, the late Anastasio Somoza.

I grew up with long guns and still own two of them. But when I was in Southeast Asia I grew out of emotional puberty—at least the NRA's brand of it. I came to see that handguns were up to practically no good, and I have never since carried one. Nor do I much like the idea of other people having them available for use, and so I unloaded this one, replaced the clip, then slipped the smooth, heavy bullets into my pocket.

So far I had sifted through most of the house and had come up with a sieve full of nothing. Maybe Kellicott should have turned his gifts from foreign suitors over to the Department of State—it seemed to me that I had read something to that effect somewhere, someplace. But it wasn't the sort of thing that either Phil Jeffers or the Senate Foreign Relations Committee was likely to get too upset over.

What remained, though, was what I figured would be the most promising area—the upstairs living quarters. I started with Mrs. Kellicott's boudoir.

Her bedside drawers held a half dozen Harlequin

romances, squirreled away out of sight. Out of whose sight? Her intellectual husband's? Apart from this, though, all I learned from my search was that she hadn't been lying about where she hid her booze. There was an opened fifth of Jack Daniel's at the bottom of her blanket chest.

In her bathroom the medicine cabinet held a jumble of pill bottles, some of the prescriptions years out of date and some of them recent. The prescriptions had been written by ten or a dozen different doctors, the sign of the pillhead. Some of the brand names I didn't recognize, but many I did. Among them were Valium, Inderal, Thorazine, Lithane—the pharmacology of the emotionally frail. There was a minimum of cosmetics and other toiletries, compared with the amazing excess you find in most women's bathrooms. No male paraphernalia was in sight.

Kellicott's bedroom didn't contain much of interest, either, except his Rolodex. I once heard someone accuse Phil Jeffers of having an upwardly mobile Rolodex. Kellicott didn't. There was no more upward to go to. The cards flapped down as I turned the little wheel: Henry, Cy, Zbig, Brent, George (Kennan, Shultz, Baker, and Bush), and on and on. I spent ten minutes copying down the private, unlisted numbers of the rich and famous. You never know when you might want to give the Ron a ring.

The books on the shelves held nothing but evidence that he had read most of them: underlinings and notes in the margin. It took nearly an hour to riffle the pages of each one, but books seemed like the best of places to hide anything small that needed hiding. The second-best place for written secrets was probably the oak filing cabinets, particularly since they were locked. I found the key hanging on a small finishing nail driven into the side of a desk drawer, so far to the rear that you had to pull the drawer nearly free of its tracks to spot it. The files could have kept me happily occupied for days, but I didn't have days. I only had till evening, at the latest, and maybe not that long. Kellicott was due at work Monday morning; he would have to catch a Sunday ferry off the Vineyard and spend tonight at home in Cambridge. And so I had to be content with thumbing through each folder to make sure that it did indeed contain only "Personal correspondence, Jan.–July 1987" or whatever else the label said. And each folder did. "Miscellaneous" was even miscellaneous, although of no particular interest.

Next I went through Emily's room, or memorial. I wondered who had made the decision to leave all her belongings in place. Maybe, like a lot of decisions, it had just got made by inertia. Much of the gear of upper-class female adolescent life was there, but it said little about the owner. There was a tape deck, but no tapes that would have indicated her taste in music. Presumably she had taken them with her. I found no diaries, letters, marked calendars, engagement books, notes to herself, sketches. Probably she had taken all that, too. The only books were old schoolbooks, and the usual little-girl collection of Nancy Drew and books about horses. I had the feeling that the answer to Emily/Nelda's death was somewhere in her life—but her old room offered no answers that I could see.

Nothing to do but to continue rooting around like a blind hog, and so I went back to Phyllis's room to search it more fully, now that the sun had risen. Nothing under the throw rugs, and no sign that the maple floorboards had ever been tampered with. The closet and the bureau drawers contained nothing unexpected; nor did her bedside tables. In the bathroom, I found a supply of birth

control pills tucked away in the back of one of the dressing table drawers. I was surprised, not that she would
hide them, but that she would have them at all. I
wouldn't have imagined that she had an active enough
love life to justify being on the pill, and yet the date on
the prescription was only a couple of months back. Good
for you, Phyllis, I thought. Maybe you'll get out of this
nut ward yet. I closed the drawer, and went back out to
the bedroom to have a look at the writing desk.

The light was good enough by now to let me see
clearly. The desk was the sort of thing you might see in
a museum. It had a row of cubbyholes and tiny drawers
above the shelf on which you wrote. The writing surface
was of green Moroccan leather inlaid into mahogany. To
the right of the kneehole were three good-sized drawers.
The hardware on them had the soft shine and blurred
edges that come from a couple centuries of polishing. In
the top drawer I found ledgers, bankbooks, and bills
sorted into envelopes or paper-clipped bundles.

Phyllis, it turned out, ran the house. Her name was
printed on the checks along with her mother's and
father's. To judge from the stubs, filled in carefully and
legibly, she was in charge of paying the help, the insurance, the property taxes, and all other household bills.
The largest single outlay was for the salaries and Social
Security for Bridget and Otto, a gardener-houseman, and
a full-time caretaker on the Vineyard. They even got
their health insurance paid, which made Kellicott an
unusually generous employer of domestic help. The
family owned a Cherokee for use on the island, and
three other cars, all Saabs of various ages. Heating oil,
utilities, major and minor maintenance of the two resi-
dences, all were high. A thousand here, a thousand
there, it all added up. Each month Phyllis got through
most of the twenty thousand dollars deposited monthly

into the Kellicotts' account by the Milton Family Trust. Very nearly a quarter of a million dollars a year. It cost more than I thought to be rich.

But it didn't cost Susan Kellicott any more to be a drunk than it had cost me in the old days. The purveyor to the Kellicotts was a liquor dealer of the old school, who sent handwritten, itemized bills monthly. Kellicott's spritzers accounted for about two bottles of his brand of white wine a week. The rest of the family also drank wine at dinner, or had when I was their guest. This seemed to account for about a bottle a day of what looked to be good stuff, although about the best I can do myself is tell white from red. I understood another regular purchase better: five fifths a week, week in and week out, of Jack Daniel's bourbon. That meant a habit of pretty close to a bottle a day, and I figured the eight bottles of sherry a month were probably Mrs. Kellicott's, too.

This only attached numbers to what I had already learned from Mrs. Kellicott, of course. What was new to me, though, was the thought of Phyllis sitting here at this beautiful antique desk, year after year, signing the bills for the slow poisoning of her mother. Was she worried about being an enabler, as they call people like her on the talk shows? Or did she just see her role in the process as part of the job Papa had handed her? What did she feel for her mother? Pity? Contempt? Nothing?

The bottom drawer of the desk was the deepest of the three, deep enough to serve as a file cabinet. The folders were labeled—auto insurance, roofing estimates, bills (paid), and so on. I began to work my way through them, pulling a couple of items from each to judge if the rest might be promising. They weren't, by and large. But inside the file marked "Appliances, guarantees &

instructions" I saw a large manila envelope. By a lucky chance, I took a look in it.

When I popped the envelope slightly open, I could see just the edge of the top picture. All that showed was a slice of dark blue, with perhaps three quarters of an inch of flesh tone near the bottom, and yet I knew what had to be on the rest of the sheet, and what the rest of the envelope had to hold. I can't say how I was so sure, what locked on to what else in my head and then on to a dozen more things. But it was like coming up with just the right letter in a crossword puzzle, the one that suddenly made sense of four or five fragments of vertical and horizontal nonsense. I pulled the whole sheaf out of the envelope.

The blue was a couch. The flesh tone was part of the ankle of a young girl, naked. The pink tips of her small breasts still had the bulbous look of early puberty. The man was spurting onto them. You couldn't see his face. The idea of these things is to not see his face, so that it can be the buyer's. The rest of the pictures in the stack were much the same, but with different girls and different men, different positions, different openings. They had evidently been culled from a considerable number of kiddie-porn magazines. A collection of all-time hits.

At the bottom of the stack was what appeared to be a blank sheet of paper, protected by a cheap transparent folder of the type that kids use to protect important homework. I turned it over and on the other side was a pencil sketch of a black man lying propped up on one elbow, his chin cupped in his palm. He was posed on a rumpled bed, facing the viewer. His upper leg was partly bent, the knee cocked in the air; his lower leg was slightly bent, too, but lay flat on the bed. His penis lay over his upper thigh, as if it had been slung to one side and abandoned. The sketch was a wonderful one, done with an assured minimum of lines, its subject suggested rather than insisted upon. The man was Pink Lloyd.

The sketch was unsigned, but of course I knew who the artist had been.

All of a sudden I had a lot of important calls to make. It was time to leave. Walking out of a house where you have no business being, in midday and in full view of the neighbors, is a scary thing to do. I had been thinking about it off and on since the break-in, and couldn't come up with any solution but to stride right out of the place as if I belonged there and hope for the best.

Initially I had thought of waving good-bye to an imaginary host, but in the end I abandoned the idea. Too cute. I just closed the front door behind me, walked with an entirely false confidence out the curving driveway, turned right on the street, and went to my car around the corner. As far as I could tell, nobody noticed a thing. That's the great, cruel lesson of the world, of course: most people out there aren't even watching when you make a fool, or a saint, of yourself. And if they were, most of them wouldn't understand what was in front of their eyes, or care if they did understand.

And so off I went, another criminal getting away scot-free while the police and honest burghers slept. On my way home, I pulled briefly and illegally into one of the parking spaces in front of the Weld boathouse so that I could toss the bullets from Kellicott's clip into the Charles. They disappeared immediately from view into water with the visibility of coffee and cream. Toward the bottom the water thickened up into blackish muck, into which Kellicott's bullets would settle and eventually become part of the earth's geological record. I headed for home, and my telephone.

10

LLOYD? LISTEN, LLOYD, THIS IS TOM BETHANY, THE GUY you talked to . . ."

"It's cool, I know who you are."

"Yeah, well, what it is, I need to know what happened to those pictures of you that Emily drew."

"Nelda."

"Nelda, right. She give you the pictures?"

"What I want them pictures for? I know what I look like."

"She kept them, then?"

"Far's I know. What you got, man?"

"Nothing, really. Not yet. I'm putting it together."

"You putting it together, you know it's not me."

"I knew that all along."

"Everybody knew that but the man. Man don't know shit. As usual."

"Probably as usual for Sergeant Harrigan, anyway. I

don't imagine he asked you what happened when you left the massage parlor, did he?"

"Didn't nothing happen. I just left."

"Out the front door?"

"Sure. If there's a back door, I don't know nothing about it."

"Nelda went down with you, right?"

"She come on down, yeah. Say good-bye, you know?"

"How? Shake hands, wave at you, kiss you? What?"

"She give me like a little peck on the cheek. You believe that shit?"

I could see what he meant. How many pecks on the cheek does a pimp get, after all? "Were you inside or outside?" I asked.

"When she done that? Inside, at the bottom of the steps. Then I went on out and she went back upstairs and that was the last I seen of her. Next thing I know, she's in the paper dead."

"So you were in that little kind of entryway, behind the glass door?"

"That's it."

"The light was on inside?"

"I guess. I didn't notice was it on, but I guess I'd remember was it off."

"So anybody outside could have seen you?"

"Sure. Wasn't no secret."

"No, probably not."

I didn't like to call Hope Edwards at home, for fear of getting her husband instead. There's a certain awkwardness about talking to a man when you're sleeping with his wife, particularly when he probably knows it. Even when he most likely doesn't care or is even glad about it, as in this case, there's still a certain awkwardness.

But it was Sunday, and home was where she'd be—and, sure enough, Martin was the one who answered.

"Hey, Tom," he said with every appearance of friendship, "how are you? Good, good. Listen, she's upstairs changing to go out. Hold on, I'll go tell her you're on the line."

Changing. I'd be up watching, but Martin would probably just holler through the door. That's what marriage does to you, no doubt, but it was more than that in his case. Or so Hope has told me; I've never discussed it with Martin and never will, never would. Plenty of things are better left unsaid.

Hope had been first in her Georgetown Law School class. Martin was second, by an insignificant fraction. The beautiful Hope, the handsome Martin, both brilliant with promise. They made the perfect couple when they were married in St. Albans two weeks after graduation. They had the perfect baby, Lisa, ten months later. And then a long pause and then the two boys, only a year apart, one born on September 26 and the other the following September 28. The boys doubled up and celebrated their birthdays on the same date, the twenty-seventh. It never particularly struck anybody but Martin and Hope that the joint birthday fell about nine months after New Year's, the only night of the year that Martin ever allowed himself to get drunk. That both nights happened to work in well with Hope's ovulation cycle was, of course, an accident. The New Year's after the second son's conception Martin got drunk again, but that time he didn't make love to his wife. He lay there like a board, almost catatonic, and told Hope it tore him apart but he had to leave her. She could have the house, the money, the children, everything. All he wanted was Louis, his partner in men's doubles.

Hope's first feeling was relief, that there was no other

woman. Next she knew that she didn't want him to leave the children. He was a wonderful father regardless of his sexuality—maybe even, now she thought of it, in some measure because of it. The children needed him to go on being their father, and he needed it nearly as much as they did. In the following days and weeks they worked out an agreement, the two of them, as much unspoken as spoken. He would have Louis, but never bring him into the life of the family. If she found some-one, as he hoped she would, she would do the same.

Hope didn't even look for someone, though. She poured everything into her children and into her career. By 1980 she was on the domestic policy staff at the White House, and that fall she took leave to do advance work for Carter's reelection campaign. I was on the road, too, trying to keep the Secret Service and local officials from getting dangerously mad at each other. That began it for Hope and me. Since then we have stayed apart, and this is the plain truth of it, for the sake of the kids.

Now I heard the two boys hollering at each other over something important to them, and Hope telling them to keep it down, and then Hope on the line. "Tom," she said. "What's up? Can't talk, just taking the dwarfs off to the zoo."

And, in the background, "Mommy, we're not dwarfs."

"Ask them how come they're so little, if they're not dwarfs."

"Can't, no time. Really. Our ride's waiting outside."

"Okay, quick. I need to know about the old rich. Who do you know that's old rich?"

"Plenty of people, from fund-raising. What do you need them for?"

"I need to talk to somebody with old money and smart enough so that he's thought about the people he grew up with."

"Somebody who leads the examined life, huh? Try Toby Ingersoll."

Her American Civil Liberties Union colleague, who had been Kellicott's aide, who wore dirty sneakers and socks with clocks on them. "Of course," I said. "Shit, I should have guessed it from his clothes."

"His town house is on Louisburg Square, but it's Sunday. Try him out at the family place in Manchester. I may have the number somewhere, but anyway it's probably listed. Old money has listed phones."

"I think I have the number already. Go to the zoo."

"I'm off. Call me later?"

I did have the number. It was one of the ones I had copied from Kellicott's Rolodex. Whoever answered went off to find Ingersoll, and I heard the deep barking of a dog. If the receiver had been more powerful, I imagine it would have picked up the sound of tennis balls being hit and the splashing at poolside and, off somewhere on the grounds, the steady growl of a power mower.

"Hi, Tom," Ingersoll said. "Good to hear from you."

"What kind of dog was that barking? A Great Dane?"

"A Lab, actually. Old now, but a wonderful dog in his day. He bit the head off a cairn terrier once."

"You're shitting me."

"No, it's true. Did you know J. Edgar Hoover used to keep cairns? That's true, too. Always had two of them. One of them called G-boy. Maybe that one was for his boyfriend, Clyde Tolson, that part I don't know. But I do know that every year he'd get District of Columbia dog tags number one and two for them. Was that what you called to find out?"

"No, I wanted to find out how rich people feel about poor boys who marry their daughters."

"Do you have our mutual friend in mind?"

"Yes."

"Then let's talk hypothetically, all right?"

"You're worried about the line?"

"Probably it's all right, but maybe it isn't. The present administration is opposed to civil rights, except for corporations."

"Hypothetically, then, what would a stupid bully with a pisspot full of money think about a poor but bright lad that married his daughter?"

"Hypothesizing that his daughter was pretty badly messed up, the old man would probably be grateful that he was able to hire her a faithful, presentable live-in nurse."

"What if he wasn't faithful? The nurse?"

"Be all right, probably. As long as he was careful, totally discreet. Or at least discreet enough so that no talk about it would get around."

"The point being not to hurt her?"

"The point being, a bargain's a bargain. I'm not talking about anything written down or spelled out here, but the old man would understand it wasn't a love match. He might have been stupid, but he wasn't blind. And very rich people live their whole lives in a state of constant suspicion that everybody else is trying to get their money away from them. Particularly everybody of the opposite sex. That's why they usually marry other rich people."

"And when they don't, they expect their money's worth?"

"Exactly right. Here's this little wounded birdie, you understand me, kind of dragging one wing through life. You pick her up and take care of her and they won't mind taking care of you. Long as you did as good a job as any man could reasonably be expected to, you could grow up to be secretary of the navy. Even a U.S. senator."

"Even secretary of state."

"Even that."

"But if you hurt her . . ."

"Oh, you could hurt her, maybe. What the hell, she's only a woman, and she was damaged goods at that. But you couldn't be seen to be hurting her. The minute you were, doors would start closing on you in certain places all over America."

"What places?"

"Bar Harbor, La Jolla, Manchester, Blue Hill, Shaker Heights, Sewickley Heights, Grosse Pointe, Red Bank. Those kinds of places."

"Would that matter? If your hypothetical ambition was to hold a very high government job?"

"Oh, it would matter."

"A lot?"

"A whole lot."

After I hung up I thought about bargains. Gladys Williams knew about bargains, too, only she called them balances. I thought about Hope and myself, and our bargain. And about Alden and Susan Kellicott with their separate domains up on the second floor, and their bargain. I thought about Emily, Nelda, whichever, and something hit me all at once. I wanted to call Hope with it, but she was at the zoo and so I called Gladys instead. She sounded a little odd, slightly out of breath.

"Is this a bad time to call?" I asked.

"Actually, yes," she said. "I'm just breaking in a new guy here."

"Shit, I'm sorry. I'll call later."

"No, go ahead."

"It's Nelda. Emily Kellicott's stage name, you know?"

"Sure, I know."

"It's one of those what-do-you-call-its. All I can think of is acronyms."

"Anagrams."

"Right. It's an anagram for Alden."

"No shit, Sherlock."

"You knew? Why didn't you tell me?"

"Never occurred to me you didn't know. It jumped right out at me, the minute you told me her father's name."

I hung up, trying to remember whether I had told Hope about the new name Emily had taken. If I had, probably it had jumped right out at her, too. You miss a lot, belonging to the slower sex. Plodding along, I called Wanda Vollmer and got a tinny version of her voice on a machine.

"You have reached Personal Leisure World," it said. "We can't come to the phone, but if you'll leave your name and number after the beep, we'll get back to you as soon as we can."

"Wanda," I said. "Listen, Tom Bethany. We were talking earlier about Nelda, okay? . . ."

"I'm here, Bethany," cut in Wanda, live. "What's up?"

"I thought of something I should have asked you before. The man who walked out on Nelda without getting a massage? The night she was killed?"

"Right."

"Did he ask for her by name?"

"No. I always ask do they want any special girl, you know, but he said it was his first time in the place."

"You've got that book with all the girls' pictures. Did he pick her out from her picture?"

"He didn't ask, so I didn't show him the book. Besides, she was the only one free."

"How did it work? Did Nelda come out?"

"She was still straightening up after the last customer.

I was busy, so I called her on the intercom to make sure she had fresh towels and stuff, then I told him go on back, number six."

"What did you say exactly? On the intercom, I mean?"

"Shit, Bethany, how can I remember? Probably something like, 'All set back there, Nellie? I got a customer for you.' "

"Nellie? *Nellie?*"

"I'd call her Nellie. It was like a pet name I had for her. A nickname, you know? There was this nun I had a crush on, I was eleven. Sister Nellie."

"A nun?"

"Don't you go getting no ideas now. I was the one had the crush, not her."

"You sure you called her Nellie instead of Nelda?"

"I'm positive."

"I was asking because you didn't seem exactly sure of what you said over the intercom."

"Nellie I'm sure of."

"Why?"

"Because she asked me that very same thing herself after the guy took off. Said she couldn't recall whether I called her Nellie or Nelda, and which was it? By the way, she asked me whether the guy had seen her picture, too. Same as you just asked me."

"How come she asked?"

"She said she was trying to figure out how come the guy took off like that."

"How would that help her figure it out?"

"I don't know."

I hung up feeling mildly pleased that there was at least one woman in this whole business who knew less than I did. Hoping that there would be another one, too, I dialed the Kellicotts' house on Martha's Vineyard. Phyllis Kellicott answered. She had a small, light, pleasant voice and a tentative way of speaking, as if she were constantly afraid of giving offense. From her voice, you'd picture the sort of girl who smiles apologetically when someone bumps into her.

"I'm afraid Papa's gone to the ferry," she said when I identified myself. "I could get Mummy."

"That's okay," I said. "You're the one I wanted to talk to."

"Me? Oh. All right."

"Quick question, that's all. Where were you the night Emily died?"

"Me? I was visiting friends on Hilton Head."

"South Carolina?"

"Yes. I got down there two weeks before Emily died, but Papa didn't call me till two days after. When they, you know . . ."

"Uh-huh." When they dug the body out of the snow-bank. "How long were you down there?"

"It was going to be three weeks, but of course I flew right back. Are you sure you don't want to talk to Mummy?"

"No, no need to bother her."

Instead I dialed Markham for President headquarters, with the idea of bothering Phil Jeffers. He might very well be available for bothering, since campaigns don't shut down on Sundays. But he wasn't. To keep my skills sharp, I tried to con his home phone number out of the volunteer on the switchboard. But either they weren't sharp enough or she was.

"I'm sorry, Mr. Tiffany, but we're not permitted to give out home numbers," she kept saying until I figured it was no use going on.

"Well, have him call me as soon as he checks in. And it's not Tiffany. It's Bethany."

"*Bethany!* Why didn't you *say* so? He's been going

crazy trying to reach you. He's had me calling some Mr. Tasty or something for hours, only you're never in."

So she gave me Phil Jeffers's number, and I was able to bother him after all.

"Where the fuck you been?" he said. "I pay you a goddamn fortune, you don't even return my calls."

"Stop shouting, Phil. What is it, you think you look cute when you shout?"

"Listen to me, goddamn it . . ."

I hung up the phone, waited a few minutes, and called him back. This time he wasn't shouting. Jeffers was a pragmatist. If one approach didn't work, he'd try another.

"Jesus, don't hang up," he said. "I'm sorry I hollered. I been going crazy trying to get you, is all."

"Well, you got me."

"You said you were going to do some last-minute poking around, right? Kellicott? Nothing came up, am I right?"

"I'd hold off on him for now."

"*Hold off?*"

"Easy, Phil. I'm delicate."

"I can't hold off, for Christ's sake. Somebody leaked it to the *Globe*."

"Somebody."

"Well, you know how it goes."

"You shouldn't have done that, Phil. I was you, I'd unleak it."

"How can I fucking unleak it?"

"You can handle it. I read where you're the consummate political insider."

"Give me a break, Tom, will you? *Newsweek* calls me something, how can I help it what they call me?"

"Maybe you could demand a retraction."

"How the hell do I always get off the subject when

I'm talking to you, Tom? What's the problem with Kellicott?"

"Nothing, really. Weirdness, that's all."

"Shit, weirdness is in the job description. Look at Haig. Look at Kissinger."

"Look at Shultz."

"Shultz?"

"Sure. He had a tiger tattooed on his ass."

"So?"

"Don't you think that's weird, Phil?"

"Not particularly."

"Are you trying to tell me you've got a tiger tattooed on your ass, Phil?"

"Jesus, will you stop changing the subject? What about Kellicott? We're on Kellicott here."

"I just told you about Kellicott. In fact, I told you yesterday, and you went to the Globe anyway. Put up a little trial balloon, didn't you? You'd asked me yesterday, I'd have told you just what I'm telling you now. Call up the Globe and shoot down your little balloon."

"For Christ's sake, what new shit have you got?"

"No new shit I can prove yet! I'll tell you when I can! And Phil? Phil?"

"What?"

"You're shouting again."

And I hung up.

Through the long summer evening I sat in my La-Z-Boy recliner, thinking. The thinking was all right to do, here in Cambridge, but the La-Z-Boy wasn't. I'd be ruined if it got out that I'd rather be comfortable in an ugly recliner than uncomfortable in an ugly Eames chair.

What I was thinking about was my hypothesis. I was holding it up every way I could against the facts, to see how it matched up with them. Sure enough, it did. It was the simplest hypothesis that could explain all the facts, so that I was on solid ground as far as Occam's razor goes. In Cambridge everybody knows what Occam's razor is, although there is some dispute over whether to spell it Occam or Ockham. If I could answer that one in 450 pages or less, they'd give me tenure at Harvard and I could spend the rest of my life in the faculty club dribbling oatmeal down the front of my cardigan.

As it was, I was doing a pretty neat job of getting a bottle of Sam Adams down me without spilling, in a La-Z-Boy recliner. And what was bothering me about Occam's razor was that while my hypothesis explained all the facts just fine, I didn't have enough facts to impress even myself. Where's the evidence, Judge Wapner would say, and I'd just be standing there like a retard. The Wapper's a lot tougher on evidence than they are at the faculty club.

Every twenty minutes or so I hit the redial button and called Kellicott's answering machine again, just on the off chance he somehow wasn't still stalled in the traffic jam that ran from Cape Cod to Boston on hot Sundays in August. It was 9:30, and dark, before Kellicott picked up. Pitching my voice high I asked for Martina, but was told I must have the wrong number. I grabbed my car keys off the top of the dresser.

11

I PARKED RIGHT IN KELLICOTT'S DRIVEWAY, INSTEAD OF around the block as I had the night before. His downstairs lights were on. He must have spotted me coming into the drive, since he opened the door almost before the bell had stopped ringing. "Tom!" he said. He didn't break into a broad, welcoming smile, but his face and his voice made it plain that I was just the person he had been waiting for all evening. "Listen, come on in. I was just getting myself some iced tea. Can I get you some? Or something else?"

Why not? We were both civilized people, after all. "Sure," I said. "Iced tea would be fine." He sat me down in the study to wait while he went for the tea.

"What can I do for you?" Kellicott said when we were both settled down in our chairs, comfortably sipping.

"I've just about got this business wrapped up," I said. "One or two more things, and I should be able to turn a preliminary report over to Jeffers tomorrow."

"Fine."

"I talked to Phyllis today."

"Phyllis? She's on the Vineyard."

"That's where she was, all right. I used the phone."

The sudden mention of Phyllis had kicked him slightly off the rails; Kellicott ordinarily was a step or two in front of a conversation, and not behind it as he had just seemed to be.

"She said she had been down on Hilton Head for a couple weeks before Emily got killed," I went on. "Must be tough on you when she's away."

"Tough on me?" He sounded puzzled, mildly curious. Now he was back on top of things.

"Doesn't she run the house normally?"

"Yes, she does. Damned well, too, although she wouldn't have mentioned that to you. Phyllis tends to keep her light pretty much under a bushel."

"I'll bet she does."

Kellicott looked at me for a moment before he answered. "This conversation is getting a little strange," he said. The conversation would have seemed even stranger, of course, if he had pretended not to notice my odd remark. Maybe he *was* the right man to sit on our side of the negotiating table at Geneva, after all.

Just then the phone rang. Kellicott made no effort to get it, and so we both just sat there listening as his recorded voice invited the caller to leave a message after the beep. And after the beep, as we both continued to sit there, came the voice of Phil Jeffers.

"Alden, we've got some kind of trouble," Jeffers said. "My guy Bethany says we should hold off till he talks to me tomorrow and for Christ's sake we slipped it to the *Globe* already. Call me as quick as you get in, I'm home all night."

We heard the click as Jeffers hung up.

"All right," Kellicott said, "what's this all about?" The easy charm was gone, utterly.

"What he said. I told him to sit on any announcement till I had a chance to clear some things up."

"What things?" It might have been Kellicott's father-in-law, laying into Kellicott's father after the town car ran out of gas on the way to the airport. I figured I wasn't going to be head of security for the State Department anymore, so what the hell . . .

"I'll tell you what things. You murdered your daughter and fucked her after she was dead."

Kellicott was silent for a moment that got long very quickly. When he spoke, the icy anger was gone. He sounded sad.

"Is that what you think?" he said. "You couldn't have any children. No one with children could say a thing like that."

I let that go. "For a long time I couldn't figure out why she was naked," I said.

Kellicott remained silent. A tiny shake of the head, almost imperceptible, suggested disagreement, or disbelief, or amazement, or who knows what.

"Think of all the things that don't fit," I went on. "It's a cold, raw night. Cars are going by on Lowell, near enough so that you'd be seen if you were crazy enough to take off your clothes and lie down in a snowbank to get laid. You wanted to get laid, you'd get in a car to do it, wouldn't you? What do you think, Alden?"

I figured this was the time to take him up on his invitation to call him by his first name.

Kellicott said nothing.

"Of course it couldn't have been her own car," I went on. "If it had happened in her car, the killer would have just left her in it. Why haul her out, stick her in a snowbank, lock her car back up, stick the keys in her purse, and stick the purse in the snowbank, too?

"Suppose it happened in the killer's car, though? Then it would make pretty good sense to shove her and her things into the nearest snowbank. Wouldn't that make sense, Alden?"

Kellicott made no answer. Get it out of your system, his mild expression said.

"Only why would she have gotten into a stranger's car, though? Force? He showed her his knife, maybe? A possibility. But not a probability, once I got to know a little about your daughter. She wasn't scared of much of anything, was she? Certainly not of her papa. Did she call you Papa? No, she didn't, did she? That was the whole trouble."

Kellicott kept on waiting for this lunatic to get tired and run down.

"Pink Lloyd's car was around earlier, of course. Maybe it was his car she got into, the way Sergeant Harrigan thinks. But why would Pink Lloyd have carved his initials into her? Harrigan probably thinks he was just leaving his mark, like a punk kid with a spray can. You probably hoped somebody like Harrigan would wander along, somebody dumb enough to think that. And of course you were right. But Pink Lloyd isn't dumb enough to do that, which is the real point. I've talked to him, and I know.

"I also know he loved her, and that he loved her because she didn't love him. And that even if she decided to throw him a mercy fuck, she wouldn't have done it naked in his car on a freezing night. And I know you were waiting in the parking lot when Emily came down to the lighted entryway and kissed Pink Lloyd good night. So that's what happened, Alden. He drove off, you hung around till she got off work, and then you got her into your car."

I took a swallow of my iced tea. Kellicott didn't touch his.

"You asked her who the guy was and she told you. That's how you knew what initials to leave on her later. How does that feel, Alden? To slice into your own daughter's dead body? A lot of people would feel a little odd about that. No? Nothing, huh? Just like cleaning fish?"

He wouldn't be provoked. I went on.

"What the hell," I said, "no harder than strangling her, I guess. Once she stopped wriggling, there was nothing to keep you from taking her clothes off and having a look at last, was there? So you did it. Nothing to keep you from fucking her, either, so you did that too. That's what you big shots do, isn't it? Whatever you fucking feel like doing?"

Now I was getting provoked, but it was okay. No need to hold back. The dumber he thought I was, the better.

"How does it work after they're dead, Papa? I mean, wasn't she kind of . . . dry?"

"This isn't really you," Kellicott said. There was no anger in his voice—just pity, and understanding. All the anger was on my side. I had gotten to like Emily, to like her a lot.

"It isn't dry with Phyllis, is it?" I said. And that got to him, to the extent of a tiny flicker of his eyelids. "The two of you look at that kiddie porn together, don't you? Does that get her nice and wet for Papa?"

"You're disgusting, Bethany."

"No, I'm not. The one who did it is the one who's disgusting, Alden. Remember how disgusting Emily thought you were when you tried it out on her in the motel, on the way back from summer camp? Did she go to her mother for help? I wondered about that. My guess is she did, but you just conned or browbeat your sick, pathetic wife the way you always have. Then you started on poor little Phyllis as soon as she got old enough.

"Poor little Phyllis has been your real wife for years, hasn't she? That's why she is on the pill and your wife's on tranquilizers. That's why the bidet is in your bathroom and not your wife's. All you need from your wife is the money and the family influence. Phyllis is the one who runs the house and takes care of her poor papa's special needs."

"I can't imagine who's feeding you all this craziness, Bethany . . ."

"Sure you can. How could I know all this shit unless I broke into your house last night and searched it?"

"That's a crime."

"Get a grip on reality, Alden. Of course it's a crime. What are you going to do? File a goddamned complaint?"

"I might very well," he said, and smiled. "If I could find evidence, that is. Which I very much doubt. And evidence is crucial in these matters, isn't it?"

"Meaning I don't have any evidence, either?"

Kellicott got to his feet and began to move restlessly around the room. He stopped by the desk and rested one haunch on it. He could have reached the Beretta before I could reach him, and I hoped he would try. He didn't know it was empty, and the attempt would make me absolutely certain that I had figured things out correctly. But he picked up the little silver bayonet instead. That didn't worry me, either. There are a dozen ways of taking a knife off a man and all of them, in a mismatch like this one, would be virtually risk-free from my point of view. Kellicott put down the miniature bayonet as absently as he had picked it up. He crossed to the window and looked out into the night.

"You can't possibly have any evidence," he said, "because I didn't kill Emily."

"If you mean physical evidence, you're right," I said. "But I've got plenty of circumstantial evidence. You're dead, Alden. You just don't know it. Let me lay it out for you."

"Yes, why don't you do that."

"You're a special customer at a porno bookstore in the Zone. The kind you buy is kiddie porn, just about the only kind that's illegal. Lou at the store can identify you. And all this daddy–daughter shit winds up in Phyllis's bedroom.

"You're saying so what, I'll dump those dirty books as soon as this asshole leaves, and Phyllis will never talk. Well, maybe she won't and maybe she will. For example, supposing she finds out that as soon as she took off for a few weeks in South Carolina, you took off to the massage parlors to get your ashes hauled by other women? That was the part that took me the longest to figure out. Right up till today I was working on the assumption that you went to Personal Leisure World to see Emily. But you didn't have any idea she worked there till you walked in with a hard-on, did you? Must have been an interesting couple of minutes, once you both got over your surprise.

"So out you go, wondering what to do next. You've got a certain problem here. A man sneaking off to a massage parlor and stumbling on to his own daughter, now that's news. Anything that weird, the whole goddamned *Social Register* would hear about it as soon as Emily opened her mouth in the right places. And she would, too. Maybe the frightened thirteen-year-old kid didn't know who to talk to, but the grown-up woman did. You have to talk to her, find out what she's got in mind.

"So you wait in your car. You see her saying good-bye to some black guy, and then you wait again till she gets off work. You call out to her and she gets into your car. Why not? It's cold, and she's not scared of you. She started standing up to you when she was thirteen. Who's your black friend, you ask her, and she tells you. Again, why not?

"My guess is you tried to tell her you heard she was working at Personal Leisure World, and you came looking for her the way you had before. Bullshit to that, she says. I checked with the manager and you didn't even know my name before you walked through that door.

"Who knows why you strangled her? To keep your rich pals from dumping you? Because you tried to screw her and she wouldn't let you this time either? Because you're a sociopath and it just seemed like a good idea at the time?

"Anyway, you do it, and then, what the hell, let's strip her and have a look. When you showed up at the Top Hat she ran you off before you could check her out, didn't she? Nothing she can do about it now, though. Long as she's bare-ass, well, what the hell, might as well spit on your dick and throw a fuck in her, right?"

His eyelids flickered once more.

"Why, you son of a bitch," I said. "That's just what you did, isn't it? You spat on it."

Nothing more showed. He had iced up again, but I knew I was right.

"When you're done you carve Pink Lloyd's initials on her to confuse the cops. What if I come over and look through your pockets, Alden? Will I find a knife of some kind there? A lot of men carry a sharp little penknife. Do you want me to come over?"

"As a matter of fact, I do carry a penknife."

"Let me have it."

"Don't be absurd."

213

"Oh, shit," I said. "All right." I got to my feet, but Kellicott produced the penknife before I had to take it off him. I put it in my pocket.

"Maybe there's some blood on it you missed," I said. "Though I doubt it, after all this time."

"You probably carry a penknife yourself," he said.

"I do, only I use mine for nails, not tits. Anyway, Sergeant Harrigan turns out to be dumb enough to think Emily was one of Pink Lloyd's whores and he killed her for some pimp reason. So everything is fine for a couple of years until this prick Bethany shows up and starts asking questions about you in dirty bookstores. Did you hear about that from Lou at the bookstore, or from Phil Jeffers? Doesn't matter. The point is, I was looking around in the part of your life that led straight to Emily's murder.

"Next thing I know this Jose Soto tries to knife me in the back. He worked as a volunteer for one of those do-gooder agencies in the basement of Old Cambridge Baptist. I figured he was an FBI plant, so for a long time I didn't make any connection between you and him. Not till I saw the toy bayonet you got from your death-squad buddy. Then I realized he probably wasn't an FBI plant at all, was he? He was a CIA plant from El Salvador. You probably knew him from the old days, when he was castrating peasants for your pal Roberto.

"Remember I mentioned Soto's name to you right afterward, asked you if you knew him? Of course you remember. It's why you killed him. You figured I'd eventually find him, since I knew his name. Maybe you even figured he told me his name, but he didn't. He was a tough little shit. I'm surprised you were able to dump him off the bridge, even with his bad arm. I suppose he trusted you, though."

Kellicott was still half standing, and half sitting on

the desk. In his shoes, I would have done the same thing he was doing: keeping quiet to find out what I had on him. So I went on telling him, because I wanted him to know that I didn't really have anything on him. Except for one thing, which I was just getting to.

"What you're thinking, Alden, is that all I've got here is a handful of air, and when I open my hand up there's nothing. Well, that would be true if it wasn't for Wanda Vollmer. Does the name mean anything to you?"

"I'm afraid I don't know Miss Vollmer, no. I don't know Mr. Soto, either, or Mr. Lloyd, or any of your other interesting friends."

"You'd recognize Miss Vollmer's picture, Alden."

"I very much doubt it."

"She recognized yours when I showed it to her," I lied. "She's the manager who took your money at Personal Leisure World."

"Really? I find that . . ."

And Kellicott caught me with a trick I had used dozens of times myself, to cut off an unwanted telephone call without seeming rude. You catch your caller off base by hanging up in the middle of your own line—hanging up, in effect, on yourself. Every time he'll blame the connection, not you.

Kellicott worked it so well on me that he managed to grab his gun and make it out the door of the study before I started to make sense. When I got to the door myself, he was disappearing around a corner. When I got to the corner, he was disappearing into a door next to the kitchen. When I got to that door, it turned out to lead into a pantry, and he was just slamming shut another door, at the far end of it. When I got to the other door, it was locked and he was slamming shut the first door. He had doubled back and locked me inside the dark pantry.

215

I knew how to handle that problem, having seen it done in scores of movies. I took a short run and smashed my shoulder into the door. It was like hitting heavy planking. So I made my way in the dark to the other end of the pantry, kneading my shoulder and hoping it wouldn't stiffen up too badly. But the other door seemed just as solid, when I tried it with my uninjured shoulder. I groped around till I found the light switch, and examined the situation. The door panels seemed to be the only possible point of attack. An old-fashioned soda-acid fire extinguisher made of brightly polished copper hung on the wall. I unhooked it to use as a battering ram on one of the door panels. Finally I was able to make a big enough opening so that I could reach through and unlock the pantry door from outside. By then Kellicott was gone, of course, and so was the car that had been parked in the driveway.

My plan had been to provoke him into making a run at Wanda, all right—but not until after the massage parlor's 10 P.M. closing. By then she would be safely away. I had figured on leaving Kellicott's house first, so that I would get to the massage parlor parking lot before him. When he showed, I would know for certain that he had killed his daughter, and probably Jose Soto as well. Then I could point the police at Wanda, and she would identify him. Once they knew for sure where to look, they wouldn't have much trouble putting together a case.

That was the plan.

But now Kellicott might be waiting when Wanda left. With her dead, the police could never make a solid case against him. It would only be my word that he had killed Wanda or anybody else. He would never be secretary of state, but he wouldn't spend the rest of his life in Walpole, either.

My first thought was to call Personal Leisure World

and warn Wanda, but all I got was the recorded message. Then I dialed 911 and it was already ringing before I thought the thing through and hung up. Even if I were able to fight my way up through the bureaucracy over the telephone and eventually get somebody in a position of responsibility, what would happen? A stranger calls with an improbable story about another stranger maybe on his way to a massage parlor, maybe with the idea of murdering someone who may have seen him shortly before a crime he might have committed? I tried Personal Leisure World once again and got the answering machine once again before I ran for my car.

When I slowed down as I passed the little shopping center on Lowell Parkway, I was glad I hadn't made a fool of myself over the phone with the police. Everything seemed quiet. I couldn't see any lights on the second floor of the building where the massage parlor was, but then I didn't know whether any of its windows were on the street side anyway. The light in the downstairs entry was on, but it probably stayed on all night. Kellicott's Saab wasn't among the dozen or so cars parked in the lot, but I was still uneasy. He could have parked in the vast anonymity of the bigger and newer mall just across Lowell. Or he might not have arrived yet, in which case the mall sounded like a good idea for me, too. Since I had been parked alongside him in his driveway, he knew my car as well as I knew his. If I parked outside the massage parlor, I might scare him off. I turned into the big mall across the parkway, and walked back to the little shopping center.

I nearly got there too late.

Wanda Vollmer appeared in the lighted entryway, probably thirty yards from me. She locked the door to the stairway, locked the glass door from the outside, replaced the keys in her purse, and headed toward her car. I began to head the same way, but stopped when a man rose up from between two cars. "Wanda Vollmer?" Kellicott said, just loud enough so that I could make out the words.

"Who wants to know?" Wanda demanded, much louder. Wanda took minimum shit off men.

Since her answer was in effect a yes, Kellicott moved instantly. He moved in too close for her to knee or kick effectively, grabbed her throat with both hands, and set out to strangle her.

"Hey," I shouted, and started to run. Kellicott pushed Wanda away and turned toward me, tugging at something in his pocket. The Beretta finally came free. As I charged, he leveled the unloaded gun at me, aimed it carefully—and it fired. The bullet felt like a sharp, hard punch to the left side of my chest. I stopped two or three steps short of Kellicott, more from surprise than from the impact.

Movement from Wanda, and a sound.

Kellicott was on the ground howling, his hands to his eyes. He was twisting around in agony, like a just-hooked worm. Wanda was holding something in her hand. She bent over and jammed the thing into Kellicott's face and it made the hissing sound again, like an aerosol bomb. He screamed louder and rolled away, leaving the gun forgotten on the pavement. I bent to pick it up.

"Holy shit," I said. "What did you do to him?"

"Mace, the fucker. I always wondered if it worked."

"You know who he is?"

She looked at him closely, the best she could with him twisting around and covering his eyes.

"No," she said. "Yes? Maybe if I could see him better. He could be the guy who came in . . ."

218

"That's right. Nelda's father."

"Nelda's fucking *father!*"

"Exactly."

"Shit, that's blood on you," Wanda said.

"I don't think it's too bad."

"What are you, a doctor?"

"I was shot once before, and it felt a lot worse."

"Yeah, well, you better come inside and let me have a look." She remembered Kellicott. "By the way, what are we going to do with fuckface?"

"Take him along."

She grabbed hold of one foot with her two good arms, and I got the other with my one good arm, and we dragged him toward the building. He was too busy trying to breathe and dealing with the agony in his eyes to fight back. As we hauled him up the flight of concrete steps his head smacked into each one like a cantaloupe hitting the floor, and after a couple of times he stopped wriggling. He was still unconscious, which was probably a mercy, when we lugged him into the sauna.

"Now let's see what you got," she said, unbuttoning my sports shirt. When she had washed off the blood—very little blood, considering—I could see a small puncture wound with puffy lips and dark red center, already coagulating. The bullet had gone in just below my left nipple, perhaps two inches off to the side. "I'll be a son of a bitch, here it is," said Wanda, fingering my back right under the shoulder blade.

I managed to reach around with my good hand to feel for myself. The bullet made a round lump just under the flesh. I had felt the same thing before once, in the arm of an old Meo woman who had got in the way of one of Kissinger's antipersonnel bombs. She had laughed when she had me feel the steel ball bearing in her. Primitive sense of humor. Kissinger would have liked her.

The shock was wearing off and the pain was starting, a dull and constant bone ache. At least there wasn't the sharp, bright, stabbing pain of a broken rib when I breathed, though. My guess was that the little bullet had found its way between two ribs, and out between two more. Now it was lodged in the meat of my latissimus dorsi muscle.

"We better get you to a hospital," Wanda said.

"The hell with that," I said. "They might keep me there. Let me use your phone, okay?"

"Okay," she said, taking me over to it. "Listen, are you sure it was her *father* that killed Nelda? Because the guy that killed her, didn't he fuck her, too?"

"That's right, and he was her father. And he fucked her after she was dead. He came after you because you're the only one that saw him here that night."

She thought that over as I phoned Gladys Williams. "Is your friend still there?" I asked when she answered.

"Hey, what do you care? You'd call anyway. As a matter of fact, though, he's gone."

"Can you cut a bullet out of me? It's right under the skin."

"Can you drive?"

"Oh, sure."

"Come on over, then. I'll take a look."

And that was it. No hesitation, no questions. I would have fallen in love on the spot, if it hadn't been for Hope.

"What do I do with fuckface here?" Wanda said when I hung up. "Call the cops?"

"Not till I figure out what to tell them. You got a closet we can lock him into till I get back?"

"None of them lock. The sauna, maybe. I could jam the door shut with a mop handle."

She dragged his dead weight in there by herself, my left side having stiffened up. "I guess we should tie him up in case he comes to," she said. "Only what the fuck with?" She thought it over and said, "Dental floss."

"Dental floss?"

"One of the girls used to have a john who had her tie him up with it. Three or four rounds and nobody can break it. Cuts in too much when you pull against it." She went for her purse and brought out a plastic container. "This is the heavy-duty stuff," she said. "The tape."

It hurt, but I helped her hoist Kellicott into a semi-sitting position on one of the benches. She explained her idea as she worked Kellicott's pants and underpants off him. Then she looped the dental floss a half dozen times around one of the cedar planks in the bench. Next she looped a triple thickness of the tape around and around his scrotum. Not tight enough to hurt, but too tight for his testicles to pass through. Kellicott was making noises now, regaining partial consciousness. He wasn't back to the point, though, where he could do anything to stop Wanda from binding his thumbs together behind him with the floss so that he couldn't use his hands to free his scrotum.

"Let's see fuckface get loose now," she said when she had finished.

Back outside, she turned the heat down to zero and wedged her mop handle between the opposite wall and the sauna so that its door couldn't be opened from inside. "Just in case," she said, although in case of what, I couldn't imagine. The man was never born who would even have tried to yank himself out of that kind of noose. I looked through the small glass window at Kelli-

cott. He was recovered enough so that he was rolling his
head around, probably hoping he could ease the pain
from his streaming eyes. I didn't know how long it took
for the effects of Mace to wear off, and I didn't much
care.

"I got to thank you," Wanda said. "It took a lot of
balls to charge that gun."

"Actually, it didn't," I said. "I thought the son of a
bitch was empty. Which reminds me." I pulled out the
Beretta and removed the clip. It was indeed empty. I
just hadn't thought to check and make sure there wasn't
a round in the chamber. Somehow there was no consola-
tion in the thought that I'd never make that mistake
again. It was the kind of situation that was unlikely to
come up twice, and so my lifetime stats were pretty sure
to remain at 0 for 1.

I left things in Wanda's more-than-capable hands and
set out for Gladys's place.

Gladys took me right to the bathroom, where I looked
unenthusiastically at the tools laid out on a cloth bundle
that she had unrolled on the top of her toilet tank.

"Why would you keep scalpels around?" I asked.

"Salesmen's samples. I've got lots of stuff. I could take
your leg off, if I had to."

"I didn't ask where you got them, Gladys. I asked how
come you had them around the house."

"To practice medicine. Hey, how else are you going
to learn? Okay, now reach over and grab your far knee,
that's it. Need to stretch the skin so I can see that
lump . . ."

I felt her fingers exploring it, and then a hard, quick
pressure, and then a lighter pressure from some wet pad
or cloth that I assumed she was using to sterilize the
area.

"Come on, get it over with," I said.

"It is over with." She began to wash something under the tap. "Popped out just like a big blackhead."

"You got a nice way of putting it, all right. Let's have a look."

She showed me the little slug, which was only slightly deformed. "My guess is it traveled around the inside of the rib cage for a few inches and then came out between two of them," she said. "If you had regular lats instead of those big goddamn slabs of muscle, it probably would have gone right on through."

"How come you didn't pass that blade through a flame before you sliced into me?"

"Not necessary. None of my patients ever get infected."

"Shit, Gladys, they're dead."

"I never think of them that way. I think of them like they were, well . . . my friends."

And so we chattered away, carefree as birds, while she put a couple of stitches into the cut and bandaged it over. She let me have the bullet and I slipped it into my pocket. Maybe I could get it bronzed. One way and another a good deal of time passed before I started to focus on the problem of what to do about Kellicott.

"Remember the detective lieutenant I told you about?" Gladys asked. "Curtin?"

"The smart one?"

"Yeah, well, you could be in pretty deep shit unless we get hold of a smart one."

"You figure Detective Sergeant Ray Harrigan might not really grasp what we've got here?"

"Might not, no. Why don't I call Billy Curtin instead, tell him we'll meet him at the massage parlor?"

"Where do you get this 'we' shit, white woman?"

"You think I'm missing this? Either it's 'we' or I don't call Curtin."

And so Gladys was with me when I returned to Personal Leisure World. Nothing that looked like a police car was in the parking lot, and so I assumed that Lieutenant Curtin hadn't shown up yet. We rang the night buzzer, and in a minute Wanda Vollmer came down to let us in.

"This is Gladys Williams," I said. "She just cut the bullet out of my back."

"Pleased to meet you, Doctor," Wanda said.

"Gladys is okay," Gladys said modestly.

"Maybe you should have a look at this guy we got," Wanda said. "He's not looking too good. Actually, I think maybe he's dead."

"Oh, shit, Wanda," I said.

"Hey, I didn't do nothing. Probably he had a bad heart. Some people can't stand the heat."

"Wanda, you turned the heat off. I saw you do it." I sounded stupid even to myself, and so I dropped it. "Oh, shit, Wanda," I said again.

"Hey, listen, he fucked her after she was dead, didn't he?"

"Probably."

"His own daughter. What could I do?"

Wanda shrugged, smiling. No doubt it was her normal smile, but it looked terrible to me. If Kellicott was really dead, that smile, through the little glass window of the sauna, was likely the last thing he ever saw.

"He's dead, all right," Gladys said after letting Kellicott's limp forearm, wrist, and hand flop back down on the cedar bench. "No pulse at all."

I had turned the heat off before we went into the sauna, and had left the door standing open. But it was still unbearably hot. Kellicott, naked from the waist

down, sat in a puddle of sweat. His wet hair was plastered to his head. His sweat-soaked shirt was stuck to
his body. I was starting to sweat myself, and so I went
out to join Wanda at the doorway. Gladys, though,
stayed inside. She examined the noose around Kellicott's scrotum, and then stuck her head under the bench
to see exactly how he was attached to it.

"Pretty neat," she said. "No way he could have gotten
to the knot."

She came out from the heat and wiped her face with
her hand. "He'd of had to leave his balls behind to get
out of that."

That made me think of something. "Where's the
broomstick you jammed the door with, Wanda?" I asked.

"Back in the closet. What did I need with the broomstick? I still had my Mace."

I considered that.

"You showed him the door was open, didn't you? And
then you cranked up the heat and looked through the
window at him, didn't you? You *wanted* the son of a
bitch to go for you."

Wanda looked pleased with herself, a big girl who had
been caught by the nuns but wasn't at all ashamed of
the bad actions she had committed.

"Well, it wasn't that so much," she said. "It was just
I needed the door open so I could throw water on the
rocks."

The thermometer had been at 102 degrees centigrade
when Gladys and I went in, just above boiling. The
human body can take it for a certain time at that temperature, but only if the humidity is so low that the evaporation of sweat can cool the system down. Tossing water
onto the hot rocks has no effect on a wall thermometer,
but it has an immediate effect on the human body. The
sudden humidity slows down evaporation. From one

second to the next, overheated but bearable air becomes scalding, suffocating.

"Jesus, Wanda," I said, "what are we going to tell the cops?"

The downstairs buzzer rang. "Shit," I said. "I guess we won't have time to work anything out. Well, we'll try the truth, or part of it anyway."

Lieutenant Curtin, the deputy chief of detectives, was with a uniformed sergeant who seemed not to have the power of speech, at least around Curtin. And Curtin was an intimidating man, although for no particular reason that met the eye. He was of short-medium height and physically unimpressive. In Laos I had known a small, scrawny case officer named O'Malley who could out-walk even the Meo born in those mountains. His last walk, before the CIA retired him on disability, was sixty kilometers through Pathet Lao territory after his Porter Pilatus was shot down. He had a bullet through one ankle and burns over most of the lower half of his body, but he made it out in nine days with no food. Lieutenant Curtin was the same kind of scrawny.

He looked in through the doorway at the body, a long look. He went inside and looked some more, at one point getting down the way Gladys had, to check on exactly how Kellicott's scrotum had been attached to the bench. He came out again and jerked his chin in my direction.

"This the guy you told me about?" he said to Gladys. He even sounded a little like O'Malley. Gladys nodded. "Okay," Curtin said to me. "Tell me about it."

"Can we do it alone?" I asked.

"The guy's okay, huh?" Curtin said to Gladys, and she nodded again. "Bethany, is that it? Okay, Bethany, let's go."

He led the way down the hall, never bothering to ask

if he could use a room, or which room. He opened the first door he came to, and we went into one of the massage cubicles. For ten minutes, I told him about it. Like me, he only fully bought it at the very end, when Kellicott began to strangle Wanda the instant he was sure who she was.

"She'll testify to this, will she?" he asked.

"Oh, sure. So will I."

"It was pretty hot in there." The lieutenant gestured again with his chin, in the general direction of the sauna down the hall.

"She turned the heat off when we put him in there," I said. "I saw her."

"I guess those rooms hold the heat for quite a while, don't they?"

"Yeah, I think you're right, Lieutenant."

"We got three things here, Bethany," he said. "First we got the murder of this girl, this Emily, plus second we got the guy in the river. On those murders we got no evidence at all. Two open cases. Unsolved."

"Right."

"This thing we got here is the accidental death of this girl's father. My guess is the guy's got it into his head that the massage parlor was responsible somehow for his daughter's death. With the grief, the brooding? Who knows what ideas people get? Lucky for the manager you happened by to save her life. Lucky for you the guy completely missed you with this." He held up the little Beretta I had given him.

"I know what you mean," I said, and I did. There was a law saying that nondoctors—police lab technicians, for instance—couldn't perform surgery without a license, particularly on gunshot wounds.

"The sergeant and I are going downstairs to radio for

227

an ambulance," he said. "It'll take us a little while, you follow me?"

I thought about what we'd have to do: cut Kellicott loose, wrestle his underpants and pants and socks and shoes back onto him, get the mop handle back out to lock him in, get our stories straight.

"Think it'll take you ten minutes?" I asked.

"Probably about that."

"What about the autopsy, though?"

"We got this pathologist, he's kind of an elderly gentleman. He delegates, you know? To one of our people with a background in pathology. About all the old guy himself does these days, he signs the autopsy report she puts in front of him."

"She?"

"Right. It's a young lady."

"Probably she'll find out that Kellicott's system was under a lot of stress. All the excitement. Mace and everything."

"Yeah, I imagine," the lieutenant said. "What it'll probably be, she'll probably find out the guy had a weak heart or something."

"You don't mind my asking," I said. "Why are you doing this for her?" I didn't have to explain that I meant for Wanda, not for Gladys. Right from the beginning of my talk with Curtin it had been plain that there was no need to fill in the lines between the dots. We both saw the same picture.

"I was talking one time with the warden out at Framingham," Curtin said. "The women's prison, you know? From what the warden said, mostly you got your usual morons in there. Whores, thieves, addicts, like that. The place would have been a nightmare to administer except for the murderers."

"The murderers?"

"Yeah, the murderers ran the office, the switchboard, the library, the infirmary, kept all the books, everything. Smart, decent, responsible. Worked hard. You know who they had killed, most of them?"

"Their husbands?"

"You got it. Some prick that'd been kicking the shit out of them and the kids for ten, fifteen years."

"No loss, a guy like that," I said.

"No loss," Curtin agreed. "Those women, maybe they were technically murderers, but you still hated to see them spending the rest of their lives in jail. I'm speaking generally here, of course. After all, the law's the law, am I right?"

"Oh, absolutely."

"Well, we're out of here, Bethany," said Billy Curtin. "See you in ten minutes or so."

Actually it turned out to be a little more than ten minutes till Curtin came back upstairs with full reinforcements. Closer to fifteen minutes, really. Plenty of time to get the distinguished Phillips Professor of Political Economy ready for company.

I even would have had time to call Phil Jeffers, but I didn't do it. My weekly check from the campaign was due at the Tasty in just a few hours from now, after all, and I wanted it to be there.

The Next Tom Bethany Mystery

STRANGLE HOLD

JEROME DOOLITTLE

A lost rich kid hungry to belong, Morton Limbach II sponsored the Poor Attitudes, an improvisational theater group, and invited them to live and work in the run-down Cambridge mansion he inherited. When he's found dead of autoerotic asphyxia, the police call it accidental death due to weird sex But Jerome Rosson, the kinetic Harvard Law professor representing Morty's estate, sees a need for unorthodox talents of "security consultant" Tom Bethany Pilgrim Mutual Insurance won't pay off on what they claim is suicide. And the beneficiary standing to lose out on a quarter of a million is the ACLU, whose Washington office is run by Hope Edwards, Bethany's long-distance lover

**Coming in November
from Pocket Books Hardcover**

POCKET
B O O K S

Pocket Books
Proudly Announces
the Next Tom Bethany Mystery

Coming Soon in Hardcover
from Pocket Books

The following is an exciting
preview of
STRANGLE HOLD . . .

Tom Bethany, Boston's iconoclastic private investigator, is enjoying a quiet beer at home when his peace is interrupted by a persistent telephone surveyor named Underwood. Bethany has a bit of fun at his expense—he enjoys putting people on—but then the fun wears thin . . .

The phone rang again. I put down the *Globe*.

"Listen, Underwood," I said, "if you *do* turn out to be in the book, you just fucked up big-time."

"Am I interrupting something?" said Hope Edwards.

"Oh, Christ," I said. "I'm sorry, Hope." I would have said darling or sweetheart, but we don't often say those things to each other, however much we mean them. "What are you doing still at the office? Why aren't you at home, being a good mother to your kids?" She has three of them. They, her job, and her husband are all down in Washington. I am in Cambridge, on the other side of the Charles River from Boston. This means that much too much of the time we are four hundred and some miles apart.

"I'm tying things up. Something came up and I'm flying to Boston tomorrow morning."

"About time, too. What's your flight?"

"No sense meeting it. I'll just take a cab."

"Stop suffering and tell me the flight number."

"US Air seven-five-eight. Gets in at 8:19 A.M. But really,

don't come. I'm going straight to Toby Ingersoll's office. Be busy downtown all day." Toby was her local counterpart; he ran the Boston office of the American Civil Liberties Union and she ran the much bigger Washington one.

"What's all day?"

"My last appointment is at four-thirty. I should make it out to Cambridge by six-thirty, at the absolute latest. Meet me then at the Charles?"

"The Charles, huh?"

"I know how you like those little refrigerators in the rooms."

"That and the fruit baskets. What's going on, you're coming to Boston?"

"That Morty Limbach business."

"Is there a civil rights angle to that? The papers said it was autoerotic asphyxia."

"The insurance company is saying it was suicide, and they won't pay off. The ACLU is his beneficiary."

"How much?"

"A quarter of a million."

"Jesus. No wonder they're sending up their heaviest hitter."

"It's not that. What it is, I spent my last law school summer interning for the same insurance company. Fighting off claims, basically. I hated it."

"But you know a little bit about the business? Maybe you even know some of the players at the company?"

"One or two. Can we hire you to look into this for us?"

"No, but I'll look into it. What do you want to know?"

"For the moment, mainly the exact circumstances of death. I thought maybe your friend, the woman in the Cambridge crime lab?"

"The one with the nice tits?"

"Stuff it, Bethany. Just stuff it."

"Yeah, right. Okay. Now about this Gladys Williams, the dog that works in the crime lab. Why don't I take her to lunch tomorrow, while you're having fun with the adjusters?"

I had told Gladys to meet me on the little grassy patch sheltered between the Weld boat house dock and the Anderson Bridge. I spread out a beach towel from my gym bag and weighted it down against the breeze with groceries. I had brought cheese and cold cuts and pâté from Cardullo's on Harvard Square, along with bottles of hot mustard, pickles, sweet peppers, and mushrooms. I had two loaves of French bread from Au Bon Pain, and bottles of sparkling cider and wine that I left in the bag, out of the sun. I was a quarter of an hour early, but I was able to pass the time constructively by watching large young women launching their racing shells from the Weld dock.

"I should do that shit," said Gladys from behind me. "Boat rowing. Maybe it would make me tall and blonde and healthy."

"Sure, give it a shot," I said, getting up. "Meanwhile I brought some cholesterol and alcohol and stuff." Neither of us cared—me because I worked the calories off wrestling, and Gladys because she didn't measure her self-image in pounds. And so we got rid of everything except a little bit of the second loaf of bread. After lunch she got a stack of color photos out of a manila envelope and showed me the crime scene. The dead man was Morton Limbach III, a rich young guy who owned an old mansion off Mass. Ave. in the direction of Central Square. He used it as the headquarters for an improvisational theater troupe he sponsored, called the Poor Attitudes. Morty had died, according to the police and the medical examiner, while playing weird masturbation games in an unused bedroom on the ground floor of the mansion. Once the bedroom had belonged to Kathy Poindexter, the TV star. In those days she had been with the Poor Attitudes, playing gigs like Central Connecticut State College. Nobody had lived in the room since she went off to New York and got famous.

"Take a look," Gladys said, showing me one of the pictures. "It's almost like the fire alarm went off and whoever lived there ran out without taking anything."

A table held a cheap makeup mirror, with four small light bulbs, two on either side. Around it were pots and jars of cold cream and makeup, bottles of lotions and oils, manicure instruments, combs and brushes and rollers and curlers, perfumes and nail polish.

"It was all stuff from the drugstore or the K Mart," Gladys said. "Not the stuff you get from the department stores with the pretty demonstrators in the doctor coats. Some of the clothes in the closet and in the drawers were good, but it was all old. Most were like the things on the dressing table, cheap. Nothing was outright filthy, but it wasn't all that clean, either."

The decorations I could see in the photos dated back to the late sixties, very early seventies. Psychedelic stuff, Max Ernst posters, a poster that said FUCK COMMUNISM, and another that showed a man puking into a toilet bowl. There was a huge official portrait, a little larger than life, of Lyndon Johnson. He was posed, stern and manly, standing with his hand on the back of a chair. In his lapel was the little red and white device of the Silver Star medal, which he had won for riding along as a passenger on a bombing run in World War II.

Morty Limbach was sitting over by the left-hand wall of the room. He was slumped to one side, saved from falling on the floor by an extension cord looped around his neck. It was strung up to an old-fashioned wooden curtain rod, thick as a broomstick, that ran along the top of a tall window behind him. The socket end of the cord dangled down his shirt front, like a string necktie with a cylinder on the end of it. The extension cord was the heavy-duty orange kind, with sixteen-gauge wires; the cylinder was its socket, which was a little bigger than a regular flashlight battery.

Limbach was wearing a striped rugby shirt that looked to be from L. L. Bean. His only other clothes were dark-colored socks, and a pair of the kind of boxer shorts that fasten at the waist with snaps. They were unfastened and gaping open. His bare legs stuck out straight in front of him, flat on the floor and spread wide. Chino pants and a pair of topsiders, probably also from L. L. Bean, sat in a clump at his feet.

"Can I get copies of the pictures?" I asked Gladys when she had finished telling me about them.

"These are extras. Just don't tell anybody you've got them."

"His face looks pretty normal," I said. "I thought your tongue was supposed to stick out when you're hung."

"Autoerotic asphyxia doesn't really work that way. The point of the ligature is to cut down on the blood flow to the brain. You can still breathe, but the brain isn't getting much oxygen. Supposed to make the orgasm more intense in theory, but hey, what do I know? I'm just an old-fashioned girl."

"Yeah, sure you are." Gladys kept two, sometimes three, men on her string at all times. Each of them knew about the others, which she figured kept them better motivated.

"No chance it was suicide?"

"Sure there's a chance. I guess there's a chance Elvis is alive."

"Physically, though, it's possible the guy killed himself?"

"Sure. All of a sudden he's had it with life, okay? He's jerked off one time too many. So the hell with it, he decides to end it right on the spot . . ."

Gladys paused for a second the way Joe Isuzu does. Then in his voice she said, "Yeah, yeah, that's it! He killed himself! *That's* what must have happened!"

In her own voice again, she said, "Yeah, and maybe Elvis lives."

"It's more or less what the insurance company says happened," I said.

"Look, Tom, the jobs I've had you see a lot of weirdness. But nobody gets ready to kill themselves by jacking off."

"Unless he's setting the stage for an insurance scam."

"I doubt even the insurance company believes that shit," Gladys said.

After driving Gladys back to work, I had gone to the reference room in Widener Library and read all the newspaper accounts of Morty Limbach's unappealing death. Then I looked up Limbach, and his rich family, and all I could find about autoerotic asphyxia. It wasn't much. Most of the relevant material turned out to be in the law library, or in the medical school library, across the river in Boston.

Hope's day had been much more active. She had met with her Boston opposite number, Toby Ingersoll, and with a roomful of insurance company executives determined to keep her quarter-of-a-million bucks in their own hands. And she had met with Jerome Rosson, who taught at Harvard Law School.

"Sure, I've heard of him," I said when she asked. "I've got a TV."

Rosson was on the guest list of every assistant producer of every news and talk show in the country, filed under constitutional law. The professor gave great sound bite.

"He was Morty Limbach's attorney," Hope said. "Now he represents the estate."

"Which means he thinks the estate should get the money instead of you?"

"No, he's on our side. Morty asked him for advice when he took out the policy in the first place, so he knows what Morty's intent was."

"What was his intent?"

"Nothing complicated. Just to support the ACLU." Limbach, as I knew from my afternoon at Widener, had been a great backer of liberal causes.

"Sounds pretty complicated to me. Why take out a life insurance policy? Why not just send you a check?"

"It was a scheme our fund-raiser dreamed up a few years back. The idea was that young or relatively young supporters could buy term life very cheaply. So they'd donate the premium money to us and we'd use it to buy policies on their lives. They'd get a charitable deduction for the amount of the premiums and we'd get a big pile of money if a truck hit them."

"Did it work?"

"Not too well. It turned out people didn't like the idea of betting that a truck would hit them. Something about it didn't work, anyway. We've been the beneficiary of a few fairly small policies, but this will be our first really big payday. If we can roll over that bastard Westfall."

"What bastard Westfall?"

"I'm sorry. Warren W. Westfall. He's the president and chief executive officer of Pilgrim Mutual."

"He's slow pay, huh?"

"Maybe no pay. We screwed up royally when we

switched carriers last year. These things are group policies, and Pilgrim offered us slightly lower premiums than our old company. The suicide clause didn't seem important at the time."

"The new company doesn't pay off in case of suicide?"

"Everybody pays off in case of suicide nowadays. Suicide exclusions aren't standard anymore, except for the first two years of a policy's life."

"And that's when you bought Limbach's policy?"

"No, it's much older than that. Only with group policies like this, when you switch carriers the new company treats all the old policies as new policies. So the clock on the two years starts running all over again, on every one of the policies. That's what gave Westfall his chance to try to screw us."

"Why would he want to screw you? You're not just some starving widow with orphans, you're a big customer. And the cops say it was accidental death anyway. Why not just pay off?"

"You never ran across Westfall's name?"

I shook my head.

"If Westfall's got any chance at all of keeping that money from a bunch of Commies like us, he'll take it. He's one of the major angels for the far right. Not quite in Scaife's class, but he isn't as rich as Scaife, either." Richard Scaife, I knew, was a fat rich kid from Pittsburgh. Actually I didn't know if he was fat, but same idea.

"Why did you switch to Westfall's company?" I asked.

"Nobody on the business side thought to check with us ideological types. And nobody on our side was paying attention. What did we care what the bean counters down in the business office were doing?"

Hope picked up her coffee cup, examined the last little bit of cold coffee in it, and put the cup back down. "Now we care," she said.

"Want another cup?"

"No, let's slip into something comfortable."

And so we took the elevator back upstairs, to Hope's room.

*   *   *

Myron Cooper, the chief of claims investigations for Pilgrim Mutual, had the kind of pig face that didn't look good in a smile. He had a pig body too, solid and thick through the middle. The hand he held out was short-fingered but wide, and felt like a broad paw when I took it. He turned out to be the sort of jerk who thinks shaking hands is a contest. I only resisted enough so that he wouldn't hurt me. "Some grip," I said, trying to sound wide-eyed at the wonder of him.

"I work on it," he said. "I do a lot of match shooting."

"Oh, yeah? Is a strong grip important?" Listen to the other fellow. Show interest in what interests him.

"Well, the way you got to think about it," Cooper said, "your hand is your shooting platform."

He waved me to one of the chairs and handed me a card. It identified him as a vice president and as Chief, Claims Adjudication Division, Pilgrim Mutual Life Insurance Company. "Chief" sounded military, which I figured was no accident. A lot of Cooper's blond hair had long since gone south, but what remained was cropped into a short crewcut. Cooper's crewcut and Cooper himself reminded me of a field first sergeant in my basic training company at Fort Dix. I had taken an instant dislike to the sergeant, too.

"What can we do you for, Tom?" Cooper said, all hearty.

I explained that, as he no doubt knew, I was employed by Jerome Rosson to investigate the circumstances of the death of Professor Rosson's client Morton Limbach III.

"Why?" Cooper said, which was actually a pretty good question.

"Because Pilgrim doesn't want to pay off on his policy."

"Yeah, but what I mean is why would Rosson give a shit one way or the other? He wouldn't get the money. Not even the estate would get the money."

"He wants his client's wishes carried out."

"Why, though? This is my business, Bethany. I know what's normal, what isn't normal."

"What are you getting at?"

"What I'm getting at is who are you working for?"

"Rosson."

"Come on. Don't try to shit an old shitter. I think you're working for the ACLU."

"Not really. The ACLU and me are just good friends."

"Funny friends you got. I'll tell you the truth, Bethany, you come through that door I said to myself, This isn't the right guy. Guys like him don't work for the ACLU, for Rosson neither. Wrong guy, I said. This is a good guy. Then it came to me, why shouldn't a good guy be doing work for Rosson, you come right down to it? I mean, it's probably just a job, right? I'd probably do the same, his position. Take their money and fuck 'em, go your own way, am I right? Laugh all the way to the bank. How much is Rosson paying you?"

"Probably you should ask him."

"Whatever it is, the estate is wasting it. This guy killed himself."

"I don't know what happened yet," I said, "but the last thing it looks like is suicide."

"First thing, buddy boy. First thing."

I had a lot of trouble with "buddy boy," but I didn't say anything about it. What I said instead was: "You must have come across something we don't know about, then. Why not just tell me about it, and then we can go away and not bother you?"

"That's exactly what the boss wants to do, is tell you about it," Cooper said. "Come on. He made ten minutes on his schedule for you."

The boss turned out to be not just some little boss, but the big enchilada himself, Warren W. Westfall. He was probably in his late fifties, still a good-looking man if you like the Tony Curtis type. Westfall's handsome head, like the actor's, seemed to belong with a much more rugged body than the one it was attached to. His voice was tougher than his body, too: angry and dead serious.

"So you're the son of a bitch thinks he can cheat me out of a quarter-million bucks, huh?" Westfall said.

"That's the son of a bitch I am, all right," I said. "Thanks, I *will* sit down."

Cooper remained standing. He looked uneasy, as if he

expected to be blamed for my bad manners. "Hey, hey," he said. "Mr. Westfall, you want me to—"

"Take a walk, Myron," his boss said. When the door had closed behind Myron, Westfall's manner changed. He selected a nice smile, one that just invited you to be his friend.

"Don't take any shit, do you, son?" he said. "I like that."

He kept on smiling.

"Your guy Myron," I said, "he said you had something you wanted to tell me."

"Well, that's right. Couple things. First thing, you understand this business over Limbach's policy is a grudge match, don't you?"

"No, I don't."

"Sure it is. This ACLU lawyer, Edwards she calls herself now, she used to work for me. You know that?"

"I know she had a summer job with the company, during law school."

"She tell you about her and me?"

I shook my head. Her and him would have been a natural, though. Like Ralph Nader and Nancy Reagan.

"Oh, yeah. Not that I ever let it come to anything, of course, but she had a thing for me. Or maybe she was angling for a regular staff job when she got out of law school. Who knows, with the split-tails? Anyway, she had been kind of coming on to me, you know, and finally one day she comes right out with it. How about we drive up to Portland, somewhere like that, spend the weekend in this little place she knows? Normally why not, am I right? Not too bad of a looker.

"But she worked for me, okay? First thing I learned in business, never shit where you eat. I tried to let her down easy, not hurt her feelings, but lots of luck, right? I don't have to tell you how they are, you say no to them. She run around hollering like she was Snow White and I was trying to rip her little panties off, rape her or something. You fucking imagine? I had to let her go, naturally. So that's what's behind this whole thing."

"You're lucky," I said. "Nowadays she probably would have sued your ass for sexual harassment."

"Hey, it happens, don't think it doesn't. What a world, huh?"

In my head, I had the son of a bitch down on the floor. I had my knee in his face and was shifting my weight onto it until the thin bones splintered and his nose went flat. I never did anything harder than make myself stay where I was, in the chair I had helped myself to.

"What I'm telling you here," Westfall went on, "your boss is trying to break it off in me for old times' sake."

"Let me get this straight," I said, in pretty good control of myself by now. "You're telling me she got this guy to jack off before he killed himself so it would look accidental? Why didn't he just blow his brains out like normal people?"

"That one, you'd have to ask a shrink on. All I'm saying is the guy committed suicide and your boss from the ACLU is trying to collect because she still wants to break it off in me after all these years."

"How do you know he committed suicide? That's the point."

"For now, let's just say this guy's got a family, all right? A family which I happen to know from some of my charity work, various charities. And the family happens to know from many years back that this guy is suicidal."

"What've they got? Papers? Notes? Letters? Medical records?"

"This thing goes to court, I wouldn't be surprised to see documents like that show up, no. I wouldn't be the least bit surprised."

"Surprise me now."

"Hey, I'd like nothing more. But the lawyers are tying my hands, you know? Once those pricks get in it, you can't talk man to man no more."

We went around a little bit on it, but he wouldn't tell me anything else. When I got up to leave, he got up, too, and started around the desk as if he wanted to shake. But I didn't know if I could control myself once I had my hands on him, so I made it to the door before he could make it to me. Myron Cooper was waiting outside for me.

On the way down in the elevator, he said, "Some guy, huh?"

"Yeah, some guy, all right."

"I was afraid he'd blow up when you sat down like that, but I think it tickled him. With Mr. W., you can never tell. He likes to keep people guessing."

We got off at the fourth floor, and Cooper led the way back into the peculiar waiting room we had been in before. He waved me to a chair, and took one himself. He clasped his hands behind his head, leaned back, and gave me a long look.

"Nam?" he asked.

"A couple times as a courier. Couple more times just across the border in the Highlands. Mostly I was in Laos, though."

"The company, huh?"

"No, the army and then the embassy."

"Sure, right. The *em*bassy. Sure." I had done a tour as an enlisted man with the army attaché's office, and then stayed on as a pilot for Air America, but let him think I had been a spook, if he wanted. "I thought it was something like that," he said. "You got the look."

"You got the look, too," I said. "MPs? Saigon?"

"Pretty close. Bien Hoa. I was in the air force. APs."

And so we talked for a while about the good old days when we still had a neo-empire and didn't have to make do with little dipshit places like Grenada and Panama. I was getting to be friends with Cooper, and friends share. What the hell, it was worth a try, anyway.

"Mr. Westfall talked about the family having proof that Limbach was suicidal," I said. "What's that all about?"

"Hey, I'd like to tell you," he said. "But I can't." So much for sharing.

"Yeah, well . . ." I said. "The lawyers, I guess."

"Yeah, I suppose it'll all come out in time."

"One of the lawyers is this Hope Edwards woman. Mr. Westfall knew her from way back, huh?"

"Yeah, you believe that shit? Actually, she's not too bad looking a cunt either."

"Not too bad looking a cunt, huh?"

"You've seen her, haven't you?"

"Actually I have, yeah."

"She can sit on my face anytime."

"You like that, Myron? You like people sitting on your face?"

"Hey, it's just a manner of speaking. No offense."

"I'm asking you, Myron. You like people sitting on your face?"

"Just who do you think you're talking to, fella?"

"A fat prick that I'm gonna sit on his face."

I stood up and started toward him, to see what he would do. I wasn't really sure what I would do, either. Maybe really sit on his face. Maybe he thought so, too, because he reached inside his jacket. I got to his hand before it could get to wherever it was going and used it to twist him around in his chair. I found a pistol in a quick-draw holster under his arm about the same time he found his voice.

"Hey, what the fuck do you think you're doing?" he said, as well as he could with his face jammed into the upholstery of the chair.

"I'm taking your gun away, dickhead." I threw it on the sofa behind me, so that he'd have to go through me to get it back.

I let him go, and he got up. He was over being surprised. Now he was outraged. "You son of a bitch," he said. "You'll be sorry."

And he charged, maybe 230 pounds of enraged porker. I grabbed his leading arm and let all that weight work for me as he rotated over my hip and down hard on his back. Before he could catch his breath I hauled him by the same arm back to where he had started. In a moment he was able to get to his feet again.

"Go get your gun, Myron," I said. "It's still on the sofa."

There wasn't any point in his getting it, of course. He wasn't going to shoot me in an office with hundreds of people around, or probably anywhere else, either. But I suspected he'd try for it again, anyway. Myron, I figured, was the NRA. Prickless when gunless.

This time he remembered his hour or two of unarmed combat training for the air police, and shot out a kick at my knee. The idea is to tear all the cartilage apart and give your opponent at least an instant trick knee, if you don't quite succeed in crippling him for good. But, like most of those hand-to-hand combat moves, it only works if you're quicker than the other guy and if he doesn't expect it. My knee wasn't where he had figured it would be when his foot arrived, but my hand was. I guided his kick up over his head, and he fell heavily on his back again. He gave sort of a squealing scream this time, which probably meant he had landed on the handcuffs I had noticed on his right hip when I was searching for his gun.

"What are you doing?" he said, once he had rolled over and scrabbled out of range. "Are you crazy?" Fair question, now that there was a pause and I could think about it. Certainly I wasn't acting completely rational. I had managed to keep myself from going after Westfall, and so now I was kicking his dog instead. Which may not have been exactly crazy, but was certainly pointless. While I was at it, though, I might as well see if I could get anything out of the dog.

"Sit in that chair, Myron," I said. "I want to talk to you."

"Fuck you."

"Hey, whatever, Myron."

I grabbed one of his arms and bent it so that the thing would break if he didn't get up off the floor, and then I made him sit down like a good boy where I wanted him to.

"Now, Myron," I said. I liked calling him Now Myron. "Now, Myron, tell me just exactly what makes you think Mr. Limbach committed suicide."

Cooper said nothing.

"Now, Myron, what we've got here is something you're probably not real used to. You're used to having the air force or a big company behind you while you push people around. You're used to having your little gun and your little handcuffs. You've asskissed your way to a little title, and you're used to having people scared of you because you're bigger and fatter than they are."

"Fuck you."

"Now, Myron, what you got to understand here is that I just turned into your superior officer. This time you're not the one who makes other people scared, you're the one who gets scared. That's because I can hurt you, Myron. Actually, the more important thing is that I *will* hurt you if you don't tell me what paper you've got on Limbach.''

"Fuck you.''

"Right.'' I got behind his chair, locked his head with my left arm, and forced the second knuckle of my right hand, slow but hard, into the bundle of nerves right below the ear. Cooper screamed, but we both knew that it wouldn't carry through that thick door.

Look for *STRANGLE HOLD*
Coming in Hardcover from Pocket Books
November 15, 1991
Wherever Hardcovers Are Sold